Brandt could be _____ and
Old Hoot faked, a killer was escaping merrily westward.
Brandt flailed wildly, grabbed hold of one of Old Hoot's
scarves, and used it to pull himself upward.

"No time!" he hissed, eyes focused on Marwick. "Assassin—"

Old Hoot gently pushed him back into the bed and
tucked his scarf back among its neighbors.

"No," the old man muttered, "I'm a physician, not an
assassin. Now, let's be done with this business."

With that, the physician began rubbing his hands
briskly together. He rubbed them longer than one would
think entirely necessary and Marwick took an interest in
the curious procedure. As Old Hoot rubbed, his hands
began to look strangely insubstantial. They flickered in
the dim light that fought through the room's grimy window and Brandt could swear that he could see the colors
of Old Hoot's robes through the man's very flesh.

"The interesting question," Old Hoot went on, as if he
had never been interrupted, "is always, 'Pregnant with
what?' "

And, with that comment, he separated his ethereal
hands and plunged them halfway to the elbow into
Brandt's stomach. With a tremendous cry, Brandt passed
out . . .

"The book moves at a rip-roaring pace . . . and by the final
chapters, knowing what happens to its characters has become an important matter."   —*Booklist*

*The Chronicles of the Unbinding series
by Robert S. Stone*

HAZARD'S PRICE
DARK WATERS

THE CHRONICLES OF THE UNBINDING

VOLUME TWO

DARK WATERS

Robert S. Stone

ACE BOOKS, NEW YORK

DARK WATERS

An Ace Book / published by arrangement with
the author

PRINTING HISTORY
Ace mass-market edition / December 2001

Visit our website at
www.penguinputnam.com
Check out the Ace Science Fiction & Fantasy newsletter!

ISBN: 0-441-00888-7

ACE®
Ace Books are published by The Berkley Publishing Group,
a division of Penguin Putnam Inc.,
375 Hudson Street, New York, New York 10014.
ACE and the "A" design
are trademarks belonging to Penguin Putnam Inc.

PRINTED IN THE UNITED STATES OF AMERICA

10 9 8 7 6 5 4 3 2 1

For my mother, who nurtured every glimmer of creativity and always kept a fresh supply of bulbs for my reading lamp.

With gratitude to Matt and John, whose boundless advice and enduring friendship have helped buoy this book along, and to Deb, for more reasons than I have pages.

For that which is bound to be freed,
That which is strong must be broken.

For that which slumbers to wake,
The hunger of ages must feed.

—FRAGMENT OF AN ANCIENT KHRINE BALLAD

CHAPTER 1

With spring's arrival, wildflowers burst with color on either side of the trade road, and the road itself bloomed with travelers of every stripe: pilgrims and soldiers, tramps and priests; farmers bringing crops to market and ranchers driving their herds; merchants hailing from Khartoum to Desh; and even carnies bent on luring townsfolk from their homes, and coin from the townsfolk, after a long winter. Fenton Swain knew the road as well as any man alive. A courier, Swain spent most of his life shuttling pouches of heaven knew what between Prandis and Belfar. Over the years, he had seen everything the road could offer, until that day.

Squinting eastward into the morning sun, Swain's first thought was that he'd come across a stray packhorse somehow separated from a merchant caravan. But his momentary fantasy of a windfall evaporated as he realized that what he'd mistaken for a large brown packing bale was a rider collapsed upon the horse's back. The body was dead weight, slumped awkwardly across the roan's right flank, arms swaying limply with each step. A man, Swain decided, perhaps in his middle years, judging by the gray sprinkled amidst the black hair. *A miracle*, Swain thought, *that he hasn't fallen off*.

Then he saw that the man would have tumbled from the horse long ago had he not been lashed in place with whip-cords.

Swain drew even with the approaching roan and grabbed its loose reins. Gingerly, he reached toward the rider's too-pale cheek, wondering what the cold flesh of a corpse really felt like. He was surprised not to find out.

As Swain's finger touched the man's face, the rider jerked upright as if a noose had closed around his neck. The man's bloodshot hazel eyes roved wildly across Swain, the road and the surrounding fields, finding nothing they recognized.

"Easy," Swain said softly. "I'm here to help."

But even as he uttered the words, he decided the man was probably beyond help. The rider was white as the moon, trembling and twitching, and even his leather riding garb was visibly soaked through with sweat. Swain glanced down at his hand as he wondered whether he'd just touched a plague victim.

Plague or not, he couldn't leave the man to die on the road. "There's an inn not far from here," Swain began.

"Belfar," the rider rasped.

Swain blinked, surprised the man was lucid, much less able to speak. "Belfar? Prandis is closer than Belfar by a day, but you won't be riding to either, my friend. Let's take you to the inn and send for a doctor—"

Swain gasped as he felt the sharp prick of steel against his belly. He looked down and saw a shaky hand pressing a dagger to his stomach. There was no doubt in his mind that he could overpower the man and force him to the inn, but if the fool wanted to die . . . well, compassion extended only so far.

"Belfar," the rider repeated. "How far?"

"Two day's ride," Swain replied, thinking, *for a healthy man. A lifetime, in your condition.*

The man looked out along the road, as if he could see across the miles of fields to the walls of Belfar.

"Back away," he ordered, giving his roan a feeble kick. He kept his eyes fixed on Swain, and his dagger drawn, until the courier dwindled into the distance. Every step triggered a new explosion of agony through his gut, but alive or dead, Brandt Karrelian was determined to reach Belfar.

On the second day out of Prandis, the pain stopped. Brandt had lived with it so long that it took him a few moments to realize it was gone, like the sensation slowly returning to a limb that had fallen asleep. He wondered how far he was from Belfar, but had no means to guess. He'd been traveling slowly—he knew that. It was likely that his prey, the bald assassin, was ahead of him now. Ahead of him and laughing, convinced that his work was done. Along with thoughts of the assassin arose Brandt's last image of Carn, his crippled friend's legs splayed awkwardly in bed. Without thinking, Brandt's fingers balled into fists—trembling fists, he realized. And not trembling entirely with fury. The pain may have vanished, but he hadn't eaten any food since leaving town—nothing but an occasional sip from the water-skin that hung from his saddle horn. He'd packed bread and cheese in his saddle-bags, Brandt remembered vaguely, but he was consumed by a single thought: *onward.*

He made excellent time for the next day, pushing the large roan, though not beyond the limits of her endurance. He wondered what the horse's name was, searching his sluggish memory. "Rachel?" he tried, though he wasn't entirely sure the horse was a mare. The roan didn't react, save for flicking away a fly with her tail and continuing steadily westward.

It was later that evening, not long before Brandt intended to find an inn for the night, that the first pang hit him, sharper than any that had come before. Brandt realized that his miraculous recovery had only been a teasing respite. A sudden spasm seized his chest, and for a moment, he couldn't breathe. His guts twisted inside him like a basket of snakes.

Seconds later, he knew no more.

He might have slept for days while his body fought the ravages of whatever disease had claimed him, but the dreams sometimes woke him. At first, they were mere images, chaotic flashes of abandoned bits of his life. A thrashing by the guardsmen of Belfar. Stealing a bottle of wine and sharing it with a tall, red-haired boy on a rooftop. Lying in an old crib in a darkened room, though he was too big and old for a crib, crying endlessly with no hope of answer.

The feel of the first gold capital, solid in his palm. There were periods lost to these sensations, and then periods of oblivion. He drifted into the latter with relief.

But the images became more insistent and more recent. Brandt stood again at the base of the Khrine shaft, watching his only friend be hauled up by the workmen above. Carn's legs were dangling like a rag doll's, smashing wildly against the sides of the shaft, though Carn couldn't feel a thing. Then the image faded, and the mocking grin of the bald-headed killer, to whom Brandt could not yet put a name, pushed forward in its place. And the visage of a dark-skinned man with angular, sweeping features, like a bird of prey, but wearing a crooked bow tie.

But the worst of it was not memory, but a strange nightmare that haunted him. In his fevered hallucinations, Brandt often found himself in a large, cold room hewn of stone, like the Atahr Vin. The sound was muted here, as if the ancient rock absorbed any irreverent word. Toward the edge of the room, he saw the silhouette of a huge man who grasped in one hand a glowing gem and in the other a dark statuette. And as the giant's hand squeezed the statuette more tightly, Brandt felt his ribs groan, then crack, and his insides explode.

It was then that he always awoke, panting for air and a vision of something—anything—else. He would try to remain awake, fixing his eyes on the horizon, but there was never a sign of a city beyond the endless fields of corn and grain. Soon, Brandt gave up guessing where he was. He tried concentrating on the passage of the featureless road, but seldom succeeded for long. He remained unconscious more often than not, nodding in the saddle while the miles passed by unnoticed. Luckily, Rachel was an intelligent and steady creature, following the road obediently without complaint.

Once Brandt awoke in the quiet hours midway between midnight and dawn, feeling almost lucid, as if the pain had burned some of the fog from his mind. Rachel stood alongside the road, grazing contentedly on tall grass. Drawing himself upright in the saddle made his stomach feel as if he were a fish being cleaned. He considered slashing the whipcord that held him in place and falling onto the grass, just for a few hours of real rest and, perhaps, dreamless sleep. But he knew that once he lay down he'd never find the strength to climb back into the saddle again.

Ruthlessly, Brandt spurred Rachel toward the road. Each jarring step sent spikes of pain shooting deeper into his bowels, but he grit his teeth against the agony and rode on, fixing the image of Hain's soulless leer in his mind like true north. He held out more than an hour, driving Rachel toward Belfar, but with every pace his body bent farther over her neck and his head swung more with the motion of the canter, until he once again found himself in the grasp of a grim man in a very cold room.

When next he awoke from his nightmare•plagued fugue, it was twilight and he found himself passing between two ancient walls of stone into the streets of Belfar. There had once been large iron gates attached to each wall—you could still see the four-foot channels where the hinges had been set—but Belfar was now a mercantile city, the largest in Chaldus. Its doors were open to anyone who came, and as a symbol of free trade, the Elders had decided sixty years ago to have the very gates removed. Henceforth, Belfar would be an open·city. Every road led there, every caravan of goods came there, and there was nothing in the world a man could imagine that he could not buy or sell in Belfar. Or, in Brandt's case, steal.

Belfar was the city of Brandt's birth, but it have never felt like home. True, there had been good times along with the bad—pranks played and small triumphs celebrated as Brandt had learned the tricks of his trade along with Marwick, his childhood companion. But there had been no regrets when Brandt had left Belfar—a cocky and skilled young thief, following a man named Carn to the capital, where the real action was.

Now, it seemed, the action had spit Brandt back, returning little more than a corpse.

It was only by chance that the reins remained in Brandt's hand. He had not the strength to use them and allowed Rachel to wander through the city at will. This early in the evening, the streets were still crowded. Dozens of vendors hawked wares from carts and stalls along the side of the road. Beggars lined walls at the larger intersections, displaying a variety of disabilities—true, false, and self-inflicted—in hopes of a coin thrown their way. At one point, a flock of beggar children crowded about his horse and Brandt suffered a pang of recognition as old visions washed over him of his own unwashed hands reaching toward mounted merchants as they rode by. Half-consciously, he fumbled in the purse at his side, spilling more money than he'd intended among the children of the street.

It was a mistake, inciting the orphan's appetite to a fever pitch. They pranced and jumped around his horse, clamoring for more, singing and shouting and drawing the eyes of every man in the street. Brandt rode on a few moments more, suffering the last sort of attention he wanted, hoping that they'd merely go away when they saw his indifference. But he knew better from experience. They circled and shouted with unabated zeal, chanting their little songs of need in the darkening streets. He knew only one way to be rid of them and although it was absurd, he put his hand to his sword-hilt. He couldn't have lifted the blade if his life depended on it, but the gesture was enough. The little beggars scattered away into the darkness.

Brandt looked around and realized that, by chance, Rachel was leading him into poorer and more dangerous surroundings—Blake's Warren, the neighborhood had been called. He remembered these narrow, grimy streets well, having lived in them long enough, and he also knew that to continue was as foolish as painting a bull's-eye on his forehead. The residents of Blake's Warren knew horseflesh and knew clothes, and they could smell from a half-mile whether you had money or not. Brandt desperately needed the comparative safety of an inn, and he knew he would have to stop at the first one he found.

It was not long before a weather-beaten sign came into view, announcing beer to be had and rooms for the night. A trio of scantily clad women were lined up outside the place—to grace it with the name of an inn would be to go too far—and the sight of their goose-bumped flesh made Brandt shiver. They huddled together, looking at him strangely and speaking in whispers as he stopped Rachel before the door. Two of the girls, desperate enough for money to hope that whatever disease wracked this odd traveler was not contagious—or if it was, not fatal—began to solicit his attention.

Brandt ignored them. Every movement cost him a fortune of energy and determination. He focused his will on pulling his dagger from its sheath. Then, weakly, he began sawing away at the first of the cords that tied him to the saddle.

He might as well have used a butter knife, for all the good it did him.

He called to the closest of the girls. With a little flourish of triumph, she smiled cattily at her competitor before sauntering to the horse's side. There, she got a closer look at the man: black hair, perhaps a little gray, plastered with sweat to his scalp; clothes likewise, but of a very good make, though an inconspicuous black. He might have been handsome if he didn't look so wasted, and if only he could manage to stop shivering for a few moments. The girl sent forth another silent prayer that she wouldn't catch whatever afflicted him. Of course, at a closer look, she doubted he'd be able to do much with her anyway. That cut down the risk of infection.

He was pushing something at her, and with terror, she realized it was a knife. She gasped and jumped back a step.

"No," he rasped. "Cut me loose."

Then she noticed the leather thongs that tied him to the saddle. The prostitute took the dagger and, with a few sure cuts, severed the cords. Tall and big-boned, she had little trouble helping him down from Rachel's back, but when she had, she discovered that she would have to hold him up or he'd collapse.

A seedy-looking fellow with a squinting eye emerged from the inn and offered to take Brandt's horse. Brandt merely nodded, hoping that the man's services would also include bringing Rachel back.

"Take the bags to my room," he ordered. It was the most he'd spoken that day.

By the time the whore had helped Brandt upstairs to a small corridor of bedrooms, the man with the squint had caught up with them, bearing Brandt's saddlebags. "This way," he grumbled, choosing one of the flimsy doors that lined the half-lit hallway.

The girl helped Brandt inside and eased him onto the bed. The innkeeper deposited Brandt's bags on the floor and, with a lewd grin, closed the door as he left.

"You want me to take those off for you, honey?" the girl asked, not waiting for an answer before she began to strip him efficiently, making a couple of lascivious observations as she went—ill-considered attempts to rouse his interest. She seemed disturbed at her lack of success. When Brandt lay naked on the bed, she proceeded to a more direct route, peeling off the skin-tight teal blouse that she wore. A pair of large breasts presented themselves to view, puckered red where someone had bitten them that day, but, she thought, still the finest on the street.

Her intended spectator was, it turned out, already asleep.

The girl waited all of ninety seconds—long enough to determine that Brandt was thoroughly unconscious—before she replaced her blouse, took all Brandt's money, and left.

All in all, she thought, it was looking like a good night.

The room was a blur when Brandt awoke, everything swimming through the tear film that covered his eyes. He knew enough to realize two things: that he was no longer on horseback, and that, very soon, he was going to die. There was a certain amount of regret in this latter realization, but if death stopped the holocaust raging in his gut, he would be only too grateful.

"Good morning."

The voice was jovial and altogether too loud. Brandt blinked and tried to move his head. There was a blurred oval not far away that could possibly be a head. He blinked again, trying to will the blur into focus.

"And how are we feeling this morning? Indulged yourself a little too well last night—and in Blake's Warren, of all places. From what I hear, you should be doing better these days. Overcome by nostalgia for cheap beer and cheaper women?"

Brandt closed his eyes and groaned. If he were to die, best he get it over with quickly, for he had recognized the voice.

"How did you find me, Marwick?" he rasped with difficulty.

The man laughed. "You're not exactly unknown in this town, my friend, and you weren't what I'd call inconspicuous last night."

Brandt shook his head. The movement cost him more pain than he'd thought possible.

"I wasn't *that* conspicuous, and it's been years since my last visit to Belfar."

"Well," Marwick replied, still in his lilting, jolly tone, "I hate to flatter you—as Mother always said, flattery goes as quickly to your head as ornery lice—but the years have been kind to you. A little gray around the ears, but otherwise—"

"How did you really find me?"

It hurt Brandt to talk, but the pain of talking, he thought, was preferable to listening to Marwick's painful drivel.

Marwick sighed. "Very well. A local hooker was a little lavish with your gold last night—"

"Hooker? My gold?"

Brandt wracked his brains to remember anything about his ride into Belfar. He certainly didn't remember a woman, and didn't think himself capable of such activity. He pressed a hand to his still-closed eyes.

"Don't pretend you don't remember," Marwick chuckled, "considering how you're lying there naked as a jaybird. Modesty was never your strong suit. Either way, old friend, you should know well enough to kick professional girls out of your bed before you fall asleep. After you started snoring, she relieved you of your purse and went on the sort of wild bender that would have made us proud in the old days. Almost drank the Baden Bar out of whiskey. By the time she was done, everyone in the room knew she'd struck it rich, and how. I simply had enough presence of mind to ask her what this visiting merchant looked like."

Brandt groaned again. In coming to Belfar, he had hoped, more than anything else, to avoid the complications Marwick would embody. Instead, he'd stumbled straight upon him, like a ship running aground on the rocks. Brandt supposed it would be necessary to open his eyes and look at his onetime friend; Marwick would hardly go away without at least that much recognition.

This time his sight functioned with greater clarity. The room still appeared blurry—not necessarily a drawback, Brandt realized, because what little he saw was revolting enough to discourage further curiosity. Whether the walls were painted green or were simply mildewed, he could not tell.

And there, in a chair next to his bed, sat Marwick. He hadn't seen the man for something like a dozen years—not since they were in their early twenties, when Marwick had chosen to remain in Belfar, rather than accompanying Brandt and Carn to Prandis. Since then, Marwick hadn't changed much. Perhaps his hairline had receded a bit, but the thief kept his curly red hair tied back in a bushy ponytail, just as he had a dozen years earlier. It was an odd habit, a style that only Yndrians favored. Brandt had once wondered if Marwick was part-Yndrian by descent—but Marwick's powderwhite skin and scattered freckles spoke of the northeastern mountains, not Yndor.

As for the rest of the man, Marwick retained a trim, lithe figure—obviously, Brandt decided, he was still in business. No ordinary job required such fitness. And, it would seem, his business was prospering. Marwick wore a deep blue velvet jacket and a pair of matching trousers. The suit was embroidered with loops of golden thread at the wrists and ankles. Rather garish, to Brandt's taste, but Marwick had always favored the garish.

"I need help," Brandt said weakly.

"That's obvious from looking at you," Marwick replied, his mouth twisting into his perennial grin. Brandt noticed that Marwick's smile lines were now deeply etched into his flesh, courtesy of an extra decade's tenancy. "Lord, Brandt, I can't remember your looking this bad since the day of the whiskey dare." Marwick leaned back and laughed, savoring the memory. "You were greener than a grasshopper, spewing like a cistern sprung a leak. Carn and I had to drag you home all the way from Parson's Inn. How is the old man, by the by? I haven't had a letter from him this month."

Brandt scowled at the mention of Carn. His friend's name sent his head spinning down that bitter rat hole that led to an image of the assassin's face.

"Marwick, chitchat aside, I need help. I had all my funds in that purse—"

"Not very prudent," Marwick interrupted, scratching the tip of his long, pointed nose. "As my mother always said, coins are as jealous as lovers, best kept out of one nest."

"I'll need you to take a letter to my Belfar banker," Brandt continued, ignoring Marwick with a skill born of long experience. Indeed, the speed with which these old habits returned was uncanny.

"Ah," Marwick interrupted, rocking back in the chair and smiling. "That's right. You've got banks in every city now. Do you own them or just keep funds there? Mother always said—"

Brandt groaned.

"Hold tight," Marwick encouraged, abandoning his previous train of thought. "I've called for a doctor, you know. You didn't look well."

An understatement to be sure, but it was Marwick's mother who had provoked the groan, not physical discomfort. Brandt had never met Marwick's mother. Indeed, he had known Marwick since they were both Belfar guttersnipes, and Marwick had had no mother then, although he had incessantly repeated her epigrams, few of which made sense. Brandt often wondered whether Marwick's mother was anything more than myth. It was hard to imagine any flesh-and-blood woman capable of bearing such a conversational force of nature as Marwick.

"Write a letter of credit," Brandt instructed, "and I'll sign—"

"Oh, no need," Marwick interrupted, fishing into his pocket. "The hooker was pretty well plastered by the time I got to the bar and it was a simple favor to reconfiscate your purse."

With that, Marwick tossed the small leather pouch onto the bed, where it fell with a bounce at Brandt's side. Rather more of a bounce, Brandt suspected, than it would have had last night, when it had looked substantially larger.

Marwick caught Brandt's look and shrugged. "I told you, a *lot* of whiskey."

No doubt, Brandt thought, as he wondered whether Marwick had owned his shiny blue suit the night before.

The reunion of Brandt and Marwick stalled as Brandt once more drifted into a tortured sleep. The dream recurred in which he himself was a statuette, the grim man's fingers twisted around his midsection, the nails digging into his stomach—digging farther and farther until, it seemed to Brandt, they must pierce through his back on the other side. And as the pain became unendurable, a new element entered the dream: an awful, acrid smell that filled his lungs and assaulted his senses.

No, this was not a new element of the dream, but of reality. There was indeed smoke in the room, Brandt realized as he came awake. His first thought was fire, but as his eyes fluttered open, he realized there was a more benign explanation. Seated at the edge of his bed was a strangely dressed old man who held a small copper incense burner beneath

Brandt's nose. As Brandt awoke, the old man withdrew the incense and handed it to Marwick, who stood behind him.

"Brandt," Marwick explained, as jovially as ever, "I'd like you to meet Old Hoot."

Old Hoot inclined his head somberly, as if he understood the gravity of the situation to an extent that Marwick did not. "It's lucky for you, young man," he began, "that I was passing through town and staying in these fine lodgings. Any further delay of medical attention may well have proved fatal."

Brandt suspected that medical attention provided by any physician likely to stay in *this* inn would prove equally fatal, but he was too weak to protest.

Old Hoot leaned over to peer at his patient, providing Brandt an unwelcome opportunity to return the favor. The man seemed to be a walking relic. His head, apparently bald, was covered with a skullcap knitted of orange wool. The color reflected a somewhat sickly hue on the face beneath it, a face deeply seamed by weather and time. Beneath his head, Old Hoot was an almost amorphous cascade of scarves and robes, both old and new, each a different, garish color, and each made of a different material.

"First," the doctor announced, "it will be off with this blanket."

Brandt was too weak to protest as Old Hoot whisked away the torn blanket. He simply lay on the bed, stripped, gazing balefully at his unwanted physician.

"Now," said Old Hoot, "let's have a look at what's bothering you. Describe the ailment."

Brandt stared suspiciously at the old man. He looked more like a beggar than a doctor, and Brandt thought wistfully of Doctor Pardi back in Prandis.

"You know I can pay," he muttered to Marwick. "Don't you have the sense to bring me a decent doctor?"

"I may not be decent," Old Hoot replied sharply, "but I'm *good*. Quite good, in fact. And although I'm not the type to force my services on anyone, I must warn you: I doubt you will survive long enough for anyone else to get here—if any *decent* doctor, as you put it, would even be willing to make a bedside call in Blake's Warren."

That was forceful logic. Old Hoot, then, it was.

Brandt briefly recounted how the pains had started in his stomach, penetrated farther inside with time, and finally spread out to affect his breathing and his head.

As he listened, the old man shook his arms, as if to work out the kinks in his muscles, and began to roll up his sleeves. Considering the multiple layers of clothing he wore, this was a lengthy process. Finally, his thin, wrinkled arms were bare to the elbow. The flesh hung off them loosely, swaying as he moved. Brandt grimaced with repugnance as the old man lay his hands on Brandt's shoulders and began to probe his body. A poke here, a rub there, a thoughtful pressing of the palm with the attitude of one waiting to hear something. It was such mummery as this, Brandt suspected, that had been keeping Old Hoot ill-clothed and malnourished for the last several decades.

Soon, the physician's gnarled hands reached Brandt's stomach, probing the area tenderly. Even this light touch was excruciating and Brandt gritted his teeth against the sharp pains that shot through his torso.

"Ah!" Old Hoot cried as his fingertips brushed along Brandt's abdomen. "I should have suspected."

The physician's cry had brought Marwick a step closer, peering over Old Hoot's shoulder at his naked ex-partner.

"What have you found?"

"It's no wonder your friend suffers stomach pangs," Old Hoot explained. "It's a common gestatory symptom."

"Excuse me?" Marwick prompted.

"Simply put," Old Hoot went on, "your friend is pregnant."

Marwick took a step backward and cast a skeptical eye at the old man. Even his vast faith in human nature was being put to the test by the odd physician, but he couldn't pass up the comic opening.

"Pregnant, Brandt?" Marwick asked, his eyes glittering. "But you never told me you'd married!"

Brandt could bear no more. While Marwick joked and Old Hoot faked, a killer was escaping merrily westward. Brandt flailed wildly, grabbed hold of one of Old Hoot's scarves, and used it to pull himself upward.

"No time!" he hissed, eyes focused on Marwick. "Assassin—"

Old Hoot gently pushed him back onto the bed and tucked his scarf back among its neighbors.

"No," the old man muttered, "I'm a physician, not an assassin. Now, let's be done with this business."

With that, the physician began rubbing his hands briskly together. He rubbed them longer than one would think entirely necessary and Marwick took an interest in the curious procedure. As Old Hoot rubbed, his hands began to look strangely insubstantial. They flickered in the dim light that fought through the room's grimy window and Brandt could swear that he could see the colors of Old Hoot's robes through the man's very flesh.

"The interesting question," Old Hoot went on, as if he had never been interrupted, "is always, 'Pregnant with what?' "

And with that comment, he separated his ethereal hands and plunged them halfway to the elbow into Brandt's stomach. With a tremendous cry, Brandt passed out.

As Brandt cried, Marwick did likewise•but rather than pass out, he pressed forward and put a hand to the dagger at his side.

"What have you done, old man?" he demanded, the former lilt in his voice replaced by menace.

"Quiet!" the physician snapped, accompanying his command with a sharp glance that silenced the Belfarian thief. "This is the delicate part."

Slowly, Old Hoot began to draw his hands out of Brandt's abdomen. There was no blood, no gore. The old man's hands withdrew as inexplicably and as insubstantially as they had plunged inside, but this time they brought something with them.

At first, Marwick could only tell that the thing was green, but as Old Hoot withdrew it farther, what looked like a leathery wing seemed to slide out of Brandt's stomach.

"Surprised you, didn't I?" the physician asked, a smile of wily satisfaction crossing his features.

"Sure as hell did," Marwick murmured, cowed by his astonishment.

"I'm not talking to you," the old man snapped, "but to your friend's 'baby' over here."

"That isn't really a—"

"Baby? Of course not—though your friend would have died in birthing it within hours."

"What is it then?" Marwick asked.

"Take a look," Old Hoot suggested as, with a final tug, he pulled the last of the creature free of Brandt's body. As the thing's long, snaky tail whipped through Brandt's navel, Brandt's skin closed up without a blemish. There was not the least trace that Old Hoot had touched him.

But Marwick's attention was not on Brandt. What Old Hoot held in his hand was a winged, tailed creature, perhaps eighteen inches tall. It was covered all over with green, leathery skin, but except for these details, it looked remarkably like a tiny replica of a bald, old man. Indeed, it bore a certain odd resemblance to Old Hoot himself.

"They're cute little tykes," the physician observed as he held up the creature for Marwick to study. "But exceptionally deadly."

Marwick slid his dagger free from its sheath, his lips curled in disgust at what he beheld.

"I'm afraid that's no use," Old Hoot explained. "At the moment, the homunculus is no more substantial than my hands. Your blade would pass through it without the least effect."

Tentatively, Marwick poked the thing with the tip of his dagger. The creature whipped its bony head around and hissed at the thief, baring a tiny set of sharp yellowed teeth. Marwick could see the shadowy outline of the blade within the homunculus's skin, but it apparently did no damage.

Slowly, he withdrew the blade, noting that it was as clean as when he'd finished polishing it that morning.

"What was it doing in Brandt?" he asked finally, still unable to take his eyes off the disgusting little creature.

"Waiting to be born," Old Hoot replied, and noticing Marwick's look of blank incomprehension, explained: "It entered your friend's body as an insubstantial thing, as it is now. That's easy. The creature then could have simply materialized, becoming solid all at once within your friend's abdomen. That would have killed them both. The hard part is to materialize without merging entirely into the medium—a trick that takes a good deal of persuasion. And that's what the creature was doing—persuading your friend's internal organs to make room for him. A little longer and it might have succeeded. Once it could coax a big enough space for it to form inside your friend's abdominal cavity, it would have become flesh."

"And then?"

The old man shrugged. "Then it would have torn its way out."

Marwick shuddered.

"Indeed," Old Hoot continued, "the entire process wouldn't have taken half so long except that your friend has quite a collection of magical protections cast upon him." Old Hoot cocked his head and peered more closely at his patient, as if he could see the protective spells that Brandt had purchased over the years. "Not a very popular fellow, I take it. In any case, all those wards must have inconvenienced the poor homunculus considerably."

"How do we kill it?" Marwick asked, tiring of the technical details.

But the physician had fallen into a contemplative mood. He revolved the homunculus about in his hands, studying it closely. "Whoever wanted to kill this man is no novice in the ways of magic."

"I'm sure he'll find that a comfort," Marwick said, casting a glance at his unconscious friend. "Unless Brandt's changed drastically since he left Belfar, he'd hate to be killed by some amateur. Can you find out who sent it?"

The physician grunted in response, and began to mutter under his breath. It took a moment for Marwick to realize that the man had not wandered into a senile fugue, but was at work on another feat of magic. The air around the homunculus and Old Hoot's hands began to shimmer and take on a bluish hue. The longer Old Hoot mumbled, the bluer the air became until, finally, a bright sphere of two feet in diameter surrounded the creature. Old Hoot finally ceased his mutterings and slowly withdrew his hands. The homunculus was left trapped in the sphere, suspended in midair. Marwick leaned closer, stretching a fingertip toward the closest point of the sphere.

"I wouldn't," Old Hoot cautioned abruptly. Marwick snatched his finger away and took a long step backward.

The homunculus's skin appeared an ugly gray through the blue light. It took a tentative step forward and pressed at the outmost curve of the sphere, but the shimmering curve seemed as substantial as a steel cage.

"How do you like your new accommodations?" Old Hoot asked merrily.

The homunculus replied with another fang-baring hiss to which it added a long, chittering diatribe. Marwick could not make out a word, if indeed there were words in the creature's high-pitched complaint.

"You understand that?" Marwick asked.

"Of course," Old Hoot replied.

"Then what did it say?"

"It said," the old man sighed, "that my mother was a witch and my father a traitor." He seemed to ponder this for a moment, his face crumpling into a frown. "It's not entirely wrong."

The creature went on chittering.

"I don't think," Old Hoot added, "that you'd like to hear what it has to say about *your* mother."

Marwick's hand went again to his dagger, but he restrained

himself, remembering his last ineffectual attempt to stab the thing.

"Now, why don't you entertain us with some more relevant details?" Old Hoot suggested to the creature.

The homunculus crossed its arms resolutely and turned away from the old man.

Old Hoot sighed. "If you'd rather be difficult . . ."

The old man gestured negligently with his right hand and the sphere slowly began to contract. The homunculus seemed to take no note of this until the edge of the sphere drew up against its head. It hissed again as it knelt to make more room in its diminishing cage.

Old Hoot lifted a finger and the contraction stopped as quickly as it had begun.

"Perhaps you're feeling more talkative now?" the physician suggested.

And indeed, the creature began to chitter away again. Old Hoot's face soured at what he heard.

"Well?" Marwick prompted.

"It's moved on to commentary about my grandparents. The cursed thing seems acquainted with my entire genealogy."

"It's got spirit," Marwick conceded.

"It *is* a spirit," Old Hoot corrected, "and it isn't yet convinced that I can harm it. It seems rather smug that it's well protected, but by whom, it won't say. Let's test its claims."

Again, the old man waved his hand and the sphere resumed its contraction. As the blue ball grew smaller, the homunculus rolled onto its back and drew its legs against its chest to accommodate the diminishing space, but still Old Hoot wouldn't stop the contraction. The thing's wings were slowly crushed into its back and its chin was forced against its chest by the narrowing arc of the blue walls.

"Well?" the physician asked.

This time the creature said nothing, merely glaring at the old man. Soon, the homunculus's body, as if made of rubber, had curled up into a sphere itself, and now it began to compress. But the creature would not speak. Amazingly, the sphere continued to contract until Marwick could no longer distinguish the thing's limbs or features. They were all pressed together into a seamless gray ball that dwindled in size. The thief expected at any moment to hear the breaking of bones, the snapping of wings, but there wasn't the slightest sound. The sphere simply contracted until it was the size of an orange, then a marble, and ultimately a dust mote. Marwick peered closer as the dot that had been a homunculus disappeared from view.

"My word . . ." Marwick muttered, his face ashen. Even for a monster, that had seemed a nasty way to die.

Old Hoot shrugged and, his professional capacity at an end, engaged himself in the lengthy process of rolling down his sleeves.

"A shame," he observed. "We might have learned something from it. I haven't seen a homunculus in . . . I can't begin to count the years. It would have been interesting to know what brought this one into the open . . . or rather, *who* brought it."

"And why it found lodging in Brandt's stomach," Marwick added, still feeling dazed by the day's proceedings.

"That, of course, as well," Old Hoot agreed, sighing as he stretched his limbs. "But I've come to Belfar for other reasons." His eyes darted toward the window, judging the time by the scant light that was still filtering into the narrow alleys of Blake's Warren. "Drat! Now I'll have to hurry . . . and I may still be late."

The physician drew himself up and took a quick step toward the door.

"But what about Brandt?" Marwick cried. "He still looks—"

"Food and rest," Old Hoot replied over his shoulder as he continued toward the door. "Must shake a leg now, but I'll check on your friend later."

Marwick watched as the old man slipped quietly from the room and pondered in dismay the fact that none of his mother's many proverbs had prepared him for a day such as the one he'd just seen.

CHAPTER 2

After four slow days' ride through open country, the Caladors had finally reached the major trade route that ran westward from Belfar, dipping gently to the south and Sartaxis. Riding through woods and farmland on little-known trails had been the best strategy for evading assassins, but they could cover only a few leagues each day. The trade route from Belfar to Sartaxis was much faster, but more likely to be watched . . . and Roland remained uneasy about riding directly toward a stronghold of the Chaldean army. How ironic, he thought. That very army had once been *his* army. He knew every inch of Sartaxis, every block of its vast basalt body. And his eldest son, Cail, was there as well.

It should have been a homecoming.

Instead, he kept reminding himself that it was the Chaldean army that had tried to kill them.

He turned to Miranda, who sat lightly upon her small chestnut mare. She wore a gray, woolen traveling cloak that warmed her against the chill winds of early spring. Her hood, though, was thrown back and her hair floated lightly behind her, the silver in it reflecting the sunlight in fluid waves. Perched atop her shoulder, swaying lazily with the rhythm of the ride, was a tiny brown spotted owl. The creature was no taller than six inches, yet it was all but fully grown. Nocturnal by nature, it was sleeping now, and Roland preferred it that way. He had never been fond of witches' familiars, and although this one seemed more mild in temperament than a certain bobcat he remembered, he still would prefer life without it.

Miranda, of course, would not. She had reminded him, as

they had ridden through the woods outside Calador, that she had forgone familiars these last ten years because she was no longer a practicing witch and she felt it cruel to restrict a wild animal to the tame and boring confines of their ducal estate. But there were few assets as valuable as a familiar to a busy practitioner of the arts, and recent events promised to make Miranda as busy as she'd ever been. Thus it was that, two days ago, before leaving the edge of the woods, Miranda had performed the ritual ancient as the trees themselves, calling for a companion on her journey.

And this tiny owl had come, settling happily on her shoulder, preening its mottled brown and black feathers, and falling quickly asleep.

It had not so much as glanced at Roland the entire time. Perhaps it was that which bothered him.

That, and riding into the midst of an army that was under orders to kill them. Worse yet, Sartaxis was simply a stopover. Their true destination was Yndor. Somehow, Roland thought, the Yndrians' reception would hardly be more enthusiastic than the Chaldean army's.

I'm a damned fool, he thought, *for going along so tamely with Miranda's plans.*

"And what exactly are we supposed to do?" he asked. Miranda's eyes twinkled as she turned toward her husband. She was used to Roland brooding over a problem for hours, then bursting out with a question as if everyone else had been privy to his internal deliberations. For anyone who hadn't been married to him for forty years, she supposed it could be a disorienting habit.

"Well?" Roland continued. "Do you intend to walk up to the gates of Sartaxis and announce, 'We're the retirees your commander-in-chief would like to see dead and we've come to visit our son. Would you mind sending him out?' "

Miranda ignored the remark momentarily, concentrating instead on the sight of Roland astride his mount. Despite her initial misgivings, she derived some inner pleasure from seeing him clad in battle armor again. The motion of the ride would sometimes throw open a fold of Roland's enormous cloak, flashing a swatch of steel beneath the wool. After all these years, Roland still looked magnificent perched atop a warhorse—this spirited black stallion a direct descendant of his first horse, from a line that had been bred by his family for generations—and it somehow made her feel younger to witness it.

"Sarcasm, my dear? How unusual."

Roland shook his head. "You seldom saw me in my professional capacity. Cynicism and sarcasm are a valuable asset in any officer's arsenal."

"One might have supposed tactics to hold a more sanctified place," his wife replied. "For instance, rather than announcing ourselves, we can simply send a messenger for Cail."

Again Roland shook his head, and his great white mane of hair swung about his shoulders. He should bind it back with a ribbon, he thought.

"Sartaxis," he lectured, "is a military installation—not simply a border city. Almost everyone is connected with the army in some capacity."

"I know that," Miranda replied mildly.

"Then where are we going to find someone to carry our message?" he demanded.

"Whoever said we needed 'someone'?" Miranda asked, and she lifted a delicate finger to stroke the tan-colored beak of her bird. "We've got Mouse here."

"Mouse?" Roland asked, his scowl disappearing as he weighed the name. "Is that what you'll call it? Doesn't seem very appropriate."

At that, the small owl opened one of its round gray eyes and fixed Roland with what seemed to be a disapproving stare. After a moment, it closed the eye again and lapsed back into contented sleep.

"Don't complain to me," Miranda replied. "*She* chose the name."

"But 'Mouse'?"

Miranda shrugged. "It's her favorite food."

Roland shook his head and turned his attention back to the road. The dense woods around Calador had thinned out the farther west they had traveled. Part of the change was the result of clearing the land for farms, the central region of Chaldus being the breadbasket of the country. But even had man not taken a hand in the work, the trees would have dwindled naturally to the west, where the land settled into a wide, rolling prairie, only occasionally broken by clumps of woods or small clusters of hills. It was this terrain that they had entered that morning and Roland did not much like it. From the road, he could see for miles around.

And that meant that, for miles around, any watchers could see him.

He thought for a moment to loosen in its sheath the great broadsword that hung strapped to his back, but he checked his hand even as it began to move. *No need to worry Miranda*, he thought. Or more honestly, there was no need to show her how worried he truly was. Life as a fugitive was a new experience for the old general. His entire career had been based on authority, on firm structures of power that ordered the world into comprehensible and efficient spheres.

No more.

He looked past the edge of the packed-dirt road beneath him and took in the fluid motion of the hip-high wild grass that swayed with the wind toward the western horizon. As if the very ground had turned into a shifting, churning, uncertain mass. And perhaps it had.

As Roland continued to gaze west, his face hardened in determination. Let the very earth buckle beneath his feet, he thought. He would jump the fissures should Thyrsus lie on the other side.

At nightfall, they found a sheltered pond to the leeward side of a small hill, by which grew a tall, solitary elm. The moon had risen before twilight and it would be almost full tonight. All in all, Miranda thought, the scene should be romantic, once darkness fell. She almost wouldn't mind sleeping on the ground.

As the last lip of the sun slid beneath the horizon, Mouse

opened her two gray eyes, blinking a few moments while adjusting to her new location. She preened some wind-ruffled feathers at the base of her neck and then turned toward Miranda, inspecting, it would seem, whether the woman was in need of preening. Miranda, however, had an unnatural facility for appearing fresh and tidy in even the most unlikely circumstances. Approving, Mouse let forth a deep, vibratory trill—like an airy purr.

"Worry about yourself," Miranda laughed as she lifted the bird from her shoulder and helped launch it skyward. "Go hunt." The field mice would not be happy tonight, she mused.

Roland, in the meantime, had judged that they were far enough from the road to risk a fire. Even if their smoke was seen, there were many travelers along the trade routes during spring, many fires dotting the plains where merchants camped. Theirs would be unlikely to draw special attention. After hunting around the occasional shrubs that grew nearby, he had enough fuel for the night and began clearing a spot for the fire. While Miranda unpacked their gear, he bent over the sticks and tried to light his tinder with a flint and steel. Soon the tinder caught, but the branches, damp from recent rains, resisted the weak flame. The best he could manage was a sickly wisp of gray smoke.

Negligently, Miranda spoke a few words and twisted her fingers in an odd gesture, a soundless snap. The sticks burst out into a steady, cozy fire.

"Perhaps I should unpack and you should start the campfires from now on," Roland murmured.

"Now, dear," Miranda chided, "don't let me bruise your manly feelings."

He smiled in return, thinking how dreary a trip this would be without her company, and turned to the business of pitching a tent. Tents were foolish luxuries for fugitives, he knew. They prevented you from seeing and hearing what went on beyond the canvas. In case of an emergency, tents hindered your response and would have to be left behind.

So be it. During the first emergency, he would abandon it. In the meantime, he wanted a tent. It eased in some small measure the sense of dispossession that had wracked him after leaving his home.

Before long, the camp was set. Roland had tethered the horses to the elm, giving them a long line to roam, and they grazed happily on the tall grass. Miranda was putting the finishing touches on a rabbit stew that smelled wonderful. The rabbit had been a gift from Mouse, who perched now on the ridgepole of the tent. The small owl swiveled its head toward Roland and let out an altogether too-amused-sounding hoot.

"Dinner's ready, dear," Miranda announced.

He ate, despite the owl's mild mockery, and found the dish so tender that he began to reconsider his feelings about his wife's familiar. If Mouse kept them stocked with rabbits throughout the journey, perhaps he would take a liking to the creature after all.

Roland's opinion of Mouse took a decided turn for the better sometime between midnight and dawn. He was awakened from sleep by a sudden eruption of screeching and jumped to his feet not yet fully awake—certainly not yet cognizant that he had gone to bed in a tent. The small camping tent was by no means tall enough to accommodate Roland's seven-foot stature, and his violent motion served only to rip the canvas free of its moorings, transforming their former shelter into an effective trap. It was Miranda whose dexterous fingers found the tent flap in the chaotic darkness and threw it wide. Roland caught a glimpse of stars and launched himself toward the swatch of sky, erupting from the collapsing canvas like a giant born of the earth. Roland's battle cry shattered the night more violently than Mouse's high-pitched screech as he reached for his sword.

The sword he had left inside the tent, by the side of his bedroll.

It would take a while longer, he knew, to recover all his old reflexes. The only question, as he stood confronting he-knew-not-what in his undershorts, was whether he would survive long enough to relearn them.

Sitting placidly by the fire was a robed figure, bent intently toward the flames in an attempt to absorb their heat. Mouse flew in tight, rapid circles around the intruder's head, screeching at the top of her owlish lungs. The robed figure made no attempt to shoo the bird away.

Behind him, Roland realized, Miranda had emerged from the tent.

"Get back!" he warned.

In an instant, she absorbed the scene.

And began to laugh.

"Roland, you can be so ridiculous when you try." Then she turned her attention to Mouse. "Stop that at once!"

The owl quit its screeching but kept circling the intruder warily.

Finally, the robed figure spoke.

"I'm glad to see that not everyone has lost all civility." The voice was low and calm. "Though these are trying times, it's still the custom to welcome travelers along the commonwealth's roads."

"Apologize," Miranda commanded, still talking to Mouse.

The bird landed a few feet from the visitor's right knee and peered at the man's shrouded face. Roland wondered whether the owl's superior sight could discern the face that hid in those shadows.

"I said, apologize," Miranda repeated, this time more sternly.

The little owl hooted something that, to Roland's ears, sounded very insincere. For once, he and the bird were in utter sympathy.

"It's a harsh world," the visitor continued, "when an old man can't reap the benefits of a friend's fire."

With that, he reached up—old, wizened hands, Roland noticed—and drew back his hood.

It was Tarem Selod.

"Don't gawk," the mage chided. "It lets too much chill air into your lungs. Indeed, Roland, if you insist on dressing like an erotic dancer, you'll have more need of this fire than I."

Roland gawked just a moment more.

"He'll get his cloak out of the tent now," Miranda said, smiling sweetly as she approached. She lay a small, warm hand on Roland's back. "Won't you, dear?"

Roland nodded dumbly and turned back toward the tent. It looked now like little more than a puddle of canvas, with a few sharp angles where the poles pressed against the fabric. It would take a few moments to find his cloak in such a mess.

"You've found a new familiar, my dear," Selod said, looking at the little bird. Mouse, whose interest in events had quickly waned, had hopped away and seemed to be worrying at an insect in the grass. Now, her head popped back up, the eyes peering like a tiny set of twin full moons at the old mage. "I would think, given the circumstances, that a lynx or eagle might have been more appropriate."

Mouse issued a low, sustained hoot of warning.

"The woods knew best what I needed and they gave me Mouse," Miranda said, an answer that seemed to mollify the owl.

"So I see," Selod replied, glancing warily at the bird. He had never paid much attention to the magic that gave rise to familiars, but he found the practice unsettling. The animals themselves could be no different from any of their species—but they seemed hyperintelligent, he guessed, through some sort of empathic link with their human masters. Somehow, when he made a remark about Mouse, it was *Miranda's* understanding of the remark that was transmitted to the animal in a way it could understand. Nevertheless, he disliked even the appearance of conducting a campfire conversation with an owl. Selod rubbed his hands briskly before the fire and sighed. "Well, we're a long way from the Council Chamber now, aren't we?"

"That's precisely what I'd like to talk to you about," Roland announced. He had returned, having found not only his gray riding cloak, but his usual, confident manner as well. He strode around the fire and offered an oversized hand to his fellow ex-minister. Gladly, Tarem Selod reached out to grasp it.

Their hands clasped together, and with one huge heave, Roland pulled the mage off the ground. Selod fairly flew into the warrior's great embrace.

"Careful or you'll break me," Selod warned. "I haven't survived assassins to be crushed by a lout of a friend!"

"Then gain some weight," Roland responded, grinning hugely. "You're still too thin." He gently put the mage back on his feet, but retained a grip of the man's shoulders. They felt frail beneath his huge hands, almost insubstantial. More soberly, Roland continued, "Survived . . . We had feared otherwise. Just before we fled, we'd heard you were dead, another of the victims. Until now, I thought we'd never see each other again, unless—"

"Perhaps," Miranda interrupted, "you would be kind enough to tell us what *did* happen to you, since it's obvious you weren't killed."

"Oh, not so obvious," Selod replied, chuckling drily. "I certainly had Hain fooled—at least until I winked."

"Hain?" Miranda asked.

"The assassin who has been murdering our old fraternity with such relish," Selod explained, his face clouding over with distaste at the thought of the man. "It all comes back to business rather quickly, doesn't it? Well, that's for the best, I suppose. There are other places I need to be, and spending the night here is out of the question."

Roland blinked in surprise. He had already begun to imagine the scenario: he, Miranda, and Selod storming the Imperial Palace at Thyrsus . . .

"Other places? Aren't you coming to Thyrsus?"

"Why should I go to Thyrsus," Selod responded, "when you won't be there to keep me company?"

"What do you mean?" Roland insisted, his voice wary. "That's exactly where we're going—"

"I'm afraid not," the mage replied. Not, he added to himself, when I need an insurance policy elsewhere.

Miranda cleared her throat. "Tarem, I can see that you're

no better than ever at explaining things coherently."

Selod spread his hands out and shrugged, as if there were nothing he could do.

"The problem is endemic, my dear, to worrying about too many things at the same time. Once you find that they're all connected, it's hard to discover how to pick them apart again."

Miranda swept back her disordered hair and tied it in a quick knot. It was back to business indeed.

"Well, Tarem, you'll simply have to do your best. Begin at the beginning—"

"That would be more than a millennium ago."

She sighed. "Then begin with Hain. How do you know the man's name? I assume you're not social acquaintances."

"Hardly. Hain has little use for polite company. Or at least, he has the same uses for them that the cat has for mice. No, Miranda, I know his name—and other select details—because I had the opportunity to probe his mind."

"Then you bested him. Your Phrase is safe, as is mine." Roland drew himself up, enthusiastic with this development.

"I'm afraid not," Selod answered. "I had hoped simply to capture him, but the man's employer has placed a few interesting wards on Hain. I doubt the assassin knows it, but he will not survive being taken prisoner. Nor will he survive failing to take a Phrase once the process has begun." Selod frowned. "That was another nasty surprise I hadn't anticipated. Perhaps I should have killed him on the spot, but we would have learned nothing."

"Which means . . . ?"

"Which means that I let the fiend have his way. He tortured the Phrase out of me. It was the only way I could gain the time I needed to learn what I needed to know."

"You simply *surrendered* your Phrase?" Roland roared with surprise.

"Surrendered? Not precisely," Selod corrected, thinking back to the torture he had endured and the ongoing ordeal of recovering from it. Any other man would have simply died and been done with it. All his magical acumen was concentrated on preserving a body that had no right to continue living. It would be weeks—perhaps months—before he had healed sufficiently to leave the rest of the process to nature and time.

"I didn't come here to chat about my meeting with Hain," Selod said quietly. "This much is important: Hain and his employer now possess all six Chaldean Phrases, and even as we speak, they have taken the road west to Yndor."

"Impossible!" Roland thundered. "My Phrase is safe."

"Yours," Selod countered, smiling sadly, "but not Amet Pale's."

For a moment, the Caladors sat in stunned silence, trying to make sense of the unthinkable. The six Chaldean Phrases, along with six Phrases entrusted to the royalty of Yndor, were the only means of undoing the Binding, a spell that had changed the very nature of the world after a war of wizards had almost destroyed the civilizations the wizards had meant to conquer. The Binding had put severe limitations on what could be accomplished by magic, and after centuries the world had become a safer and more predictable place, where wizards were seldom considered more powerful than engineers or businessmen or politicians—politicians like Calador, who had eventually come to think of the Phrases as little more than a ceremonial responsibility. Ceremonial, that is, until an assassin had begun murdering them, one by one, for their pieces of the ancient formula. To doom the world again to the chaos of unchecked wizards was utter madness, but a madness that Yndor's emperor seemed bent upon.

Finally, Roland shook off the shock of the news and his face hardened with resolve. "Then let's get on the road and fly to Thyrsus!"

"A sad course of action," Selod said, smiling, "considering that they're behind us."

"Better still. We'll ride east—"

"I'm afraid not."

"But—"

"You would not be able to stop Hain if you tried. Or rather, you would not be able to stop the one for whom he works." Selod did not bother to add that, if the Caladors headed east to intercept Hain, they would be walking beneath the noses of hundreds of army and intelligence agents who were looking for them. And that would yield no good for anyone. "No, Calador, your road lies neither east nor west."

"Please, Tarem," Miranda entreated, "don't be cryptic. It's an awful habit."

Again, Selod smiled. "Very well, I'll be plain—although it rather spoils the Delphic pleasure of my trade. There are very few besides, my dear."

"You're getting worse," Miranda warned.

The old mage sighed and held his hands before the fire, as if he were reluctant to go on. "How well acquainted are you with the Ulthorn?"

Roland shuddered. "Not at all. That's no place for an army."

"Not of men, anyway," Selod murmured in assent. "Upon the easternmost reaches of the Woodblood River, roughly north of Belfar, there is a solitary hill in the forest. It stands high above the trees and you will know it for the ruined tower that stands at its crest. This is known as Happar's Folly."

"An odd name," Roland mused. "Surely, there's a story behind it."

Selod pulled his cloak more tightly about himself and nodded. "A simple story. Happar was the man who built it, and to build it was folly indeed. It's the only edifice made by human hands in the heart of the forest, and for good reason. Dwelling there cost Happar his life." He went quiet again, leaning over the fire to warm his hands. His eyes caught the light of the flames and flickered. "I warned him."

"And how are we supposed to find a single tower in the midst of a forest the size of Gathony?"

"I know it," Miranda said softly.

Roland's eyes narrowed as he turned toward his wife. "How would you—?"

Miranda shot him a quick look, lips pursed disapprovingly, and he let the remainder of his question die in his mouth.

"I know it," she repeated. "And we can find it."

Frustrated by the sudden, confusing turn of events, Roland huffed out a long breath before rejoining the conversation. "I still don't see why we don't simply hunt down this Hain and finish things quickly."

"Some things don't finish quickly," the mage replied. *No, indeed*, he thought. This business had been centuries in the finishing already. And if there were a dram of justice left in the world, it would be over without any need for the Caladors' further involvement. With a bit of justice—or luck; he was not about to get picky—Tarem Selod would meet the Caladors at Happar's Folly and tell them they could go home to their quiet lives. But in case anything went awry . . . "Believe me, old friend, it is important that you be at Happar's Folly."

Roland's gaze met Selod's, fell into it, in fact. In the thirty years he had known the wizard, Roland had experienced only a few glimpses of the inner man. Tonight, he saw pain (what exactly had Selod meant, that Hain *tortured* the Phrase out of him?), and a deep sorrow, and an all-abiding patience. Selod had waited an awfully long time for something—Calador was not exactly sure what, although now he began to have suspicions—and the mage would continue to bide his time until the moment was right.

"And what do we do at Happar's Folly?"

Selod chuckled, as if Calador should already know the answer. "You'll know when the time comes. And speaking of time, it's time that I go." Slowly, he rose to his feet and dusted off his cloak.

Calador looked around. "And where is your horse?" he asked, a sly smile coming to his lips.

Selod's mouth curled with an answering humor. "Ah, dear Roland, you should know better."

And with that, the mage lifted his cowl over his head and disappeared.

CHAPTER 3

When Brandt awoke, he found Marwick seated in the same position by his bedside, as if he had not moved in hours. The Belfarian thief looked deeply lost in thought. His hands were pressed hard on either side of his head, little shocks of curly red hair spilling between the fingers. It was rare to see Marwick, a jester by nature, look so reflective.

Brandt gazed about the room and noted, with relief, that Old Hoot was nowhere to be found. He couldn't quite recall what the man had finally done for a cure. Some potion or unguent . . . ? Brandt's memories of the strange physician seemed like a nightmare, and he began to wonder whether Old Hoot had been nothing more than a figment of his fevered brain. But whether Old Hoot was dream or real, whether it had been the physician or time's curative powers, what mattered was that the pain was finally gone. Finally, he could resume the hunt in earnest.

"Marwick."

The thief looked up, a bit startled that Brandt had awoken without his realizing it.

"You look better," Marwick observed, noting the pink that had returned to Brandt's cheeks. "How are you feeling?"

Brandt propped himself up on his elbows. He really felt much better, he realized, save for a ravenous appetite. How long had it been since his last meal—or more remote still, the last meal that he had not thrown up? He would need to build his strength back before he faced the assassin . . .

"It's gone, you know," Marwick added when it became

apparent that Brandt was not going to answer his previous question.

"It?"

"The homunculus," Marwick replied.

Brandt's brow wrinkled. "What are you talking about?" he asked irritably, but Marwick's words had stirred something, a hazy memory. A memory of Old Hoot's gnarled hands plunging into his flesh—

"What happened here?" Brandt asked suspiciously. "What did that old man do to me?"

Marwick smoothed his hair back as he pondered how to describe recent events. "Well, Brandt, as Mother used to say—"

"No twisted proverbs," Brandt interrupted. "Simple facts, please."

"Nothing that happened here was simple," Marwick replied with a laugh. "But if you need an explanation you can balance on your fingertip . . . Basically, a homunculus was trying to materialize inside your guts in order to tear its way out and kill you, but Old Hoot outwitted it—" He paused a moment in contemplation of what he considered a profound enigma. "Funny," he said finally. "The odd bird didn't even charge a fee."

Brandt stared at his former friend, disbelieving. If only he could reassemble his confused recollections of the past few days into a coherent narrative. But all he could summon were disjointed sensations: the road passing as a jarring blur, some woman undressing him, the strong odor of his horse, pulling a knife on some traveler, the feel of leather cords biting into his thighs, the swirl of Old Hoot's motley robes . . .

"A homunculus?" he muttered.

Marwick nodded. "Little green-gray demon, long as your forearm."

"I know what they are," Brandt muttered. He had forgotten Marwick's habit of tweaking him at every turn. He feared he didn't have the strength left to deal with the prankster. "At least, I know what the bedtime stories *say* they are. And where is this homunculus now? Playing with its fairy friends?"

"Old Hoot became annoyed with it and destroyed it."

Brandt peered about the room suspiciously. There was no evidence of this bizarre encounter. "And where's the corpse?"

Marwick smiled, remembering the creature's unexpected demise. "There is no corpse. Hoot—well, he shrunk it into nothing."

"That old charlatan drew a homunculus out of my belly and obliterated it?" Brandt asked, eyes narrowed suspiciously.

Marwick shrugged. "You asked for the simple facts. There they are."

Brandt sat up and swung his legs over the edge of the bed. Amazingly, the movement incurred no ill effects.

"You're working some sort of angle," he accused. "I thought even you could cook up a better story—"

"If you recall," Marwick interrupted testily, "I had the entire contents of your purse in my hands earlier this morning. It would have been easier to leave you here delirious—in fact, never to have come here at all—if I'd been after your money."

Brandt turned to see his leather purse resting on the rickety night stand. Perhaps Marwick was telling the truth. Perhaps it was Old Hoot working the angle. Chances were, the old man hadn't the foggiest idea what had been wrong with Brandt and had used some mummery to fool Marwick into thinking he'd actually done something. But why hadn't Old Hoot asked for payment? Possibly, Brandt considered, they were in cahoots—and the return of the purse was the classic gesture of the confidence man, instilling enough trust to soften up the mark for the big score. And Marwick surely knew that Brandt was worth far more than he carried about in his purse.

"I saved your life, old friend," Marwick went on, his voice deepening, "and I think I deserve better thanks than an accusation."

Brandt sighed, sure he knew what Marwick meant by "better thanks."

"Just send a letter to Carn and tell him how much you want—"

"I don't want your money, Brandt," the thief reiterated wearily. They had spent as many years apart now as they had once spent together, and still, Marwick reflected, nothing had changed. "I never wanted your money. If I coveted mountains of gold, I'd have gone into espionage with you and Carn. But government work? Plenty of money, but boring as Governor Tam's daughter."

Brandt raised an eyebrow at that last comment. "You know the governor's daughter?"

Marwick grinned rakishly. "Intimately. She likes her love made quickly, with liberal doses of tearful penitence thereafter."

Brandt's other eyebrow followed suit.

"A wasted conquest," Marwick continued. "As Mother always said, it matters not what position the father enjoys, but which ones the daughter does."

"A wise woman, your mother," Brandt growled, wishing that Marwick had just stolen his purse and disappeared last night. "So, Marwick, if you're not after my money, why have you been hanging around here all day?"

The corners of Marwick's mouth curled downward in an uncharacteristic frown.

"I'm beginning to wonder, myself," he muttered, pushing a stray wisp of red hair out of his eyes. "Let's pose a riddle for you, Brandt. Suppose that, after a dozen years' absence, your childhood best friend finally comes to town—and he's more dead than alive. What would you do?"

A long sigh escaped Brandt's lips. "Fair enough. Thanks for making sure I recovered. But now that I'm better, I need to get moving."

"Moving toward what?" Marwick asked. He leaned forward, chin on clasped hands, elbows on knees, in the posture of a man who had all the time in the world to listen.

"I thought you said government business bores you, Marwick."

The thief replied with his usual lopsided grin. "I'm willing to make an exception. No musty old files this time, I'll wager. No, Brandt, you look to me like a hunted man."

Slowly, Brandt balled his hands into fists. Marwick and his damned taste for drama . . . They sat here chatting and, meanwhile, the assassin's trail grew colder.

"There's no hunting being done," he replied grimly, "except what I'm doing myself."

"Ah," Marwick replied, leaning back in his seat as if everything had become clear. He made a steeple of his fingers and tapped them against his chin. "That's why you rode into town with a mythological creature gnawing at your guts."

Brandt stood up. "Where are my damned clothes?" The cheap room took only a moment to examine—the cot, a small bedside table with decades of names whittled into the wood, and not a drawer in sight. As he walked to the closet, he continued speaking, hoping to bring the conversation—and the reunion—to an end in no longer than it would take to be dressed. "Let's be blunt, Marwick. I've got someone I have to find, and find quickly, so there's no time for chatter and delay."

Marwick threw his head back and laughed harshly. "Dying from a homunculus attack isn't a delay? In any case, Brandt, if you're looking for someone in Belfar, I'm the man to talk to. Say I was looking for antique shops in the Prandis suburbs, you'd be the first man I'd ask for directions—but Belfar is *my* city now. If I can't find a man here, that man simply doesn't exist."

Brandt paused for a moment to consider the suggestion. Marwick had found *him* as soon as he entered Belfar, after all. Had that just been coincidence—or were Marwick's contacts really that extensive?

Brandt pushed those questions roughly aside for more practical matters when he discovered that the closet was empty.

"Marwick, where are my blasted clothes?"

The thief wrinkled his nose in memory of the departed garments.

"They were stinking up the room. I couldn't think from the fumes so I sent them downstairs for a washing."

Naked, Brandt sat down on the bed. There would certainly be some delay now, until he could get his clothes back. For the first time, he glanced at Marwick's ostentatious blue suit with something resembling envy.

"All right," he sighed. "I'll describe the people I'm looking for, and if you can help me find them, I'll pay you well." Brandt hardly expected that Marwick would find them, but at least the quest would get Marwick out of the room. "The first is perhaps four inches taller than me and completely bald. Built like a rock, moves like a cat. He may be traveling with another man, about my height. Black hair with a sharp widow's peak. Long, thin features, and swarthy—probably a foreigner, though you wouldn't know by the accent."

Marwick absorbed this information quietly and waited a moment, seeming to expect Brandt to go on. In a moment, it became apparent that he wouldn't. "Brandt, that's not much to go on. Surely you can do better than that."

"Surely I can't," Brandt snapped. "The first one I met during a sword fight in the dark. I had other things to worry about than the color of his eyes. The other I met only once, almost a month ago, and had no reason to think I'd ever want to see him again. I didn't pay particular attention."

Marwick said nothing, but Brandt could guess what he was thinking: too much of the high life was making Brandt soft.

"Can you find them or not?" Brandt growled between grinding teeth. "I'll pay good money—"

"For the last time," Marwick interrupted, "I don't want or need your money. Oh, I'm no damned industrialist magnate, but I keep leather on my feet, whiskey in my glass—and a tidy nut tucked away against winter. So the answer is no, Brandt, I won't help you for money. I'll help you only if you acknowledge that you need a partner and an equal." *That*, Marwick did not bother saying, was more than Brandt had ever been able to admit, even as a child. "So, what will it be?"

Brandt leaned back against the wall, indifferent to the peeling green paint that stuck to his naked flesh. Here he was again, twelve years after leaving Marwick, back in the same rut. How they had once been such good friends, he could no longer imagine. The undiscriminating nature of childhood friendships, he supposed. But even long ago, the more serious he had become, the more glib Marwick had turned, as if to maintain some overall balance. And now, here was Marwick still toying with him, when what Brandt needed was simple help.

Brandt sighed. There would be no way to get that help without humoring the old guttersnipe.

"Partners," he breathed, barely audibly, and then added with force, "only so long as I remain in Belfar."

Marwick's smile broadened by a hair. "Now tell me why you're here."

Brandt realized that, if he kept grinding his teeth together, there would be nothing left of his molars by the time the conversation was over. The last thing he wanted was to discuss *why* he was here in Belfar, why he was hunting an assassin—because he had been too slow-witted to stop him in the first place, because he'd been too weak to kill him when he'd had the chance. This was exactly the last discussion he wanted to have, but Marwick was clearly unwilling to move his blue velvet ass until he made Brandt confess.

"The bald one crippled Carn—"

"What?" Marwick cried, rising from his seat, his face drained white.

"He'll never walk again," Brandt went on.

"How . . . ? No, never mind." Marwick strode toward the door, his eyes narrowed with fury. "Time for the explanation later. Mark my words: Those are dead men by dawn."

When Marwick swung open the inn's front door late that afternoon, the low sun swept across the grimy dining room floor to reveal Brandt seated before a bowl of what looked to be porridge. Brandt put down a steaming cup of tea and motioned his old partner to join him.

"Well?" Brandt asked.

"I've never seen porridge quite that color before."

Brandt shrugged. "I feel almost my old self, but my stomach isn't quite up to solid food. I thought I'd go easy on it for a while," he explained, raising his spoon to the light with a profound look of distaste, "assuming you can call this easy."

"As I recall," Marwick responded lightly, "it was you who chose this particular lodging. Good thing they don't have any of your electric lights, though. Can you imagine eating that stuff if you had a really good look at it?"

Brandt took the spoonful into his mouth and swallowed as quickly as he could manage, trying to eliminate the painful process of taste.

"What did you find?"

Marwick sighed. "Belfar is a large city and this is the busy season. Merchants are pouring through the eastern gates and pouring out through the western ones just as swiftly."

At that moment, the proprietor, a greasy-haired man wearing an apron stained gray and brown, stopped by the table.

"What'll it be?"

Marwick assumed an ingratiating smile. "You know, I had such a large lunch, I'm just not hungry yet."

The man glowered at him but left the table without an argument.

"Perhaps we should do something about the accommodations," Marwick muttered.

"To hell with the accommodations. Did you find them or not?"

"Give me another day," the red-haired thief replied. "If they're in Belfar, they haven't made their presence obvious—"

Halfway through Marwick's sentence, Brandt put down his spoon and pushed back his chair.

"I knew I should have taken care of this myself," he announced as he rose to his feet. "I'm wasting my time with you, as usual."

Marwick scowled as Brandt rose shakily from his chair.

"You shouldn't be moving about!" cried a scratchy voice.

Both men turned to see a swirl of color descending the staircase from the boarding rooms above.

"It was too much to hope that he wouldn't remember payment," Marwick muttered beneath his breath.

"I've just been looking for you," Old Hoot explained as he crossed the wide room. Without ceremony, he pulled up a chair and settled between Brandt and Marwick, not seeming to notice that Brandt was standing, ready to leave. The old physician sniffed warily at the porridge left in Brandt's bowl. "That stuff could kill you," he announced curtly. "I didn't save your life for you to throw it away on the food here."

Save your life, Marwick reflected. Nine times out of ten, those words preceded a pitch for money.

"Save my life," Brandt grunted. "Yes, so Marwick tells me . . . although he takes more than half the credit, by virtue of having hired you."

"Mm," Old Hoot hummed in assent, "true enough, I suppose. Few physicians have experience in the removal of homunculi. Had your friend sought a different practitioner, you would probably be dead."

Brandt eased back into his seat and peered intently at the old man's face. Old Hoot's eyes were almost obscured by drooping and spotted folds of flesh, but behind those wrinkles were a pair of engaging and, Brandt had to admit, honest-looking eyes.

On the other hand, Brandt reflected, as a con artist, Old Hoot clearly had at least a forty-year advantage over him in experience.

"So," Brandt finally announced, hoping to cut short the negotiation, "how much do I owe you?"

Inaudibly, Marwick groaned. To *remind him,* of all things . . .

"Nothing," Old Hoot replied, and Marwick's eyebrows shot up like rockets. "In cases of life and death, I never charge. You were, after all, in no position to accept or reject any fee I might have offered, and it's unfair to impose payment after the fact."

"That's . . . quite generous," Brandt replied, as puzzled as Marwick by the old man.

"Of course," Old Hoot went on smoothly, "there's no telling when another homunculus might come your way, and you have no protection against *that*."

Involuntarily, Brandt smiled. "And I suppose you have a way of preventing relapses?"

"Certainly," the old man replied.

"For a certain fee?" Brandt continued.

Old Hoot got to his feet. "We can discuss that back in your room."

The odd physician turned away and, without waiting for Marwick and Brandt, disappeared up the stairs.

"Coming?" Marwick asked as he rose. Brandt seemed to have no intention of moving.

"I suppose," he replied, but he got up slowly. He had supposed that Jame Kordor was the only man trying to kill him, but Kordor would hardly be the type to send homunculi his way. Brandt considered this for a moment. Homunculi—except for the brief flash of green that had registered in his mind before he had passed out, Brandt had never seen a homunculus. As far as he knew, no one on earth had. They were legends, scary stories for ill-behaved children—or perhaps, like the Khrine, they had once existed, before the Binding. But this was the modern age, an age for motors and electricity, not monsters and frights. The idea of a homunculus—Brandt's hand went reflexively to his stomach as he pondered this—the very idea was preposterous. Especially a homunculus lodged in his belly.

The physician was waiting patiently outside Brandt's room. Brandt drew a skeleton key from his newly laundered trousers and unlocked the door. Old Hoot slipped inside and, without ceremony, dropped himself into the chair that Marwick had occupied all morning.

"Well, well," the old man said. "Let's see about preventing any further infestations, shall we?"

He beckoned Brandt to stand close and peered intently at the thief's belly, although what he hoped to discern in Brandt's shirt was uncertain.

Disconcerted by the physician's odd posture, Brandt took a step back.

"Don't move!" the physician snapped. "I'm an old man and my eyesight isn't what it once was."

Brandt obliged by stepping forward again.

"How many homunculus attacks have you dealt with?"

The old man looked up and grinned. "Oh, yours is the first. Usually the patient dies far too quickly to be saved. On the other hand, I've seen the remains of a homunculus attack . . . oh, I'd say nine or ten times." Old Hoot leaned back in his chair with pride. "That makes me one of the continent's experts on the subject."

"Charming," Marwick muttered.

"Now, I was in the process of examining you." Once again, Old Hoot leaned forward and began peering inexplicably at Brandt's belly. "I don't think," he announced, "that I have ever seen a man quite so loaded with magical protections as yourself."

Marwick cleared his throat, as he often did before an official proclamation. "As my mother always said, the popular man saves money at the armorer's."

"What the hell is that supposed to mean?" Brandt snapped.

Marwick grinned amiably in reply. "Short on friends, long on foes, few days on earth, but eternal repose."

"Your mother as well, I suppose?" Brandt grumbled.

"Why, you've even got a spell protecting you against lice," Old Hoot exclaimed. "I've never seen that one before."

Brandt frowned, remembering a long-distant day with disgust. The lice had been a competitor's revenge for a piece of espionage that Brandt had done.

"Try having your body shaved when you're suffering a pox of lice, and you'll think of consulting a mage as well."

"A wise decision, no doubt," Old Hoot proclaimed. "I was

just taken by the novelty of it." The old man sat back. "Well, it's done."

"What's done?" Marwick asked.

"The spell. Your friend should be protected against any homunculus for the remainder of his life."

Brandt and Marwick looked at each other. For all the world, it seemed that the old man had done nothing but stare at Brandt's belly for the past five minutes. Sheer fakery . . . *Still*, Brandt thought, *he had known about the lice.*

"I see you're skeptical. You've very little confidence in anything, have you?" the old man asked Brandt, who did not deign to reply. "Well, no hard feelings. Mine is a profession in which one is called to prove himself from harvest 'til market, market 'til harvest. So come, have a seat and as a gesture of goodwill I'll tell you your fortune."

Brandt snorted in open derision.

Old Hoot's face twisted with sly humor. "Of course, I'm not the type to thrust unwanted services on a customer . . . but I will tell you this before I leave. That friend of yours will never find the man you seek in Belfar."

"What—" Marwick sputtered, but Brandt cut him off with a sharp, surprised gesture.

"What do you know about him?" Brandt asked, his voice low and dangerous. Old Hoot did not seem to notice the menace of his tone.

"So you *would* like your fortune told?"

Brandt frowned as he took a seat on the bed. "Get on with it."

Old Hoot nodded and reached into the folds of his garish clothing. After a moment of groping about, he produced a small, oval mirror and placed it on the bed beside Brandt.

"Think of the one you seek and press your hand to the glass."

Brandt kept a suspicious eye on Old Hoot as he slowly lowered his hand onto the cool surface of the mirror. When he lifted his hand again, the glass was clouded—misted over where his skin had touched it. Oddly, the mist did not evaporate. Instead, it began to swirl about within the confines of

Brandt's handprint. The vapors darkened as they writhed, slowing until they resolved into a hazy image. Hard as it was to make out, there was no mistaking it: the mist had formed the picture of Hain's face.

"This is the man?" Old Hoot asked.

Brandt nodded quietly as Marwick leaned over to stare at the vaporous image.

"He and his companion arrived in Belfar this morning."

Brandt's eyes narrowed at the news. So he had been ahead of them, despite his illness. That simplified things enormously.

"You can find them tonight in dusky arms. I will say only this in addition: do not interrupt them, but wait. After midnight, your time will be ripe. Seek to rush things and you will lose more than you might imagine."

With that, Old Hoot reached for his mirror and secreted it away in whatever hidden pocket it had come from.

"That's gibberish—" Brandt began sourly.

"Perhaps you have *heard* gibberish," Old Hoot countered. "What I've spoken, quite simply, is the truth. And now I must leave you. Good luck, Brandt Karrelian. I do not envy what I see ahead for you."

"Wait!" Marwick cried, but Old Hoot had already risen and opened the door. Marwick jumped nimbly to his feet and sprang toward the old man, but Brandt caught the thief by the arm.

"Let the charlatan go," he muttered, "and good riddance."

The physician had just slipped past the door and into the hallway. Marwick shook himself free of Brandt's grip and vaulted into pursuit. He would be, perhaps, a step or two behind the old man.

Fools chasing fools, Brandt thought with disgust as he threw himself prostrate on the bed.

A minute later. when he returned to the room. Marwick's face looked paler than usual.

"He vanished," the usually exuberant thief said quietly.

"Naturally," Brandt replied from the bed. "He knew well enough to flee before we had him jailed as a fraud."

"No," Marwick replied, "I mean he *vanished*. He shouldn't have been more than a step ahead of me when I got into that hallway, but he was gone. Completely gone, as if he'd never been here."

Brandt shrugged. "He probably ducked into an adjoining room. More than likely, he's having a good laugh right now, eavesdropping on you."

"I checked the nearby rooms," Marwick replied, a bit of an edge creeping into his voice.

Brandt sighed. "What does it matter where he went? The old fool obviously had nothing of use to tell us."

Marwick lowered himself into the chair by the bed and sat quietly for a moment. "Brandt, Dusky Arms is the name of an inn that opened seven, eight years back, no more than a mile from here. We'll find your quarry in Dusky Arms."

Brandt pulled on his lower lip as he considered that. He thought back to the image that he'd seen in the mirror: Hain's mocking leer framed by the outline of Brandt's own hand. Brandt burned to get his hands on Hain, but in a much more physical fashion. He would take any opportunity, even if it came from as unlikely a source as Old Hoot, and even if it involved enduring Marwick's company that much longer. *Besides*, he thought, glancing at Marwick's lanky figure, *his old partner was more than an ordinary asset in a fight*. Brandt might need someone to occupy Hain's employer while he dealt with the assassin himself.

Marwick smiled as he watched Brandt's face darken into a contemplative scowl. He could fairly read each bitter thought as it wheeled through Brandt's mind. Amazing, he reflected, that after all these years Brandt had changed so little.

"Then, tonight, at the Dusky Arms?" Marwick extended his hand toward Brandt.

Slowly, Brandt exhaled, then nodded. "Tonight," he replied, making no move to take Marwick's hand.

"Still partners?" Marwick half-asked, half-stated, leaving his hand suspended between them.

Reluctantly, Brandt gripped it in his own. "Partners," he agreed, "for now."

The two partners looked to be in vastly different moods as they trod the darkened streets of Belfar. The red-haired man who led the way spoke volubly and cheerfully on a variety of subjects, but most enthusiastically on the triumphs and tragedies of the local sporting teams. His companion, who strode grimly along with a hand on his sword, said nothing during this monologue. Indeed, he wondered how he'd forgotten Marwick's mania for sports.

"The Highlanders have more than enough talent to win," Marwick was explaining blithely, "but their owner—"

Suddenly, Brandt's interest awakened—not from Marwick's appraisal of the sporting situation, but by a weather-beaten wooden sign that swung beneath a weak gaslight. It crudely depicted an aproned woman, middle-aged and wide around the belly, holding out her arms invitingly. Beneath the amateurish painting were two surprisingly neatly stenciled words: DUSKY ARMS.

Brandt drew his black cloak tightly around him and picked up his pace, overtaking Marwick in a couple of steps.

"Brandt? Where are you going?"

Brandt offered no answer. He merely increased his pace and began to outdistance Marwick farther. The red-haired thief scowled and broke into a run even as he looked upward at the sky. The city bells had not yet tolled midnight and, he could tell by the position of the moon, it would be another fifteen minutes before those bells would announce the new day. Marwick had no idea whether Old Hoot's words amounted to good advice or prophecy, but after what he'd seen during the past day, Marwick was reluctant to cross the old man's words, even by a few minutes.

He caught up with Brandt just as the smaller man reached the long window that ran along the front of the inn. Years of smoking and cooking had left a deposit of filth on the window, but if you didn't mind pushing your nose to the glass, you could still discern the inside of the main room. Several men were clustered about a few different tables, a few eating a late meal, but most of them merely drinking. Marwick searched the crowd but could not find a bald man among them. No doubt, they were lying low in a room upstairs. It would be simple enough to bribe the innkeeper to tell them which. And by that time, midnight would have arrived . . .

"I don't see him," Marwick began, squinting against the fitful light cast off by tallow candles. "You know, they could use one of your electric lamps in there." Marwick laughed at the idea of the shoddy inn buying one of Brandt's expensive generators. "Just think, Brandt, if all of Blake's Warren went to electricity, you'd be the richest man in Chaldus. Imagine what it would take to light up this hellhole . . ."

Marwick heard Brandt inhale sharply and he turned to watch his old friend. Brandt's face was transformed, twisting with emotion, as he peered at something toward the far corner of the room. There, through the swinging doors that led to a back room, a bald man emerged, his right arm wrapped around a woman's back in a way that left his thumb casually nestled beneath her breast. The man glanced down at the woman the way a diner might inspect a piece of meat, casually assessing whether it had been cooked to his liking. Marwick studied the hard lines of the man's face. He recognized the type—the pure predator—and was usually wise enough to steer wide of them.

One of the patrons had been tuning a guitar and chose that moment to begin playing. Hain took the opportunity to spin the woman around, crushing her against him in a more-than-suggestive manner as he moved in time to the music.

"The bastard is *dancing*."

Brandt had been talking to himself, but it was enough to make Marwick turn. He wasn't sure what it was about the dancing that made Brandt react so, but if his old friend had seemed furious before, there were no words left for how he seemed now. Brandt's chin was quivering, his nostrils flared wide, a single vein in his temple throbbing green. He jerked the leather drawstring that kept his cloak in place and let it slip from his shoulders onto the ground.

"Brandt," Marwick cautioned, wishing the damned town bells would ring in the new day, "remember what Old Hoot said—"

But Brandt was paying him no attention. "Dancing," he muttered again, as if it were a curse. He drew his sword, then lurched forward. Almost as an afterthought, he realized that the dirty window stood between him and the inn's common room.

"Brandt!" Marwick protested. "For pity's sake, this isn't the way!"

Before the last word had left his mouth, Marwick ducked down, covering his head with his arms. With one sweeping blow, Brandt had swung his sword round and shattered the window-front of the bar. Glass shards sprayed in every direction, more than a few biting into Marwick's flesh.

"Now do you see him?" Brandt asked.

Hain, it was certain, saw them. Some of the inn's patrons had ducked beneath the tables upon the explosion of glass; others had jumped to their feet, equally stunned. Hain abandoned his grip on the girl and looked up. He greeted Brandt with a slight nod of his head and pushed the woman out of his way. A slight grating of metal announced the drawing of his sword.

Brandt smiled.

"No!"

It took Brandt a moment to realize that, although the cry had come from behind him, it wasn't Marwick's voice. He glanced over his shoulder to see two figures slide out of the shadows of an alley across the way and sprint across the street toward the inn. Both were clad in loose-fitting, black outfits that covered their entire bodies, down to gloves and masks. Each carried a short, light sword.

"Attack *now!*" the foremost figure cried as he hurtled past Brandt, clearing the broken glass with one fluid leap and landing in the barroom.

At this shouted command, two similarly clad figures burst into the room through the inn's kitchen. All four directed themselves at Hain.

The assassin's smile widened at this new turn of events. For a moment, Brandt seemed rooted to the ground, amazed at what he had unwittingly set in motion. Hain's hand flashed twice—two sharp flicks of the wrist—and two of the black-clad strangers fell in their tracks, circular razors embedded in their throats.

Two more, however, charged down the stairs from an upper room, and a third emerged from behind the bar. At this rate, Brandt realized, he would forfeit his chance to kill Hain personally. As Brandt leaped into the inn, another figure appeared at the top of the stairs—a swarthy man, not much larger than Brandt himself. It was, Brandt realized, the man who had tried to hire him weeks ago. How much pain and trouble Brandt would have saved by killing him then, he could not guess.

Madh stood unarmed at the top of the steps, scowling at the proceedings as if they amounted to an annoyance. Two more black-clad assassins emerged from the shadows and sprang at him. The first he sidestepped and, with a neatly placed kick, sent the man sprawling down the steep flight of stairs, splintering wood and bones as he tumbled. The next man aimed a swinging blow at Madh's head but, somehow, before his arm could get fully into motion, Madh stood only inches away from him, almost as if they were about to embrace. It would be the man's last embrace, it turned out, as Madh reached up and twisted his opponent's head sharply, breaking the neck.

Meanwhile, Hain had gutted the remaining three assassins as neatly and easily as a farmer slaughtering livestock. The room was a riot, with furniture overturned as the screaming patrons sought to flee the place. But in the street, they saw only a newly arrived throng of the black-clad killers—at least a dozen—and many of the bewildered customers stampeded toward the rear exit, not knowing whom to fear most.

Hain stood amid the carnage, waiting for the next challenge. He licked clean a spot of blood that had splashed upon his lips and laughed. Then, through a break in the crowd, he caught another glimpse of Brandt and lifted his blood-slick sword in salute.

"Come, Karrelian!"

Brandt needed no invitation as he hurdled tables and patrons toward Hain's corner, with Marwick only a half-step behind him.

But Madh had reached the ground floor and, calculating quickly what the approaching throng of attackers meant, cast a venomous look at Hain. For a moment he paused, as if pondering whether to leave the assassin, but instead he bent over and struck a fist to the floor. The floorboards erupted into a huge, crackling fire that leapt toward the rafters, forming a ribbon of flames that cut the room in half. One of the black-clad intruders, a little in advance of the others, was caught in the conflagration and staggered backward, screaming. The flames quickly lapped up the walls' wood paneling and danced upward toward the ceiling rafters. Marwick and Brandt stopped short of the fiery wall, unable to approach the intense heat any further.

"Brandt, let's go!" Marwick cried over the noise, grabbing at his old friend's shoulder. "This place is a tinderbox!"

Brandt pushed him away. He could still see, through the flames, the distorted, retreating figures of Hain and Madh. Desperately, he searched the room and found a table that had not been overturned. He sprinted toward it, vaulting onto the tabletop, and launched himself wildly over the fire. The flames licked at Brandt's flesh and singed his hair as he dove over them, landing heavily on the wooden floor. He rolled to his feet, taking only a moment to snuff a spot on his sleeve that had caught fire.

But a moment was too long. Hain and Madh were gone. In their place, Brandt was greeted by a gaping hole that grinned crookedly at him in the back wall of the bar. Splintered remnants of beams and studs lay strewn across the floor, a jumbled threshold to the riotous night beyond.

Brandt screamed in frustration as he dashed through the opening into a street that became more crowded with each passing second. The fire was flushing people out of nearby buildings and attracting the jaded denizens of Blake's Warren, who came merely to watch the show. In the distance, the firefighters' bell rang chaotically. Brandt ran pell-mell through the jumbled throng, trying to examine each bald head that bobbed among the masses.

Within minutes, the firefighters had arrived, spraying down the building with water pumped by magical means from a large, horse-drawn tank. The flames had already spewed a vast cloud of black smoke that obscured the sky, leaving the street lit only by the lurid reflection of the fire against wet cobblestones. Firefighters and panicked pedestrians ran past Brandt in either direction, their faces shining a demonic red in the night.

In one direction, the street ran toward the water truck; in the other, Brandt could see a large square in the distance. It was Hunin Square, he remembered from his Belfarian childhood, from which streets ran in a dozen different directions. If he were fleeing, that would be the path to take. He set off down the street at a breakneck pace, waving his sword through the air to clear a path through the onlookers. Halfway to the square he saw a form sprawled in the midst of the cobblestones: another of the black-clad assassins, a gaping wound in his neck.

He was on the right path. That knowledge lent further speed to his pursuit. He felt as if he were flying as he rounded the corner into Hunin Square, and a moment later, he *was* flying. A slim, well-placed foot shot out of the shadows, catching him in midstride, and he sprawled to the pavement, landing hard on his right elbow.

Foolish, he thought. That body was too obvious a sign. Hain had set a trap—

He rolled over, thinking only of getting to his feet, when that same foot connected squarely with his jaw, snapping back his head sharply. In another moment, he felt strong hands grip either arm and haul him up. A telltale pricking informed him that a knife had been set none-too-gingerly against his throat.

Slowly, his vision swam back into focus, and what had been a black blur resolved into a black-garbed assassin about Brandt's height, holding a long, wicked dagger. Two larger assassins stood behind him, pinning his arms against his back.

"Tell me why I shouldn't kill you now."

He could see, but his thoughts had not yet refocused. He realized only dimly that he recognized that voice. Who . . . ?

But an obliging black-gloved hand reached up and pulled off the mask that, until now, had hidden Elena Imbress's livid face.

Brandt groaned.

"You're not persuading me, you stupid bastard," Imbress observed, pushing the knife a little deeper into his flesh. "Do you realize what you've done? *We had them!* Another hour at most and they would have been in their rooms, asleep, easy prey—but then you arrive to blow the whole thing wide open."

Brandt glanced to either side, hardly in the mood for debate. The two intelligence operatives who pinioned his arms were too strong and had too much leverage to allow even a chance of escape. In addition, there was the matter of Imbress's knife at his throat. Cursing, Brandt realized he would have to talk his way free.

"We're letting him get away," Brandt declared urgently. "While we waste time squabbling—"

"They already *are* away," Imbress replied. "As soon as they got to this square, they vanished. I have twenty agents in this area, still looking, but it would take a thousand men to search Blake's Warren properly."

"And just who are you, anyway?"

They all turned their heads at this new intrusion, and Brandt found himself fighting back a smile, despite the dagger that remained pressed near his carotid. There stood Marwick, wearing his eternal jaunty grin above his now sooty velvet suit. His question was addressed to Imbress, at whom he waved his sword negligently.

"I don't believe we've been introduced," Marwick said. Then, seeming to realize that he was pointing a sword at a woman, he dropped the point of the blade and bowed his head slightly. *A fine-looking woman at that*, Marwick thought, despite the furrowed brow beneath her red hair. "Forgive my manners," he added, winking at Imbress before he turned back toward Brandt. "Keeping such fine acquaintances a secret from an old friend like me? I'm appalled, Brandt."

Brandt cleared his throat—a delicate operation to undertake when the throat was at knifepoint.

"Marwick, this is Elena Imbress of the Ministry of Intelligence."

Elena Imbress, Brandt would have added, if not for the knife at his throat, *my personal curse*. Ultimately, Brandt understood that it was Taylor Ash, the Minister of Intelligence, who had mixed him in this mess, but Imbress was the particular operative whom Ash had chosen as Brandt's scourge—and Imbress relished the job more than duty seemed to require. It was Imbress who had helped frame Brandt for the murders of Chaldus's ministers; Imbress who had shot at Brandt from Prandis's rooftops, trying to trick him into hunting the assassin; Imbress who had lied and manipulated him, doing everything to prevent him from learning the truth about the Phrases; and now whose interference was putting easy miles between the assassin and Brandt. In leaving Prandis, one of Brandt's few satisfactions had been the thought that he was leaving Imbress for good.

Marwick, for his part, bowed. "I've always admired the fine work Intelligence has done in Belfar. I've read many of the Ministry's reports."

At this, Elena arched an eyebrow and, with something approaching outrage, turned back toward Brandt.

"Who's your friend?"

Brandt rolled his eyes. Hain was getting away, yet here he

stood making formal introductions. "Marwick, a former associate of mine in Belfar."

Imbress nodded. "Ah, the thug days of your youth."

"You do us an injustice. We were energetic," Marwick responded, sounding hurt, "but hardly thugs."

Brandt's nostrils flared as he sucked in a long, annoyed breath. Between Imbress's meddling and Marwick's flirting—which might well last the rest of the night, Brandt realized—Hain and Madh were gaining miles.

"Let me go!" Brandt bellowed.

Marwick smiled again. "I was getting to that." He motioned toward the two operatives who held Brandt's arms. "Annoying as he can be, I'm still fond of him. Let him go," he suggested mildly.

"By no means," Elena ordered. "We have much more to discuss."

Marwick shrugged and turned as if to leave. Then, with stunning speed, he wheeled around and struck Elena's dagger out of her hand. With a dancer's agility, he let the movement carry him in a full circle as he pivoted behind Imbress, coming to rest with his sword at her throat.

The thief smiled engagingly. "As Mother always said," he observed, "you can't bargain with a squirrel unless you've got his nuts in your hand. Now, let's try again, shall we? Let him go."

"No!" Imbress snapped.

One of her operatives nodded curtly and released his grasp on Brandt's left arm with one hand, only to draw a dagger and put it to Brandt's throat, a fraction of an inch lower than where Imbress's had been.

"Why don't you all just kill each other and have done with it?" a hoarse and very testy voice interrupted. "It seems that's about all you're good for."

Marwick didn't need to turn around to recognize the voice. "Finally come to collect your fee, old man? It's an inconvenient time for it."

Old Hoot walked into the square and placed himself directly between the two deadlocked parties.

"Inconvenient?" he repeated. *The venerable physician*, Marwick thought, *was looking more than his age—whatever that might be.* His back was bent wearily beneath his motley outfit as he cursed his ill luck. "The inconvenience is entirely mine. After giving you such explicit directions, I never dreamed you could bungle on this scale."

Imbress, meanwhile, was peering intently at the old man's face, wishing that the light in the square was better. "I know you," she said softly.

"And I know you, my dear," the old man replied. "Or at least I thought I knew you better than to think you'd stoop to such idiocies. I sent you that note, after all, in hopes that you'd act on the knowledge effectively."

"*You* sent the note?" Imbress said. If only she could place the face . . .

Brandt smirked. "So you didn't find the assassin on your own, did you?"

Old Hoot fixed Brandt with a piercing glance. "Neither did you, if you recall. Now, Marwick, release Imbress. And you two, release Karrelian."

There was a moment of tense silence as Marwick watched the two men from Intelligence, and they watched him, neither party moving an inch.

In the distance, the town bells chimed midnight. The old man laughed harshly, reflecting that, by now, this whole affair should be over. *Well, it was over*, he thought. Just not the way he had intended. If only he'd possessed an ounce of his former strength, none of these machinations would have been necessary . . .

"I'm going to lose my patience very quickly," Old Hoot warned testily. His voice sounded more tired with every word..

"If you don't mind my asking, old man," Marwick began, "why should we listen to you?"

"Perhaps because I saved your friend's life already. Perhaps because, without me, none of you would have found Madh or Hain—"

"Madh?" Brandt interrupted. "Hain? Which—"

"The assassin is Hain," the old man explained. "His employer, Madh. Without my help, none of you would have found them. And without my cooperation, none of you will find them again."

Even now, he thought, he could feel them drawing away. At least, he could feel the movement of the gem that had touched his skin ever so briefly two weeks ago.

Silence fell over the square, save for the distant shouts of firemen echoing through the streets.

"Do it," Imbress finally commanded. "Let him go."

Marwick released her as soon as he saw Brandt freed.

Brandt took a few steps away from his captors and put a finger to his neck. It was bloody from a cut made when Marwick had knocked away Imbress's dagger.

"You almost killed me yourself," he observed.

"It was that or stand by and watch them do it," Marwick explained. "And I assumed you'd rather die by a friend's hand."

"A kind assumption," Old Hoot observed. "But if you don't mind, there is the rather more pressing matter of Madh to consider."

"Where is he?" Brandt insisted. With a little luck, he would be given a second chance that night—

"On the road north," Old Hoot said simply.

"That makes no sense," Imbress replied. "He should be in a blind panic now to get to Yndor. I'm certain he's taken one of the trade routes west. It's merely a matter of discovering which one."

Old Hoot fixed her with a scornful eye. "You may ride west if you like, but you'll have a difficult time explaining to Taylor Ash why you've failed." He turned toward Brandt. "Your colleague seems intent on a tour of the western trade routes. I suggest that *you* ride north."

Brandt frowned, undecided. It was true that only Old Hoot seemed to know Hain's whereabouts, but that very knowledge was disturbing. Who in the world was this old man, who conveniently happened to be nearby during Brandt's homunculus attack, and who knew so much about everything? Brandt began to suspect that Old Hoot himself was some sort of mage who had caused the attack and had then "cured" him in order to worm his way into Brandt's confidence. Had the Dusky Arms tip-off actually been a setup, spoiled by Imbress's unexpected appearance? No, that didn't quite add up—

"I agree with her," Brandt said cautiously. Imbress raised a skeptical eyebrow at that remark. "Why would they flee *north*? They'd be crossing the plains for no good reason."

The old man rolled his eyes and muttered something in a language that Brandt did not recognize.

"There's a perfectly good reason," he snapped. "Thanks to your bungling, Madh now knows that he is being pursued. Having you behind him, he doesn't care to face the bulk of the Chaldean army before him."

"He'll still have to cross the Cirran River," Imbress observed. "Our troops patrol the entire river regularly, and the farther he moves from the major roads, the more he'll slow himself down. It seems a losing proposition."

Old Hoot nodded. "He counts on such reasoning. And in part, you're right: he would run into substantial army forces . . . if he were intending to cross the Cirran in Chaldus, in the plains."

"The alternative is the Ulthorn," Marwick pointed out skeptically. No doubt, half the tales that were told of the haunted forest were spun of pure imagination. But if even half the tales were true . . . Marwick remembered the homunculus and reminded himself that, if even one of those tales were true, he wanted nothing to do with the Ulthorn. "Give me a choice between the army and the Ulthorn, and I'll risk the soldier boys any day."

"Madh is not afraid of the Ulthorn," Old Hoot replied.

"Well, then there's no need chasing him," Marwick exclaimed. "He's signed his own death warrant. I suppose this means we can go get a drink, Brandt."

Brandt scowled in reply. Damned Marwick, ever joking . . .

"I'll catch them *before* the Ulthorn," he said darkly, "so I can kill them myself."

"Neither outcome seems more likely as you stand here and chatter," Old Hoot fumed.

As the discussion progressed, Elena had meandered closer to the old man to get a better look at him. She knew that she knew him, but she couldn't say how. Not dressed in these clothes, she realized. They had met long ago . . . For the first time she looked directly into his eyes, and as he looked back, an instantaneous spark of recognition flared in her mind.

"My God," she cried, half-awed, half-outraged, "why didn't *you* simply kill him and save us the trouble?"

The old man smiled. "The answer, my dear, is that in my present condition, I'm in no shape to be standing out here in the middle of a chill night, where I'm liable to catch pneumonia, much less vie against a skilled opponent. These days, in truth, I feel much more like Old Hoot than I do Tarem Selod."

"Tarem Selod," Brandt repeated softly, almost under his breath. "Then you survived the assassin's attack . . ."

"Just barely," the man who had called himself Old Hoot agreed. He shook his old head once more as he considered what he'd said. "Just barely. But I have little time for reminiscence. As I said, Madh and Hain travel north. It is important that you catch them *before* they reach the Ulthorn. Once they reach the forest, Madh becomes far more dangerous. And the Ulthorn is dangerous enough on its own. Imbress, you must go with Karrelian and Marwick—"

"She's not going *anywhere* I go," Brandt began to object. Then he thought further of it. "And neither is Marwick. Listen, old man, I don't care who you are, but let me straighten you out on something. I don't work with anyone except—" He stopped short, scowling. "I don't work with *anyone.*"

"Explain to Carn why you failed," Tarem Selod replied, shrugging. "I'm no prophet. I know nothing of the future, but I do know this: alone, none of you can stop Madh and Hain."

Brandt glowered at Imbress but said nothing further.

"I'll go with Karrelian," Imbress said after a moment. "But I'm taking Harnor and Laz with me," she added, indicating the two masked men who had captured Brandt.

"Where you head," Selod cautioned, "numbers will be of no avail. Ignore me at your peril."

"They're going," Imbress repeated, not a trace of compromise in her voice.

"Very well," Tarem Selod sighed, "We don't have time to argue the point." The old man took a few steps back toward the street of the destroyed inn, then paused. His eyes touched upon Brandt's and held the younger man still for a moment. There was a great calm in those eyes, Brandt felt, and while he swam in them, his rage seemed to melt away.

"If you are wise, Mr. Karrelian," Tarem Selod said, "you will not think wholly of Hain. The assassin's work would never have been done had not Madh been there to direct him. It is Madh who must be caught. Bend your thoughts upon that."

Then, slowly, the man Brandt thought of as Old Hoot walked off into the night, leaving the five new colleagues in the square to contemplate each other uneasily.

" 'or the Body is but Dross,' " Carn read. The book in his lap was one of the expensive leather-bound editions of philosophy that he suspected Brandt had never opened, its spine so stiff that Carn had to hold the tome open with both hands. " 'It serves only as the Crucible in which the Mind may be heated to its whitest Flame, and is for that worthy but of Despite.' "

The crackling flames in the fireplace of Brandt's library were only reddish-orange, but they would have to do. To their embrace Carn consigned the book, hurling it across the room in disgust, pleased only at the eddies of ash and sparks when the volume struck the logs.

"Philosophy," Carn muttered, "serves as the bloody crucible in which the sausage may be heated to its brownest crust, and is for that worthy but of despite."

Holding one wheel in place, Carn spun the other wheel of his chair with two quick thrusts, turning him toward the door. He was surprised to find the door ajar, a small headless figure framed there in silhouette by the blinding electric chandelier in the hallway beyond. Carn's eyes adjusted after a moment and he realized the figure was Katham, inexplicably standing on his hands. How long the boy had been standing there, watching him upside-down, Carn had no idea.

"I like it when you read aloud, Master Carn," the boy said, walking nimbly on his hands into the library, "though it pains me to see you roast the book."

"The book was worthless," Carn muttered gruffly.

Katham laughed, his boyish soprano ringing through the room. "It's been years since your days of thievery, Master

Carn. Value on the street? Well, that book was worth a couple of caps, at least."

With that, he bent his arms until his head almost touched the floor, then catapulted himself backward. The boy landed gracefully on his feet and bowed.

"You should have come to Minister Kordor's funeral," the boy said. "It was great fun."

"I sent you," Carn replied, "because I knew you would enjoy it."

In point of fact, Katham had complained for an hour about the heavily starched white shirt and the itchy woolen suit he would have to wear in order to sneak into the funeral. But the sneaking itself—that was worth the world to him.

"What did you learn?" Carn asked. He noticed that Katham had not hesitated to change his clothes before coming to report the news. The boy's face, thank goodness, seemed well scrubbed, and his hair not as unkempt as usual, but those clothes—Carn could easier convince a snake to wriggle back into its shed skin than to persuade Katham to keep on a decent set of clothes. Except for occasions when he was strictly forbidden, such as Kordor's funeral, the lad insisted on wearing the same rags that Brandt had found him. *I'd stand out like a crown on a whore,* the kid had argued, *once I got back to the streets.* Carn sighed, remembering the conversation. So stubborn . . . and young though he was, a mouth like a sailor's.

"I learned," Katham replied, dropping his voice to a conspiratorial whisper, "that Minister Ravenwood hasn't been worth a slim copper in bed for the last three months."

Carn closed his eyes and sighed. Twenty years ago, he'd have been calculating the market worth of that tidbit, but now it just seemed dreary.

"Andus Ravenwood took you aside to tell you this, no doubt?"

Katham laughed again, his eyes twinkling in the firelight. "Of course not. The Ministers are a bunch of sly, mean old goats. They watch everything and say nothing when anyone is within eavesdropping distance. No fun at all. Especially that General Pale." Katham smiled crookedly. "He looks like some of my friends have been playing X's and O's on his face . . . with knives."

Carn remembered the reports of Amet Pale's near-fatal encounter with Hain and nodded, waiting for the boy to go on.

"But their wives talk, and if they stop to notice an innocent boy like me"—Katham was grinning broadly now—"it's only to tousle my hair."

Katham omitted telling Carn that, toward the end of the event, when he had learned everything he wanted to, he had responded to one of those hair-touslings by goosing the wife of an Underminister of Finance.

"And did you learn anything from the good ladies besides Minister Ravenwood's amorous problems?" Carn asked wearily, beginning to run out of patience.

The boy shrugged. "A few things. I learned that General Pale acts as ugly as he looks. He caught one of his aides staring at his scars and he beat the man senseless with the flat of his sword."

"Sounds like typical Pale," Carn mused.

"Then Pale took the aide's knife and carved his initials on the man's cheeks," Katham added, noting the way Carn winced. "Seems, though, the general is eager to carve up more than his own aides."

"How do you mean?"

Katham shrugged as he sauntered over to Brandt's desk, lifting a fountain pen between his nimble fingers. He held the pen up to the light, admiring the lustrous black enamel with its golden ornamentation. He raised a quizzical eyebrow toward Carn.

"It's yours," the man sighed, but he was almost amused at the grin of delight that illuminated Katham's impish features. Usually he found it difficult to remember how young the boy really was—no more than fourteen, Carn guessed. But despite Katham's waifish looks, there lurked a hardness and edge that Carn remembered only too well: it was difficult to remain a boy for long on the streets.

Katham tossed the pen casually into the air, hardly watching the blur of its swift rotations until it began to fall. Then his hand shot out, and in an instant, the pen disappeared entirely. Only a few men other than Carn would have noticed the swift twist of the wrist that had slipped the pen under Katham's sleeve. *A small enough price to pay*, Carn thought, *for Katham's information . . . or even for the distraction.* And Carn would rather give the boy a pen or a book than any of the other things Katham might have asked for. No doubt, the boy simply wanted the pen to sell, but still—

"General Pale wants to make war on Yndor."

Carn rolled his eyes. "Any milkmaid in Perth knows as much."

"But he may finally have his way."

Carn gripped the wooden handles of his wheelchair and leaned forward. "What makes you think so?"

Katham's brow creased for a moment and he crossed his arms, assuming a grave posture. Carn had learned quickly that the boy possessed an uncanny ability of mimicry. He could do fair imitations of any voice that was not too deep, and he seemed able to remember entire speeches verbatim. Mostly, Katham employed his abilities to poke fun, but there were moments when they came in handy.

" 'The escalation of forces along the Cirran is progressing at a breakneck pace,' " Katham said in as deep a voice as he could muster, his eyes glazing in a faraway look. " 'Pale has already collected enough forces and materiel to withstand a massive attack . . . or to launch a preëmptive one.' "

"Do you have any idea what 'materiel' means?" Carn asked. "Or 'preëmptive'?"

Katham shrugged. "More or less. I got the gist of it."

"So I see," Carn said to himself, nodding absently. "You should look those all up afterward." He turned and pointed to a large blue book on a nearby shelf. "Consider that dictionary yours."

Again, the boy's eyes lit up. He didn't hesitate to snatch

up the book and, after a single appraising look, tuck it under his slim arm.

"That is, it's yours," Carn added, "only if you promise not to sell it. Now, did you overhear anything else?"

"Not much," Katham replied. "Something about needing more 'armaments.' That's another one I should look up, I guess."

"It is indeed," Carn said, dismissing the boy. He ran his fingers through his curly gray hair as he watched Katham run down the hall, looking now like any normal, carefree boy.

More armaments, he thought. War munitions for the Chaldean army. They would want the finest materials. Deshi steel.

Carn sighed. He could foresee trouble brewing, and none of it very far off.

Five days. Carn thought, *and already he had put this off far too long.* He sat in a small room deep beneath the mansion, a room protected both by powerful wards and the nastiest traps that Brandt's engineers had been able to devise. The room itself was sparsely furnished—a small desk with an oil lamp. Indeed, the place was so small that Carn's wheelchair could not maneuver behind the desk, so he had asked two of the servants to carry him inside. Positively claustrophobic, and for more reasons than size alone. With the exception of the door that led upward toward the main basement, every wall was a bank of filing cabinets, from floor to ceiling. Carn had pulled a few of those drawers open and laid out their contents on the desk—thick files in either red, yellow, or black folders. Different colors for different hues of sin.

And who the hell are we, Carn thought, *to judge?*

These files had lain in this room for years, unread, untouched until a few weeks ago. They formed an encyclopedia of everything that was wrong with the human soul. And Carn would have happily left all this buried if not for Brandt's last words before he disappeared down the road to Belfar:

Fire burns yellow and red, leaving black ashes for all to see.

It was a coded message that only Carn would understand—to burn the yellow and red files, the records of folly and indiscretion, and release the black files, which detailed acts of murder and treachery. Yes, he could well imagine burning these files. Carn shared Brandt's urge to destroy them, to excise the tumor that lay within the foundations of the house, to see whether there was no possibility of making a clean start in life. But then why not burn them all? Weren't the people who had earned a black file also somehow deserving of a fresh chance?

Perhaps not. Carn opened another black file, perusing it quickly, hoping to find evidence of something so heinous that he would agree with Brandt that these crimes could not be erased. There were, he knew, some shocking secrets contained within these walls, and he would have to steep himself in them before working up the courage to send even the first file out. *How much better*, he thought, *to spend the day upstairs with Masya*. Perhaps take a coach into the countryside. The woods were exploding with spring buds and the outside air was heavy with tree pollen. Masya had been wearing a calico dress that showed off her still-trim figure to best advantage . . . But he had put off this room, and this task, long enough.

He leaned forward and pulled the lamp a bit closer before he began to read.

CHAPTER 5

" **I** sn't it about time that we rest?" Marwick asked.

Spring was masquerading as summer that day, the sun beating down upon the endless fields of corn . . . and upon a soot-streaked suit of heavy, blue velvet that was most definitely not made for traveling. But though Marwick had counseled a thoughtful preparation for the chase—a good night's sleep and thorough packing—both Brandt and Imbress had insisted that they leave as soon as possible. *The need for speed*, Marwick reflected, *was about the only thing they seemed capable of agreeing upon.* Neither Brandt nor Imbress had even admitted to becoming partners in the chase after Madh and Hain. Rather, Brandt had hurried back to the inn to saddle Rachel, giving Marwick only a few minutes to equip himself. Then they had galloped off to the north, Brandt making no mention of Imbress the entire time. Marwick had gotten the distinct impression that his old friend would be perfectly happy never to see the agent from Intelligence again.

As luck would have it, though, Imbress and her two men had arrived at Belfar's ancient north gate only a few moments later. It had not been a rendezvous so much as a chance meeting of five people who were all trying to get out of the city as quickly as possible. Not a word had passed between Brandt and Imbress, and throughout the night, Imbress's group had remained thirty yards behind Brandt and Marwick, just as they had been upon first reaching the hard-pack road.

All night and all morning, Brandt had pushed the pace, hunched over Rachel's neck as he rode, eager to overtake

Hain. He had said little, except for an occasional threat of what he would do to Old Hoot if the old man had misled him. Brandt still called him Old Hoot, though now that they knew he was really the mage Tarem Selod.

Tarem Selod, the former Minister of Foreign Relations, posing as an old healer and interested in Brandt? Marwick found this irresistibly fascinating. Add the intimation that Selod had almost been killed—by Madh and Hain, Marwick supposed—and things became more curious still. What on earth would prompt anyone to attack a wizard as powerful as Selod was reputed to be? And why cripple Carn? The connection there escaped Marwick entirely.

An hour into their ride, he had simply asked Brandt to explain. Marwick was no fan of unnecessary guile . . . and after the past days' events, he supposed that Brandt owed him at least a little information.

"Thanks to Hain," Brandt had snapped, "Carn lies crippled. What the hell else do you need to know?"

Marwick had shaken his head with frustration. "Brandt, he's my friend, as well as yours. And if he's had some trouble with these men we're chasing, I think I should know what lies behind it."

"If you're looking for conversation," Brandt had muttered in response, glancing backward toward Imbress on the road behind them, "ride with them. I'm saving my breath for fighting."

And that had been their only conversation since leaving Belfar. At times, Marwick was almost glad to have the mystery to chew on. It kept his mind spinning so quickly that he didn't always notice the hard ride—until, that is, the sun threatened to bake his brains if he did not find shade.

"Brandt," he urged again, "we have to rest sometime."

Brandt stared along the road as he answered. "They're ahead of us," he said. "Somewhere up the road, I know it. The old man didn't think we could catch them before the forest, but I know we can if we sleep less than they do, if we ride harder and longer."

Marwick sighed and rolled his eyes.

"You won't catch anyone," he replied, "if you drop out of your saddle from exhaustion, or if you kill your horse underneath you by running the poor girl too hard."

"I plan to trade for fresh horses as we travel," Brandt explained. "That will give us a better chance of catching them."

Marwick nodded. At least that made sense . . . to a point. A point they had already exceeded. Marwick seldom ventured outside of Belfar, but he knew something of the surrounding countryside.

"Brandt, the next village of any size is Barhelm, and that's got to be another fifty miles. There's no way we can make Barhelm without a break."

Brandt said nothing in reply, pushing Rachel northward with the same determination as before. Marwick shook his head in disgust. Perhaps he had been a fool to come along. He was powerfully curious about the mystery that drove Brandt forward, and he had other reasons to go along, as well. But they were useless, Marwick thought, if you looked at them in the cold light of reason. No measure of revenge would heal Carn's legs. And though he was willing to sacrifice a lot for Brandt, even if Brandt did not understand why, he would not suffer being perpetually ignored.

It surprised him, then, that Brandt slowed Rachel to a trot and led her off the road as they approached the next farmhouse. It was a large, ramshackle affair—new rooms added haphazardly over generations of construction, whenever the need arose.

As Brandt swung off his saddle and began speaking to the aproned woman who opened the door, Marwick looked back toward Imbress. She and her men had paused in the middle of the road, quietly conferring. After a moment, she turned toward the farmhouse, glaring at Brandt. Then she spurred her horse and, with Harnor and Laz following her, continued to the north.

Marwick sighed as he dismounted and joined Brandt. Brandt had just dropped a silver coin into the woman's hand.

"—only for my friend and I. The others will have to negotiate their own price."

"There be no others, sir," the woman replied gently, her eyes darting toward the dwindling trio of riders.

Brandt turned about, catching a glimpse of Imbress as the agents from Intelligence disappeared past a small copse of trees.

"I'll be damned," he muttered. "If they can go on, Marwick, so can I. And so can you."

"No," Marwick replied quietly, but with a firm edge to his voice. "Imbress won't stop here because it would show that you're leading this little expedition. But they need rest as badly as we do. They won't be going far. And we won't be going farther than this goodwife's spare room, unless we want to drop dead of exhaustion. As my mother always said, the tired fox dances poorly."

And with that, he slipped with a smile past the bewildered goodwife and beyond the range of Brandt's scowl.

Marwick was young again in his dreams—a freckled boy of fifteen, his copper hair forever straying in front of his eyes as he and Brandt loped through the quiet, darkened streets of Belfar. Although Brandt was a year older, Marwick was the bigger of the two boys, and he found it difficult to match Brandt's quick pace. That was the way of it: Marwick always a step behind his serious friend, always following Brandt's lead. And tonight Brandt was leading them into the richer precincts of Belfar, where the merchants and the aldermen lived. This neighborhood made Marwick nervous, not that he would ever admit such a thing to Brandt. It was different from the labyrinthine slums that he and Brandt called home. Here, the tall, brownstone rowhouses were set well back from the street, making Marwick feel exposed. He preferred the twisting paths of Blake's Warren, where there was always a shadow at hand, always an alley for escape.

But Brandt seemed at ease amid the long blocks of townhouses. He said, as men get richer, they become less watchful. They confuse their big houses with fortresses. And so, as Brandt saw it, a fat merchant made easier pickings than the lean carpenter who lived above his shop and understood the fragility of his well-being.

Brandt came to a sudden stop and turned around. His dark eyes were glittering in the feeble light of the moon.

"That one," he said, pointing at a house near the corner. His voice was too deep, the voice of the grown Brandt rather than the boy, but Marwick, dreaming, took little note of it. Marwick knew no one else who so often dreamed episodes of his past, sometimes reproduced precisely, sometimes mixed with whatever fantasies his slumbering brain conjured. Either way, he typically enjoyed his dreams, floating along their currents with pleasure and usually remembering every detail when he awoke.

The scene shifted to the front doors of the house, Brandt bent over the lock, deftly probing its interior with his make-shift wire tools. Marwick searched the opposite side of the street nervously, sure he had seen someone in the shadows of one house's steep front steps. *A large man*, he thought, but the image disappeared as he strove to secure it, and Brandt merely laughed when Marwick suggested they go home.

The dream now melted into a succession of fluid impressions: cleaning out the contents of a large, velvet-lined jewelry box while its owner snored fitfully a few steps away; Brandt pocketing a small, obsidian statuette found upon an antique desk in a library; Marwick sliding open the drawer in the butler's pantry that held the silver, one polished spoon slipping between his fingers and ringing against the floor. And suddenly, three of the merchant's guardsmen, half-dressed but bearing swords, at the kitchen door, charging at them. Brandt, dark as the night, insubstantial as a ghost, slipping between them all, tripping one, pushing another over the kitchen table. And Marwick, heart pounding, trying to dodge the last as the glittering blade whipped around and sliced the flesh of his forearm. The bag of silver seemed to fall very slowly as he cried out, the forks and spoons tumbling from the velvet bag without a sound. Then, as the blade rose for a final stroke, something dark cut the air and hit the man's forehead with an explosion of blood—the statuette that Brandt had taken.

Somehow they were racing down the steps, the other two men right behind them. Marwick's chest felt tight, knowing they would never escape the long, open streets before the city guard arrived. But then another image appeared in their midst: the large man he had glimpsed before entering the townhouse. Just a touch of gray glinted in the man's tight, curly black hair. Strangely, there was an amused smile on his face as he stepped into the center of the chaos upon the steps, swinging a walking stick as if it were a twig. In a moment's time, the cane blurred from the head of one man to the other and they were both laid out on the steps, as unconscious as dreaming Marwick. And the boys were running through the streets of Belfar with the laughing man who said his name was . . .

"Marwick!"

He was being shaken by the shoulders. The crisp immediacy of his dream slipped away as he awoke, staring into Brandt's lined face. That face seemed so much older now.

"Wake up," Brandt ordered. "It's time to ride. We've slept more than five hours."

Marwick simply nodded as he swung his legs off the pallet that Brandt's silver had bought for the night. He wondered what Brandt had dreamed of, whether Brandt ever dreamed of Belfar days—of his youth with Marwick and Carn. And then, remembering what Brandt told him of how Carn had been crippled, Marwick wondered how that large, laughing man could ever suffer confinement to a wheelchair. For the rest of his life. Marwick was glad, suddenly, that he had never followed his two friends to Prandis, that he had not been there to see Carn broken. It was an image he did not need haunting his dreams.

As Marwick pulled on his boots, he glanced out the window. It was twilight, the sun only just having dipped below the horizon. Marwick could have wished for a real night's sleep, but he supposed that traveling all night would at least keep him out of the sun.

The first time Brandt stopped to trade horses, Marwick decided he would be best off trading suits.

When Marwick was finished dressing, he joined Brandt in the large common room that adjoined their rented bedchamber. He found Brandt filling a burlap sack with corn muffins, still steaming from an oven tended by the goodwife.

"Those muffins smell delicious," Marwick effused, earning an appreciative smile from the woman.

Brandt, however, was in no mood to exchange pleasantries. He looked as grim as ever in the flickering light of the goodwife's tallow candle. An afternoon's sleep had done nothing to improve his disposition.

"We would be interested in purchasing two spare horses," Brandt said tersely. "We have a long ride ahead."

The goodwife bowed her head, looking down at her baking as she spoke.

"I am sorry, sir, but we own but two draft horses—fit only for the plow, not for a gentleman like yourself."

Brandt scowled with frustration. No doubt the farmer would sell the horses and plow both if Brandt offered enough money, but draft horses were too slow for a chase. Brandt picked up the sack of muffins and turned toward the door.

"Thank you for your hospitality," Marwick said, bowing slightly, as he followed his silent associate outside. *It was a shame*, he thought, *how obsessive Brandt had become*. All the effort Carn had spent trying to teach Brandt manners . . .

The two men saddled their horses in silence and set off along the darkening road. The horses' spirits seemed high enough. A few hours' respite, along with oats and hay, had swept away some of the past days' labor. *They would be able to make good time*, Marwick thought.

The road was empty of other travelers—all fled to some snug resting spot for the evening—and Marwick found himself missing Imbress, Harnor, and Laz. Not that he expected much in the way of amusement from the three agents, but the simple sound of more hooves against the hardpack was a mite to fight off loneliness. As far as loneliness was concerned, he reflected, Brandt figured more as affliction than cure.

"I wonder how much further Imbress and the others pushed on," Marwick said, but Brandt's only reply was an uninterested grunt.

An answer of another sort, however, was not long in forthcoming. About four miles into the evening's journey, they passed a tiny farmhouse to the west. The uppermost lip of the moon had crested the horizon and a cheerful wreath of smoke climbed from the house's chimney, lending it a pleasant, homey look. But as they trotted past the place, a cry arose, and only a few moments later Marwick saw one of the male agents—he had no way to tell one from the other—run from the house toward the barn, still struggling to pull his shirt over his flaxen-haired head.

Marwick glanced at his friend and was surprised to see, for the very first time during their journey, the slightest of smiles cross Brandt's lips.

Within fifteen minutes, the sound of a gallop began to reach Marwick's ears. The noise grew to a thunderous crescendo and then stopped abruptly as three horses were reined in. Marwick did not have to turn around to know that Elena Imbress had come within thirty yards of them—the same distance as yesterday—and then slowed to match their pace. She would not be left behind, she certainly would not join them, and she was too smart to push her men a little ahead of Brandt. Provoking Brandt like that would simply precipitate a costly game of mounted leapfrog, one group pushing past the other again and again, thereby wearing out the horses for no good reason. So Imbress would simply stick to their track, a stone's throw behind them. *Stubborn woman*, Marwick thought, *grinning*. He wondered if Brandt, intransigent as a mule, had finally met his match. This Imbress would bear more attention, he decided.

Accordingly, about two hours later, when the night's black

cowl had tightened around them, Marwick began to let his mount slip back. Nothing noticeable—just a tiny lag that let Brandt gain a step on him every few seconds. Within a moment, Imbress's dappled white-and-gray horse had almost overtaken his own.

"You belong up there with Karrelian," Imbress said curtly.

Marwick pressed his hand to his chest in mock surprise. "Have you known Brandt long? I had heard that after moving to Prandis he improved the quality of his acquaintances."

"Ride with your friend," Imbress snapped, accustomed to being obeyed.

"But you're so much more talkative than Brandt," Marwick argued, his blue eyes twinkling. "And frankly, more pleasant to look at. As my mother always said, among a basket of sour apples, choose the one with no spots."

Imbress's brow creased with irritation, but she said nothing. Instead, she lifted a hand and gestured with her smallest finger. A moment later, the larger of her two escorts galloped to her side—*Laz*, Marwick thought, though he was still unsure of the agents' names. What was certain was the threatening manner in which Laz loosened the sword in his sheath.

"Oho," Marwick chuckled, "and here I was worrying that we were settling into a boring routine. Such a disappointment after that promising beginning—black-garbed operatives, a mysterious mage and a bald assassin, a spectacular fight and an inferno to match—"

"Best you not listen to your friend's ravings about murdered ministers and Thyrsian plots," Laz growled, but a sharp glance from Imbress cut him off before he could say anything more. Laz, Marwick decided, was the man he'd seen running out of the farmhouse last night—a large, blond, blue-eyed man, probably from the northern plains. Harnor, was smaller—though still taller than six feet. A bruiser, by the looks of him, with that crooked nose and a fat scar that ran across his chin like a second lower lip.

"As a matter of fact," Marwick replied, his grin as wide as the cornfields at his back, "Brandt hadn't said a word about a Thyrsian plot to murder government ministers, but now that you bring it up, I suppose I had better ask him. Unless you'd like to spare him the bother."

While Marwick was talking, Harnor had moved his horse nearby. Swiftly, the rough-looking agent drew his sword and swung the flat of the blade sharply against the rump of Marwick's horse. The beast bolted down the road, neighing with distress, but Marwick only laughed as he clung on, his coppery hair shaking and shimmering in the moonlight.

"A pleasure chatting," he cried after regaining control of the animal, only a few paces behind Brandt. "Perhaps we'll talk again in Barhelm."

The village of Barhelm was little more than a few small houses clustered around an old grain mill, perched on the banks of the Redham River. The Redham was not much of a river, only fifty spans across. In the dry season just before winter, the current dwindled to a trickle that could no longer turn the waterwheel and the millstone that the wheel drove. But all through spring and summer, the water flowed steadily between the brown banks, and farmers for miles around carted their grain to Barhelm to be processed and barged downstream to the markets at Belfar. Indeed, the river had almost reached its highwater mark, and in this season Barhelm's little rope-and-pulley ferry was one of the few convenient places to cross the Redham and continue north.

A small town like Barhelm would have held no interest at all for Brandt under ordinary circumstances, but now, an hour before noon, he found himself spurring on Rachel beneath the hot sun to reach the hamlet more quickly. There he would find provisions, fresh horses, and with a little luck, information about Madh and Hain. Unless the Thyrsians knew other places to ford the river—which was unlikely, for even Brandt knew little about the sleepy heartland of Chaldus—or were willing to waste time searching for one, they would have passed through town to use the ferry. And if that was so, some of the townspeople, or at least the ferryman, would remember their passing. Brandt was itching to speak with the residents of little Barhelm and finally learn how far behind Hain they were.

A clattering of hooves broke Brandt's concentration and he turned to find Marwick overtaking him. Dark rings of sweat had turned the color of the thief's velvet riding outfit from blue to black and his coppery hair was plastered to his skull. Brandt almost smiled, remembering how much Marwick hated looking anything but dapper. But Marwick was thinking less about his own sweaty state than about the thick lather on the horses and the white flecks of foam at the corners of their mouths.

"First thing," Marwick said, "we'd better see to buying new horses. These would need a full day of rest before we could ride them hard again." *His ass*, he thought wryly, *could use twice that long, but Brandt would never afford them such a rest.* "Then we can buy some food and ask a few discreet questions."

Brandt nodded. "I think we may have some luck with the horses." He pointed toward a building that had the unmistakable look of a stable. In the pasture beyond the structure, several colts frisked and grazed.

Marwick sniffed the air and pointed at a thick column of smoke that was rising from behind the stable.

"You know," he added, "we may be able to take care of two chores at once. Smells like a barbecue. Remember the grilled lamb at Fodar's Tavern, the way they bury the whole thing in a coal pit? Fodar still makes it, you know. I would have taken you there if we had more time in Belfar."

Brandt said nothing in reply, but a smile rose involuntarily to his lips as he remembered the spicy, skewered meat that he and Marwick had often indulged in as children. He spurred on Rachel, his spirits feeling somewhat lighter than they had since the journey had begun.

A few minutes' ride brought them to the stables and they dismounted gratefully, hitching their horses to a post outside the door. Marwick was stretching his legs happily as Imbress, Harnar, and Laz came up behind them.

"Fresh mounts?" Imbress asked curtly.

"For us, at least," Brandt replied. "I won't be buying horses for you."

"Oh, but you will," she answered tartly. "Thanks to some of those taxes you pay, Karrelian, the Chaldean Treasury can afford a few horses."

"Well, the pick of the stable is ours," Brandt said gruffly. "We were here first."

Just then, a small door opened and a large, balding man wearing a leather apron walked from the dim interior of the stable into the bright light of the late-morning sun. He blinked a couple of times, taking in the visitors with a crooked frown. He had the look of a man with a perpetual stomach ache.

"Good day," Marwick said.

"Good day," the stableman replied, bowing slightly to the party. His voice was not quite gruff but, perhaps, distracted. He seemed not in the least pleased to see potential customers. "Name's Kolom and I own these stables. If I overheard you aright, you've come to buy horses. You want 'em for breeding?"

"For riding," Brandt said. He gestured toward the five horses that they had hitched to the stableman's post. "These are all good mounts, but we've ridden them hard and we need fresh ones. You can have these and we'll pay you fair value for what your horses are worth in excess."

Kolom craned his neck toward the party's horses, gnawing at a fingernail as he appraised them. "Not bad," he admitted, "but I breed the best horses in the county—"

"Show us the horses and name your price," Brandt interrupted.

"Problem is," Kolom went on, ignoring the interruption, "I can't sell any for riding just yet. Fact is, can't sell any at all for a while, and then only the geldings."

"Why might that be?" Marwick asked amiably before Brandt could snap out another curt remark.

"Plague," Kolom replied, and now a distinct bitterness suffused his voice. "Two dozen fine animals just died of it. Up and sickened last night, and the pox took most every one.

Burning the last of 'em now so the plague don't spread."

At that, Marwick's stomach lurched. There would be no barbecue today after all.

"We saw horses in your pasture," Brandt said, eyeing the stableman with distrust.

"Mostly colts and fillies," the man said. "Each one from this spring's foaling and none ready to be rode. Especially not rode hard like you've done to these here. The few adults that survived are too weak to carry a child, and I'll be needing them for breeding stock."

At that, they all peered past the corner of the building to the pasture and saw that, indeed, most of Kolom's livestock was spindly-legged, only a few months old. There were four or five full-grown horses, but these animals moved listlessly, their heads swinging low to the ground although they were not grazing. Patches of hair had fallen out of their coats and a dull yellow sheen covered their eyes.

"Who does have horses to sell?" Brandt asked.

"I'm the only breeder in town," Kolom replied. "Most folks only have one or two, and they wouldn't have parted with 'em—"

"If I pay well enough, they'll part with them."

Kolom paused and scratched his head. "They'll part with 'em now, rightly enough, whether you pay well or not. If you'd waited for me to say it, I would have told you that the plague done struck us all. Ain't but a few horses left in all of Barhelm now, and them that's alive will need consid'able nursing."

Brandt ground his teeth together in frustration, staring first at the feeble horses in Kolom's pasture and then at the exhausted ones they had just ridden into town.

But before he could think of anything else to say, Imbress had walked up to the man, sweeping her rich red hair back from her eyes and smiling sweetly. It was an utter transformation from the Imbress Brandt knew.

"Tell me, Master Kolom," Imbress began, "this plague must have been terrible. Where I grew up, we had one similar that lasted weeks as one horse after another fell ill."

"That's the odd thing, miss," Kolom replied. "I've seen diseases spread around before, but this one was different. Quick as lightning. This morning, we just woke up and all our horses were dead or dying."

"This morning?" Brandt repeated.

"Yes, sir, all this morning. Last night, they were hale as you or me. Like the hand of God visiting us."

"Or the hand of Madh," Marwick muttered to himself, remembering what he had seen at the Dusky Arms.

"And nothing else took ill?" Imbress went on. "Not the cows or any other livestock?"

"No, thank goodness. Just the horses," Kolom answered, "and that's bad enough for me."

"One last question, Master Kolom. Did any other travelers stop here to buy horses, yesterday perhaps? Two men, one dark-skinned, the other bald?"

"Not last night, but real early this morning. Roused me from bed before sunrise, looking like they had been riding harder than you. I was going to send them on their way for waking me up like that, but they offered good gold for my two best horses, and plenty of it. Didn't know there was a plague coming round, of course, or I wouldn't have sold 'em. I expect those horses took sick and them fellers are walking back this way mad as hornets."

"I wouldn't count on it," Imbress said, frowning. "I wouldn't count on it at all."

For a time, everyone brooded over the news as they climbed back on their tired mounts and set off slowly toward the river.

"After what I saw at the bar," Imbress finally said to no one in particular, "nothing should surprise me, but I would love to know how Madh killed every horse in Barhelm."

"We don't *know* it's Madh," Harnor countered, but his scarred face betrayed his real suspicions.

"They could have simply poisoned the horses," Brandt grumbled. "No great mystery about that."

"Poisoned every horse in town?" Imbress asked, laughing harshly. "I think not. It would have taken hours."

"I think I know how he did it," Marwick said, and everyone turned his way. Marwick took a moment to straighten his velvet lapels before he continued, enjoying the looks of thwarted curiosity on his companions' faces. "He left a homunculus to do the dirty work."

"A *homunculus*?" Imbress repeated incredulously.

And then Marwick told the story of how he had found Brandt wracked in pain and only hours from death, and how Old Hoot had destroyed the ethereal homunculus.

"For all we know," Marwick concluded, "Madh may have a dozen of the damned things at his command. It was probably a simple thing for them to kill or sicken all the horses in town."

The mention of time reminded Brandt of something else— more bad news. "They were here this morning, before dawn. Hard as we've been riding, they managed to gain a good five hours on us. How on earth will we catch up now?"

"Well," Marwick replied, "one thing is for sure. We won't catch up today. If we keep riding our horses this hard, they'll wind up as dead as Kolom's. I say we find an inn and rest for a few hours at the very least."

Imbress stared at their horses, shaking her head with frustration. "We'll have to rest them and water them," she agreed, "but on the far side of the river. Just in case this plague is real."

The plague was real enough, whether or not Madh was responsible for it, for everyplace they passed thereafter, they found heaps of dead horses, or woefully ill beasts being tended carefully by frightened owners. It became clear that the travelers would have to rely upon their original mounts, and that they would have to adopt a reasonable pace that the animals could sustain for days, rather than hours. More frustrating still, as they reached each village or hamlet, they found that the plague had preceded them by ever-wider margins. With each passing day, Madh and Hain were building a more substantial lead.

"We'll never catch them at this rate," Brandt grumbled.

"You may be surprised," Marwick replied, wiping sweat from his brow with a velvet sleeve. They had switched back to traveling during daylight, despite the heat, because they could make better time. "Ten hours' lead is hardly insurmountable when you're talking about a cross-country chase. And if they're headed for the Ulthorn . . ." Marwick paused for a moment, staring ahead along the road as if the dark fringe of the forest was already visible, although it still lay almost two hundred miles away. "Do you think they're truly headed for the Ulthorn?"

Brandt shrugged. "That was the old man's idea, not mine," he said, sounding unconcerned. Although he had started accustoming himself to the idea of a long chase, the details seemed not to matter, as if Brandt would be as happy chasing Hain over mountains or across oceans as he was riding the trade roads. "But it certainly seems that way. The trail of dead horses keeps leading north."

"I wonder if that could be a ruse," Marwick said after a moment's thought. "It would be an awfully convenient way of leading us astray, don't you think?"

"That farmer outside of Jollum's Ferry got a pretty good look at them. Described them well enough to suit me."

Marwick shrugged. "Jollum's Ferry was two days ago. They could have changed course since then."

"To do what?" Brandt asked, shaking his head. "Cut through miles of fields, dodge army patrols at the border, and swim the Cirran? I doubt it. Hain is headed for the Ulthorn . . . to be with the rest of the beasts."

"You don't have to put it *that* way," Marwick complained, half under his breath. Brandt didn't seem bothered by the idea, but the closer they came to the forest, the more Marwick began to think of the legendary beasts of Ulthorn. The bears and the big cats would not think twice about attacking a man. And it was said that other creatures dwelled farther in the woods, in Ulthorn Deep—creatures that had not been seen by man since the days of the Binding. For Marwick, who had spent his whole life in Belfar, the forest sounded like a strange and unfriendly place. Give him bricks before birch any day, he thought.

"Well," he said, sighing, "we'll have at least one advantage if they decide to try the Ulthorn."

"What's that?" Brandt asked, turning toward his companion with a glimmer of interest in his eyes.

"There are no towns in the forest, so there won't be any fresh horses. Once they enter Ulthorn, they'll be stuck with the mounts they brought in, just like us."

Brandt nodded and nudged his heels into Rachel's flanks, urging her to a trot. Marwick had found that Brandt often sped the pace whenever he thought about catching Hain, which was far too often for their horses' good. But for better or worse, Marwick understood that Brandt had become the de facto leader of their uneasy expedition. Driven by an inner necessity that surpassed any Marwick knew, Brandt sacrificed sleep, rest, and food almost thoughtlessly in order to keep moving. Wracked by illness when Marwick had found him in Belfar, Brandt had still retained traces of the good living that he had indulged in for years: the subtle padding of fat that obscured what had once been the sharp line of his jaw, the comfortable bulge that gathered above the waistline of his trousers . . . Over the last few days, though, Brandt's body seemed to have journeyed backward through time, shedding itself of the luxuries of Prandis, paring itself back down to the hard lines and rigid edges that Marwick remembered. Only Brandt's face bespoke his true age now. It had thinned, too, but it had not reverted to the daring, carefree smiles of Brandt's Belfarian youth. Instead, its seams deepened, adding a severity to Brandt's mouth and eyes and brow that Marwick could not remember seeing before.

You should have stayed with me in Belfar, Marwick thought. *You would be less rich, Brandt, but far happier.*

A rare burst of conversation among the government agents behind them interrupted Marwick's reverie, and he looked up at the horizon to find several lines of smoke writhing into the air.

"A town," Marwick announced. "Should be Dandun. Perhaps we can finally find some fresh horses."

"If we do," Brandt grumbled, "it means that we've lost Hain."

But as it turned out, Brandt had nothing to worry about. After an hour of trotting through ripening fields of corn and amber wheat, the party came to the outskirts of Dandun. Like most of the towns in the plains, it amounted to no more than a few dozen houses and a smattering of businesses built up along either side of the road. There was a general store, an inn, and several hundred yards away, down a broad cart path that was the only cross street in Dandun, a small mill by the side of a fast-flowing stream.

Marwick pointed to a large, red-painted structure toward the northern end of the town. Behind it lay a considerable expanse of grass enclosed by split-rail fences. Hundreds of head of cattle were gathered within, chewing contemplatively at the tall grass or lying down by a small pond in the middle of the pasture.

As they drew closer to the building, they were able to make out the sign above the door. Crudely hand-lettered, it read LIFESTOCK.

"Life stock," Marwick laughed. "I wouldn't mind buying shares if Hain is headed for the Ulthorn."

But as they passed the inn, the screen door swung open and four large men filed out, each dressed in weathered leather riding clothes and sporting beards that spoke of a long journey without benefit of a razor. One of them, a man who looked as if a bear somehow belonged in his not-too-distant lineage, had twisted his beard into a braid six inches long, capped by a jade bead, held in place by a final knot of hair. His already-pinched eyes narrowed when they fell upon Brandt, weighing silently.

"Hold on a minute, stranger," he called out, walking quickly out into the middle of the road. "I'd like a minute of your time."

"We have very little time to spare," Brandt answered, slowing his pace only marginally.

His eyes flicked from one man to the next, noting their broad, muscular builds and the swords that hung by their hips. The leather hilt-wrappings on those swords had been burnished smooth by years of use. Mercenaries, if he had to guess. Soldiers of fortune were common enough within a hundred miles of the Cirran, employed by both Prandis and Yndor to monitor the movements of troops on the other side. Brandt turned for a second toward Marwick, who answered with a barely perceptible nod.

"Nice horses," the mercenary continued, and at that Marwick could not help but laugh.

"There's our answer," Marwick said softly.

"We're not interested in selling our horses," Brandt announced, letting his right hand fall from his stirrups to the long knife at his hip.

"We'll pay you well," the mercenary countered, his eyes still squinted so tight that Brandt could not tell how he meant the phrase—straight up, or as a private joke, a punning reference to a different type of payment he intended to mete out.

"Not nearly well enough," Brandt replied, smiling slightly, and then he spurred Rachel back to a trot.

The mercenary reached back toward the pommel of his sword, but at just that moment, Imbress thundered by at a gallop, nearly running the man down. He glared at her, but backed off farther as Harnor and Laz rode by with dangerous gleams in their eyes. Reluctantly, the man herded his fellows back toward the inn.

Imbress reined in alongside Brandt. It was the first time the two had traveled side by side since leaving Belfar.

"Madh is a clever fellow," she said softly, with a note of ironic appreciation. "This shortage of horses is liable to slow us down in more ways than one. Best we don't spend the night in Dandun."

"Agreed," Brandt said curtly, his eyes focused down the road.

"If I may put a word in?" Marwick asked, not waiting for a response before he continued. "Little as I like Dandun, we should stop long enough to buy supplies. Are any of you familiar with this territory?"

Brandt shook his head. Elena merely watched Marwick with her usual impenetrable expression, lips pursed as if continually biting back a cutting comment.

"Well," Marwick went on, "our map shows grazing land between here and the Ulthorn. This is the last town south of New Pell, at the verge of the forest. That's a good four, five days' ride. So," he concluded, patting one of the drooping saddlebags behind him, "it seems to be the moment to fill our larders."

Simultaneously, Brandt and Imbress nodded—and then each looked sourly at the other, unhappy to have been caught in agreement.

"You four buy supplies, then," Brandt replied. "I want to talk to the owner of that stable and see if I can find out how far behind we've fallen."

"Harnor will go with you," Imbress added. She had made a habit of sending the closed-mouthed agent along with Brandt on his little intelligence forays, unwilling to let the former spy discover more than she knew herself.

But Marwick was glancing back over his shoulder at the inn.

"Perhaps we had better all stay together."

"I hope you're not worried about those thugs," Imbress said, a faintly smug tone to her voice.

Brandt slipped his purse free of his pocket and tossed it to Marwick. "I don't care who comes with me, so long as someone buys supplies." With that, he spurred Rachel toward the stables, followed immediately by Harnor.

Marwick shook his head, following Imbress and Laz toward the general store. "Mother used to say my father was stupid enough with one brain," he muttered to himself. "But two would spell disaster."

The owner of the **D**andun stables was in an expansive mood when Brandt and Harnor came to talk. His

name was Roddy, he said as he smoothed his coarse blue
shirt and pulled a bottle of homebrew from a nearby cabinet.

"Have a drink, fellers?"

Brandt had opened his mouth to refuse when Harnor
slapped his thigh.

"That'd be right kind," he said, adopting the accents of
northwestern Chaldus with what seemed to be a born fluency.
Brandt merely shook his head. He was not surprised by the
sudden transformation of the taciturn agent into an affable,
talkative fellow—he had witnessed similar metamorphoses
each time they stopped to gain information about Hain and
Madh. But Brandt chafed at the time wasted on pleasantries.
Slap enough money on the counter, he reflected, and men
will tell you what you want, whether they like you or not.

"That's a lot of head of cattle you got there," Harnor commented, nodding toward the grazing herds that were visible
through the open window behind them. There was something
about his homely face, something about the brown hair thin-
ning far in advance of his thirty-four years, that made Harnor
seem like a solid country fellow.

"Sure is," Roddy agreed, taking a swig from the bottle and
then passing it to Harnor. "Ain't mine, though. Sometimes
I'll buy the cattle outright from some of the small ranchers,
then drive 'em to Belfar or Penthus. Penthus, usually. Them
military boys eat a lot of steaks, and the Council Tower pays
good money, bless Amet Pale's heart. Mostly, though, local
ranchers pay me a cut to gather their cattle here, then take
'em to market in one big drive. I can usually get a better
price than they can, them being ranch folk and not used to
bargaining."

Brandt ground his teeth together, wondering whether Harnor ever intended to turn the conversation toward Madh and
Hain.

"But them cattle there," Roddy continued, "is Red Par-
vitt's. Old Red got tired of paying me a cut, so he just arranged to take them to market himself. Only paid me to keep
the cattle here while he waited for his other herds to come
in from the east. Well, they all got here last night, but this

morning, just before Red and his boys could take off, all their horses up and died. So Red done outsmarted himself. He can't drive them cattle anywhere on foot, and at the rate he's paying me to board them every day, I'll own one head out of ten by the time he gets fresh horses out of Jollum's Ferry."

At that, Harnor began to laugh—a surprising gale of hearty, unfeigned humor. "This Red, is he a big fellow with a braided beard and bad manners?"

"Yup, that's Red. He and the boys are staying back at the inn." Then Roddy's eyes narrowed with comprehension. "I bet he tried to buy your horses."

"Sure did," Harnor replied, adding under his breath with a chuckle, "Mercenaries." They had been nothing more than a group of disgruntled, stranded ranchers.

"Well," Roddy went on, "I see you didn't sell them, and that in itself is worth a drink."

This time he waved the bottle toward Brandt, who merely shook his head and glared at the crooked-nosed agent.

"Well, Roddy, I wouldn't worry about Red getting any horses out of Jollum's Ferry."

"How so?" the stableman asked.

"All the horses there are dead of the plague. Sounds like the same one that killed Red's horses. Strikes quick. I wonder how it's spreading."

Roddy grunted. "I think I know how," he said, "and I was fool enough to help it. Couple of fellows came in here just past dawn, riding horses that looked two steps from the grave. Wanted to buy two fresh horses, so I sold 'em and off they all went. Strange thing is they kept their old horses, too. Chances are, they're probably all dead by now—but if any of 'em make it up to New Pell, well, the foresters won't like that none."

"What did these two men look like?" Brandt asked, opening his mouth for the first time. Harnor shot him a cross look.

"The one who did the talking was pretty small, maybe your size," Roddy said, too pleased with the news of Red's further bad luck to notice Brandt's tone. "Dark-skinned. Nice and polite. His helper was bigger and had real short hair, mean-looking."

"That's them," Brandt muttered, heading toward the door. "You say they were here just past dawn?"

"No more than an hour past sunup. You looking for them fellows?" Roddy asked, sounding curious.

"We are indeed," Brandt replied as he slipped through the door, Harnor hurrying to catch up with him.

"Thirteen hours," Brandt growled as the agent reached his side. "Our horses become more and more tired, and we fall farther and farther behind."

"A few hours more will make no difference, Karrelian," Harnor replied. "We'll win or lose by our wits, not our horses."

CHAPTER 6

t was late before Carn finally called for the servants to carry him upstairs from the basement, so late that he expected Masya to be asleep. He realized ruefully that he had spent an entire day without her—not that she could have helped him with the awful work he'd done. And since no light seeped from beneath her door, he had at first thought she was asleep, until he heard the steady, rhythmic creaking of her rocking chair. Rocking chairs in the mansion seemed almost laughable—not the sort of thing that Brandt would have chosen as a furnishing. But Tomas, one of the staff, had heard Masya wonder aloud whether there were any rocking chairs on the premises and had then taken it upon himself to ensure that there was one.

How long, Carn wondered, *had it been that he'd fantasized about just this, about having her here where she could radiate warmth through the mansion he'd shared with Brandt?* Almost as long as the two years they'd been lovers . . . But Masya was a proud and stubborn woman, unwilling to be kept when she could make a simple, honest living on her own. She had always avoided Brandt and the mansion, not entirely out of jealousy, Carn felt, but because meeting Brandt might in some way force her to acknowledge that his claims on Carn's loyalty were real. Carn was unsure whether it was fitting or somehow ironic that the one thing capable of bringing Masya to the mansion was tragedy, and the very tragedy that had driven Brandt away, perhaps for good.

Given the late hour, Carn paused a moment before knocking, but decided that if she were up, she might be glad for the company. A moment later, Masya opened the door, wearing a robe over her dressing gown, her brown hair let down to its full shoulder-length for the night. It was only as she turned that Carn was able to catch the moonlight's glint against the few steel-colored strands interspersed among the brown.

She said nothing as she walked across the room, past the large canopy bed with its heavy velour drapes, and settled back into her rocking chair, shifting slightly to find a comfortable position on the embroidered seat. There, by the window, she was limned by the light of the moon and Carn lingered near the room's threshold, pleased to gaze at her far-off silhouette. There was something about that pug nose, despite her fifty years, that spoke to Carn of an impish girl, once prone to mischief and prone to mischief yet.

"It was a long day," he began, regretting the way his voice cracked the still night. "I'm sorry I didn't take a break to see you—"

"I understand," she interrupted quickly, "that you have your work."

And Carn could hear in her voice the unspoken conclusion to the thought, that she did not have hers—the cleaning and washing and other domestic chores that had been her livelihood these many years. That there was nothing for her to do in this mansion that a paid staff did not already do. That there was nothing for her to do in this place but tend to him, but that, even crippled, Carn was still somehow so busy tending to Brandt's business that he had no time for her.

"You smell like smoke," she said. "Even from this far away . . ."

At that, he realized that he was still at the very edge of her room, the door open to the hallway beyond. He wheeled himself inside, paused to swing the door gently closed, and continued across her room, stopping just far enough away from her to allow for the scope of her chair's rocking.

And he did smell like smoke, he realized. How long had he been in that room, feeding files to the fire? The smell had suffused his clothes, perhaps his flesh itself.

As she rocked, he had the sudden impulse to dart forward

and kiss her as her face swung closest to him. But the wheel-chair had foreclosed any hope of such spontaneity. Once more, the overwhelming tragedy of his accident swept over him—and he realized that Masya deserved more, deserved better than to be trapped in a house she hated, with half a man who reeked of guilty pasts.

As the rocker swung forward again, Masya leaned nimbly out of it, coming to her knees before him. She took his hands in hers and kissed him gently on the lips.

"Let's leave this place," he said. The words were flying out of his mouth before he even knew where they were coming from. But suddenly it was clear—Brandt was gone, the files were either destroyed or beyond the mansion's walls—that there was no reason for him to be here anymore. "To-morrow, if I can manage it. To your house. If you'll have me."

Even without a moon, Carn thought, *Masya's smile would have been enough to light the room.* She leaned forward to kiss him again and stopped only long enough to wrinkle her pug nose.

"Of course I'll have you," she replied, the mischief creeping back into her voice, "provided you let me give you a good scrubbing first."

CHAPTER 7

The five travelers left Dandun as a single group, Marwick noted to his satisfaction. Laz had learned from the shopkeeper that Madh and Hain had stopped in the general store, Madh filling their saddlebags with supplies while Hain wandered aimlessly. Afterward, the shopkeeper had noticed a pouch of his best tobacco missing from behind the counter, and he swore about it considerably to Laz, although he couldn't imagine how the shifty-eyed stranger could have stolen it. Laz had also asked about the land to the north. It was all grazing land, the shopkeeper had said, without more than a ranch house or two between there and New Pell.

"Better still," Marwick said, pleased with the news. "With any luck, they won't be able to change horses until New Pell. And if they keep driving their steeds at the same pace, not realizing there aren't any more towns until New Pell, they just may ride their horses to death fifty miles south of the forest. We could catch them before the Ulthorn after all," he concluded, sounding very pleased by the thought. "Unless, of course, we drop dead from exhaustion first."

So they trotted north along the trade road with a somewhat more enthusiastic prospect than before. Imbress and her men drifted back to their customary position behind Brandt and Marwick, but not, Marwick noted, quite so far behind as they had been that morning. Marwick had no great desire to make lasting friends of Intelligence agents, but he felt a growing conviction that, if they were going to enter the Ulthorn forest in search of Madh and Hain, it would be helpful if Brandt and Imbress hated each other at least marginally less than they despised their quarry.

*   *   *

An hour north of Dundun, it was beginning to grow dark and Brandt reined in Rachel by the side of the road. Within a moment, the agents from Intelligence had pulled up by their side.

"Isn't it a little early to camp?" Imbress asked, peering at the sun's position, still halfway above the horizon. In the past, Brandt had squeezed every last minute out of the lengthening days, and just as often, his only concession to nightfall was to slow their pace until a suitable lodging came along closer to midnight.

Rather than answering, Brandt pointed to the northwest where, perhaps two hundred yards away, a group of large, black birds were wheeling above the ground.

"Crows," Marwick said with disgust. "Filthy creatures."

"Filthy or clean," Imbress persisted, "why are we stopping?"

"Do you remember Jollum's Ferry?" Brandt asked.

Marwick raised an eyebrow at the non sequitur.

"About an hour's ride north of Jollum's Ferry, I saw a large group of crows, also off to the left side of the road. We know they bought fresh horses in Jollum's Ferry, and again in Dandun—but they never trade in their old mounts."

"So what?" Imbress asked, glancing skeptically at the circling crows. "If you think that *their* old horses will be in any shape to replace our own, fatigued as they are—"

"Judging by all those crows," Marwick said, his face still twisted with disgust, "whatever's there is fit for little more than fertilizer."

"Either way, I want to see it," Brandt said, and with that he nudged Rachel into the tall grass.

"All you're going to find is what our horses are going to look like if we keep pushing them this hard," Marwick grumbled, but he spurred on his own mount after Brandt.

After a moment, they passed a patch of grass that had clearly been broken by the passage of a horse. The trail led onward toward the crows, and after only a few moments more, they drew near the birds. Some of them scattered, caw-ing raucously, but most, bold as crows can be, continued to circle above them, just out of reach, enraged to have been driven away from whatever they had found.

Marwick looked up, a grimace on his face. "We'll prob-ably get dropped on."

But Brandt was looking at a large depression where the grass had been matted down. He swiveled out of his saddle and slipped to the ground, almost disappearing in the shoulder-high grass. Reluctantly, Marwick did the same, with Imbress following just behind him.

A few steps brought Brandt to the edge of the depression, and thrusting aside the last tasseled blades of grass, he drew his breath in sharply at what he saw. Two horses lay on their sides, but they seemed hardly substantial enough to crush the grass beneath them. Their coats were the dull gray of the sky during an approaching storm, although one had a slight brownish tinge, and the other a whitish one, that revealed their true colors. Through the dried parchment of their skin, every bone seemed visible. The horses' ribs jutted gro-tesquely toward the sky, and their glassy eyes bulged ob-scenely from otherwise shriveled heads.

Brandt bent over and reached toward a nearby hoof. Mar-wick shuddered, expecting the whole corpse to fall to ashes upon being touched. Instead, as Brandt lifted the leg, they heard a distinct, brittle snap. He dropped the leg and rubbed his fingers idly against his trousers.

"Light as straw," he said softly. "It's unnatural."

"It is indeed," Imbress agreed. "But now we know how they've been pulling ahead of us."

All eyes turned toward Taylor Ash's prized operative. She paused for a moment, brushing her red hair from her eyes as she weighed what was best to say.

"It's an old spell," she finally announced. "I've never heard of it being used since the Devastation. But one of the histories of the ancient wars recounts the battle of Senia, which was Tyr Senil before the Binding. Parth Akhana had been lured north by a group of Chaldean cavalry, but the cavalry proved to be a feint, intended to draw Akhana and his forces away from the city so Duke Penthus could overwhelm it. When they realized the plot, Akhana's mage cast a spell on the troops' horses so that they could return to Senia in time. Akhana reached Senia in only two days, despite a journey that should have taken three. But according to the book, all the horses died thereafter, the life sucked out of them by the magic, sometimes their bones breaking beneath the soldiers as they rode."

Slowly, the five Chaldeans backed away from the corpses and remounted their own horses. Now that the humans had retreated, some of the crows began to plunge downward toward the carrion, but the birds always veered away at the last second, reluctant to settle on the unnatural flesh, cawing instead in hunger and dismay.

Marwick tore his eyes from the dead horses and focused instead on Imbress. She had spotted another trail leading northeast from the depression, back toward the road, and had turned her gelding in that direction. Clearly, she had said all she was going to.

"That doesn't make very much sense," Marwick said. "If Madh can cast this same spell, and it allows a horse to travel three days' distance in two days' time, they should have reached the Ulthorn long ago."

"Perhaps," she replied after a moment. "But the Ministry and Karrelian seem to spare little expense on horseflesh. I doubt you can buy better thoroughbreds than the ones we've been riding. Meanwhile, did you take a close look at the remains of Madh's horses? Very broad in the shoulders once, I would guess, but short in the legs. Draft horses, more used to pulling a cart than bearing a saddle. What else would he be likely to find in Jollum's Ferry? And I'm willing to wager that their other horses haven't been much better. Farmers breed for strength, not speed. Take my horse and a draft horse on a fresh day, and Ramus could carry me half again as far. Cast a spell on his horse and let Ramus grow tired—they gain an hour or two each day."

Marwick nodded, a smile growing upon his lips. "But if this spell kills off the horses every two days, Madh and Hain are going to find themselves unexpectedly on foot . . . a good five days' walk south of New Pell."

And with that, he spurred his horse back toward the road, ignoring the protests of his saddle-sore rump, dwelling instead on all that he had learned. With just a little bit of luck, they would never have to see the interior of the Ulthorn forest.

Almost a hundred miles north of Dandun, Hain hauled viciously on his reins, bringing his horse up short. The beast was beginning to look bad. Its roan coat had faded to a dappled, sickly gray and much of its mane had fallen out. Only a few pathetic strands of its tail remained, to shoo the flies that kept pestering it, drawn by the scent of death. But gaunt as the horse appeared, it had continued along at the same brisk trot they had used since leaving Roddy's stables.

"Treat the beast more gently," Madh said in his usual tone—slow and carefully neutral, masking the loathing he felt for his associate. With each passing day, with each of Hain's whorings and petty thefts and indelicacies along the road north, Madh continued to question the utility of keeping the assassin by his side. Hain was dangerous and unpredictable . . . but that, Madh reminded himself, held generally true for any powerful weapon, and there seemed to him a chance that Hain's savagery would prove convenient again before they found themselves upon Yndrian ground.

"Treat it gently?" Hain repeated, laughing harshly. "Why? It's only going to die like the others. Sooner, if you ask me. This one seems to be dying sooner."

"That's what you said two days ago," Madh replied dryly. "The horse will survive as long as we need it, so long as you treat it gently."

"Like you do?" Hain countered, sneering.

But the response only provoked a slight, satisfied smile

upon Madh's lips. Despite Hain's uncanny instinct for butchery, Madh's eldritch rites somehow unnerved him. And for all that Hain would gut a man like a pig without a second thought, there was something about watching Madh force-feed the crows' blood to the horses that made the assassin shiver to the core. Madh had suspected as much; now he knew.

"There's nowhere to camp out here," Hain said after a moment, choosing a different complaint to change the subject.

"I told you this stretch of road would be barren. We will have to sleep in the open again."

And that, too, gave Madh cause to smile. He knew how Hain hated to be deprived of his women and his card games, of men he could intimidate, of soft feather pillows and softer breasts for his prickly head. Chances were, the murderer's hypodermic would be filled a little more than usual tonight.

Hain scowled in response. "Well, if we don't run across *something* by this time tomorrow, we'll be walking all the way to New Pell."

"I have no intention of walking," Madh replied evenly. "We will find new horses when we need them."

And then he nudged his withered mount gently into a trot northward.

A curse upon his lips, Hain watched as his employer moved away. Foolish, he thought, that he had not insisted on the entire payment in advance. He could have been relaxing in northern Gathony right now—where the women tended not to be quite so religious—safe from Chaldeans and Yndrians alike . . .

He lifted his legs and delivered a savage kick to his mount. The horse launched into a gallop, as Hain had desired, but there was more: his stirrups sliced through the beast's dead gray skin as if it were paper, and he felt the thing's ribs crack beneath his heels. As the horse vaulted past Madh, the Yndrian stared at him with cold enmity.

"Pray, Hain, that you have not damaged the beast irreparably."

But no amount of prayer would help, for two hours later, blood-flecked foam began to gather around the horse's mouth. It continued to trot through the night with the same mindless persistence as ever, but when, a little later, it began to drool a sickly yellow-red blood, Hain realized he had killed the thing. Madh said nothing, but he steered his horse off the road, into the thick, tall grass to the left. Hain's beast attempted to follow, but after only fifty yards, it seemed ready to falter. Madh wheeled his horse around and, drawing the foot-long knife that hung from his pommel, decapitated Hain's mount with one smooth motion. The head bounced to the ground only a second before its body collapsed beneath the assassin, sending Hain sprawling to the dirt.

Hain was back on his feet in less than a heartbeat, his sword drawn and glittering in the moonlight.

Madh slid from his horse, ignoring the bared blade, and bent over to retrieve the severed head.

"You have slowed us considerably," the Yndrian said casually. *It would be interesting*, he thought, *to see whether Hain attacked*. A humiliating insult combined with an exposed back would prove a mighty temptation, perhaps not outweighed by the fortune that Hain had been promised in Yndor. This would prove a useful test of the assassin's reliability. At least, the reliability of his avarice.

Behind him, Hain stood perfectly still.

"We will have to share a horse," Madh continued in his matter-of-fact tone. "And that will prove the death of the beast before noon. I fear we will have some walking to do after all."

Madh stared at the head he held, and abruptly, it burst into flames—blue-white tongues of light licking upward into the night, launching a twisted wreath of smoke into the air. The flames flickered over Madh's fingers but he paid them no attention, turning his face skyward instead.

"It will take a few moments," he said, seemingly to himself.

Hain remained where he was, two paces behind Madh's back, sword stretched out as if it was frozen in place.

After perhaps five minutes, a familiar rustling sound greeted Hain's ears, and even before he could see it land on Madh's shoulder, he knew that the mage had called one of those dirty homunculi he commanded. As soon as the creature squatted upon Madh's shoulder, the Yndrian dropped the horse's head, its flames guttering out as it fell from his fingers. Then, as he always did, Madh lowered his mouth by the homunculus's ear and whispered his directions. The hunched-over creature nodded and sprang upward into the air, visible for a moment before its leathery wings spread wide, catching the currents, and it disappeared.

"That should afford us whatever extra time we need," Madh said.

And behind him, he heard the distinct snick of Hain's hand-guard sliding into place in its scabbard. Madh smiled. Hain had indeed proved himself as treacherous to his owner as any bared blade. But Hain's foolishness with the horse amounted to no more than a nick, and there was not a swordsman on earth who abandoned his sword for such a scratch. No, Madh would keep Hain by his side. For now.

Three hours north of Dandun, Marwick was realizing the full implications of what had so upset Hain: since there were no towns or farmhouses along the road, they would have to sleep on the ground. Although Marwick had slumbered through more than his share of uneasy nights on the cobbled streets of Belfar, he had grown fond of beds long ago. If this was to turn into a camping expedition, they might at least have supplied themselves with tents and waterproof bedrolls. Indeed, he said as much to Brandt.

Brandt merely shrugged. He had spent the worst nights of his life strapped to Rachel on his way to Belfar. Five hours on the ground would hardly kill him. But he agreed that they should outfit themselves sensibly upon arriving in New Pell. The Ulthorn would prove even less hospitable than the republic's trade roads.

"Well, I suppose this will make as good a camp as anywhere else," Marwick said, reining in his horse and dismounting. Behind him, he could see the three government agents doing the same. *If it was any consolation*, Marwick thought, *Imbress probably dreaded the idea of camping more than he.*

But Imbress merely led her horse to the opposite side of the road, through the tall grass toward a lone elm that stood atop a small elevation. Her red hair glimmered prettily in the moonlight and, Marwick thought, she seemed perfectly at ease tethering Ramus to the elm and spreading her bedroll beneath its branches. Indeed, he realized, she had chosen a better campsite than he had. The higher ground would keep her dry if it rained, and the elm's shade had prevented the grass beneath it from growing so annoyingly tall.

"A little young to be leading an important intelligence mission, if you ask me," Marwick grumbled.

"I don't know how old she is," Brandt replied, untying his bedroll from its straps behind his saddle, "but I do know Ash considers her valuable. Don't underestimate her."

It was a grudging compliment, and one that he would never have uttered within Imbress's earshot. *Hell*, Brandt thought, *if she really was as good as Ash thought, she would have found Barr Aston herself and saved them all this trouble.* And that, for about the hundredth time that day, conjured the image again: Carn, lying on the hot stones of the defile, his legs twisted uselessly. *It would haunt him*, Brandt thought, *until his last days.* And as it had many times during the last several days, the fleeting traces of his good mood vanished.

Marwick, however, busy stamping down the tall grass to form an area for his bedding, was not done talking.

"Brandt, what is the Atahr Vin?"

Brandt started visibly, shocked as thoroughly as if Marwick had truly read his mind. But his old companion seemed to be paying no particular attention, working instead at smoothing down his blanket.

"Why do you ask?" Brandt replied, carefully even-toned. Damn Marwick's prying . . .

"It's something you mumbled the night I found you. Whenever you seemed to be coming closer to consciousness, you would start talking. Mostly Carn's name, over and over again, but a few other things as well. And I heard 'Atahr Vin' two or three times. Didn't have a chance to look it up before we had to leave Belfar."

Brandt drove a stake into the ground using the pommel of his knife. Silently, he tethered both their horses to it.

"The Atahr Vin," he finally said, "is an old Khrine ruin outside of Prandis." He would say no more.

They both unsaddled their horses, and then Marwick began rummaging through his saddlebags for the makings of a cold dinner. It wasn't until he had begun chewing on a tough piece of dried beef that he spoke again.

"What on earth does Carn have to do with Khrine ruins?"

"That's where he was crippled," Brandt answered tersely.

"Crippled," Marwick said softly, "by this mysterious assassin that the government is interested in catching. Interested in catching . . . why? Because he attacked your personal assistant? I doubt it. So my question stands. What were Carn and Hain doing in a Khrine ruin? You're too rich to bother with treasure hunts, Brandt."

Brandt sat down on his bedding and stared at Marwick in the moonlight. The call and response of the crickets were the night's only sound. Finally, Marwick sighed. "All right, Brandt, I'll tell you what I think. I think something upset your little applecart in Prandis, something threatened to reveal your past as Galatine Hazard. Not a savory background for an industrial magnate with important government contracts, eh?"

Brandt raised his eyebrows in response. "Concocting another of your mother's tall tales, Marwick?"

The thief chuckled, his hair shaking like kinked strands of wire in the moonlight. "Oh, I'm smart enough to figure this one out without my mother's sage teachings. After all, I can't think of anything else but dangerous publicity that would have jogged you from the featherbed you were enjoying in Prandis."

Enjoying, Brandt thought, *was the wrong word*. But he said nothing, intrigued by Marwick's logic.

"Anyway, it had to be something to do with your past. Otherwise Ash's leading lady across the road would have little interest in you."

This time, Brandt could not hold back a laugh. "Now you *are* dead wrong. She couldn't be less interested in me."

"I didn't say she *liked* you," Marwick countered, a mischievous gleam in his eye. "In any case, the common link seems to be the murder of retired government ministers."

Brandt arched an eyebrow. "What gives you that idea?"

Marwick shrugged and carved a generous slice of cheese from a wedge he had retrieved from his saddlebags. "Something Harnor let slip. The murder of ministers would interest those Intelligence types. Meanwhile, the fact that they were *ex*-ministers is what convinced me they were linked somehow to you, back to the days when you made a living by prying into their secrets . . . and their pockets."

Brandt stretched out on his blanket, staring upward at the dizzying array of stars. It was the first time he had slept outdoors in ages—not counting his delirious ride to Belfar—and the intensity of the starlight seemed overwhelming to him. *The night would be quite pleasant*, he thought, *perhaps even relaxing enough to put him to sleep, if it weren't for Marwick's chattering.*

"Anyway," Marwick went on, "the one thing I can't figure out for the life of me is why anyone would want to murder an ex-minister. Not much sport in offing retirees, nor much profit, as far as I can tell. And from what I've seen of him, I would imagine that your friend Hain would prefer more vigorous challenges."

Brandt fought down a smile. He was glad to see the progression of Marwick's reasoning frustrated . . . especially by the very point that had stymied him for so long. It would be amusing to see how long it would take Marwick to unravel the secrets of the Binding. Probably forever.

"What, then," Brandt asked, a hint of amusement creeping into his voice despite himself, "have you concluded?"

Marwick made no immediate answer, pulling off his boots instead and wrapping himself inside his blanket. For a moment, there was only the determined stare of the starlight and the crickets' discordant concerto.

"I have concluded," Marwick finally said, almost too quietly to be heard, "that you will begin treating me like the friend I have been to you. Or come morning, I will turn my horse south toward Belfar, and to hell with Ulthorn forest and you with it."

For a moment Brandt lay there in stunned silence, and then he began to laugh. It was only fitting, after all, that Marwick had resorted to extorting the story from him, just as he had extorted it from Barr Aston. He lay there for a while, unwilling to say anything just yet, although he knew immediately that he'd talk. After all, he would need someone at his back when he finally caught up to Hain—someone who could occupy Madh while he dismembered the assassin. And irritating as Marwick could be, he was now—as he had been all through childhood—a loyal companion. Aside from Carn, the only man he trusted in a fight.

If only, he thought, *looking at Marwick wasn't so much like looking at a mirror.* Or closer to the truth, at a portrait of the two of them, Marwick looking just as he had at fourteen and Brandt—Brandt looking just as he did now.

"You know," Brandt finally said, "it really is a shame you didn't come with me and Carn to Prandis. You have a natural talent for spying and blackmail."

"That's the first compliment I've heard from you in twenty years. But what's your answer?"

"My answer," Brandt sighed, "is a story that's too implausible to believe."

But Brandt told him anyway, all of it, from the night that Madh had arrived at the mansion, hoping to hire Galatine Hazard as an assassin, to the way Madh had framed him when Brandt had turned him down. He told him how Taylor Ash, using Imbress, had mired Brandt deeper in the mess, leading to Carn's crippling in the Atahr Vin and Barr Aston's confession. He told him that the very laws of nature were no more immutable than the laws of the state, and that the mages who had wrought the Binding had also left a way to undo their work. He told him that those six Phrases—Prandis's half of the spell that would undo the Binding—were the true object of Hain's quest, and that the assassin had succeeded in finding them.

Throughout the story, Marwick remained motionless beneath his blankets, eyes closed, listening with such quiet intensity that Brandt began to believe the man had fallen asleep.

"So," Brandt prompted, "what do you think?"

Marwick said nothing at first, but he did open his eyes. Then he propped himself up on one elbow and turned toward Brandt. The Belfarian thief wore an expression that Brandt had never seen before. All the characteristic mirth, the incorrigible grin of the ageless smart aleck, had drained away.

"I think," Marwick answered, "that it's a damned good thing I decided to come along."

And then he lowered himself back to the ground, pulled his blanket over his chin, and wished he could find some way to sleep.

Marwick's unexpected flash of gravity had disappeared by morning. Brandt was woken by the freckled thief's singing—it was an old bawdy from their tavern days, Brandt recognized—as he broke camp and began saddling his horse. Only the uppermost lip of the sun had curled above the horizon. Brandt struggled to his feet, sore from a night on the ground, and cast a curious eye at his old friend.

"Move that middle-aged body of yours," Marwick cried out, affecting a lofty, theatrical tone. "High time to greet the road. See? The spooks across the way have already broken their fast and are almost ready to depart."

Indeed, Ash's agents had saddled their horses and mounted.

"You ate, too?" Brandt asked.

"Of course," Marwick replied, grinning at Brandt's frown.

"I would have woken you earlier but I thought you had sworn off food for the remainder of your quest."

Brandt shook his head. It seemed an utter transformation from last night, back suddenly to Marwick the clown.

Inured to the routine of Brandt leading the way in the morning, Imbress no longer set off first, forcing Brandt and Marwick into a gallop to catch up with them. It would only foolishly waste their horses' energy. Instead, they crossed the road and remained in their saddles as Brandt pulled on his boots, strapped his sword and knife to his belt, and began to saddle up. It was when he knelt down to fix the cinch strap that he looked past Rachel's belly and noticed the small tab of leather hanging down from Imbress's cinch.

"Better check your strap," Brandt advised. "Looks like it's tearing."

"I check my gear every day," the agent replied with her usual hauteur, "and it's perfectly fine."

Annoyed by her tone, Brandt walked over to Ramus and knelt down by the horse's side. The cinch strap was fine. But more oddly still, a small, greenish triangular tab of leather seemed to be hanging down from the gelding's belly, as if it had been pasted there. And as Brandt watched, the tab seemed to be getting smaller, as if it were retracting into the horse's stomach. There was barely enough left to grasp.

"Well?" Imbress asked icily. "Are you satisfied?"

Brandt ignored her, very far from being satisfied. Instead, he reached out and pinched the leathery tab between his thumb and forefinger. It felt oddly light—insubstantial against his flesh, except that it shivered palpably. Brandt tugged at it and was surprised to pull a foot-long, triangular flap of leather from Ramus's belly.

"Oh my," Marwick said under his breath, watching Brandt. Slowly, the thief slid from his horse. "Mother always said, no one has more friends than a roach."

"What are you babbling about?" Imbress asked testily. She leaned over to get a look at what Brandt was doing, but Ramus's broad midsection blocked her view. "If you loosen my saddle while I'm up here . . ."

To Brandt's surprise, the leather flap yanked back, and he almost lost hold of it. Several inches disappeared back into Ramus's gut. But now that Brandt was prepared, he gripped the thing with both hands and pulled with all his strength. The thing came free as if it had been hauled from under water and Brandt looked at what he held in his hands: an old man, it seemed, but only eighteen inches tall. The thing was hairless, completely naked, and thin as a rail, its bones straining at its leathery skin. Two gnarled horns jutted from its brow above tiny red eyes that stared at Brandt with hatred and disbelief. But the most amazing thing about the little man, Brandt thought, were its two batlike wings, one of which he had a firm hold of.

"What on earth . . . ?" he asked.

"Homunculus," Marwick growled, slipping his dagger from its sheath. "Don't you recognize them?"

But then he remembered that Brandt had been somewhat incapacitated at the time.

"What on earth are you talking about?" Imbress snapped.

Brandt looked up. The three agents were looking down at him from their saddles as if he were a lunatic.

"I'm talking about *this*," Brandt snapped back, shaking the thing in Imbress's direction. "It was trying to kill your horse."

"You've gone mad," Imbress said, as if the idea surprised her very little. What on earth was Karrelian doing standing there, waving his fist at her?

But Marwick had come between them.

"Brandt, I think we're the only ones who see it."

"See *what*?" Imbress insisted.

Marwick ignored her. "Do you think we can kill it?"

Brandt peered at the disgusting creature. Suddenly, its head flashed forward and its little teeth sank into Brandt's wrist. Brandt screamed, more in surprise than real pain, and the homunculus sprang free from his loosened grip. But Marwick was there, plunging his dagger at the creature's belly. The homunculus rolled to the side, avoiding a deadly blow, but the point of Marwick's dagger bit through the creature's wing, pinning it to the ground.

"Bloody hell!" Imbress swore as the creature finally melted into her sight.

Glowering at the thing, Brandt drew his sword and directed a careful stroke at the creature, lopping off its right arm. Yellow ichor spurted onto the ground, bubbling hotly in the morning air. Grimly, Brandt severed its left arm as well.

"Just kill it quickly," Imbress said with distaste.

"I don't want to kill it."

"What then?"

Brandt leaned close to the thing. He could smell its fetid breath.

"Tell your friends we're coming for them," he said, a savage undertone to his voice. "Tell them they don't have very much longer."

And then Brandt pulled Marwick's dagger free of the creature's wing. The homunculus rolled instantly onto its belly and, using its good wing as a crutch against the ground, levered itself to its feet. It hissed a final time at Brandt before launching itself feebly into the air. At first, Brandt thought that he had killed it after all, for it almost collapsed back to the ground. But it beat its wings harder, the left one moving much more freely than the right, and it rose unsteadily into the air, little by little, until it was gone.

"Do you think that was entirely wise?" Imbress asked, her face turned skyward toward the point the homunculus had last been visible.

Brandt paused before he answered, wiping his blade diligently against the grass to get rid of the yellow ooze that dripped from its edge.

"With any luck, letting the thing go will accomplish two things. First, it may convince Madh that he shouldn't risk sending more of those vermin our way. It was just luck that I caught that one, but I want him to think it was something more. If he sends any others, we might not be so fortunate."

"Especially if we can't see them," Laz added darkly. His

blue eyes narrowed as he looked from Brandt to Marwick. "Why could *you* see them?"

Marwick smiled. "I think we have Tarem Selod to thank for that. When he pulled one of that fellow's brothers out of Brandt's stomach a week ago, he said he would put a spell on Brandt that would protect him from the things. Apparently, it was one hell of a spell. And he seems to have included me in the bargain, because I was able to see the creature as soon as Brandt grabbed it."

"It would have been nice if the old man had been so generous to us," Laz said, but Imbress ignored her assistant's complaint.

"You said you let it go for two reasons," she prompted Brandt.

He nodded. "The second is, it may make them nervous. And nervous men make mistakes."

"I wouldn't count on it," Marwick said dryly as he climbed back in his saddle. "From what I saw in Belfar, neither Madh nor Hain is the nervous type."

That day, the five Chaldeans began riding as a single group. It happened by tacit agreement, Brandt and Imbress both remaining unwilling to discuss anything that resembled a unified effort. But as they rode away from the campsite, Imbress and her men remained even with Brandt and Marwick, not falling back as they usually did. Everyone understood the reason: in case Madh had left any further surprises along the way, it was best to keep the whole party together, watching out for one another.

Nevertheless, the day was mostly quiet, save Marwick's sporadic efforts at banter, asking the agents where they were from, how long they had worked for Intelligence, whether they knew what the women looked like in New Pell. That last question drew such a piercing stare from Imbress, however, that it quieted him for the next hour.

But it was Laz, the most taciturn of the group, who noted late that afternoon, "Lot of stray cattle around here."

And there were. Several minutes ago, they had passed a large, black-and-white cow by the side of the road. The cow seemed entirely unconcerned, chewing happily at the tall grass. Soon afterward, a couple of steer were visible west of the road, perhaps fifty yards away. Slowly, the frequency of the cow sightings increased until the body of the herd was visible east of the road. Offhand, there seemed to be a good hundred head, but they were far more dispersed than any responsible rancher would allow in the proximity of the road. And stranger still, there were no ranchers anywhere about.

"You see what I see?" Marwick muttered.

Brandt followed his friend's line of sight out into the field. "Crows," he said. "You think they changed horses again."

Marwick nodded, frowning. "Unfortunately for the ranchers."

They rode reluctantly toward the crows, passing by cattle that cared not a whit about their presence. Once again, as they drew closer, they could see where an area of grass had been flattened. Marwick steeled himself for the sight that was about to come.

Sprawled in the grass were the bodies of two horses and three men.

"Something's wrong here," Imbress said quietly as she took in the scene.

Only one of the three ranchers had even had time to draw a weapon. His two partners had been killed with ruthless efficiency, their necks sliced open as deep as the carotid artery. *At least*, Imbress thought, *they seemed to have died with more merciful speed than Hain's usual victims*. The third rancher was a different story. He had tried to resist, and apparently, Hain had punished him for it. The man's clothes were hanging in tatters, sliced open by innumerable cuts, none deep enough by itself to be fatal.

Brandt, however, was working on the arithmetic. "Something is *wrong*, Imbress? Actually, it seems for once that something is right."

He pointed at the horse closest to them, its emaciated

frame covered with the same desiccated skin they had seen the day before.

"We expected this," Brandt said, "but not that."

He gestured now at the second horse. Though a dozen yards farther away, it was obvious that this horse had been perfectly healthy—a normal rancher's mount, untouched by Madh's arcane talents. It would have proved a fine horse except that, just like its former rider, its throat had been cut.

"Hain killed the extra horse to keep it from us," Brandt said quietly, still adding up the implications in his head. "But where is the other shriveled horse that Madh and Hain used to get here?"

They rode a quick circuit around the vicinity, but there were no more corpses to be found. After a swift search, they gathered again at the scene of the fight.

"Something must have happened to their other horse," Brandt said, "and we just missed the corpse down the road. But it seems certain that Madh and Hain shared a horse to get here, and if that's the case, we may have gained time."

"There's one way to find out," Imbress said, sliding down from her saddle. She knelt by the side of one of the corpses and grabbed his arm at the wrist. Her cheeks twitched as she touched the cadaver, but rather than let go, she moved the arm. It bent easily at the elbow.

"This body is still warm," she said. "I don't think we're more than an hour behind them."

Brandt wheeled Rachel back toward the road.

"Time to ride, then. Maybe we'll catch them before New Pell after all."

"And miss our chance to visit the Ulthorn?" Marwick asked, his voice heavy with sarcasm.

But Laz simply sat atop his horse, staring down at the corpses. "We should bury them," he said quietly.

"Without a pick or a shovel?" Imbress asked as she climbed back into her saddle. "It would take all afternoon . . . and most of tomorrow morning. We're less than an hour behind them, Laz, so let's catch them before New Pell. Otherwise, there may be many more bodies to bury."

CHAPTER 8

The horse beneath Hain's legs was flesh and blood, free of Madh's sorcery, and Hain preferred it that way. No matter how hard he spurred the beast or reined it in, there would be no unnatural crackings of bone, no tearing of fragile flesh. And most important, he would not have to watch the creature turn gray beneath him, withering into a wraith before, stripped of its last ounce of muscle, even Madh's magic could hold it to life no longer. No, when things died, Hain preferred to be the man in charge—the symphony's conductor, rather than a member of the audience.

Nevertheless, the fact that Madh declined to ensorcel these mounts only reminded Hain of the long, treacherous ride that awaited them in the Ulthorn forest. There would be no fresh horses, no inns, none of the hot food and lukewarm women that had kept him at least mildly contented along the road thus far. Add to that Madh's insistence that they hurry because Hazard and his companions were only a few leagues behind, and the proposition of a journey through the Ulthorn began to look like a bleak, uncompromising flight.

Hain looked around him at the boles of the trees that had grown more frequent and more imposing since they had left New Pell. North of Dandun, upon the grazing lands, trees had begun to spring up: stands of pine dotting the plains, an occasional willow limned against the horizon. As they had traveled north, the land had grown ever more hilly and wooded until, just south of New Pell, the plains disappeared completely, and almost with a start of surprise, Hain had realized he was within the southernmost fringe of the Ulthorn. The trees had still been small and young there—the pioneering pines that had reclaimed the land after Chaldeans had cleared it for farming. While the plains might surrender easily to the plow, the Ulthorn stubbornly insisted on its rights, and the ten or fifteen miles south of New Pell that had once been cleared into ambitious stretches of fields were now almost entirely wooded again. The frontier town of New Pell found itself being swallowed by the forest.

North of the town stood the trees that had never been touched by an axe: walnuts and willows whose branches spread overhead, obscuring the sun; white elms and black oaks as tall as Prandis's Council Tower; and monstrous black cherries within whose spreading limbs entire families could hide. Hain found that he liked the forest better than the plains. Dark and cool, a warren of obscure trails and a refuge of half-glimpsed movement, the Ulthorn seemed like home. More the pity, then, that they be forced to rush through it at a breakneck pace.

"If Hazard is as close as you say," Hain announced, pleased with the way the leaves swallowed the sound of his voice, "we would be foolish to exhaust ourselves with a protracted chase, only to have him catch us when we are tired."

Madh did not look up from the trail. Since they had entered the Ulthorn, he had concentrated with his usual, peculiar intensity on the weaving web of half-erased tracks that laced the forest floor. Every few minutes, one of his homunculi would swoop down through the leaves and perch on his shoulder for a hushed conference, taking wing again into the woods—scouting ahead, Hain supposed. Growing familiarity with the creatures had enabled him to tell the things apart, to distinguish the one whose green skin was lightly dappled with gray, to diffentiate between the twisted dwarf whose forehead horns curled outward and his seeming twin whose horns curled inward. There were five of them, as Hain counted. Six if you included the creature Madh had sent back to hinder their pursuers. But by Hain's reckoning, that beast should have returned half a day ago. Madh had not said a word about it, but Hain suspected the creature's absence worried him, and this, too, contributed to their flight through the forest.

"They will not catch us," Madh said finally, his voice a mere whisper above the rustling leaves.

"Is that so?" Hain replied, as always more jeering when Madh seemed subdued. "I would be more inclined to believe you if you hadn't left dozens of fresh horses in New Pell for them to buy."

Madh reined in, also bringing to a stop the spare mount that was tethered to his pommel. Then he turned about to look at Hain. He did not seem angry, as Hain had expected, but simply annoyed at having his concentration broken.

"The residents of New Pell are a peculiar lot," Madh said quietly, "living so close to the Ulthorn. Before the Binding, the town was just called Pell and the men who lived there were all that stood between the great beasts of the Ulthorn and the vulnerable plains to the south. Among them numbered some of the finest mages and warriors of the age. When the beasts passed beyond memory after the Binding, so did many of the Pellians, but even still they remain a hardy breed. Though nothing truly monstrous ventures beyond the confines of the Ulthorn in this age, there are more than enough lesser beasts, hungry for human blood, that trespass upon New Pell. Those who live there are well used to dealing with them. A homunculus in their midst would have been quickly detected and just as quickly dispatched. And it would have set the residents upon our heels, for no homunculus wreaks mischief without its master directing it."

"Well, then," Hain said, "since we are safely past the town now and Hazard is close upon our heels, why don't we arrange a little ambush? After we deal with him and his friends, we can proceed to Yndor without having to look over our shoulders."

"In the Ulthorn," Madh replied dryly, "we shall always be looking over our shoulders. If you're interested in bloodshed, I expect there will be more than enough to satisfy you along our way. In the meantime, it is foolish to seek a fight that we can easily outrun."

"Fight in the time and place of our choosing, I say."

Madh's face remained impassive, but his eyes twinkled with mischief. "The bowels of the Atahr Vin were the time and place of your choosing," he reminded the assassin, "and you could not best Hazard there. What makes you think you will do better here, when he has several companions to help him?"

Hain's fingers twitched toward the knife at his belt, but he reminded himself of the fortune that awaited him and held his temper.

"My job is to bring the Phrases to my master with as little risk as possible," said Madh. "That means no ambushes simply to please your thirst for blood. If you are so eager to try your blade against Hazard's again, hope he catches us. But in the meantime, ride. And ride quietly."

"I thought New Pell was at the *edge* of the forest," Marwick complained, shifting his painfully swollen rump in the saddle. There was no amount of fidgeting, however, and no redistribution of weight that would help. Ever since Hazard had caught Madh's homunculus, they had practically lived on horseback, hunched wearily over their horses while the plains passed by them unnoticed, growing humped and heaving into wooded, rolling hills. Finally, Marwick had taken a good look at the country around him and decided that, at some point, he knew not when, they had actually entered the forest.

"New Pell *is* at the edge of the forest," Imbress answered.

"Then what do you call this?"

Tired as she was, covered with road dust until it seemed to choke her, Marwick's complaint made her smile. She had never met, she had decided, a creature more purely of the cities than Marwick.

"Can't you tell the difference between woods and the forest?" she asked, glancing at the sparse stands of trees that here grew to the very edge of the road but, elsewhere, might give way to clearings a mile wide.

"No," Marwick replied, "I suppose I can't."

"Well, as soon as you see the Ulthorn, that will change," Imbress replied. "You know, you should pay me for the education you'll get on this trip."

It had been an education already, Marwick thought, *though not perhaps in the ways that Imbress and Brandt expected.* In the end, he suspected he would have to educate them—Brandt, who was so driven for vengeance that he could not see the true danger, and Imbress, whom he suspected considered this expedition, while dangerous enough, mere politics.

But all he said was, "What's the matter? Doesn't Taylor Ash pay you well enough?"

And then Imbress laughed because, of course, Taylor Ash didn't pay her a tenth of what she deserved for this—for chasing Yndrian assassins and conspirators; for spending her thirtieth birthday, two days ago, on a thankless and back-breaking cross-country race; for sacrificing every semblance of a real life for the good of her countrymen, none of whom recognized her sacrifices or, in most cases, deserved them; for enduring the silent hostility and hauteur of Brandt Karrelian and the mindless jabbering of Marwick. She should find out Marwick's last name, she realized, and alert the Belfarian tax assessors. God only knew what revenue lay untapped there.

She *should* report Marwick, Imbress thought, but she wouldn't. She reflected, not for the first time, that Marwick, with his endless banter and pointless anecdotes, with his off-color jokes and his mother's warped proverbs, had wormed his way into her good graces.

"Let's hope that we catch Madh in New Pell, then," she said, "so we can get you back to your city as soon as possible."

Marwick smiled. "Whenever Brandt talks about the chase, he talks about catching Hain. Whenever you talk about it, you talk about catching Madh."

Imbress raised her eyebrows in admiration of the logic. "I suppose you're right," she admitted. "The problem with Karrelian is that he refuses to see the big picture."

"True enough," Marwick agreed as he spurred his horse, heading back toward Brandt's side. "But do you?"

Imbress watched Marwick draw away, standing in his stirrups in order to spare his behind until he pulled even with Brandt. There, he began volubly reminiscing about old taverns in Belfar. But the odd thief, she decided, might bear even more watching than she had first thought.

The trade road beneath them stretched almost three hundred miles back to Belfar, then another hundred east to Prandis and half a thousand more along the coast to Desh. It was part of a seemingly endless web that had been spun from city to city, town to town, in an intricate, interrelated circuit. But one hundred yards ahead of them, that circuit came to a dead stop. The trade road that had stretched endlessly before them for days reached the doorstep of a small wooden building that, ramshackle as it was, defied further progress. The road could neither go through nor around the building that had been labeled the FORESTERS GUILD, and so New Pell proved its end.

"*This* is New Pell?" Marwick said, sounding incredulous. As far away as Belfar, he had heard of New Pell, the city that stood at the gateway of the Ulthorn. And as such, he had expected something . . . well, something more like Belfar. But the "city" of New Pell consisted of the guild hall before them, a travelers' inn immediately to its left, and a general store to the right. Small horse trails led off in several directions into the trees, and where the woods were not so dense, Marwick could glimpse several cottages, but this was nothing like what he had expected.

"At least," he muttered, "it won't take us long to search the place."

Harnor snorted in amusement, reining in his horse by the hitching post that stood before the guild hall. It was an ambitious hitching post, stretching the full twenty feet of the hall on either side of the door, but before the party arrived, there had been only one other horse tethered to it. Nevertheless, that horse was on its feet and seemingly healthy. Harnor caught Imbress's eye and she nodded.

"It seems the plague spared New Pell," Brandt said with satisfaction, coming to the same conclusion. "Perhaps Madh's little pet isn't as vicious without hands."

"Or perhaps," Marwick suggested hopefully, "they're still here somewhere."

After tethering their tired horses to the post, they slipped through the open door of the building into the cool, dark confines of the guild's common room. There were a dozen men lounging about the tables in a few small groups, leaning over glasses of amber liquor, talking in harsh voices that carried a peculiar twang in the vowels. All were dressed in rough woodsmen's garb—garments crudely stitched together from buckskin and boar and whatever else they had killed. Though they were inside, several wore wide-brimmed leather hats that cast their faces in deeper shadow. Marwick peered beneath those brims and, with a start, realized that four or five of the guild members were women. They were dressed no differently from the men and, for the most part, were tall and solidly built. Well, he decided, there was no reason that thieving should be the only equal opportunity profession in Chaldus.

As the travelers filed inside, a large, bearded man looked up from his card game.

"Welcome to New Pell," he said gruffly. "Name's Imming. I'm the guildmaster. You'll be looking for a guide, I take it. Long-Nose here is next in line."

At that, one of Imming's card partners, a wiry man who indeed possessed a remarkably long, slender nose, tipped his hat.

"Actually," Imbress said, "we're looking for two men who we think passed through here."

Then, as Imbress began describing Madh and Hain in some detail, Imming gathered his cards into a pile and set them neatly, facedown, on the table. He pushed himself to his feet and began a slow, meandering walk around the party, paying special attention to Harnor and Laz.

As Imbress finished her description, Long-Nose snorted a laugh. "If them's who you're looking for, then you'll want a guide, all right. The fools rode in here right past the hall. Just stopped at Payter's next door to buy fresh horses and three weeks' supplies. I went over there to offer my services, seeing as I got next draw and all, but they wouldn't hear a word of it. Small, dark-skinned one chased me off with a nasty look. He'd better have more than that evil eye, though, 'cause his friend and him rode off into Old Beauty alone."

"Old Beauty?" Imbress asked.

"The Ulthorn," Long-Nose explained, grinning crookedly. "That's our pet name for her. Anyway, you'll be wanting a guide if you're looking to track them down in the forest."

"I suppose we will," Imbress allowed. "How long ago did they leave, Long-Nose?"

The man scratched his head. "No more than an hour, maybe. Damn fools, with the sun going down. Even this far out from Old Beauty's heart, it's foolish to spend an extra night inside for the sake of one or two hours' ride. I wouldn't do it. And I won't guide you until morning."

"We need to leave now," Imbress argued, "just as soon as we can buy fresh mounts."

Long-Nose grinned again. "I s'pose that's why they went in at dark after all, knowing they was being chased. Though if I was being chased by a lady with your looks"—and here his smile broadened to show the gaps where a molar should have been—"I wouldn't be running too hard."

Imming had completed his circuit around the company, but rather than return to his seat, he took a position between the party and the guild members, feet astride, hands on his hips.

"And why *are* you so anxious to follow those men into the forest? What have they done?"

"That doesn't concern you," Imbress answered tersely, pulling a coin from her pocket, "as long as my gold shines the right color."

Imming ran his tongue over his teeth and frowned. "That, lady, is where you're wrong. Because these two men," he said, pointing at Harnor and Laz, "are government, and you probably are, too, as far as I can see."

At that, a clamor arose among the foresters, many of them rising to their feet and walking toward the party, scrutinizing them anew.

"What are you talking about, Imming?" Long-Nose asked, clearly anxious to secure the gold in Imbress's hand, and more, if possible. "What makes you say they're government?" In his mouth, the word was pronounced *gummint*.

"Take a look at their swords. Same make," he said, pointing first at Harnor, then at Laz. "Alike as two acorns. Same with their boots, and city-made boots, too. They carry themselves like army, and they come in here chasing folk. Maybe army, maybe Intelligence. Either way," Imming concluded, turning back now to Imbress, "the New Pell Foresters Guild don't do business with the government."

Scowling, Brandt pushed past Imbress and walked right up to Imming. "That's fine with me," he said, approving the guildmaster's decision. "*I'm* not government, and neither is he," Brandt said, pointing at Marwick. "If you want to know what those two men did, I'll tell you. They crippled my best friend. And if you want to know what I mean to do about it, I'll gladly tell you that, too. I mean to kill them."

Brandt paused, taking a moment to regain control of himself. His voice had grown deeper as he had spoken, until he finished in a guttural choke. Imming, all the while, watched him with keen curiosity.

After another moment, Brandt pulled a roll of bills from his pocket and peeled off the top five, each of them revealing a 100-capital denomination.

"That's to hire *you*," Brandt said, offering the money to Imming, "and a like amount for every other man here who rides with us into the forest. And the same amount again every week we're there."

Imming laughed, pushing the money away. "I think I believe you, stranger, and you have my sympathy about your friend. But none of us use that fancy paper money of yours up here in New Pell. Coin only. And even if you had it, you rode in here with government . . . and that's how you'll ride out. With your government friends, and not with no one else."

Then, with a shrug of his large shoulders, Imming returned to his table and picked up his cards, examining them as if they had just been dealt.

"I'll double the offer," Brandt proposed. Though Imming had apparently abandoned further interest in him, Brandt could see that a few of the other foresters had let their gazes linger on the money in his hand. "And I can arrange for gold coin, if that's what you need."

"Don't make me kick you out of my guild hall," Imming said calmly, still examining his cards. Slowly, the other foresters returned to their tables, affecting the same air of indifference as their guildmaster.

Furious, Brandt reached for his sword. One of the foresters smiled crookedly at the gesture—as if he'd been threatened by a child.

"And I won't guide you neither with a hole in me," Imming went on, still calmly thumbing his cards. "And you won't catch those two friends of yours any better if maybe I put a hole in you. Now, I don't have no argument with you, and you don't have none with me. Let's keep it just that simple."

Slowly, Brandt let his sword slip the few inches he had raised it back into his scabbard. He turned sharply and stalked out of the hall.

Harnor, Laz, and Marwick also turned to go, but they were surprised to hear Imbress ask one last question.

"Maybe you will tell us this," she said. "Where can I find Callom Pell?"

Finally, Imming looked up from his cards, his eyes alight with laughter. "You think you're going to get Callom Pell to help you? He hates the government worse than me."

"Maybe," she said. "Now, where can I find him?"

Imming shrugged. "If he ain't in Old Beauty, he'll be at

his house. Take the eastern trail out of here, branch left, left, right, left, left, left again, and right. He's two hundred yards north of the blasted oak, no path to his front door. Hope you got that because I ain't repeating it."

"I got it," Imbress answered with a sweetness calculated to get under Imming's skin, "and thank you so much."

When they walked out into the waning twilight of the street, they found Brandt standing a hundred feet past the guild hall, staring north at the Ulthorn. Imbress, frowning with impatience, was the first to reach him.

"I would have thought you would be ready to go," she said sourly, "rather than admiring the beauty of the trees."

"The only thing I'm admiring," Brandt replied, his voice carefully neutral in tone, "is the fact that, without a guide, we are going nowhere. Take a look at these trees. They're bunched so close together that you can't see fifty yards. Willow and oak and elm and I don't know what else. I'm no woodsman, after all. But that's exactly the point. Hain and Madh entered that overgrown mess without any guide. We can bloody well guess that at least one of them knows where he's going."

He turned on his heels and began walking back toward the horses. "We would have had a guide, Miss Imbress, if your men were not so obviously who they are. *You've* put us in the position of losing Hain in the Ulthorn without a guide to help us. So I don't see what your hurry is."

Imbress stared coldly at Brandt for a long, tense moment before replying.

"My hurry, you bastard, is to go find us another guide."

With that, she untied Ramus's tether, mounted in one smooth motion, and set off down the eastern trail at a gallop, leaving everyone else to follow.

Imbress had to slow down soon, however, to watch the trail. She was sure she remembered Imming's list of trail forks, but deciding what was and wasn't a fork was a far more complicated matter. The trail was only a foot-wide ribbon of dirt that had been traveled just often enough that the underbrush had not yet managed to intrude upon it. Frequently, a track would break off to the left or the right, but whether it was clear enough to call a fork Imbress was unsure.

"I think that's the first left turning."

Imbress swiveled about in her saddle to find that Marwick had come almost abreast of her. The last thing she needed now was a distraction, but if Marwick had come to help her sort out the trail, she would be thankful for it. Maybe the city boy actually had a better grasp of such things than she.

Although the trail itself was only a foot wide, the trees fell back on both sides five or six feet. There was plenty of room for two horses to ride abreast, but except for Marwick riding even with Imbress, the others followed in a single file, Harnor and Laz each silently chiding himself for giving away their origin, and Brandt last of all, stewing at the thought of Hain having escaped. They all wound quietly into the forest for a few hundred yards, passing beneath the oaks and the willows that threatened to obscure the dying embers of the day.

"Another few minutes and we won't have enough light to follow the trail," Imbress commented.

"There's the second left right there," Marwick said by way of response, pointing ahead to a clear fork in the trail where a well-beaten path branched off to the right to a shingle cottage that stood a hundred feet back in a small clearing.

Taking advantage of the easy marking, they hurried their pace for a few moments, winding northward into a thick copse of younger elms and spruce. Toward the middle of the copse, Marwick thought he could make out the collapsed remains of another cottage, perhaps fifty years old. The forest quickly reclaimed its own.

"There's the right," Marwick announced, again pointing the way.

In other circumstances, Imbress was sure she would have regretted the thief's sharp eyes, but in the dimming light of the forest, she breathed a silent thanks and let Marwick draw a half-pace ahead.

"Funny," Marwick said, almost to himself, "that the New Pellians, or whatever they call themselves, are so wary of the government, don't you think?" He paused for a moment, slowing his horse's pace. "That might be the next left at that moss-covered rock."

It proved indeed to be. To the right, a small, indistinct trail twisted off into a thick stand of oak, to what purpose they could not say. Another fork in the trail came by and the party filed again to the left. Marwick, meanwhile, chewed on the puzzle. "Well," he said finally, "you realize that I have absolutely no experience in illegal commerce, and therefore I'm wholly ill-suited to speculate on this sort of matter. But if I had to take a guess—a random, stab-in-the-dark, last-chance guess—I would say that our friends at the guild run a cozy smuggling ring. Times must be bad, considering all the free trade agreements Yndor and Chaldus have signed over the last twenty years, but there are still plenty of individual items that get hit with hefty excise taxes. Jewelry, for instance, and fine arts. In fact, there's been quite a steady black market for rubies and jade in Belfar—at least, that's what I heard from a friend—and those are predominantly southwestern Yndrian stones. Now, I might not choose the Ulthorn and you might not either. But if it's all these boys know and their best way of collecting a little coin, well . . ." He paused and grinned. "That's what the entrepreneurial urge is all about."

Marwick turned to look back at Imbress and found the agent smiling in spite of himself.

"You know, Marwick," she said, "if you weren't so thoroughly corrupt, you would have a future in Intelligence. Is that the last left turn?" Abruptly she forged ahead to a spot where the trail began to rise along a mild hill, down the slope of which an indistinct horse path appeared to descend to the west.

Marwick pulled even with her and examined the break in the foliage that ran to the west. Until now, all their forks had been fairly clear, and the route they had taken had uniformly been the better marked. Whether this was truly a fork, or simply a point where some errant horseman had decided to lead his mount into the woods, it was almost impossible to tell.

"Well?" Imbress prompted.

Marwick shrugged. "Love and war, my mother said, are mere matters of interpretation. She should have added trails to the list."

"That's no answer," the agent snapped. "Another five minutes and we won't be able to see a thing out here."

Marwick looked left, then right, then left again, and shrugging, set off down the leftward trail at a trot.

"Just one more right," he called backward. "Everyone keep a lookout."

But as he kept riding, his eyes riveted on the trail before him, Marwick again took up his casual conversation with Imbress.

"The New Pellians hate us. So why will this Callom Pell of yours agree to help?"

"The Ministry has agents and informants in almost every village and hamlet of Chaldus. New Pell is actually somewhat important because it's close to the Yndrian border, so I happen to be acquainted with the name of our local informant—Callom Pell."

"Hard to forget when he's named after the town," Marwick observed.

"This town," a rough voice interjected from the woods before them, "is named after *me*."

Immediately, the party stopped their horses, peering into the dark path before them. After a moment, a broad shadow detached itself from the general murkiness of the woods, sliding quietly toward them. It was a huge man, they saw, though extraordinary in breadth rather than height. He was perhaps as tall as Brandt, but half again as wide, his burly shoulders possessing almost the span of a horse's. He walked with an odd heel-to-toe gait that somehow made very little sound on the forest floor.

"I'm Callom Pell," the woodsman said as he drew close

to the party. Now they could make him out clearly: the hand-stitched buckskin of his clothes; the broad-brimmed hat that hung by a leather thong behind his head; the small, deep-set eyes that were lost in the darkness beneath his furrowed brow. Indeed, Pell's expression seemed impossible to read, what with his eyes lost in shadow and his mouth obscured by a curly brown beard that grew up his face to the ridge of his cheekbones. The little flesh that remained visible was seamed and weathered, making it hard to tell whether Pell was thirty years old or fifty.

"Well, Master Pell," Imbress began, "I'm glad we found you—"

"*I* found *you*," Pell interrupted, correcting her, "and I have a bad feeling I'm going to regret it."

Then, without another word, he turned his back on them and headed northward along the trail, not particularly seeming to care whether the others followed. After a few hundred yards, the trail curved gently eastward, but Pell didn't follow it long. Rather, when he reached a tremendous stump—the remains of an oak that had watched ages pass before a lightning bolt had shattered it to its core—he slipped off the trail into the woods to the north. They followed his circuitous lead, skirting around thick stands of trees, pushing through close-grown brush, until finally they could make out the faint glimmer of a lantern ahead.

"Pell Manor," the woodsman grumbled.

After a moment more, Pell Manor came into view, and it was all Marwick could manage to suppress a laugh. In the middle of a small, natural clearing at the crest of a hillock stood a split-log, one-room cabin, perhaps ten feet wide and fifteen long. A stone chimney rose along the middle of the wall that faced them, a small window flanking it on either side. The windows, Marwick realized, possessed no glass; there were only shutters to keep out the rain in bad weather—and with it, any light. These, it turned out, were the only windows, set in the south wall to take advantage of the winter light. There was a stout door with an iron lock in the eastern wall, but otherwise just the bluff rows of rough timber and the mortar that sealed the cracks between them. *Belfar*, Marwick thought, *was looking better all the time*.

Nevertheless, he realized that Callom Pell was not a sloppy homeowner. The tiny cottage was solidly built, the heartwood of the Ulthorn as sturdy as any Belfar brick. And the ground around the house did not grow wild, as he had expected. Rather, neat beds of flowers and vegetables ringed the house. Many of Pell's plants were still bare this early in the season, but an impressive array of tulips fronted the southern wall. Set against the rugged logs, the flowers stood out all the more, their large, colored petals cupping toward the sky. *Amusing*, Marwick thought, *to imagine gruff Callom Pell fussing over flower beds* . . . but the thief was not daring enough to make public sport of the fact.

"Hitch 'em there if you need to," Pell grumbled, pointing to a thick post near the door. Then, without waiting to see what they did, he walked inside, the door slamming shut behind him.

"If we *need* to?" Harnor repeated, shaking his head. When he frowned, the scar across his chin puckered thicker.

As Brandt dismounted, he caught Imbress's eye.

"Imming seemed more pleasant than your Callom Pell," he said, his voice dark with warning.

She said nothing in reply, simply hitching her horse and following Pell inside.

The interior of the cabin was spartan. There was no rug on the split wood floor and very little furniture: a cot in the southwestern corner, by the fireplace; a table and two stools at the center of the room; and a few cabinets between the fireplace and the southeastern corner, holding some cast iron pots and wooden trenchers. The only surprise was that the northern and western walls, unbroken by windows and doors, were lined from floor to ceiling with bookshelves. And by the look of them, if Callom Pell bought even one more volume, he'd have to start building more.

Makes sense, Marwick thought. *If I were stuck here my whole life, I'd probably spend every last penny on romances and adventures myself.*

Pell had taken a seat by the table, propping his boots upon the opposite stool—which, for all Marwick could guess, was its only function. Callom Pell did not seem the type of man who entertained guests often. What was certain was that he was going out of his way to discomfit Brandt and Imbress, both of whom stared hard at the man as they stood in the center of the room, looking uncomfortably out of place.

"My name is Elena Imbress—"

"So?" Pell interrupted.

With difficulty, she fought back a harsh reply, composing herself before she went on.

"I am an agent for the Ministry of In—"

"Intelligence," Pell said, finishing the word for her. "Yes, yes, I know all that. Heard you talking in the forest. The forest air carries voices farther downwind than you'd think. So, what do you need from me that my little reports don't give you?"

"We need a guide through the Ulthorn," Imbress answered.

Pell's eyebrows danced upward as he laughed, and for the first time they were able to see the sparkling brown eyes that resided deep in those sockets. But just as quickly, they disappeared again, as did his laugh.

"Absolutely not," Pell said. He glanced at the door, as if he were suggesting the conversation had reached its end.

"It's my understanding," Imbress countered, her voice growing sharper with irritation, "that you are employed by the Ministry. As an employee—"

Pell rose smoothly from his seat and walked up to Imbress, leaving his nose a scant inch from her own.

"Your understanding is wrong, lady, so let me correct it. I write a little report for your ministry every few months and send it down to Prandis, where them fancy boys read it and decide that nothing much is going on up here in Ulthorn. And nothing much is. The only reason I write the reports at all is that somebody's got to, else them fools in Prandis will decide they have to send one of their own boys up here full time. Now, if that happened, that boy of yours would get himself killed before the second sun set, and then old Barr Aston—"

"It's Taylor Ash," Imbress interrupted curtly, pursing her lips. "Barr Aston retired years ago."

"Whoever," Pell replied, unconcerned. "Your boy would get killed and *whoever* is in charge down there would get his fur up like a bear woken two months early, so he'd send a couple more boys, and they would get their fool selves killed twice as fast as the first one, and pretty soon we got Prandis paying an awful lot of attention to us. Deal is, I write the little travelogues that your type loves to read, and you leave us alone. Nice arrangement. I intend to stick with it. So why don't you just get out of my forest before you wind up being that first fool to get killed and all the trouble starts?"

Imbress stared hard at Pell, a look that would wither other men. But Pell just stood there, close enough to bite her nose, returning her gaze impassively.

"I could tell Imming and his men that you've been working for us all these years," Imbress suggested. "That would make your life considerably less comfortable."

Pell laughed. "There's very little, city lady, that could make my life *less* comfortable. Man wants *comfort*"—he pronounced the word as if it were a curse—"he sets up home somewhere outside the Ulthorn, or he's a damn fool. Besides, Imming and the boys know about our deal. If I didn't send those reports your way, we'd have to find someone else at the guild willing. Problem is, most of them boys can't read, much less write a lick."

"Really?" Imbress countered, her lips twisting with distaste as she tried to find some lever stout enough to move this bear of a man. Her ears began to burn red as she realized that Brandt was staring coolly at her, his expression unreadable but only too easy to guess. She had sounded so confident that Callom Pell was a loyal Intelligence man, yet here . . . "And you wouldn't mind if we ask Imming ourselves, just to be sure?"

Pell shook his head with annoyance, his shaggy eyebrows creasing together. "Go back there and all you'll manage is to get your throat cut." The woodsman returned to his stool and sighed. "And that's my problem. I'm afraid if I lead you back to town to spend the night, one of you will say something stupid and rile the boys. Don't want no deaths on my conscience that I can avoid. So I suppose you'll be sleeping on my floor."

With that, Pell seemed to consider the conversation complete. He fished a pipe out of his pocket, stuck it into his mouth unlit, and tramped out of the house, leaving the party alone.

"Any suggestions?" Imbress asked, sighing as she lowered herself onto Pell's vacated stool.

Harnor and Laz said nothing, but looked at her sullenly.

"I have a suggestion," Brandt said sourly, walking forward and leaning over the table toward Imbress. "Why don't you head back for Prandis tomorrow and request a transfer to a desk job? As for me, I'll take my chances in the forest alone . . . unless Marwick chooses to come along."

And then he stalked outside, bringing back his bedroll. Without another word, he spread out the blankets on Pell's floor, crawled beneath them, and closed his eyes. Scowling, Imbress proceeded to do the same, and within a few moments more, everyone was disposed for the night, the lantern's light extinguished.

And it was too bad, Marwick thought. For a day or two, everyone had actually been acting like they knew how to get along.

Brandt had expected to awaken at first light, and so it was a surprise that he found himself kicked rudely in the shoulder well before dawn.

"Get up," growled the rough voice of Callom Pell. "We'll want all the light for the trails if we're going to catch your friends, so we'll need to buy horses and supplies before dawn. Those horses of yours are little better than meat on a hoof right now, and even if they were fresh, they don't know the Ulthorn. You don't want a horse that spooks easy. Hell, you don't want a horse that spooks at all."

Throughout his speech, the woodsman continued to kick awake those who were too slow to spring up at the sound of his voice. But when they did get up, they all wore the same expression: a look of shock that the resolute Pell would have changed his mind overnight. At least, they all looked shocked except Marwick, who was already awake and dressed in his blue velvet suit, a mysterious little smile on his face.

Half an hour after the others had fallen asleep. Marwick noted that Callom Pell had not returned to the cabin. That suited him just fine. Marwick slipped quietly from beneath his blanket and, with the sharp skills of a veteran cat burglar, slipped from the tiny house without making the least noise.

Outside, the night air bit through the light linen traveling gear he'd bought back in Dandun, and for the first time in a while, Marwick found himself wishing for his blue velvet. He hugged himself for warmth while his eyes adjusted to the clearing's silvery moonlight. It seemed to Marwick worth a try to talk with Pell alone, when neither Imbress nor Brandt were around, chafing each other's egos and alienating the woodsman. Just Callom Pell and himself, Marwick thought. There seemed some hope that way of conducting a rational conversation. A rational conversation about irrational fears.

He had grown a little more used to the cold, and so he cast his eyes skyward, admiring the brilliance of the stars against the coal-black field of sky. He wondered whether, as his mother had said, those stars were really suns like his own, only very far away; and whether, if they were, those suns lit worlds like his own, with people upon them; and whether, if there were any people out there, any of them had to live with such gut-churning aggravation. And it was then that he noticed the faint swirl of smoke trailing upward toward the moon.

Smiling, Marwick walked quietly across the clearing toward an ancient black cherry tree. Marwick had seen plenty of cherry trees in Belfar—the tiny, ornamental kind that merchants planted before their houses in order to show off the ostentatious spring blooms, but he could hardly believe that they were related to the black cherries that grew within the northern woods. This tree, situated at the very edge of the clearing, was so wide around the bottom that Marwick doubted three men could link arms around it. Half as big as Pell's house, it seemed. The trunk rose up fourteen or fifteen feet, thereafter splitting into two dozen stout branches that stretched toward the sky, ever proliferating, until they reached eighty feet into the air. And somewhere in the crotch of that tree, where the trunk divided into those branches, sat Callom Pell, invisible but for his smoke.

It took Marwick only a moment to find an old scar in the bark that would serve as a handy foothold, bringing him up to a large knot from which he was able to climb into the crotch of the tree. He was level now with the roofline of Pell's house, but surrounded by so many branches that he could hardly see the cottage. Or the woodsman who sat on the far side of the broad, woody cup, his back against a broad branch.

"Welcome, city boy," Callom Pell said quietly, apparently unsurprised to find Marwick joining him. The woodsman then sucked on his pipe, and by the mild glow that radiated from the bowl, Marwick caught a better look at his face. The man seemed to be smiling, amused at something.

Marwick eased himself down against the old, rough bark.

"I was wondering," he began softly, "how it is that the town is named after you."

The forester chuckled. "Remembered that, did you? Vanity will be my undoing, someday." He paused for a moment, puffing on his pipe. "Town's not really named after me, of course. It was my great-something-grandfather, about a hundred generations removed, who founded it. Back then, there was no Chaldus, really. No Yndor, neither. Just a ragtag collection of assorted dukedoms and principalities trying to sort themselves out, figure out who was nastiest, who could learn more from the Khrine quick enough to whip the others' butts. But there was always the Ulthorn, and the Ulthorn was a real problem, those days. Before the Binding, magic ran rampant, unlike now. We live on a trickle of the stuff by comparison. The beasts of the Ulthorn were born as much of the magic as they were born of their mothers. Giants and dragons and manticores, all sorts of horrible creatures. Well, the man who called himself the King of Chaldus back then—which is to say, he had more soldiers, at the moment, than any of the other dukes—couldn't spare those troops to keep the monsters of the Ulthorn from making snacks of the local farmers. So this king offered my many-times-great-grandfather a deal: hold the northern lands safe until the troops could be spared and the entire forest is yours—a dukedom larger in size than any other."

Like telling a man that, if he plugged up a volcano with his body, the volcano was his to keep, Marwick thought.

Pell drew a deep puff from his pipe. "And that," he concluded, "is how the Pells came to own the Ulthorn forest. And it is also how we discovered our singular destiny: every Pell, over dozens of generations, has been born to be cheated by the government of Chaldus."

"How's that?" Marwick asked, growing legitimately interested in Pell's story. While Brandt and Imbress had been arguing, Marwick had busied himself surveying the titles of Pell's library, and he was surprised to find that the books were not entertainments, as he had supposed. Rather, many of them were ancient texts and, if his appraising thief's eye told him right, probably worth a fortune. There were histories of cities and kings, wars and mages that Marwick had never heard of, retreating back into the haziest memories of the continent, even before the Binding. Many of the books' titles were written in languages he did not know—languages he did not even recognize, belonging to the long-dead tongues of whom he could not say. But the books had obviously been preserved at great cost. Most of them would have withered to dust long ago, he was sure, if not for some sort of preservation spell cast upon them. The Pells were a people who valued their history.

And as if to confirm it, Pell chuckled at Marwick's question, asking, "How many weeks do you have to hear this story?"

"My mother always said, a sip from the pot tastes better than the whole."

"Well, then," Pell explained, "after agreeing to the king's deal, old Fallcom Pell brought a group of stout warriors and subtle mages with him to the Ulthorn, and there they beat the monsters back into the heart of the forest, into Ulthorn Deep. They fought day after day, week after week, waiting for the king to solidify his political position and send his troops. We're waiting still.

"You see, the king's power was never secure enough to risk his troops on a foolish errand to hold sparsely populated northern lands. With Fallcom Pell here, the monsters no longer raided the plains and so the king was content to let matters lay. Yet, without masses of Chaldean troops, Fallcom's dream of pushing back the monsters to the Grimpikes and clearing the land as his duchy could never be realized. He could drive them from the margins of the forest, but no farther."

Marwick shook his head, wondering at the combination of fierce warrior and inept negotiator that Fallcom Pell must have been. "Why didn't your ancestor simply leave the forest? When the monsters came south again, perhaps the king would send the troops and hold to his end of the bargain."

Callom laughed. "We Pells are a stubborn breed. Stubborn and stupid, some say. In any case, Fallcom and his associates built a walled town as the months went by—the original Pell. There they continued to fight back the monsters . . . and to receive the king's worthless excuses explaining why, as time dragged on, the troops could not be spared. The town became their home, and after a few years, they thought no more about leaving than you would think of moving from *your* home. Generations passed and still we stayed. Many times the town was destroyed, and thus New Pell was built . . . again and again. Kings came and went, and before long, there was no one left who would even acknowledge Fallcom Pell's royal pact, though we've always kept the original deed to prove it."

At that, Pell paused, slipping his meaty hand within his buckskin jacket. From an inner pocket he produced a rolled piece of parchment, tied about the middle with a ribbon. He held it up in the moonlight only a moment before returning it to its hidden resting place.

"Worthless, really," he grumbled, "but we keep it with us anyway. A sop to our pride, I suppose."

"If you don't really believe that one day the Ulthorn will be chopped into kindling and plowed into farmland," Marwick asked, incredulous, "why on earth do you stay?"

The thief could barely make out the forester's huge shoulders shrug in the darkness.

"I stay because I'm the stubborn son of stubborn fathers. I stay, as most Pells have stayed, because the forest is ours, our only patrimony, and we will not abandon our inheritance after so many years and so much work. I stay because I'll be damned before I live my life on another man's land, and this is the only land I can call my own. But mostly, we Pells stay because we have fallen in love with the Ulthorn, dangerous as it was before the Binding . . . and dangerous as it remains, even now. You couldn't pay me enough, city boy, to leave this forest. And you couldn't pay me enough to chop it down, despite old Fallcom's dream of a duchy. The Ulthorn is here to stay, and the Pells will stay with it.

"And so," the woodsman concluded, "I live as I like, walking the forest and hearing its voices, and I work only to keep Chaldus away. I want none of their promises and none of their help, and I will give them nothing in return. As that long-dead king kept my ancestor waiting by sending his messengers with their deceitful excuses, I send my reports to the Council Tower . . . excuses for them *not* to come to our aid."

There was a lot more to the Pellians anti-Prandian attitude, Marwick thought, than either he or Imbress had guessed. And more to Pell, as well. The deeper Pell had delved into his family history, the more articulate he began to sound. Marwick guessed that Pell's typical, gruff vernacular was a way of speech he had adopted around Imming and the other foresters, but beneath it lay a surprising education. He thought again to all the books crammed within Pell's cabin.

"If you're trying to keep the government away by pretending cooperation," Marwick asked, "isn't it foolish, then, to be telling me all this?"

Pell laughed again, louder than before, and Marwick got a sense of the booming laughter that the man was capable of if he were ever truly seized by mirth.

"You don't worry me," Pell said as his chuckles died away. "You may be a city boy, but you're no ministry lackey. Not the way you move, as quiet inside a house as I am outside one. If I had to guess, I'd say you're a thief—"

"Now, wait just a minute," Marwick began to protest, shaking a finger at the woodsman.

"Oh, no," Pell laughed again, waving off Marwick's excuses. "You needn't lie to me. I'm the one man you'll ever find who doesn't care whether he lets thieves into his house. I have nothing worth stealing but this forest, and that, city boy, should you be the most nimble thief in history, you'll never manage to slip into your pockets."

At that, Marwick had to laugh, although he was thinking that Pell clearly had no notion of the market value of his library.

"So what," Pell asked, "brings me a thief—indeed, two thieves, if I count aright—in the company of the Council Tower?"

Marwick grinned and leaned back, happy that Pell had come around to the question himself. It would make things easier. And he knew, even before he opened his mouth, what Callom Pell would think of an Ulthorn once more ruled by dragons and giants and manticores.

"Well," Marwick explained amiably, "we're all chasing the same two fellows. My friend Brandt is chasing them because one of those men crippled his best friend. Also, perhaps, because he has nothing more to live for in Prandis and, if he had stayed, he would have become no better than a piece of his upholstered furniture. Elena Imbress and her two agents have joined us because the men we chase possess something that the Yndrians could use as a political advantage over Chaldus."

"You still haven't answered my question," Pell rumbled.

Marwick kept his smile to himself, knowing the hook had been well baited. He paused for a moment, listening to the crickets and owls before he added his own voice to the chorus.

"And I have joined this merry band," Marwick concluded, "because the something that those Yndrians possess is not just a political secret. It's the spell that would reverse the Binding and plunge us back into the chaos your family shed so much blood to drive back. And the thought that such a spell even exists scares me to my very bones."

For a moment, Pell sat there silently, the bowl of his pipe glowing and dimming rhythmically as he smoked. His sharp eyes cut through the darkness and concentrated on Marwick's open face. *A city boy and a thief*, he thought, *but not—at least, not now—a liar.*

"We'd better get back to the cottage," Callom Pell said finally, "if we want to get enough sleep for the trail tomorrow."

The hours passed quietly. Hain contemplating the pleasures of vengeance while Madh studied the trail, sometimes taking inexplicable detours after a conference with a returning homunculus. Hain had almost ceased to notice the creatures when one of them glided right past his very nose. He struck out in annoyance, but the creature was already beyond his reach, dipping low toward the ground as the air current it had been riding dissipated. Something seemed a bit odd about this one, Hain noticed, as it struggled to rise back into the air, flapping its left wing vigorously, but its right wing hardly at all. As a result, it rose in a feeble, clockwise spiral, in danger of plummeting to the ground. When the

thing had gained a few yards of altitude, it spread its wings
again in a glide and headed toward Madh's shoulder. Its feet
stretched out desperately for the perch, claws digging through
the Yndrian's shirt, making him turn sharply toward the creature.

"Sycorax!" he exclaimed, lifting a hand toward the homunculus.

Curious, Hain nudged his horse to a faster trot, clucking
encouragement for the spare mount behind him to keep pace.
As he drew nearer, he recognized the homunculus that was
chittering, distressed, into Madh's ear as the one that had
been sent back to Hazard's party. But now, with its wings
folded back, Hain could see clearly what was wrong with
the beast: its arms had been cut off.

No, not completely cut off, he realized as he came within
a few yards of Madh. There appeared to be short stumps left
. . . or, not stumps precisely. Rather, tiny, curled appendages
that ended in five delicate nubs. Hain drew in his breath
sharply as he realized what he was seeing: the homunculus,
its arms severed, had begun growing a new pair. Stubborn
little things to kill, he noted. That might be important to
remember on the day he exacted his vengeance from Madh.

But, for now, the homunculus bore more important news.

"What does it say?" Hain insisted as the creature continued
to chitter into Madh's ear.

Madh said nothing until, a few moments later, Sycorax
finished its monologue. Then he scooped the beast from his
shoulder and, opening a saddlebag behind him, deposited the
creature into its cool, dark interior.

"Hazard caught it," Madh said softly, sounding as if he
were swearing. "I don't know how, but I was afraid he might.
At least he didn't destroy it as he did the last."

"The last?" Hain repeated, confused.

"I sent one to stop him from reaching Belfar, but somehow
he did away with that one also. I was told that he had no
magical abilities, but perhaps one of his companions is more
talented than we know. It doesn't matter. He merely maimed
Sycorax, as a boast, a scare tactic. As injured as it was, for

some time it could not even travel as quickly as Hazard. It overtook them in New Pell, though. Apparently, they made it there a little after dusk, only an hour after we had left, and spent the night. I expect they are back on the road by now."

"And so we begin to run again?" Hain asked.

To his surprise, Madh shook his head. "If they are that close, we need to take action. We may have very little time to prepare before they reach us."

Grinning, Hain drew his sword, inspecting its edge in the muted forest light.

"That is precisely what you will need," Madh agreed dryly. "Make sure that you choose only fresh, living limbs to cut, and that you cut them close to the trunk. They must be supple, and they must be black willow—no other tree will do. We shall need Parson's Vine as well."

Hain looked at his employer as if the man had gone mad, but Madh had already slid off his horse and walked to the spare they had bought in New Pell. The men had loaded the heavier saddlebags onto the spare horses, spreading the weight in order to keep all the horses fresh. Within one of the black mare's leather saddlebags, Madh retrieved his ewer, his bowl, and the small, polished wooden box that contained the deadly kahanes root. Only then did he look up to find Hain, still astride his horse, staring at him.

"Get moving," he snapped. "We have very little time, and you have a great deal of willow and vine to fetch."

Then, as Hain dismounted and slipped off into the trees, Madh's homunculi began to gather for directions, even wounded Sycorax climbing from the hospice of Madh's saddlebag, and the real work began.

CHAPTER 9

Landa Wells, Minister of the Interior, drew her quilted robe tighter about her body, although the bedroom fire was sufficient to drive away the chills of a spring morning. She should be dressing, she knew, preparing herself for the work of governance. But she could almost hear the murmur of evil tidings rise on the streets of Prandis.

Marco, her husband, walked out of the bathroom, wearing one white towel around his waist while using another to dry his hair. Here and there, drops of water glistened like gems amid the matted hair of his chest. On most days, the sight would have proved distracting, but today Landa hardly noticed.

"Get any sleep last night?" Marco asked, his lined face all but invisible beneath the towel.

Landa laughed, as if the possibility of sleep were absurd. She ran a hand through her wiry gray hair and wondered what she must look like—frightful, no doubt, with dark crescents under her eyes.

I must look like a guilty woman, she thought, and wondered how the other Council members would react when they saw her later in the day. But then, none of the Council members had been looking less than hunted over the past two months.

"What's bothering you?" Marco asked. He stood in front of her, towel in his hands, his salt-and-pepper hair charmingly tousled. Landa smiled and tapped his dimpled chin with her forefinger. Faithful Marco, naïve Marco—how would he take the news if it ever came to light?

Shouts rose from the river and they both turned involuntarily toward the window. The windows were ceiling height and opened inward in pairs, the morning breeze filling the linen drapes with playful billows. Beyond lay the River Mirth and, in the distance, a crowd gathering along the quay beneath Jury's Bridge. Two massive stone pillars rose eighty feet above the water to the roadway of the bridge, creating a high arch that would allow sailing ships to pass beneath. At eighty feet, Jury's Bridge was one of the tallest public structures in Prandis, and therefore a favorite spot for jumpers.

A couple of men had stripped on the quay and plunged into the chilly waters, hoping to rescue whoever had jumped. Landa could have told them they were wasting their time. Any jumper from Jury's Bridge would not be seen again until they dragged the river for bodies.

"That's the third since last night," Marco muttered, incredulous. "A whole season's crop. What's happening to the world?"

He hadn't expected an answer, but Landa thought she could supply one. It had started yesterday afternoon, as near as she could tell, when a flock of innocent-looking white envelopes began turning up across the city. Some were delivered to the newspapers, others to government agencies, still others to the city guard or private citizens. Each envelope contained a file. And each file contained the seeds of someone's destruction.

The files of Galatine Hazard, she was sure.

Landa had spent the night worrying about those files—or rather, about one file in particular. Her file. For more years than she cared to count, she had made her payments to Hazard in precisely the way he specified. The right amount, on time, year after year. So Hazard had no reason to expose her.

If I really believed that, she asked herself, *then why couldn't I sleep?*

What worried Landa Wells was the number of exposures that had happened yesterday. She'd heard of a dozen herself, but feared she knew only a fraction of what was happening across the city. It was absurd to suppose that scores of Hazard's victims had summarily decided to boycott their payments. And if Hazard was releasing the files of paying customers . . . She shuddered and wondered what would happen to poor, sweet Marco.

She blamed this on Taylor Ash, that meddlesome turd. Somehow, the release of Hazard's files was related to the murders of the ex-ministers. From the very first murder, the assassin had been trying to frame Hazard, but the Council knew that Hazard himself was not to blame. Taylor Ash had said as much a month ago at a Council briefing, but he had also said that he was going to use Hazard's appearance of guilt to secure the ex-spy's help. Somehow, Ash had managed to threaten or insult Hazard. And this was the result. Chaos. *With the whole city going straight to hell,* Landa thought, *who cares who's got the bloody Phrases?*

A sharp breeze blowing off the coast, Hyram Meens noted, his heart dancing to an optimistic tune. The middle of spring typically heralded the beginning of the slack season at his shop downstairs, the Port District Fuel Concessionaire. Business had been dry for ten days now. Although Meens had no official competition—he was the city's sole licensed concessionaire for fuel in the district—the spring thaw was all the competition he needed. This was the season when people kept the fires banked low, coaxing their diminishing stock of winter coal to last until summer's first blush. A few days of these brisk coastal breezes, though—that could turn lumps of coal to gold in his pocket one last time this season.

Meens hesitated by the dressing mirror at his bedroom door. It was a large, oval mirror in a standing mahogany frame and Meens fit it perfectly, as if he'd chosen the oval shape to avoid wasting money on extra glass. From his small feet and spindly calves, his figure blossomed into thighs gone fat with age and an abdomen swollen like a snake after a meal, then contracted into a shrunken chest and his long, pointed head. There was lint on his gray suit, he noted, and he paused to brush himself diligently before descending to the shop.

The shop itself was little more than a single room bisected by a long counter. There was no need for much space. The shop existed only to take orders, which were then relayed to a distributor (another city concessionaire—how Meens wished he had been able to finagle that license!) who delivered the coal. Although tall barrels of coal flanked the door, and a coal shovel leaned upright nearby, these were just props that Meens used for decoration. You couldn't physically buy a single lump of anthracite there if you wanted to, according to the law. And on spring days, Meens mused, a single lump might exceed the sum of his sales. He sighed, resigning himself to the lonely morning hours. During the high season, Meens hired additional clerks to help him take orders, but he would work alone this morning until his one summertime assistant arrived to spell him for lunch.

Someone pounding on the outside door prompted Meens to smile. The coastal breezes were already blowing good fortune his way. A customer already, and he hadn't even had the time to clean a nib or open his inkpot. Meens unlocked the door and was surprised to find not a single customer but a small crowd of them clustered outside his shuttered shop front.

"Why, Master Diesen," Meens said, recognizing a stout shipowner whose offices stood just across the street, "what a pleasant surprise. And Master Azerian as well. And Mistress Cloyse."

Perhaps thirty people were gathered round—too many for him to find space to open the shutters.

"If you'd be so kind to move away from the shutters," Meens began.

"Your shutters can wait," Diesen grumbled beneath his beard. The man had been a ship's captain for twenty years before leaving the sea for an office, infamous among the sailors for never smiling—not even upon landfall. But even for dour Diesen, there was something uncharacteristically dark about his tone.

"I can hardly write orders in the dark," Meens countered, glancing nervously now at the crowd. Even on the coldest winter's day, he realized, thirty people had never lined up outside his shop before it opened.

"You won't be taking any orders today," Diesen countered as he pushed Meens roughly back toward the shop. The old navigator still possessed the burly frame of a man who wrested a hard-earned living from the sea.

"We're here for our bloody money," cried another voice. Master Helman, Meens thought—the owner of two warehouses upon the docks.

And then someone else shoved Meens backward. He tripped over the threshold and sprawled to the floor, hitting his head hard against the wide planks. People were towering above him, pushing their way into the store through the scant space between Meens's body and the coal barrels. Meens levered himself upright, then scrambled backward from the doorway, scuttling like a spider on his hands and feet. But they were all around him now, blocking off any possibility of escaping upstairs or even hiding behind the counter. He glimpsed a few more faces and realized that he knew them: Barrows, who lived around the corner, a customer for thirty years; Tenzer, who ran the seaman's inn and the old sailors' home; Allarian, who owned the Rose and Anchor pub; several of the stevedores who worked the docks. All good customers.

"I don't know what you're talking about," he protested, stuttering. His voice sounded high and cracked, he thought.

"Liar!" cried several at once.

"We *know*, Meens, you bastard."

"Whore-son!"

"It's out, Meens, you and the other concessionaires fixing prices with the commissioner."

Someone kicked him in the side. Meens cried out and curled up into a ball, panting hysterically.

"Like taking the food from our mouths."

"From the mouths of our babes!"

Something hard struck him in the back, then clattered to

the floorboards. Meens ducked his head under his arms and pulled his legs up tighter against his chest.

"How much is this *really* worth?"

Something pelted him in the back of the neck and Meens realized someone was throwing coal at him.

And then, amid the hail of words, the hail of coal increased. They were all grabbing lumps of it from the barrels by the door and hurling it down at him. The pellets stung and bruised, but Meens knew they could not kill him. And he knew something else they did not yet know—that the barrels had false bottoms only a few inches below the surface, so there was only a little coal in each. Full barrels of the stuff would have been too awkward to move around.

Still curled up, eyes clenched, Meens heard their ragged curses when they found the false bottom and realized that their weapons were running out.

And then someone discovered the coal shovel leaning by the door.

On every working day. Spelman Tooms sat for breakfast at the long communal table of the Turnabout Inn. He smiled at Missy, the morning waitress, who had long ago stopped asking for Spelman's breakfast order. She would bring out his eggs, white sausage, and beer just the way he liked it—sausage half-burnt and eggs runny. Spelman scratched his stubbled chin as he unfolded the morning newspaper. He'd been lucky to get one today; they seemed to be flying off the stands. The supply had been so low, Spelman had first thought he'd overslept, but a glance at the sun had reassured him that he had a full hour before he was expected at the construction site. A sliver of sunlight splashed across his thick, callused hands and the gray newsprint, and something about the sight made him smile.

Although reading was a pleasure for Spelman, and something he was proud of, it did not come easily. He skipped an article about some banking scandal, which he supposed might be interesting to the types who had enough money to keep in banks, and moved on to the next—something about an old election. Apparently, some new information had come to light through files that had been sent confidentially to the newspaper. Spelman began to read only because he was curious about why a twenty-year-old election would make front-page news. It took him only a few moments to understand.

He turned to his neighbors at the long common table—a pair of dock workers—and stabbed the article with his finger.

"You seen this, boys?"

The younger of the pair, a broad-shouldered man wearing a bandana around his neck, shook his shaven head and pushed the paper away. "I came for breakfast, not school."

But the man's older companion leaned forward. "What's it say?"

In his thick, halting voice, Spelman read the first few paragraphs. As he read, the dock workers began leaning closer. Heads looked up from farther down the table and conversations at the surrounding tables stopped.

When Spelman finished, he found a dozen men crowded about him. A dozen men and a dozen angry looks.

"Bloody damned wizards," the older stevedore muttered. His face was flushed, as if he had just finished loading a whole galleon by himself.

"They sacrifice children there," the younger man chimed in, "in that building, the one near Council Tower. They should be bloody burned to death, each one of 'em."

Spelman found himself nodding. "Unnatural bastards, they are."

"The devil's own," chimed in a teamster, slamming his fist into the table.

"Slave-makers," Spelman growled.

It was only a few moments later that Missy came back from the kitchen, bearing a piping-hot plate of sausage and eggs. But the dining hall was empty.

* * *

Landa Wells had just finished dressing when the door to her bedroom burst open, slamming violently into the wall behind it. She was too shocked even to scream as the soldiers filed inside, pushing past Marco and his protests as if the man did not exist. There were six of them, she noted, and all but the captain had his sword drawn, as if, preposterously, they expected a fight from a woman over fifty. Their black lacquered armor bore the seal of the Chaldean Dragoons, the military police that were typically charged with administering discipline and investigating crimes within the armed forces. This made no sense. If anything, she had expected the city guard . . .

"What is the meaning of this?" Marco stormed, pushing his way past the soldiers to stand at Landa's side. He had been slow getting dressed and wore only a pair of brown pants, but his dignity remained intact. "How dare you storm into our home—"

"But it's not your home," the captain interrupted. A large man with a slim mustache, the captain carried himself with a somehow preening air. He smiled knowingly as he offered further explanation: "This property belongs to the Republic of Chaldus."

Marco paused, confused. "What are you talking about?"

The captain's small teeth glinted in the early light. "Your wife paid for this house with kickbacks—bribes from businesses that wanted government contracts for building roads and schools. Like most property in such cases, I expect the courts will repossess it."

Marco took a step backward, hit the edge of the bed, and sat down heavily. His face had drained of color. "Kickbacks? Landa, explain to them—tell them it's not true . . ."

"It is both true and well documented," the captain argued. "But I have no more time to waste on conversation. You can ask your wife for the details when you visit her in prison."

"Prison?" Marco bellowed, rising from the bed. "This is outrageous. I know enough of the law to know you can't arrest a sitting minister. Separation of powers—"

"As of six this morning, your wife was no longer a sitting minister."

With that, the captain drew a pair of irons from his pocket and reached toward Landa's wrist.

Marco stepped forward, slid his body in front of Landa's. As the captain's hand swung upward with the iron, he slapped it away.

The captain's smile never wavered. "You just earned a cell of your own."

One of the Dragoons brought the flat of his blade down across Marco's head. The blow spun him around and he dropped to his knees. A second Dragoon stepped forward and struck Marco in the face with his pommel. Marco fell backward onto the floor, unconscious. Landa glimpsed her husband's white cheekbone between split flesh before the blood began to flow. And then she heard the faint snick of a thread being caught by the tip of a sword that came to rest against her belly.

"And would *you* care to resist arrest as well?" the captain asked.

Echoing across the waters beyond her window, Landa Wells heard another distant splash, followed by the horrified screams of the republic.

CHAPTER 10

While Brandt strapped his bedroll along the top of a saddlebag, he leaned toward Marwick and whispered, barely audibly, "How on earth did you change Pell's mind?"

Marwick shrugged. "Who knows? We just had a little chat about the forest."

Pell had ushered them outside the cabin shortly after waking them, announcing that they should pack quickly. There would be time for breakfast in the saddle, he said. In the meantime, he had only to prepare the cabin for his departure and then he would join them.

After a few moments more, the door to the cabin swung open and Pell stepped out, locking the door behind him with a large brass key. Brandt's eyebrows rose as he surveyed the forester's working outfit. Pell wore the same buckskin suit, but he had added elements to his costume that spoke volumes about the days ahead: a double-bladed, short-hafted axe hung from a belt-loop near his left hip, and a large, spiked mace hung upon the right; long daggers were strapped to sheaths upon each ankle; he held a long, unstrung bow carved from ash; and over his back he had slung a large quiver of arrows.

"He likes to ride prepared," Brandt muttered to Marwick.

"Apparently," the thief answered, "Old Beauty has a heart of stone."

Pell also held a pair of voluminous leather saddlebags, but since there were obviously no stables attached to Pell Manor, Brandt assumed the woodsman would buy a horse in town. Instead, upon reaching the clearing, Pell stuck the forefinger and pinkie of one hand into the thick bush of his beard, and from where Brandt presumed the man's mouth to be, a shrill whistle issued. Brandt and Marwick exchanged a look of amused curiosity.

"A man of nature, indeed," Marwick whispered.

And then, a moment later, a tremendous stallion trotted past an old willow into the clearing, lifting its hooves high in anticipation as it approached Callom Pell. The horse stood a full hand taller than the largest of the party's mounts, and it was jet black, its coat and mane lustrous in the day's first light. The only marking was a star-shaped patch of white around its left eye.

"Ah, how are you, One-Eye?" Pell asked, a carrot in hand as the stallion halted a few feet in front of him. He fed the horse, patting it energetically on the neck, and then moved toward One-Eye's hindquarters, securing his saddlebags. From one bag, he pulled a small brown blanket that he tossed over One-Eye's back. Long leather straps dangled from each of the blanket's corners, and Pell knelt beneath the horse, cinching those straps securely. But that, apparently, was all the saddle he required, for he straightened up and mounted One-Eye with a smooth, easy leap.

"Time for the road," he announced, steering the stallion toward the woods to the south while the others watched, both amused and amazed.

They stopped in New Pell only long enough to buy a few weeks' supplies and to bargain with old Payter Temmis for fresh horses. Behind Payter's general store there was a stable full of fine horses—none of them quite so impressive as One-Eye, but all of them a vast improvement over the tired mounts that had brought them north from Belfar. The trouble was, Payter named a price for each horse that should have bought a champion racer, and that was in addition to trading in their old mounts. The old beasts, Payter claimed, were half ridden to death, and even if they recovered, they were unused to the Ulthorn.

"And if they ain't Ulthorn horses," Payter concluded with

a shrug, "they ain't worth much 'round here."

Brandt suspected that old Payter was holding out for his extortionist prices because he knew there were no other horses to be had. After a few minutes, Brandt tired of Imbress's attempt to economize on Chaldus's behalf, and he simply pressed the money into Payter's seamed hand, adding more when Payter complained about paper instead of specie.

"It's robbery," Imbress muttered, glaring darkly at Brandt for having interfered.

They transferred their gear quickly to their new mounts. Imbress had chosen another chestnut gelding, whom she named Ramus like the horse it resembled. Brandt decided that he might as well keep the same name for the sturdy, dappled, black-and-white mare he had bought. Marwick, though, took a moment to name the roan gelding he had chosen. It was a fine horse, but not the prettiest of Payter's lot. Its lips seemed somehow too small for its mouth, giving it the appearance of an eternal grin.

"You're an ugly fellow," Marwick announced, walking around the beast. "I suppose I'll call you Andus. In honor," he added, "of our valiant prime minister."

And at that, old Payter and Callom Pell erupted into thunderous laughter. But when Callom's mirth subsided, his mind had returned to the business at hand.

"Which trail did your customers take after they left you yesterday?" the forester asked Payter.

The old man pointed west. "Sorrowful Heart," he responded.

Pell nodded, turning to survey his new charges. "We've lost half an hour of light already," he announced. "Let's ride."

Brandt could not imagine why the trail was called "Sorrowful Heart." The thin ribbon of clear ground wound its way sinuously through the deepening forest of spreading willows and ancient oaks, keeping where it could to higher ground by passing from ridgeline to ridgeline. Where there were breaks in the foliage high above, light streamed down in distinct rays, illuminating isolated parts of the underbrush that grew thick upon the forest floor.

He stayed close behind Callom Pell, scrutinizing the woodsman whenever Pell paused to examine the trail. Brandt realized he would not become a master of Pell's woodcraft from casual observation, but he wanted to get some idea of how Pell tracked Hain—in case the broad forester changed his mind, or in case something happened to him. And so he began to notice the broken branches in the underbrush, the scuff marks of hooves against the dirt. He had no idea, however, an hour into their ride, how Callom Pell knew to rein in One-Eye and dismount, leading the horse off the road across a broad shelf of rock.

"They camped here last night," Pell announced, kneeling upon the rock and pressing his fingers to its surface. He stared at the face of the stone as if it were some rich text, making Brandt feel all the more illiterate. "Both of them. Tethered their horses to that elm," he added, pointing to an old white elm nearby. "You can see where they grazed. Payter told me right. They bought four horses, and that's what they have with them still."

"I wonder what happened to the ranchers' horses," Marwick said. "We haven't found any corpses."

"Corpses?" Pell asked, looking up at the thief with interest gleaming in his deep-set eyes.

"You're not paid to ask questions," Imbress said as she stepped forward onto the rock shelf, hoping to avoid Pell's inquiry.

"I don't track what I don't know," Pell growled, his eyes narrowing at Imbress. Then he turned back to Marwick. "Go on, city boy."

Quickly, Marwick described the horses they had found, gray and dried, as if the last ounce of life had been sucked out of them before they had been allowed to die.

"Kind of you to mention we're chasing a mage," Pell grumbled. He turned momentarily to Imbress. "My fee just doubled."

*   *   *

As they continued along the trail, Brandt noticed
that the twigs broken by Hain's passage seemed greener
where they had split, often still glistening with the interior
moisture of the plant. "We're not very far behind them, are
we?" he asked Pell eagerly.

Pell took his eyes from the trail to glance at Brandt, nodding to himself as if he saw something he had missed earlier.
"You pay attention, city boy."

Brandt grimaced at the title. He suspected that Pell was
no more than a few years older than he was, and of the two,
Brandt certainly had more gray hair. He could do without
the condescension.

"Maybe you'll do all right in Old Beauty," Pell continued,
not noticing Brandt's discomfort, or ignoring it if he did.
"She's forgiving enough if you pay attention—as long as you
stick by the hem of her skirts. Go beyond," he added, his
voice dropping to a forbidding rumble, "and no amount of
attention will do. She's got ways to kill even I can't guess
at."

"And where exactly does 'Sorrowful Heart' go?" Brandt
asked, suspecting that he now understood the meaning of the
name.

"Exactly where you'd think, city boy. Exactly where you'd
think."

And then Pell turned his attention back to the trail and
spurred One-Eye to an easy gallop, as if he knew he was
headed for the very center of Ulthorn Deep, so he might as
well get there faster.

Two hours later, Pell came to another sudden
halt, slipping gracefully from One-Eye's back.

The party gathered around, staring at a clear space by the
side of the trail. It didn't take sharp eyes to notice the activity
that had recently taken place: footprints all over, twigs broken and branches bent back all around the area. Pell pushed

the brim of his wide brown hat farther back on his head and strolled a few paces deeper into the forest, lifting his hand to one tree and then another. He walked a little farther, disappearing from view for a minute, and returned with a genuinely puzzled look on his face.

"These men you're chasing have anything against willows?"

"What are you talking about?" Imbress asked.

The woodsman shrugged, kicking at a broken twig that lay on the ground. "I wish I knew. All I can say is, one of your friends ran amok with his sword out here. Chopped off dozens of young willow branches."

"Maybe they wanted to build a fire," Marwick suggested.

Pell threw his head back and laughed. "Next time we need a fire," he replied, still chuckling, "I'll let you try that, city boy. Chop living branches for a fire? You could cook your dinner in the sun faster than that."

"Then what did they want the branches for?" Imbress asked.

"Hell if I know. Never seen a thing like it. Cut down a lot of vines, too, it looks like. That makes sense if they wanted to tie up bundles of branches, but why anyone would want to tote bundles of willow branches through the Ulthorn, I'll never know."

"Well, I for one don't care," Harnor announced. The flaxen-haired agent glanced toward the trail impatiently. "If we were only two hours behind them before, we must be closer now. The more time they waste playing in the forest, the better off we are. So let's not make the same mistake."

At that, Harnor and Laz remounted and headed back to the trail. Imbress paused a moment more, staring at Pell, and then followed her men.

Pell, however, paused to kneel in the clearing a final time, studying the chaotic impression of prints that the earth bore.

"Funny," he mumbled. "They weren't going to meet anyone else on this trail, were they?"

Brandt shrugged. "Could be. I have no way of knowing. Why?"

Pell shook his head. "No, I'm just going daft. For a second, it seemed . . ." Pell shook his head again, still staring at the ground as he walked back to the trail and mounted One-Eye.

"Daft," he muttered, and then they began riding again.

Brandt rode just behind Pell for the remainder of the day, keeping his new Rachel to a moderate pace during the heat of the day, and then, after a short midafternoon break, riding hard again until twilight. Brandt rode hunched over Rachel's neck, straining always to see around the next bend in the trail, expecting at any moment to catch that glimpse of Hain he had been waiting for so long. But although the tracks confirmed that the party was only a short distance behind, Madh and Hain maintained their slim lead.

"Time to camp for the night," Pell announced, staring up through a break in the leaves at a sky that had grown gray with clouds.

Brandt hesitated, watching the forester steer One-Eye off the path into the lee of a broad hillock that would make a good campground. Rather than following, Brandt turned back toward the trail, watching the path disappear into the maze of trees ahead.

"Why don't we put an end to the chase tonight?" he suggested. "We can overtake them while they're camping and be back in New Pell tomorrow."

At the very least, he thought, that last idea should appeal to their guide.

But Pell had already dismounted and begun removing his saddlebags from One-Eye's back.

"We go nowhere at night."

"But—"

"There are no buts," Pell growled. "It is foolhardy to travel anywhere in the Ulthorn, even this close to its edge, in the best of circumstances. Tonight, the moon is slim, the clouds are heavy, and even I would be hard-pressed to keep us on the trail—a trail which, if we were lucky enough to follow it half the night, would bring us stumbling through the dark into the camp of a mage."

Brandt opened his mouth to protest, but he realized it would do no good. As the last rays of light disappeared beneath a horizon that they had not seen all day, the forest cloaked itself in the gathering darkness. Brandt had forgotten how alien the forest seemed at night, when you could hardly make out the bole of an oak an arm's distance from your face. Now that sense of danger came rushing back to him and he understood why even Callom Pell would not travel the Ulthorn at night. Darkness, it seemed to Brandt, served as a wake-up call to the forest, and in the rustle of the leaves in the breeze, Brandt imagined he could hear the stretchings of unseen beasts as they shook off their daytime slumber. Hain and Madh, no doubt, welcomed such company.

Turning back toward the camp, Brandt found that Pell had organized the group into an efficient frenzy of activity. The forester had already cleared a space, ringed it with stones, and set a small fire. He had instructed Marwick and Laz to fetch more firewood, adding sardonically that Marwick had best choose wood that was already dead. Harnor had been sent to fetch a pot of water from a nearby stream. Imbress, whether under Pell's direction or her own, was tending to the horses.

"Well, city boy," Pell called to Brandt, "I don't suppose you can cook, can you?"

Tired as they were, it took the city dwellers longer than they had expected to fall asleep. The first couple of nights out of Belfar had taken some getting used to— sleeping out in the open, becoming accustomed to the sounds and smells of the outdoors. They had not thought that the Ulthorn would be any different, but it seemed to conspire against their rest, emitting rustles and hoots and shrieks of alarming volume.

"Ignore her," Pell advised tersely, referring as always to

the forest as a woman, "or she'll keep you up all night. She likes those tricks."

And then, after setting a rotating watch on the camp, he showed them the proper way of ignoring the forest, by pulling his bedroll up over his great thatch of hair and promptly setting to a raucous snore.

In the morning, however, Pell could see by the dark eyes of his clients that they had not been able to take his advice. Frowning, he reached into his saddlebag for a small burlap bag of bitter-smelling beans, which he proceeded to grind and then steep into an inspiriting infusion.

"I had hoped to save these for later, in case we needed it," he grumbled. "From now on, make sure you get to sleep quickly."

"And how do we do that?" Marwick asked, rubbing his eyes irritably. He had drawn the fifth watch and been forced to shake himself awake three hours before dawn. The brief nap that he'd been allowed after his watch only seemed to have made him more tired.

But Pell did not answer, peering upward instead at the faint glimmer of light in the sky.

"Let's get moving," the woodsman said, "before we lose more time."

They rode harder than they had the day before, the horses from New Pell sustaining what would have been a punishing rate for the party's old mounts—and what proved to be a punishing rate for the riders themselves. The path grew narrower as the day progressed, often forcing them to travel single file under the boughs of the overhanging trees. But Brandt paid scant attention to the forest's increasing gloom, his novice eyes riveted instead on the evidence of Hain's passage. Glistening beads of moisture clung like pearls to the tips of broken stems among the underbrush. At the bottom of hills, where the trail remained soft from the spring rains, hoofprints were imbedded in the dirt with a clarity he had not seen before.

"We're very close, aren't we?" he asked Pell quietly as they rode.

Pell simply nodded.

"Do you think we can catch them today?"

The large man shrugged. "Not for certain. Sometime this afternoon, we should reach a fork in the trail. Sorrowful Heart continues northward into Ulthorn Deep, where I doubt even these men are willing to go. A small trail will lead westward—Beauty's Tress we call it, for it meanders slowly toward Yndor, following the higher, safer ground, until it ends upon the eastern plateau of the Jackalsmaw. It's that way I suspect they'll choose, but we'll see. A fork is the best place for them to try some trickery, so we'll have to be careful. And careful means slow, so they may gain time if they ride hard."

And then, as if even that much conversation had hurt their chances of catching Madh and Hain, Pell spurred One-Eye to greater speed, leaving Brandt alone for a moment to contemplate what the forester had said.

It was Marwick, still as sharp•eyed as a youth, who finally spotted them. The party had just crested a small hillock that gave a tolerable view of the wooded valley below. The trees were still thick here, but only as thick as they had been at New Pell—not like the utterly impenetrable curtains of foliage they had been passing through for the last several hours. Marwick had been able to trace their trail downhill into the valley and, as it dwindled from sight, up the rise to their north. And there, near the top of the next hill, he spotted a flash of color moving through the trees.

"I see them!" he cried, bringing Andus to an involuntary stop as he pointed across the valley to the trail on the other side.

"Where?" Imbress asked, straining to follow the line of Marwick's arm, even as Brandt asked, "Are you sure?"

"Good eyes," Callom Pell muttered to himself. "Yes, the

city boy is right. I just glimpsed them myself, passing over the next ridge. Perhaps half a mile away."

"Then let's ride!" Brandt called out, striking Rachel sharply with his heels. The mare exploded down the trail, kicking up dirt and rocks as she galloped along.

A mad race followed, each of the companions spurring their horses to keep up with Brandt. Imbress, astride Ramus, soon caught the onetime spy and hurtled along the trail at his side. Hot behind them followed Marwick and then the two agents from Intelligence. Only Callom Pell seemed interested in refraining from an all-out steeplechase, and although One-Eye kept pace behind them, Callom's eyes were not for the horizon, but for the trail beneath his feet.

It took only a few minutes for the band to plunge through the depths of the valley and gain the heights of the next hill, where Marwick had glimpsed their quarry. Brandt would not consent to stop, but he slowed his pace as Callom Pell called out for the party to rein in their horses.

"Why stop?" Brandt cried out above the rushing wind. "They're within our grasp!"

"I want to check their trail," the forester replied gruffly.

"We *saw* them," Imbress argued. "For once I agree with Karrelian. If we can see them, we don't need to check their trail. Check it from your horse if you must."

Pell glowered at the pair, but said nothing in argument. Instead, he nudged One-Eye into a faster run, easily outdistancing the others after only a few moments. In front, at least, he could see the trail before his companions trampled it into oblivion. As he sped beneath the trees, his eyes picked out the fresh hoof marks of their quarry—truncated semicircles dug sharply into the earth.

"We're not the only ones with good eyes," he announced.

"What do you mean?" Brandt asked as he hunched low over Rachel's neck, trying to absorb her jarring gait.

"I mean that they saw us when we saw them. Their marks here indicate a gallop. They're trying to flee."

"Let them try," Brandt answered darkly, reaching to his

hip to check that his sword was loose in its sheath. "They have reason to fear."

The rest of the afternoon passed as a blur. like the foliage that brushed past them on either side, sometimes etching tiny cuts along their faces and hands. They thundered along the path, ignoring their aching bodies and the flecks of foam that gathered at the corners of their horses' mouths, ignoring the twisted roots that snaked across the trail, threatening to trip them. They lived only for the glimpses of distant movement through the trees that told them they were just behind their quarry. Only Callom Pell ever held back, stopping occasionally to examine the tracks, then allowing One-Eye full rein to catch the others. Pell stopped longest where a slim ribbon of trail snaked off to the left, unseen by the rest of the party. But diligently as he checked, there was no sign that Madh and Hain had followed Beauty's Tress toward Yndor. Why they would continue to race northward toward the very heart of Ulthorn Deep, Callom Pell had no idea. He knew only that it was imperative to catch them soon. This part of the forest was safe enough, but Happar's Folly lay only a few leagues away, along the banks of the Woodblood River, and beyond those banks the forest allowed none but its own.

Brandt knew none of this as Rachel pounded along the hard-packed dirt of Sorrowful Heart, nor would he have cared. The chase had seized him, and ever since he had glimpsed that first flash of color through the trees, he rode on in the certainty that he would shed Hain's blood before the night fell. He imagined how sweet it would be to sever that hateful head from its body and bring it back to Carn. And then, finally, everything would be right with the world.

But even as he thought this, he realized how hollow it rung. Everything would not be all right: Carn would be avenged, but not whole. And Brandt . . . He would be back in his mansion, half-ignoring the businessmen who plagued him with deals, the engineers who bored him with technical details of their improving generators. For a moment, Brandt's stomach twisted at the thought, but then he summoned the image of Hain's face back to his mind. The assassin's leer floated before his eyes, searing away any other possibility of thought.

Imbress, riding almost alongside him, read the expression on Brandt's face and thought she could guess what it meant.

"When we catch them," she called over the clatter of the hooves, "our aim is to *capture Madh*. Do you understand, Karrelian? The assassin doesn't matter. Do with him as you like, but only after we've taken Madh."

Brandt turned slowly toward her, his hazel eyes glowering.

"You seem to forget that I'm not on Taylor Ash's payroll."

With that, he spurred Rachel sharply and pulled a few paces ahead, leaving her to stare angrily at his back.

Marwick knew it must be his imagination, but the forest seemed more menacing. The elms and walnuts of a few miles back had given way to a forest of ancient black oaks, each gnarled tree stretching more than a hundred feet into the air, and the spread of its limbs just as broad. Those limbs intertwined above their heads, branch locked against branch like wrestlers with death grips around each other's neck. What Marwick found more disturbing still was the way each oak sent a number of massive branches curving down toward the ground, like thick legs that braced up the enormous weight of the tree above it. Beneath those ground-bent branches lay countless woody caves in which anything might hide—even two men upon horseback. It would be simple enough, Marwick thought, for Madh and Hain to lose themselves in this wooded labyrinth should they grow tired of being chased. And it would be equally easy for them to become the hunters thereafter, surprising the party under the cover of darkness. Indeed, the sky had dwindled to an occasional patch of light glimpsed between masses of shifting leaves, and that light had begun to gray with the approaching sunset. In fifteen minutes, they would be left in utter darkness.

Marwick steered Andus toward Callom Pell, waiting to speak until the sides of their horses were almost touching.

"We'll have to stop for night soon, won't we?"

Pell shrugged. "I think we'll find them before then."

Marwick's eyebrows rose in surprise.

"What makes you think so?"

Pell smiled. "Listen hard, city boy."

All Marwick heard was what he had heard for days, it seemed: the pounding of the hooves and the rustling of the wind in the leaves. But as he listened, it seemed to him that the leaves had added another voice to their chorus—a deeper, rushing sound.

"Is that water?" Marwick asked.

"There's hope for you yet," Pell rumbled in return. "That's the Woodblood River you hear, rushing on its way toward the Cirran. This time of year, it should be a torrent, carrying the spring melt-off from the Grimpikes."

Marwick shrugged. "What does that have to do with Madh and Hain?"

"At low water," Pell explained, "the ford ahead is passable . . . barely. This time of year, it would take great preparation to cross the Woodblood. Stringing lines, I'd think, to guide a raft."

As he began to understand, a smile spread across Marwick's face.

"So we'll catch them with their backs to the river," he concluded. "No place to run."

Pell shook his head darkly in response.

"We'll be catching a *mage* with his back to the river," Pell reminded the thief. "And an assassin to boot."

"Put that way," Marwick answered, "it does sound less pleasant."

"Well, it gets worse," Pell continued, his brow furrowing beneath his shaggy mane of hair. "Along the banks of the river stands the ruins of Happar's Folly. If the stairs to the tower still stand, the mage will enjoy a very defensible position. Even if he had not an ounce of magic left, he could spend a week raining stones upon our heads."

For hours, Pell had brooded upon this possibility. The only reason the mage would have bypassed Beauty's Tress was that he knew about Happar's Folly—and knew that getting there first would provide the ideal place to make his stand.

Marwick grimaced. "The first building we run across in two days, and they get to use it as a fort. I was hoping for an inn. Or a bar."

"You won't be joking when you see Happar's Folly," Pell responded gruffly.

"What *is* Happar's Folly, anyway?"

Pell waited a moment before he spoke.

"Happar Pell," he said at last, "was a cousin of mine. Lived a few decades after the Devastation. By then, most of the big beasts had died out, starved of their magic by the Binding, and we Pells began to venture deeper into the forest than we had ever gone before. Happar fell in love with the Ulthorn's vicious beauty, and he swore he'd live within it, rather than upon its verge. And so he brought a team of workmen to the banks of the Woodblood, where he built a strong stone keep with a tower that reached above the trees. It was a glorious place, devoted both to the beauty of the forest and to that of his new bride, Rissa. He wrote in his journal that, from the roof of the tower, with his bride by his side, he could see his two loves at once, and he was at peace."

Pell paused for a moment, staring off along the trail as if he expected to see Happar himself around the next bend. Marwick waited anxiously for the man to continue, noting again how the woodsman sounded as if he were reading aloud whenever he told a story of the olden times. Had Callom Pell *memorized* all those books, Marwick wondered.

"But Rissa," Pell continued, his voice dark and bitter, "did not share Happar's love of the forest. After only her first night there, she swore she would leave. They quarreled, and in his anger, Happar struck her. Rissa stumbled backward and fell from the tower, her body breaking on the ground below. Happar rushed to her side, only to see the earth swallow the last of her blood."

"What did Happar do?" Marwick asked quietly.

"It is said," Pell sighed, "that Rissa's was the first human blood the forest had tasted since the Devastation, and once reminded of its need, little Rissa could not sate its black thirst. And so the forest killed Happar, as well, and shook his fine keep into ruins. And since that day, we have marked Happar's Folly as the edge of Ulthorn Deep, beyond which a man dare not go lest he expect to forfeit his life."

Pell turned his attention back to the trail, but Marwick would not let the story go so easily.

"What do you mean, the *forest* killed Happar?" he asked, looking around uneasily. "How does a forest kill someone? Isn't it more likely that Happar simply killed himself in his grief?"

Pell shrugged, his mouth lost beneath his thick, brown beard. "Perhaps, perhaps not. Happar's journal does not do me the favor of recording his own death. And it's best that we not discover how he died ourselves."

Marwick nodded in agreement. To think of dying in this dark and quiet place, killed by your own love . . .

"Such a story," he muttered, almost to himself. "My mother once said—No, my mother never said anything that would explain a story as terrible as that."

"No," Callom Pell answered, "I don't suppose she could."

"Something is wrong," Pell muttered a few minutes later.

There was something about the trail that seemed different, but it was hard to say what. Certain that they would find their quarry holed up in Happar's Folly, Pell had been content to let the others ride ahead, but now their marks obscured the signs of Madh's passage. Cursing, Pell signaled One-Eye to draw forward, and the black stallion leaped effortlessly along the path, slipping past Harnor and Laz, Marwick and Imbress, as easily as the breeze. With only Brandt ahead of him, the trail was clear enough for Pell to read, but it rushed beneath him so quickly that, in the twilight, he could barely make out the marks. He bent low over One-Eye's back, concentrating on the indistinct crescents that bespoke Madh and Hain's passage. Then he realized what was bothering him. All the marks thus far had confirmed that the fugitives had brought an extra pair of horses to help them through the forest. Those horses had always left tracks just behind the lead horses, as any trained mount would, staying in line behind its leader. Now those rear marks were drifting away, drawing apart.

"They've cut loose their extra mounts!" Pell called out.

Brandt spared a moment's glance backward at the forester. "They're afraid we're going to catch them. And we will."

Pell shook his head. "Or they are planning to split up, and they know that four separate trails will cost us time and confusion."

It was a smart plan, Pell thought—or it would have been, if not for the Woodblood River, whose rushing water could now be heard clearly over the breeze. Perhaps the Yndrian simply didn't know how deep the river was, but somehow Pell doubted that. Thus far, the mage had moved with all the sureness of a Pell through the forest, and thus the splitting up bothered him. It didn't make sense when Happar's old fortress lay so close at hand.

At that moment, the trail burst over a small ridge, and suddenly, the trees disappeared. Instead, there was a large grassy clearing that stretched almost a quarter-mile to the banks of the rushing Woodblood. And brooding above the river stood the moss-covered ruins of Happar's Folly.

"There they are!" Brandt shouted, pointing ahead. "Splitting up won't do them a bit of good."

Pell's eyes narrowed as he searched through the twilight. At first, he saw little but the ruins by the river: the tumbled blocks of stone that had once composed the body of Happar's keep, piled one on the other as Happar and Rissa's cairn; and the circular tower that had withstood the centuries, rising a hundred feet and more above the ground, despite the gaping hole in its side that let in the weather and the darkness. It was toward that darkness that a hunched figure rode, a gray cloak fluttering behind in the wind. *A smaller man,* Pell thought. *The mage.*

Fifty yards to the right, another rider was driving his horse furiously toward the jumbled ruins of the keep, lashing the beast again and again with the flat of his sword. As Pell watched, the horse stumbled, its front left leg crumpling beneath it. The rider flew from the saddle but tucked into a ball before hitting the ground, rolling easily to his feet. Without sparing a moment's thought on the suffering horse, he took off at a sprint toward the ruins.

Pell was not the only one to see Hain fall. Brandt cried out—a scream of pure fury that had nothing of language in it—and spurred Rachel on toward the ruins, drawing his sword as he rode.

Odd, Pell thought, *that the spare horses were nowhere to be seen.*

"Damn you, Karrelian!" Imbress screamed. "It's the mage we want!"

And she spurred Ramus into an all-out gallop, racing toward the tower with Harnor and Laz only paces behind her. Marwick rode between Brandt and the agents, yelling after Brandt. Pell spared a glance at the thief, surprised by the anguished look on the man's face. Marwick was screaming something at his friend, but Pell could not make out the words over the pounding of One-Eye's hooves. For a few moments more, Marwick continued riding between Imbress's party and Brandt, but finally, with a disgusted jerk of his reins, veered away to join Imbress.

So the thief hadn't lied during their tree-borne discussion, Pell thought with a little satisfaction as he kicked One-Eye into a still-faster gallop. Still, it would be nice to know where those other horses could have gone . . .

It took only a moment for Pell to pull even with Imbress's group.

"The last time I was here," he shouted over the roaring wind and clattering hooves, "the stairway to the top was still passable, but that was four years ago."

Four peaceful years, it seemed to him now; four years that he should have enjoyed more, for he suspected his peace was done. It had been a pleasant trip to the tower, that day, standing high above the forest and drinking it in much as Happar had done centuries ago. Tonight would be different.

"If the stairs have fallen," Pell continued, "we will trap him in the tower's base. If not, he will be well positioned at the top. We need to plan—"

But Imbress seemed not to be listening, hunched low over Ramus's back as the large chestnut devoured the ground with each stride. Already, the party had cut the distance to the ruins in half. Madh had reached the tower's base and rode his horse right through the rift in the building's side, there disappearing into darkness. Hain had meanwhile reached the ruins of the keep, where he began climbing nimbly from stone to stone toward the top of the fallen heap. Karrelian had already passed the assassin's dying horse, Pell saw, and would arrive at the ruins only moments later.

Marwick watched Brandt ride the last two hundred yards. The thief shook his head as Brandt jumped from Rachel's saddle.

You still have to do everything alone.

And then Marwick was forced to turn his attention back to the tower. It loomed up before them, only yards away, and Imbress was finally reining in her mount. Marwick did likewise, trying to make out the details of the tower in the vanishing twilight. It seemed to be a plain stone cylinder, half-covered by ivy, and interrupted nowhere by windows. Indeed, there seemed to be no door—only the giant rift, ten feet wide and nearly as tall, in its western side. The musty smell of the old granite was overpowering, mingled with the cloying odor of the river behind it.

"Let's be careful now," Callom Pell rumbled, but the three Intelligence agents, swords drawn, had already slipped inside the hole in the tower's base. Callom Pell merely shook his head and took hold of the great, double-bladed axe that had hung at his side. Then he, too, slipped past the ageless granite blocks into the darkness beyond.

Marwick hesitated for a moment. Surely those four would prove a match for Madh, while Brandt had been left alone to deal with Hain. Again, Marwick was torn between impulses: the purely rational impulse of getting the hell out of the Ulthorn forest; the far stronger impulse to go help his friend, even if Brandt would curse such aid; and the reluctant knowledge that finally triumphed, which told him that it was Madh who was important, Madh who needed to be stopped. And so Marwick took a deep breath, drew his long dagger from the sheath on his belt, and slipped quietly inside the tower.

It seemed to take forever to pass by the stone walls, each block four feet thick and the wall itself two blocks deep. It was no wonder the tower had stood all these centuries, despite the gap near its base. But the tower's very strength made Marwick wonder what on earth it had been built to keep out. Once again, he found himself wishing for the familiar dangers of Belfar rather than the Ulthorn's unknown.

The others had paused within the tower's base, waiting for their eyes to adjust to the scant light. Only a little illumination leaked through the hole in the wall, and a patch of twilit sky was visible through a trapdoor in the distant ceiling. Although there once had been eight stories to the tower, evidence of those floors had entirely disappeared over the centuries, leaving the tower itself as hollow as a silo. As Marwick strained at the darkness, a nervous nicker surprised him, and then he realized that Madh's horse had remained at the tower's base, pawing anxiously at the huge, mossy flagstones that comprised the floor.

"We'll be defenseless climbing up there," Pell warned.

"No more vulnerable than we are down here," Imbress countered, and with that she headed toward the base of the stairs.

It was clear why the stairs had survived centuries that had slowly claimed each of the many floors above. While the floors had been made of wood, the stairs were carved into the stone itself, a slim helix that wound upward along the interior of the granite cylinder to its roof. It would be a steep climb, rising a foot for every foot it traversed, interrupted only every five or six yards by a wider platform that jutted out from the wall. These, Marwick guessed, marked the former location of the tower's floors. A quick examination confirmed his suspicion: just beneath each platform, there was a ring of square insets around the tower wall in which the timbers had once been set. There seemed to be nothing left of them but splinters.

"At least there's nothing flammable," Marwick muttered, but the comment earned only a quick glare from Imbress.

"Quiet!" she hissed. "Let's get up there quickly, overpower him, and be done with it."

But somehow, Marwick thought as he took his first step up the stairs, eyes riveted on the empty square of sky above, he doubted it would be quite that easy.

As a child. Brandt had played king•of•the•hill. but never with swords. Nevertheless, that seemed to be Hain's idea, and Brandt was willing to indulge him. The assassin stood atop the massive pile of jumbled granite blocks that had once been Happar's Keep, waving his sword above his head in challenge.

They were destined to meet, it seemed to Brandt, in ruins—and once again the image of Carn's shattered body being hoisted out of the Atahr Vin rose to his eyes upon a hot rush of blood.

"If you have any last words," Brandt muttered, "now is your chance."

The ancient building-stones lay heaped upon each other at crazy angles, but they presented little danger to a man who had spent years scaling sheer walls. Brandt leaped nimbly from one block to another, steadily mounting toward the apex. Within moments, he stood mere yards from the assassin, on a level area of stone only a few feet lower than Hain's own perch.

The assassin ran his left hand over the half-inch stubble

on his scalp and smiled. Then, without warning, he leaped down to Brandt's ledge, bringing his sword around in a smooth overhead stroke. The blades rang against each other as Brandt parried Hain's cut. Then both men sprang backward, eyeing the other warily. Brandt feinted to the left, then cut upward toward Hain's free arm. The assassin beat back the blow, but Brandt smiled coldly at the clumsy riposte that followed. Hain seemed as strong as ever, but not half as agile as he remembered. The chase had worn him down: Brandt could see it in the dull sheen of the assassin's eyes, in the sickly pallor of his skin. Hain was not well, and this would prove to be no contest.

Brandt feinted again, smiling as Hain held out his sword to parry. Brandt struck quickly, sliding his blade down the length of Hain's, then hooking the curved bar of his crossguard beneath Hain's own. A quick wrench of his arm and Hain's sword came flying out of his hand, clattering along the rocks below.

Brandt opened his mouth to cry something—some final statement of revenge or justice—but the words eluded him. Instead, he screamed with rage as he brought back his sword for the killing blow. But before he could deliver it, the assassin sprang forward, wrapping his strong arms around Brandt's waist in a grip that threatened to crush the life out of him.

For a moment, as the breath burst out of his lungs and his eyes swam in their sockets, Brandt feared he had underestimated the man. The assassin's strength was unbelievable. Desperately, Brandt gasped for air and almost choked on what he got: a breath full of decay, smelling like the decomposing mould of the forest floor. Dizzy and sickened, he tried to slice his sword across Hain's back, but at such close quarters, the long blade was worse than useless. Every time the assassin shook him, Brandt's arms flailed helplessly, and he finally dropped the sword in despair.

Hain tightened his grip further, crushing Brandt against his chest. Brandt could feel every corded muscle hard as stone beneath Hain's shirt. Beyond a doubt, the assassin was strong enough to kill him this way.

Brandt sucked in another sickening breath and whipped his fist forward, striking Hain across the chin. The assassin's head bowed and snapped back, the grin still immutably in place. And for his trouble, Brandt's hand throbbed in agony. It was like hitting a wall.

He raised his foot instead and struck viciously downward at an oblique angle, aiming at Hain's right knee. A sickening snap cracked through the air, and from the corner of his eye, Brandt could see Hain's leg collapse inward. But Hain refused to release his grip—refused even to relinquish his grin—and as he toppled over, he brought Brandt crashing with him to the granite. His embrace had only grown tighter.

Feeling as if his chest were about to burst, Brandt struck at the assassin's face, again with no effect. Hain continued to smile, continued to stare at him in that unnerving, emotionless way as his arms coiled ever more tightly about Brandt's chest. Desperate, Brandt jammed his thumbs into Hain's eyes, digging deep into the sockets, feeling the soft orbs burst liquid onto his hands. It was a blow that would incapacitate any man, but it only weakened Hain's grip momentarily, and when Brandt peered through the darkness at what he had done, he found that the sticky fluid upon his fingers was not red, but green.

He would have screamed, had he the breath to do it, but all he could manage was to raise Hain's head, still using the man's eye sockets as a grip, and bring it down sharply against the rock. Again and again, Brandt raised Hain's head and battered it brutally against the granite. And finally, like a man splitting open a coconut, he felt Hain's skull burst beneath him, spilling its convoluted contents out upon the rocks.

What passed for Hain's brain was green and mossy.

And finally, as the last of the fluid spilled out of the thing's cracked head, the strength of its grip departed. Still gasping for air, Brandt reached behind him to push away the creature's arms, but it was like trying to move a tree branch.

Instead, he wriggled out of its unnatural embrace, collapsing on the rocks by its side.

But over his ragged breathing, he could hear the sounds of running steps from the tower above.

"Marwick!" he shouted with the last of his strength. "It's a trick!"

The wind whipped across the top of the tower, coldly carrying away the sweat of the long, nervous climb, and carrying away Brandt's words with it. All Marwick could make out was his friend's desperate tone—a desperation that evoked a renewed blossom of guilt in Marwick's breast. How could he have left his friend alone with the assassin, especially when the mage had turned out to have exhausted his tricks? Never, during the anxious climb up Happar's tower, did Madh show his face through the trapdoor, raining down lethal spells. When they crept cautiously out onto the tower's roof, they found the man pressed up against the low parapet at the very edge of the circular platform, hands raised in surrender.

"Cooperate with us," Imbress said, "and it will go easier with you."

Madh said nothing in return, his dark features illegible in the failing light.

"First, I want to know who you're working for," Imbress went on. "Is it Mallioch?"

The mage maintained his stubborn silence.

Imbress sighed. "One way or another you'll talk. I promise you."

And then Brandt's faint cry came rushing along the wind again, swallowed up beneath the air's elemental howl.

"I have to help him," Marwick cried, turning back toward the stairs.

It was then that Madh sprung forward at the man closest to him—Laz, who had stood only feet from his side, sword pointed menacingly at the mage's neck. The agent swung the sword around sharply and it bit deeply into the flesh next to the mage's right shoulder, but the blow could not stop the momentum of Madh's mad rush. The mage wrapped his arms around Laz's waist as he continued on like a juggernaut toward the parapet behind them.

"No!" Imbress screamed, jumping forward. Her fingers grazed the back of Laz's hand as he was swept by, carried by the mage's momentum to the parapet, where the two men struck hard and toppled over the side of the tower. And then there was nothing, as the whipping wind swept away the sound of their impact.

Pell shouldered his way past the others, leaning over the parapet, a cold dread beginning to knot in the pit of his stomach.

"He killed himself," Marwick began, puzzled. Why on earth hadn't the mage put up the kind of fight Marwick had seen in Belfar?

"He killed *Laz*," Harnor spat, his blue eyes narrowed with rage. A muscle in his cheek twitched, twitched again.

"Perhaps not," Imbress suggested, edging toward the stairs. "There may be a chance . . ."

Marwick looked up and caught Pell's eye. Despite the ruddy glow of the sun as it hunched against the horizon, the woodsman seemed ashen.

"By god," Pell swore, "by god, this may mean trouble."

But the others had already leaped into motion, scrambling toward the trapdoor that led to the stairway down.

"Careful!" Pell shouted as he followed. "There's nothing we can do for Laz, but we can make sure he's the only one to fall from this cursed tower."

But no one seemed to heed him as they scrambled down the two-foot wide ribbon of darkened stairs, taking them two or three at a time in their mad dash. It was, Pell thought, their only stroke of luck that day that no one was hurt in the descent.

When they spilled through the rift in the tower wall, they found Brandt, looking tired and battered, kneeling by a tangle of undergrowth.

It was Imbress who tried to speak.

"Did you see—?"

Brandt merely nodded, his eyes hard.

Imbress continued scanning the ground near the base of the tower. Despite some brush and debris, the bodies should have been easy to find, yet they seemed to have disappeared.

"Where could they have gone?" she asked, looking up for a moment, as if Laz might have caught hold of the tower's edge.

"Right here," Brandt growled, touching the undergrowth by his side. And then he reached into the tangle of vines and branches upon the ground and yanked them savagely aside. "*This*," he cried, shaking the useless waste in Imbress's direction, "you thought was Madh. And there's another pile," he added bitterly, pointing at the ruins, "that I took to be Hain. We've been fooled."

With that, he threw the foliage aside, picked up another armful of it, and cleared that away as well. Beneath it, they could now make out the ruined body of Laz, his limbs bent unnaturally beneath him.

Pell knelt beside the corpse and began gently to clear away the rest of the brush that remained tangled with Laz's limbs.

"Willow," he said quietly as he tossed a branch to the side.

Marwick stepped closer. Beneath the remaining twigs and vines, he could now see Laz's corpse—and was glad for the darkness, lest he see it more clearly. The agent's head had struck a stone and split open, the involuted curls of brain glimmering slickly in the silvery light of the now-rising moon, dark blood seeping into the darker ground.

A bloodcurdling shriek split the night air and Marwick fairly jumped in shock, his heart threatening to beat its way out of his chest. But he realized that the shriek had merely come from one of the countless screech owls that populated the forest and that, for so many nights already, had disturbed his sleep. The small bird had swooped down through their midst, emitting its piercing cry as it passed by, before circling back toward the forest behind them.

"Damned flying vermin," Marwick muttered.

But Pell was watching the creature disappear with a more speculative eye.

"Odd," the forester rumbled, and he bent down again to examine Laz's corpse, feeling the bloody ground with his forefinger. "We'd better leave this place. Go gather the horses."

Imbress stepped forward, shaking her head. The skin of her face seemed pulled tight around the bones, and her native prettiness had been obscured by the severity of her expression.

"We're not going anywhere until Laz is buried," she announced, the tone of her voice indicating that she expected no argument.

"Not wise—" Pell began.

"We're losing time again," Brandt added harshly. "Imbress, you can dig all day for all I care. Pell and I will go after Hain."

"There's more to this than time," the forester began by way of explanation.

Marwick had ignored most of the argument, staring again at Laz with morbid fascination. To be killed by a mass of moving foliage, hurled a hundred feet to your death . . . He grew dizzy at the thought, disoriented as if the world had lurched beneath him.

"What the hell was that?" Imbress cried, spinning around as if there was something to see.

Brandt, too, seemed alarmed. His weariness seemed to vanish as he snaked his sword out of its scabbard.

"I was afraid of this," Pell grunted to no one in particular.

Then, before Marwick's eyes, a small grassy hump about twenty feet away *shuddered*—there seemed to Marwick no other word for it. The shudder spread their way, the silky tassles of the wild grass swaying in a great wave, and this time Marwick was nearly thrown off his feet.

The world *had* lurched beneath him.

"Get to the horses!" Pell cried, springing away from the ruins.

But the horses, all save One-Eye, had decided to flee long

before their masters. At the first of the tremors, they had trotted nervously toward the cover of the forest. With the second tremor, they took to full flight, galloping madly away.

"I thought Ulthorn horses were trained not to panic!" Brandt snapped as he sprinted toward the tree-line.

"Nothing is trained for *this,*" Pell replied, swinging smoothly onto One-Eye's saddle. *Not even One-Eye*, he thought. It was loyalty that had kept the horse by his side, lessons never being stronger than love.

But as they began their dash toward the trees, a long, grassy mound in their way suddenly convulsed, soil erupting into the air as the mound listed sharply to one side.

"Damn!" Pell swore. "Back to the tower! It's our only chance."

They wheeled about and dashed toward the ancient stone shelter, listing perilously as the ground continued to shift beneath them. Only Pell stayed where he was, astride One-Eye's back with his battle-axe in hand. His eyes were riveted on the convulsing landscape, as if it were crucial to remember every detail of what was happening.

What *was* happening none of them could understand: the land, it seemed, had suddenly become a turbulent, grassy sea as broad mounds and long ridges pulsed sinuously like waves lashed by a storm. Huge flaps of turf ripped loose from the ground like sails torn from their yardarms. And beneath this turmoil, something was rising from the ground.

Pell glanced over his shoulder to ascertain that all the others had made it safely into the shelter of the tower, but instead of following them, he turned back toward the writhing land and tightened his grip on his axe, looking like a man who was about to attack the world itself.

Something was becoming visible beneath the earthen quilt that had covered it for so many centuries—since the very time of Happar and Rissa, Pell suspected. As he watched the field spasm before him, it was his library he was thinking of—the hundreds of musty, timeworn books, and his own leather-bound journal, until now a slim addition to the collection. Callom Pell expected that he was about to learn what had really killed his ancient cousin Happar. It would be his first real contribution to his family's ongoing history of the forest. The only question in his mind was whether he would live to write about it.

The twisting mass beneath the earth reared up high into the air and a long sheet of sod slid from its back, exposing its skin to the air for only the second time since the War of the Devastation. Dark skin, Pell saw in the moonlight, like a deep gray.

No, more like the blackest purple.

And then Pell had his answer, for in all his reading, he had come across only one creature whose skin was reputed to be of such a hue.

"Great mother of mercy," the forester whispered as he watched the Druzem arise.

Something broke free of its grassy shroud—a hand as broad as the forester's body. It tore at the soil that covered it with yellowed nails as long as daggers, brushing free large swaths of dirt. In a moment, another hand appeared, helping to clear off legs as thick as ancient oaks. Then, finally, as if an afterthought, the Druzem cleaned off its head and stood.

Pell had long wondered whether his ancestors had possessed a gift for exaggeration equal to their gifts of narrative, for despite all he had seen himself of the horrors that the Ulthorn contained, he could never quite credit the mind-boggling descriptions of the beasts that lived before the Binding. Perhaps surpassed only by dragons and the great leviathan was the Druzem—presumably an individual rather than a species, as only one had ever been seen. Its singularity was a stroke of luck for mankind, for, by Pell's best guess, the Druzem stood forty-five feet tall, its mountainous chest almost thirty feet around. In form it appeared almost like a man, save for the large, curved horns that grew from its knee-caps and elbows, and the long, powerful tail that helped to support its weight. Its head alone was taller than a man, the mouth a savage door bristling with yellow, foot-long fangs. The thing possessed small, pointed ears and a broad, fleshy nose that resembled a dog's snout, its nostrils dilating and contracting as it sampled the air. Thick black hair hung from its head like a mane, and hair almost as long covered its upper arms, its back, and the inside of its legs. The rest of the beast was bare.

The Druzem raised a hand to its eyes, brushing away the dirt that had sealed them for so long, and finally opened its lids. To Pell's great surprise, the creature's eyes were milky white, with no hint of an iris or a pupil, as if an opaque membrane had grown over them in the long years of its slumber.

Beneath his thick beard, Callom Pell's lips curled into a grim smile. If somehow the Druzem had gone blind, perhaps they stood a chance.

Just then the beast's nostrils dilated and it breathed in noisily, leaning forward with interest. Its mouth opened wider and it spoke, its voice strangely quiet but deep as the ages.

"My thirst is great," the Druzem said.

Pell shuddered, thankful only that the beast spoke an ancient dialect derived from the Khrine tongue—a rough patois that had once been used as a trade language. Several of the old Pells had written in it and so Callom had acquired some fluency in the language. Few others would be likely to understand a word of the dead language, and so much the better. The city folk were better off not knowing what the Druzem said.

But Hazard had edged out of the tower, followed closely by Harnor.

"Hsst," Brandt called quietly to Pell, "get back here, you fool!"

The Druzem's head shot up, its pointed ears twitching.

"More than one. Good. I've a thirst it will take thousands to slake."

Pell wanted to shout at them to get back under cover, but that would only give away his location. Instead, he waved them back toward the tower, not looking to see whether they obeyed, for he dared not take his eyes off the Druzem.

The creature took a few steps toward the tower, the earth

trembling beneath his feet as he walked, but then he stopped
and cocked his head uncertainly.

"Speak again, little ones. Your voices are so pretty."

Not bloody likely, Pell thought. Quietly, he backed One-
Eye away from the Druzem, circling slowly behind it. He
could see the others now, clustered at the base of the tower,
staring at the Druzem in horror. Pell raised a finger to his
lips, but none of his companions was paying attention.
Thankfully, in their awed terror of the Druzem, they had lost
their tongues. Perhaps, Pell prayed, fear itself would save
them.

"The other time," the Druzem mused, *"there was a man
weeping at the sight of my majesty. Perhaps he was blinded
upon seeing me, as I was blinded when I looked upon the
final battle. No matter, though. He wept and he was mine,
and my thirst was eased by his soul, paltry though it was.
Not enough to fend off the sleep that weighed on my limbs,
and weighs thus still."*

And then, as if its words were literally true, the Druzem
fell to its knees and brought its tremendous fists thundering
against the ground, which leapt and buckled beneath the on-
slaught. Feeling the earth move beneath him, One-Eye reared
backward and trumpeted in alarm. Instantly, the Druzem
wheeled around, its head bent low toward the ground, nostrils
dilating, a deadly grin upon its black lips.

One-Eye reared back again, and Pell realized that even the
finest stallion in the Ulthorn would not calmly meet the
charge of the Druzem. The forester slid nimbly from his
horse's broad, black back and slapped it sharply across the
rump as his feet came to the ground. One-Eye wheeled about
and stretched his body out toward the tree line.

The Druzem lunged forward, smashing down his open
palm against the ground as if swatting a fly, but the horse
proved an instant too fast, jumping into a mad gallop for the
woods.

Pell fought to keep his balance as the ground shook beneath the Druzem's blow. Then, before the creature moved
again, he jumped forward and brought his axe down in a

great, two-handed blow against the Druzem's exposed forearm. The monster bellowed—in surprise more than pain—and snatched its arm away, throwing Pell backward ten feet in the process. Black blood was oozing from the gash in the Druzem's arm, but it did not seem to mind. Instead, it took a step forward, sniffing at the air, both hands extended in Pell's direction, seeking to snare the man.

"Prick me again, little one."

Pell backpedaled, hoping to circle behind the monster, but the Druzem was bent low to the ground and advancing quickly, its forearms brushing through the grass like a great net. The creature was bringing those arms together, like a shrinking corral, and Pell knew he would not be fast enough to escape.

Just then a small, dark blur fell from the sky and sped just past the Druzem's ear, emitting a piercing shriek. It was another screech owl, Pell thought, or perhaps the same as before. But why any owl would do something so inexplicable—

The owl had provided a distraction, though, as the Druzem whipped its head around, sniffing the air in agitation.

Something flashed silver through the night and buried itself in the Druzem's side—one of Marwick's daggers. The dagger was less than a pinprick, but the creature took a moment to brush it away. Immediately, a dark figure blurred over the field, slicing at the Druzem's shin with a sword. This was more irritating still, and Brandt was barely able to roll out of the way before the Druzem's other hand came crashing into the earth.

"Yes, prick me, prick me," the ancient monster cried happily as it spun around, fingers spread wide to snare whomever it found first.

The fools! Pell thought as he glanced around. At least Harnor and Imbress had stayed in the tower, disciplined enough to keep their minds on the ultimate goal of catching Madh. But here were Brandt and Marwick, circling the Druzem with their blades in hand, like a pair of flies who meant to take honey from a bear. Pell had been trying to catch the Druzem's attention and lure it to the woods, where he would have been able to evade it, circle back for the others, and lead them to safety. The last thing he had wanted to do was encourage them to attack the thing themselves.

Marwick was closest at hand. Pell ran the few steps to the thief's side, grabbed hold of the man's arm, and swung him bodily back toward the tower. The Druzem was occupied with Brandt now. Somehow, whether by hearing or smell, it possessed a good sense of location for anything within arm's reach, and Brandt had been playing a dangerous game, dashing between the Druzem's legs and under its arms, slashing at it each time he ran and dove past. But the Druzem leaped forward with surprising speed and, fingers outstretched, reached straight for the man.

He'll never dive away in time, Pell thought.

But Brandt didn't try to dive. Instead, he fell flat on his stomach, bracing his sword upright against the ground. The Druzem's left hand came swinging down upon the blade, the steel point plunging directly into the creature's palm. It bellowed in pain and jerked its hand away, dragging Brandt ten feet through the grass before the sword finally pulled free. But now the Druzem knew where Brandt was, and he swung his other arm around for a deathblow.

Pell jumped forward, axe over his head, although he knew the attempt would be futile. But before he could cover the few yards between himself and the Druzem's taloned right foot, another figure stepped in front of him. It was a woman, he realized with surprise, and not Imbress—an old woman with a screech owl perched on her shoulder. One of her hands was cupped, palm upward, and the other held a tiny copper baton. She sounded as if if she were talking to herself.

Anyone standing three yards from a Druzem—*the* Druzem—and talking to herself was most likely crazy, but Callom had lived on the fringes of the Ulthorn long enough to recognize that this woman was not crazy. She was a witch.

The forest seemed to be lousy with them these days.

The witch snapped the copper baton down into her cupped palm and some powder that had lain within burst into flames. It was a small blue bonfire contained within the palm of her hand, and it looked just like the flames that suddenly exploded all over the body of the Druzem.

He should have let go of his sword, Brandt knew, but it had been sheer instinct to hold on. Or perhaps the truth was he was so terrified of the inexplicable monstrosity before him that his hands had wrapped around the hilt in a death grip. Either way, all that mattered was that he get up, but that simple task seemed beyond him. When his sword had finally pulled free of the thing's hand, Brandt had fallen hard to the ground, and he couldn't seem to catch his breath. He couldn't seem to do anything other than watch the Druzem's enormous hand come swinging around for him for the last time.

And then that hand burst into crackling blue flames.

The scream that split the air seemed to split his head as well, and he wondered whether he would ever hear again.

Then two strong hands—large for a man, but they seemed puny after seeing the Druzem's—reached down through the night and caught Brandt around the waist, hoisting him far up into the air and swinging him over a massive shoulder. *Pell*, Brandt thought. But as his stomach landed on that shoulder, his breath exploded out of him yet again, and his face slapped against an impossibly cold, hard back.

Callom Pell had not been wearing armor, Brandt thought.

Nor did Callom Pell possess the long mane of white hair that fell across Brandt's face, obscuring his vision as his rescuer set off at a labored run across the field.

"Watch where you hit me with that sword!" Brandt's rescuer ordered, his voice deep and commanding, yet holding a note of amusement. Brandt's sword was still dangling from his hand, and as the older man ran, the blade slapped rhythmically against his rescuer's mailed posterior. Must be a maniac, Brandt thought, to find anything funny with a monstrosity like the Druzem only yards away. And suddenly he knew his rescuer.

"You're Calador, aren't you?" Brandt wheezed, still gasping for breath. "The old minister of defense."

"*Ex*-minister of defense, if you don't mind," Roland corrected. "And perhaps the late minister, if I don't get us into that tower."

But even as he said it, he was passing through the massive stone walls of Happar's monolith and swinging Brandt down to the flagstone. Brandt finally caught a moonlit glimpse of the man's face—nobly proportioned, the white beard and moustache neatly trimmed, his blue eyes glimmering brightly. But there were deep furrows across Calador's brow and creases at the edges of his eyes. It was not until a handsome woman joined them a moment later, her black hair fluttering in the breeze, that Roland seemed marginally to relax.

"You didn't have to get that close to cast it," the old warrior said quietly.

"And when did you take up magic?" Miranda responded archly.

Brandt ignored the conversation, pushing himself up onto one elbow and peering through the rift in the wall. The blue fire was still playing over parts of the Druzem's body, but most of it had guttered out. The creature had fallen to the ground and was rolling around crazily in an attempt to smother the eldritch flames.

"Did you kill it?" Brandt asked.

Miranda looked down, paying attention to Brandt for the first time. She laughed sharply, but there was no humor in it.

"Kill it?" she asked. "I'm not sure it *can* be killed. If that is what I think it is, the monster should have been long dead. If it can survive the Wars of the Devastation and the Binding, it will survive anything I can do."

Imbress and Harnor had approached from the other side of the entryway.

"And who exactly are you?" Imbress asked.

But it was Brandt who answered, pushing himself back to his feet. "Someone I can trust in a fight."

Roland turned toward Miranda and raised an eyebrow in question. By reply, she shrugged ever so slightly. Then, as if someone had called her name, she turned sharply about, her eyes cutting through the darkness as if it were noon.

"Mouse says the Druzem is about to rise again."

At that, they all turned back toward the field, straining to make the best of the moonlight. Every trace of Miranda's blue fire had disappeared, and the Druzem was beginning to pull itself to its feet, though more slowly and tentatively than it had been before. Its nostrils oscillated rapidly, searching for the scent it had detected just before it had been hurt. It found nothing and nodded in satisfaction, then cocked its head with interest. Between the beast and the tower lay Callom Pell. He had been glanced by a flailing hand during the beast's convulsions and the blow had dazed him. Now Marwick was by the man's side, trying to pull Pell to his feet as the forester cleared his head. Slowly, the thief succeeded in helping Pell up and the two of them began scrambling toward the tower.

The Druzem shook its head, whipping its great mane from side to side.

"You will taste all the better now. And the mage shall be the sweetest. An unexpected pleasure, and so very nutritive."

"Oh my," Miranda whispered. "It appears I've angered the thing."

"You can understand that?" Imbress asked sharply. "What did it say?"

But just then Marwick began bellowing almost as loud as the Druzem's unnatural voice.

"Back!" he was shouting. "Back! Back!"

The Druzem had lurched into motion, only a few of its twenty-foot strides behind the pair. They were all headed straight for the tower.

"Back!" Marwick screamed, only a few yards away now.

"Good advice," Roland muttered, and he began ushering everyone across the flagstones to the most remote edge of the circular chamber, perhaps twenty-five feet from where the door had once been.

Marwick and Pell burst into the tower, a monstrous hand following them like a gigantic bird of prey, mere inches from their heads. The men kept running, leaning forward with each stride as if they could feel the Druzem's talons behind them, and with each step they took, another yard of the creature's forearm flew through the rift in the wall. A moment brought the men to the center of the chamber, and the Druzem's elbow came into view, its curved horn striking sparks against the floor.

"Mercy above," Miranda whispered, "they won't make it."

But they managed three more strides apiece as the Druzem's maned upper arm filled the opening, almost cutting off all light. And then, just as the thing's fingers brushed against their backs, the men threw themselves forward, rolling across the floor until they stopped at Roland's feet. The Druzem's talons flew after them and, abruptly, a tremendous crash resounded through the tower, throwing them all to the ground.

The Druzem's shoulder had hit the tower's outer wall. It could reach no farther.

Bits of mortar rained down upon them, dislodged by the enormous impact. Marwick glanced nervously upward as he pushed himself to his feet, surprised to discover that the roof had no intention of falling. Then he turned toward the giant hand that had failed by only a second to catch him. The Druzem was straining to reach farther into the tower. Its massive fingers felt their way across the floor, yellowed talons clicking against the flagstones as it searched blindly for its quarry. There were, Marwick estimated, perhaps ten inches between its forefinger and his boots.

"Mother always said, when building a house, leave space enough for guests. Seems that Happar left no room for error."

The Druzem's hand continued to explore the floor, fingers rising and falling like the legs of a giant spider. Each time it passed close to them, they had to press hard against the wall to avoid its touch.

"It will try something else before long," Pell said, lifting his axe once again as he glanced at Roland. "Unless we discourage it."

The old warrior nodded and reached a hand behind his left shoulder. Then, from a scabbard strapped across his back, he drew forth the longest sword Brandt had ever seen. Keen-edged and glittering even in the murky light, the blade alone was five feet long. Brandt doubted he was strong enough to swing the thing once, but Roland was a giant of a man. Beside him, even Pell seemed tiny. Brandt might have derived some satisfaction from the observation if not for the groping hand of the Druzem, which made even Roland look like a gnat.

As if by some silent agreement, Roland inched one way along the wall, Pell the other. They waited for the Druzem's hand to come between them and then both leaped forward. Pell's axe was first to strike, laying open the Druzem's pinkie finger to the bone. Roland took a full step forward, bringing his sword around with a two-handed swing that spun the blade around his head before it whistled down at the monster's wrist. Thick skin sliced open and flesh parted as the sword continued its stroke, not stopping until the blade had disappeared entirely amid gouts of blood. A terrible scream rent the air and Roland wrenched free his sword just as the Druzem snatched back its hand, knocking free another of the building stones as he withdrew the wounded limb from the tower.

"That will give it something to think about," the old warrior said with satisfaction.

"And something for us to think about as well," Pell added, sounding distinctly less happy.

"How do you mean?" Roland asked.

"I fear," the forester explained, "that we are about to find out exactly how Happar Pell's great keep fell in."

They all looked at Pell quietly, and then at the massive granite blocks that they had moments ago considered their only shelter. An eternal shelter, it might prove.

"Surely there is something we can do," Elena Imbress snapped, her voice taut with anger at being trapped. She turned toward Miranda. "Duchess Calador, if I'm not mistaken."

Miranda inclined her head. "I haven't the pleasure of knowing your name, though," she said.

"Introductions can wait," Pell rumbled, his eyes darting back and forth from Roland to Miranda, dark and unreadable. "The agent has a point."

"What did you do to the creature before?" Imbress asked. "Can you do it again?"

The older woman sighed and shook her head. "Fiend's Fire? It's no help, I fear. It looks impressive and it burns while it lasts, but that is only for moments. Despite the show, the fire does no real damage. Now, before the Binding . . . that would have been a different story. And that's what I was counting on. The Druzem remembers what Fiend's Fire once was. Its attempts to extinguish the flames were more a reaction to memory than reality."

Suddenly, Marwick cried out and they all turned their attention back toward the outside. The Druzem's fingers had reached gingerly inside the tower again—clearly, it had no great desire to be hacked at anymore—and curled around the stone wall, taking a firm grip of the granite blocks. Then the creature strained at the wall, and with a tremendous grating sound, one of the enormous stones tore free. It looked like a mere brick in the Druzem's hand.

"Finishing what it started centuries ago," Pell grumbled, once more lifting up his axe.

The Druzem's hand withdrew, and after a moment, the party was greeted with the crash that the granite block made as it was tossed casually aside. The Druzem reached in again and tore loose the next block.

Marwick looked up at the ceiling overhead.

"At least this place will make an impressive mausoleum."

Pell scowled and stepped forward, axe in hand, but Roland caught the forester by the arm. Pell looked down at the nobleman's hand, scowling, but Roland would not let go.

"We could attack it here," Calador explained, "because it could not reach us. If we venture within its range, we're doomed, especially in this confined area. All it needs do is swing its arm from side to side and sweep us into the wall."

"You suggest we let it bring the roof down on our heads?" Pell asked.

"I don't think that's what it's after," Miranda said quietly. Everyone turned toward the small woman.

"I don't suppose any of you recognize the language the Druzem speaks," she began, wondering why Pell's scowl darkened at the comment, "but what it said is important. Before tonight, I would have laughed at a suggestion that the Druzem—or any of the great beasts—had survived the Binding. The histories say that the strongest of them fled the Devastation before they were destroyed, but after the Binding was wrought, the magic they depended on for life slowed to a trickle. I suppose you could say they starved to death."

"That thing hardly looks like its starving to me," Brandt muttered.

"Ah, but it is," Miranda replied. "It spoke of its thirst for souls. According to the histories, the Druzem lived upon human souls. The essence that flees our bodies upon death is what sustains the beast. Weakened by the Binding, the Druzem must have fallen here, helpless for years as the grass grew over it, until something—I have no idea what—aroused it."

"Laz's soul," Imbress whispered, a horrified expression on her face.

"One soul?" Miranda said. "Hardly a meal after such captivity. The Druzem is weak and desperately hungry. It can't afford to bury us under this tower. The Druzem needs our *blood*."

The protest of stone accompanied yet another block torn out of place.

"Then why is it doing its best to topple this place?" Marwick asked.

The witch shook her head.

"It isn't trying to topple Happar's tower," she explained. "It's simply making a big enough door to get in."

*   *   *

No one spoke for a moment as they pondered what
Miranda had suggested. Now that they considered it, they
could see that the Druzem had been working neatly. It had
removed an entire column of stones, three blocks high. The
rift in the wall was now twelve feet wide and just as high—
nearly large enough for the Druzem to crawl inside. As if to
confirm their worst fears, the creature bent down and thrust
its enormous head through the gap in the wall. The smell of
its fetid breath quickly filled the small space.

"Yes," the Druzem said in its oddly quiet voice, *"you
smell of fear. In that other age, men did not smell so afraid."*

Then it grinned at them, showing teeth like stalactites, and
withdrew.

Calador was searching the tower for another way out. "It
appears our only alternative is to go up. If the thing refrains
from bringing the whole tower down, the roof will be the
most defensible spot."

They looked at the stairway that spiraled up toward the
small patch of sky that glimmered beyond the trapdoor in
the roof. Where they stood, the stairs had already climbed
twenty feet, far beyond their reach. To get onto the stairs,
they would have to venture back toward the Druzem, where
the staircase began only feet from the tower's entrance.

"Watch me," Brandt whispered.

He slid his sword back into its sheath and turned toward
the foot of the stairs. Then, holding his arms out to either
side, he walked slowly across the flagstones, lowering each
foot gently, his heels never meeting the floor. When he had
crossed half the floor, Marwick broke out into a wide smile
and followed. Within seconds, both men had reached the
stairs without making a noise the Druzem could hear. Imbress nodded and followed, Callom Pell close by her side.
Pell was used to walking quietly through the Ulthorn and
found the brief trip easy. The pair joined Brandt and Marwick
on the steps and began climbing quietly toward the roof.

It was Calador that Pell worried about, although the forester saw no reason why he *should* worry about a damned Chaldean nobleman. The man was weighed down with enough metal to forge a church bell, and Pell imagined that when the old minister moved, his armor would prove just as loud. But the bronze plate armor that protected Calador's chest and back had been fashioned from only a few pieces and was held together with strong leather straps. It did not clink with every step as chain mail would, and Roland crossed half the tower's floor without incident, Miranda walking at his side, her hand in his. Calador paused then, watching the Druzem as it strained at the next block. Finally, in a cloud of burst mortar, the block ripped free and, simultaneously, the Caladors dashed to the stairs under the cover of the noise.

Only Harnor was left, his short sword in hand, staring white-faced at the Druzem as the monster went about its work.

"What's he waiting for?" Brandt whispered in Marwick's ear.

The thief shrugged. Another block or two and the monster would be able to crawl inside. Harnor had precious little reason to wait. But reason, Marwick thought, probably had little to do with it. As he watched the Druzem's monstrous hand find purchase around another building stone, he could understand what kept Harnor rooted to the spot—the sick, unreasoning hollow in one's chest that rose when you looked upon something that *simply could not be*.

The Druzem ripped another stone free and Harnor sprang ahead, sprinting noisily across the tower floor. Instantly, the Druzem dropped the granite block and shot his hand forward. Harnor spun out of the way, slicing his sword across one of the Druzem's knuckles as he turned, and flung himself upon the stairs. Undaunted, the Druzem plunged his entire arm back into the tower, sweeping across the floor. Finding nothing, the hand swung back, feeling its way along the tower's curved wall, headed directly for the stairs.

"Up!" Brandt cried, and what had been a quiet, orderly climb dissolved into a mad dash along the narrow stairway.

Harnor barely scrambled onto the first landing before the Druzem's fingers slithered across the lower stairs, only a yard beneath them.

Disappointed, the Druzem finally drew back its hand and disposed of the building block it had been removing. Then, quickly, it tore away the block that had lain beneath it.

"Quickly!" Pell called to Harnor as the forester passed the second landing.

Both of the Druzem's hands appeared now, and both arms followed it. Then the monster's head ducked through the opening, nostrils dilating in pleasant anticipation.

"So sweet you smell," the Druzem rumbled.

Its arm shot upward twenty feet, but Harnor, who had just reached the second landing, remained a few steps above it. Shaking its huge, maned head in frustration, the Druzem began to slide its torso through the rift, belly up, driving with its legs from outside. The creature had to bend its chin to its chest in order to bring its waist inside. Then, pushing up against the floor, it levered itself into a sitting position, its trunklike legs slipping into the tower as well.

"Hurry!" Imbress shouted between ragged breaths, seeing that Harnor was still lagging behind, only at the third of the six landings. She, Pell, Marwick, and Brandt were a few steps from the top. The Caladors were only fifteen feet behind them.

Slowly and awkwardly, the Druzem rose to its feet, bringing its head even with the third landing. Harnor had almost reached the fourth now, but that was still easily within the beast's reach. The Druzem's shoulders, though, only cleared each side of the tower by a few yards, and it found it difficult to raise its arms above its head, having to press its back to the ancient stone wall in order to make room. And then, with Harnor's steps ringing clearly against the granite, the Druzem's hand shot upward.

Harnor fell flat against the steps, hoping to duck beneath the Druzem's reach, but the beast's hand never completed its strike. Something large plummeted from above, knocking away the Druzem's forearm before falling to the flagstones with a great, metallic clatter. As Harnor scrambled back to his feet and began dashing up the steps, he saw that, somehow, Lord Calador had shed his armor.

The agent could feel nothing now, not even his legs moving beneath him, although the tower steps sped by in a blur. And again he saw the Druzem's monstrous hand explode toward him, talons outstretched . . . but it came to an abrupt halt a few feet short, at the edge of its reach. Finally, Harnor was safe.

Roland was helping Miranda through the opening in the ceiling that led outside, and then the Duke followed her out of view. It took only a few moments more for Harnor to stumble up onto the tower's roof, falling to his knees as he gasped for breath.

"Well," Brandt said, "we made it. Now what?"

They looked about. The top of the tower was level with the canopy of the forest. It was a clear night, and the gibbous moon washed over the tops of the trees for miles in every direction, illuminating a stippled green-black field. The only break in the endless foliage was the clearing around them and the thin ribbon of the Woodblood River behind them as it cut through the Ulthorn, eventually disappearing as it twisted toward the west.

And beneath them, through the roof's opening, they could see the Druzem standing calmly at the bottom of the tower, like a man down a well waiting to be lowered a rope.

"A stalemate," Imbress said quietly.

"I wouldn't be so sure," Pell muttered, glaring down at the beast below.

"How patient do you suppose it is?" Marwick asked, kneeling at the edge of the trapdoor.

"It's waited centuries between meals," Pell observed. "I don't suppose a few hours more will inconvenience it."

But the Druzem had no intention of waiting. Feeling the wall with its hands, it wrapped its fingers around the stout ledge offered by the fourth landing. Then, pressing its back against the tower wall and finding a toehold upon the lower stairs, it levered itself ten feet up the tower wall, as a man might climb up a chimney. Grimly, Brandt drew his sword. One by one, the others followed suit.

The landings provided solid outcroppings for the Druzem to grasp or step upon, and it took only a few moments for the creature to bring its head only scant yards beneath the tower's roof. The Druzem pressed its left arm against the far wall for better leverage, the fingers of that hand smearing blood on the ancient stones from the wounds Pell and Calador had caused. Then it reached upward with its right hand along the stream of fresh air it could feel rolling in from above. Everyone scrambled backward as the hand shot through the opening, the forearm following it, until it a tremendous concussion rocked the tower's roof, sending everyone staggering off-balance.

"The horn!" Pell cried. "That curved horn that grows from its elbow will never fit through the opening."

Indeed, it would not, and with its joint beneath the roof, all the Druzem could do was reach straight upward, ten feet into the air. The thing's forearm filled the entire opening, allowing no latitude for the arm to move from side to side.

"Sate your thirst on this!" Pell bellowed in the ancient patois the Druzem used, and then he sprang forward, swinging his axe in a great two-handed stroke that laid open the beast's forearm.

Calador was only a second behind him, his great sword biting deep beneath the purple-black skin of the Druzem's arm. And then, save Miranda, the others darted forward around the arm, blades flashing, as they sliced and hacked at the thing. To his surprise, Brandt found that his sword barely cut through the creature's tough skin, then rebounded back, sending a jarring shock through his arms. It was almost like chopping wood, Brandt thought, wondering at the enormous strength behind Calador and Pell's damaging blows.

As Pell's axe bit again, the Druzem snatched back its arm, howling in pain.

Calador's lined face was set in a grim smile.

"No easy prey here," the old general said.

But the Druzem did not hesitate long, for once again the

hand shot through the opening, far faster than the first time, and a shower of stone exploded outward as the beast's hooked horn shattered the granite that had at first held it back. Already slick with the monster's blood, the floor now bucked beneath their feet, and Brandt could barely remain standing. From the corner of his eye, he could see Harnor, Pell, and Roland go down. And then the Druzem bent his arm, bringing his hand down to the tower roof, casting about in search of a victim.

The great arm came rushing Brandt's way and he jumped nimbly over it, but as he turned around to watch the end of its pass, he saw the Druzem's fingers brush over Harnor's back. The agent rolled to the side, but not before the Druzem closed its fingers in a fist around Harnor's head. Brandt sprang forward, hacking at the Druzem's arm, but though he drew blood, the monster would not release its grip. Instead, the Druzem straightened its arm in order to bring its catch back into the tower.

"No!" Imbress cried, but her dagger was unable to do more than scratch the creature's tough skin.

The arm began to sink . . . but it came to an abrupt stop with another roof-shaking collision. This time, the Druzem's hook had caught on the outside of the tower, and it couldn't seem to twist it about properly to slide back through the hole it had made.

Instead of trying to pull its arm down again, the Druzem merely snapped its huge wrist, and Harnor went flying across the roof, landing in a heap on the granite.

"He's free!" Imbress cried, and she turned toward her companion, but Marwick caught her roughly by the shoulders and spun her around, having seen what she hadn't: Harnor's body had been thrown back down, but the man's head remained within the Druzem's closed fist.

"Yes," the thing rumbled from within the tower, *"as sweet as the very first."*

And then, in a grotesque acknowledgment of the fact, the Druzem slowly straightened its forefinger, as if pointing to the sky.

Pell rushed forward, axe whistling about in a great arc, but this time he did not strike at the thick, fleshy part of the monster's forearm. Instead, the blow ended above his head, slicing into the creature's wrist. A sharp twang broke the night air, like a giant bowstring snapping, and the Druzem howled beneath them at the pain of a severed ligament.

Seeing Pell's strategy, Calador jumped to the other side of the Druzem's arm and delivered a hacking blow that cut a foot deep into the yard-wide wrist. Desperately now, the Druzem banged its elbow against the roof, but its horn remained caught against the low stone parapet of the tower behind it.

And then the two men struck as one, axe and sword slicing through flesh in a shower of blood, their metal meeting with a resounding ring where the middle of the Druzem's wrist had been. Slowly, like a falling tree, the Druzem's hand toppled stiffly down to the stone, still curled into a fist except for its outstretched forefinger. Black blood fountained from the exposed arteries in the stump of its arm, and the Druzem brought down its elbow in a final, thundering crash that pulled its arm back through the stone floor.

And then the entire tower rocked as the monster lost its balance and fell to the ground below. For a moment, they thought the force of its fall would send Happar's monument crashing to the ground, like the remains of the keep to its side, but the tremors quickly subsided, leaving the survivors atop the tower in stunned silence.

"You've killed it," Imbress said after a moment, too exhausted for her voice to betray any emotion, whether elation, relief, or sorrow.

"Mouse says not."

They all looked up at that, not quite understanding what Miranda had so quietly said. But then Brandt felt a telltale vibration from below. He glanced through the jagged hole in the roof, but the base of the tower was pitch-dark. Then, peering over the side of the parapet, he saw the Druzem crawling out of the tower, its bloody stump pressed beneath its left arm as it tried to stanch the bleeding. Slowly, the beast rose to its feet, swaying for a moment before it could gain its balance. And then it began to stagger toward the forest.

"It's fleeing," Marwick said.

But after ten paces, it stopped and turned back toward the tower. Slowly, the Druzem opened its mouth and emitted an awful, inarticulate roar—the bellow of centuries' hunger and pain. Lurching into an awkward run, the creature sped back toward the tower and smashed its right shoulder into Happar's ancient stones. The roof leapt beneath the Druzem's prey, sending them crashing down again to the granite. The stones felt as if they were still slowly shifting beneath them.

Brandt was first to his feet, his head throbbing and his knees shaky. Someone was screaming—no, it was the owl again, he realized, screeching madly as it flew around the doomed tower.

"It's going to come down!" Brandt cried. "Quickly, to the steps!"

Already, he could see the Druzem drawing back for its next—and probably last—charge.

"Not the steps," Miranda said firmly, her voice still quiet. "We'll be knocked off them instantly."

Instead, the woman turned toward the parapet behind her.

"Mouse says fly," she said, and with that she ran toward the parapet, throwing herself over the side.

Instead of the sickening thud Brandt expected to hear after a few seconds, there came the immediate cracks of breaking branches, the rustle of leaves. He had forgotten the two great black oaks that stood between the tower and the river, their spreading branches reaching all but the last few feet to the stone.

"Miranda!" Roland cried, and without another thought he hurled himself after her. Marwick took only a second to glance down at the Druzem, preparing itself for its next charge, before he dove neatly after them.

Pell, Brandt, and Imbress stood across the roof, closer to the eastern oak. It was a longer jump, but Imbress didn't hesitate, her legs pumping through the air as she fell into the ancient tree's embrace, disappearing in a sea of leaves. As the Druzem began to lumber forward, Pell threw himself over the parapet, his thick body plummeting more quickly through the slim branches at the top of the oak before Brandt lost sight of him.

The Druzem was only a step away.

Brandt surged into motion only a second before the monster crashed into the tower. The broad stone roof listed forward as Brandt launched himself into the air, flying peacefully for a moment before he struck the tree, stinging branches cutting at his face, boughs buffeting his body as he fell one way, then another. The snaps of the oak were accompanied by the tortured groan of stone shifting, and it seemed to Brandt he was not the only one hurtling through the oak's branches, but that great dark masses of stone were tearing through the tree, cracking off stout branches, battering the trunk.

And then there was an enormous crack, sharper than any of the others. The world rotated sickeningly beneath him and Brandt fell free of the oak, feeling nothing again until he struck the cold, hungry waters of the Woodblood.

CHAPTER 11

This was the type of glorious spring day that made one yearn to live forever, Doctor Pardi thought as he slowed his horse to a walk. He was due back at his office soon, but the sky was too brilliant to hide indoors. Better to linger on the way home—just a few moments longer—and work a bit faster the rest of the day.

Too bad about Carn Eliando, Pardi thought, *stuck inside on a day like this*. The doctor was on his way back from the Karrelian estate. The night of the accident, Karrelian had insisted that Pardi check on Carn every week. It seemed that Karrelian was leaving on some kind of trip (insensitive of the man to go on the very eve that his friend was crippled, Pardi thought) and he wanted to be sure that Carn received frequent medical attention. It was a useless gesture, the doctor knew; Carn Eliando was as stout and healthy as a bull— except that he would never use his legs again. Pardi sighed. Soon enough, Carn would grow tired of his repeated, useless visits, which would serve only to remind the man of his injury.

With a touch of regret, the doctor turned his horse onto the tree-lined street that, in three blocks, would bring him to his office. *Patients*, he thought glumly, *and work*.

"There's one of them!" a voice cried.

Pardi looked down to find a shopkeeper emerging from his vegetable stand, his ample belly covered by a green apron. As the man pointed at the doctor, his lips twisted with the sort of disgust one might reserve for a cockroach. Pardi did not know the greengrocer's name, but he purchased fruit from him most every week. Confused, the doctor turned around, half-expecting to find some disreputable figure behind him to be the true target of the shopkeeper's cry.

"One of them mind-twisters!" the shopkeeper continued.

At this, several nearby pedestrians paused to watch the growing commotion.

"Mind-twisters?" Pardi asked, genuinely puzzled. He spread his fingers, gesturing for further explanation and was surprised to see the grocer shrink backward.

"Don't try any of your wizard tricks on me!"

Wizard? At that, the man's meaning began to sink in. There had been a spate of strange stories circulating through the city this week, some published in the newspapers and others simply spreading mouth-to-mouth like a wildfire. One of those stories concerned the election of a prime minister more than twenty years ago. A Prandis daily had received evidence that a group of wizards had conspired to influence voters in favor of Kermane Ash. Pardi knew enough about magic to detest the news coverage, which had made it sound as if the wizards could change a man's mind as easily as snapping one's fingers. Even before the Binding, tampering with minds was difficult, beyond the power of any but the most powerful. mages. Now, Pardi doubted that a wizard could do more than nudge someone through the power of suggestion—perhaps enough to sway a few undecided voters, but little more. Even still, that had been enough for Ash to promise the wizards that, in return for their help, he would sanction the National Arcane Authority as a governmental organ and reward the NAA's chief with the Ministry of Magic—a seat that had centuries ago been established as a watchdog agency for wizards, during the days when people remembered the wars of the Devastation all too well. Or at least, so the article claimed.

Pardi scratched his head and laughed. "Fear no tricks from me," he responded, trotting out his best bedside manner. "I'm no wizard at all, simply—"

"Liar!" someone shouted behind him. Pardi turned to see Mistress Speth, a longtime patient of his. "You've laid hands on me and my skin has turned clear as glass," the old woman continued. "I've seen parts of my body that God meant to keep covered from sight. And you've stuck your hands inside me with magic!"

And pulled out a tumor that would have killed you, you stupid cow, Pardi thought, although he hesitated to say so.

"Well, of course," Pardi answered instead, keeping his voice soothing. Heads had begun to pop out of nearby windows and a crowd was starting to gather. With each passing minute, people were leaving nearby stores to watch what was happening on the street. "I'm a healer."

"A healer or a wizard—no difference!"

Pardi did not recognize that voice, which came from some man behind him, but he knew the man was only half-wrong. Healers belonged to a class of mages sometimes called small-wizards: people who had learned a little specialized magic in order to perform particular jobs, such as healers or herbalists or the Whisperers who allowed the rich to communicate quickly across vast distances. But he was no wizard. Hell, he didn't even belong to the NAA . . .

"This is ridiculous," Pardi snorted. "These things you're talking about—they happened when I was a boy. Leave the past alone . . ."

Abruptly, the greengrocer shrieked and fell to his knees, clutching his head between his hands. *The man was in need of his professional help,* Pardi thought, frowning.

"He's doing it!" the shopkeeper screamed, his arms flailing as if he were fending off an invisible assailant. "I can feel him inside my skull! Out—get out of my mind!"

Doctor Pardi had no time to decide whether the greengrocer was a lunatic or a liar before the citizens of Prandis dragged him from his horse.

By neither temperament nor habit was Orbis Thale a man who let events slip beyond his grasp, but even his reach was not sufficient for the events of the past few days. Between the assassinations, the upheavals in the Council membership, and Pale's incessant clamoring for war, Thale would have had more than his hands full. But this business with the vote . . .

Not for the first time, Thale cursed his predecessor, Abrinius Loft, who, at the tip of the assassin's dagger, had met nothing less than a fitting end. Three decades ago, Orbis Thale had barely received his journeyman's certification from the NAA, yet even then he would have known better than to have thrown the association's weight behind a surreptitious plan to brainwash the populace. Thale threw back his cowl and ran a spidery hand over his shaven head, frowning all the while. What galled him most was that Loft must have considered the deal with Kermane Ash a triumph—gaining a seat on the Council in exchange for the use of Wizards' Suggestion during Ash's election. Any decent wizard—even a wretch like Loft—knew that Suggestion worked only to reinforce underlying tendencies. A voter against Ash could not be made into a voter for Ash, and so Loft would have effectively traded nothing for everything.

Or so Loft had thought. What Loft had never considered, in his scramble to consolidate power, was that it had taken centuries to wash away the terror of wizards that the Devastation had branded into the people's hearts. Even after the Binding, which had rendered mages little more than uncertain shadows of their former power, that fear had lingered—dormant, but ready to spring to life if given just a whisper of encouragement. And news that wizards were manipulating the highest elections of the land . . . That was no whisper; it was an accursed shout.

Thale had traced that shout back to its ultimate source—the same source, it seemed, as so many of the recent disruptions around the city. Galatine Hazard had released his files, and the information within them had shaken Prandis to its roots. But knowing the source of the turmoil was not the same as knowing the solution. The knowledge, once free, would not be bottled again.

Thale had spent the past few days working tirelessly to stem the swelling backlash of public sentiment. He had been besieged on one side by his allies in the government, who felt betrayed; on the other side, by his own constituency—from small-wizards to arch-magi—who felt outraged to be implicated in a secret pact that endangered their community standing. And then there were the communities themselves, the vast horde of common people who, it seemed, were ready to rise up against anyone who could so much as light a match with magic. That was the real problem and it seemed to defy even Thale's subtle talents. The sad truth was that Suggestion worked poorly indeed, or Orbis Thale would have been sorely tempted to use it on the people of Prandis again.

At the knock upon his door, Thale lifted his cowl over his head and lowered himself into his chair. His eyes narrowed suspiciously. That had not been the knock of Pilar, his assistant. Who then . . . ?

"Come," he growled, impatient for the door to open and for the mystery to be solved.

The solution lingered teasingly for a moment before striding inside, clad in the black-lacquered armor of the Minister of War. Where the assassin had mutilated Amet Pale's face, the scars seemed deeper than ever, as if the general's head had been diced into a dozen awkward cubes, one perched atop the next like a haphazard arrangement of children's blocks. Behind Pale, Thale could see Pilar gesturing an apology. The general had stormed right past the woman.

"Minister," the general began, still using that odd whisper he had adopted since the attack at Hawken Heights. Like the point of a knife rasping lightly across stone. Thale understood that the general had almost choked to death on a coin the assassin had slipped into his mouth. He wondered whether the experience had somehow damaged Pale's vocal cords or whether this new voice was an affectation.

"Minister," Thale replied. "To what do I owe the honor? I fear my vote is not subject to change."

Thale shrugged as if the matter of the vote were inconsequential.

"Water passed grinds no more," the general said offhandedly, picking a piece of lint from the edge of the black cape he had taken to wearing. The scar tissue that crossed his face formed tight bands from ear to ear and chin to brow, so whenever Pale spoke, the rest of his flesh twitched at slight, unpredictable angles, like a marionette disturbed by its master's restless sleep. "And to prove there are no hard feelings, I want to show you something of interest."

Thale paused, took a deep breath. It required no particular genius to understand that something unsavory lurked behind Pale's offer. Nor did Pale seek to hide the fact. The general wanted Thale to know that he was there on the sort of wretched business that only he could take pleasure in . . .

Thale spread his hands, indicating the stacks of paperwork that covered his desk.

"The needs of my ministry press, I fear. Perhaps another day?"

A smile flickered across Pale's lips, disappearing before it could settle in place. "You'll want to see this as it happens. Trust me. And my carriage, as luck has it, stands ready downstairs."

It was clear the general did not intend to take no for an answer. Thale inclined his hooded head.

"Then I am in your debt," he said, keeping his tone carefully decorous.

Not a fraction yet, Pale thought, *of what it will soon amount to.*

When Spelman Tooms left the Turnabout Inn, he had no clear sense of where he wanted to go or what he wanted to do. He knew only that he was a man, not a slave to wizards, and that he meant the world to know it. He walked out onto the street, blinking in the sunlight, and paused to watch the rest of Prandis intent on its own business. People frowned as they stepped around Spelman and his newfound dockworker friends, hurrying on toward their jobs.

Damned sheep, Spelman thought, *and they didn't even know they'd been fleeced.*

He wanted to shout at them but had no words for it, so he shook his newspaper at the passing crowds instead.

One of the stevedores clapped him roughly on the shoulder.

"Can you spare a minute for the docks?" the man asked.

Still squinting against the morning sun, Spelman nodded, following along as they set off at a bandy-legged trot downhill to the harbor. The tide had not yet begun to ebb, so the piers were crowded with sailing ships, each a nucleus of chaotic activity as sailors and stevedores alike swarmed about. By comparison, Spelman thought, the construction site where he worked was a model of order.

"That's the Tryal," said Liman, the worker who had suggested a detour to the docks. He indicated a three-masted, broad-beamed ship that had been moored along the left side of the pier. A dozen men were laboring at a winch, slowly raising a cargo net that had been filled with a single, large crate. "We're loading her with cloth and farm tools, bound for Gathony."

"And when do you sail with her?" Spelman asked.

The man laughed. "We're no monkeys for the ropes. We work pier sixteen, loading and unloading the ships. No sailing for us."

As they approached the Tryal, the nearby workers hailed Liman by name.

"Late again, Liman!" one called. "Couldn't find your way out of bed . . . or did your ass get stuck in the pot again?"

All the men roared at that, Liman included.

"Your friend looking for work?" the joker continued, motioning toward Spelman.

Liman shook his head. "No, but he has something to tell you all. Gather round, lads! Gather round!"

As Liman continued his exhortations, the stevedores and even a few of the sailors paused long enough to turn their attention toward Spelman. His ears were burning, Spelman realized, and for a moment he wondered what on earth he was doing wandering around the docks, shirking the morning's work. So many eyes pressing in upon him . . .

"Come on, then," Liman said, clapping him on the back. "Tell 'em!"

Spelman's mouth opened and he paused, uncertain. He was embarrassed and mad to feel embarrassed. Mad at himself, and at Liman, and at the wizards who had tried to make him less of a man. *A real man,* Spelman thought, *would know how to speak among other men.*

The breeze filled his nostrils with salt air and rustled the pages of his newspaper. Spelman looked down at the paper for a moment. And then he began to read.

By midmorning. Spelman had read the article a dozen times more—at several other piers, at his construction site, at the harbor-side market. With each reading, his voice grew more confident with the words. He began to like the sound of his raised voice, carrying across the streets of Prandis. And the look of men as they listened.

By the time he read the article to his own friends at the construction site, he knew what he wanted to do. And by the time the mob spilled through the city streets into the square that held the headquarters of the NAA, they were three hundred strong.

The NAA was housed in the sort of nondescript government building that characterized much of the city's center. It was a four-story affair, but an entire block long, built of drab yellow bricks and designed to house the maximum number of bureaucrats and functionaries. It could as easily have sheltered the Farm Authority, but for the three letters that had been inscribed over the open double doors. Spelman walked right up to those doors and opened the bucket of red paint he had brought with him from the construction site. With one jagged swipe of his paintbrush, he shot a bolt of red across the letters "NAA." And then, beside the doors, he began carefully painting some of the letters he had taken such pains to learn, each one the sort of lopsided capital that a child might make.

When he was done, he took a step backward to survey his work.

SLAVEMAKERS, it read.

But behind him, Spelman could make out a growing, dissatisfied grumble. He could not pick out anything specific that had been said, but the men were shifting about uncomfortably. Marching through the streets had been a kind of activity, a purpose in itself . . . but just standing there? They were expecting something more decisive, Spelman realized, than his merely painting SLAVEMAKERS on the side of the building.

The rumbles grew and Spelman could feel the tips of his ears turning red.

He raised his brush again and carefully painted a large "D" onto the granite.

Above him, heads were beginning to pop out of windows as the mages of the NAA realized that a crowd had formed outside their building. The laborers of Prandis hurled curses and jeers at the faces that appeared in the windows above them.

With one long stroke, Spelman added an "I" to the wall.

He heard the sound of broken glass as one of the workers hurled a brick through a window on an upper floor. The sound was followed by curses above and below, by both the wizard who had been the target of the brick and by the men upon whom the broken shards of glass had fallen.

Spelman finished his work, noting that the "E" was smallish and lopsided, but easily recognizable.

"Slavemakers Die," read a voice nearby.

Spelman looked up to find that the door of the NAA had opened, letting out several men onto the front steps of the building. Two wore long brown robes, looking quite the essence of wizardry, while another half-dozen were dressed in suits like any city bureaucrat.

"What's the meaning of this?" the wizard continued, his voice calm but stern.

"It means bloody *die*!" screamed Liman, who had stayed close by Spelman's shoulder the entire time. The stevedore grabbed Spelman's paint bucket and hurled it at the wizards, covering them with red paint. Amid the mages' curses, one brought up his hands in a broad, expressive arc.

"Watch him!" one of the dock-workers shouted.

"He'll burn you!"

Liman was not willing to wait to see what spell the mage had been preparing to cast, if indeed he had been intended to do more than wipe the paint from his eyes. Instead, Liman launched himself at the wizards, fists flying, and was followed by a crush of men behind him.

A few moments later, when there was little left of the wizards worth beating, the workers of Prandis flooded into the building.

The ruins of Amet Pale's face betrayed only the slightest hint of pleasure as he ushered Orbis Thale onto the roof of the townhouse he had commandeered. He had chosen this house, summarily evicting the elderly couple who owned it, because it was the tallest on the square. At four stories, it fully matched the height of the NAA's headquarters, which stood two hundred feet away, separated only by the small park that occupied the middle of the square . . . and the thousand-odd rioters who occupied that.

If only Thale didn't wear that damned cowl, the general thought, the morning would provide even greater amusement. He doubted that even a man as stoic as Thale could watch his life's work ruined without so much as a visible trace of misery. Yet the wizard's brown hood hid everything except a shifting play of shadows—a teasing glimpse of nose, the contour of a cheek, but never even a hint of Thale's eyes.

"When do you suppose they'll find the wits to burn it?" the general asked with the air of a man watching an anthill being smoked out.

Thale said nothing, taking a moment to survey the situation from the edge of the roof. Much as he detested Pale, he was forced to acknowledge that the soldier had chosen an admirable perch. In the square beneath him, he could see the seething mass of people—mostly men, but not a few women mixed in—shaking their fists and throwing things at the NAA headquarters. There was not, Thale noted, a single window left intact. And through their broken remains, he could see the fleeting figures of the rioters, dashing to and fro, bent on destruction. There was not, Thale surmised, a stick of furniture left intact, a document left unshredded. The only thing that had stopped the rioters from putting the building to the torch was the fire-inhibiting wards that had been placed on the property. Those had been difficult wards to cast, and they did an admirable job of retarding accidental fires, but the spell was not foolproof. While the wards made it less likely than any individual spark would blossom into flame, some lucky flint would inevitably meet equally lucky steel.

But it was only when Thale directed his gaze toward the NAA's roof that he saw the true problem firsthand. Clustered on the roof were perhaps four hundred people—the men and women who worked for Thale at the agency. Before it had housed the NAA, this building had been home to a trade association of metalworkers. It had not been built to withstand attacks, nor had the NAA ever anticipated such a need. With several doors and dozens of first-floor windows, the place was indefensible, so as the mob had poured into the building, the workers had only one direction in which to flee: upward.

Of the four hundred besieged on the roof, perhaps one hundred were true wizards (and many of them mere small-wizards), while the rest were clerks, secretaries, hired bureaucrats. It was, after all, dreadfully difficult convincing a real wizard to work a desk job . . . Nevertheless, one hundred wizards were enough to rip this crowd to shreds, given a little time to prepare and the will to work together. From their position atop the building, they had both . . . and that was what worried Thale. Someone with wits had been holding the workers together, organizing a purely defensive posture and cautioning restraint. But for how much longer would wise heads prevail?

Some of the men from the docks and nearby construction sites had gone back for coils of rope and tools that they could use as grapnels—cargo hooks, winch cranks, a dozen odds and ends. From time to time, one of these homemade devices would catch securely over the NAA's roof and rioters would begin climbing upward. Quickly, someone on the roof would pry loose the grapnel or cut the rope—but not always fast enough to prevent the rioters from being hurt by the fall. Given a little time, the crowd would become smarter and force the wizards into a broader life-or-death confrontation.

Thale wondered how many rioters had died already. During the ride from Council Tower, the general had told him that the count exceeded two dozen—most, Thale was sure, from the stupidity of their own actions: crowd tramplings, furniture foolishly thrown from upper stories . . . But the real cause did not matter. Orbis Thale knew that, when this madness was finally over, every death would be blamed on the wizards. And heaven forbid, should the wizards on that rooftop become scared enough or desperate enough to try to fight their way out—using fire or lightning or some other powerful, elemental magic—it would mean the end of centuries of the NAA's careful work.

Back to the days of wizards being burned at the stake, like the years just after the Devastation.

An improvised grappling hook caught hold of the NAA parapet. Men on both the third and fourth floors leaned out of windows to take hold of the ropes and began to climb up toward the roof. Someone above dislodged the hook and both men plummeted into the crowd below. There was a resurgence of shouting and more rioters bulled their way into the building. Thale wondered how the wizards were holding the roof—by means physical or magical—but nothing could last long against a determined crowd of this size. A melee was inevitable.

"It will be interesting to see how the dailies write this up tomorrow," Amet Pale mused.

He is *trying* to provoke me, the mage thought, suppressing a sigh. He would not be able to defer for much longer the conversation that awaited him—the real reason that Pale had brought him here.

"A public relations disaster, don't you think?" the general continued.

Thale swept his arm across the vista of the square and turned toward Pale. "You are the expert, Minister, at battle tactics. What would you recommend in such a situation?"

Now, Pale did not even try to hide a wolfish smile. His scars contorted with the movement.

"The only way to win," he said in his rasping whisper, "is not to fight. To send the crowd home peacefully, before every wizard in the land is branded an enemy of the republic. Even still, more citizens die down there by the minute. It would take an agency of unimpeachable integrity to stand behind the NAA if you would escape . . . ugly repercussions."

"An agency such as the army," the wizard said, supplying the foregone conclusion.

The scars on his face swam at swift angles as the general nodded.

"Suppose that this crowd were dispersed by the army," Pale proposed. "Suppose that we arrested the criminals who fomented this riot and made clear that any crime against a wizard is a crime against the state. Suppose we proved to the citizens of this land that every member of the NAA, from the youngest wisp of a small-wizard to the most powerful arch-mage, was as stout a defender of Chaldus as the soldiers that risk their lives daily along the Cirran River. Do you not suppose, Minister Thale, that such a course of action might solve this problem of yours?"

The mage exhaled as if a vise were physically crushing the air from his lungs. Every minute that he let pass increased the chances of a free-for-all on that roof—a battle that would kill either the members of his agency or their reputation. Or quite likely, both. But to be beholden to a snake like Pale . . .

"And what is your interest in this, General?"

Pale crossed his arms over his black-lacquered armor, studying the crowd below with hooded eyes. He lifted one foot onto the low wall that marked the edge of the roof, the better to look down at the furious masses.

"My interest?" Pale repeated. "Why, that should be obvious, Minister. My interest is the preservation of the honor and safety of this nation. Chaldus requires a strong NAA.

Should a war break out, facing Yndor without the NAA behind us would be like fighting without cavalry. However, we also require a nation safe from the tampering of mages."

Fleetingly, Thale thought of a spell he knew—a simple thing that wove air into a small column that could move a foot or two before dispersing. It could blow a stack of files off a nearby desk . . . or perhaps a precariously perched general off a roof. What service, ultimately, would he render his country by ridding it of Pale, the wizard wondered?

But there was the matter of the rioters . . . Was Pale leaning over the edge on purpose—subtly underscoring the message that neither Thale nor the NAA posed any threat to him?

"Kermane Ash's election is ancient history," the wizard said emphatically. "It was a different time and a different NAA."

The general shrugged. "What can happen once can happen again, Minister. I would be a fool not to require assurances."

From below, Thale could hear a backward count called out, from three down to one. At once, two dozen grapnels flew toward the roof and half of them found purchase. Again, rioters used the upper windows of the building as a starting place for their climb, requiring only a few feet to reach the roof. This time, Thale realized, not every rope could be cut in time. Some of the climbers would make it.

"What type of assurances?" he asked, cursing the words as he heard them leave his mouth.

"A vow," the general replied—a beat too quickly, the wizard thought. This, it seemed, was the end toward which Pale had been headed since picking up Orbis Thale that morning. "A simple vow that every member of the NAA shall take to foster the best interests of this nation."

"We already take such a vow," Thale replied, his suspicions growing, "when we join the NAA."

Across the square, a half-dozen rioters had gained the rooftops. More grapnels were flying upward as they spoke.

"Clearly," the general rebutted, "your current vow is too open to interpretation if it allows the subversion of the electoral process. This new vow will remedy things by ensuring that every member of the NAA is sworn to uphold the policies of the agency only as they are confirmed by the Minister of War."

For a moment, the wizard's mouth hung open in amazement. He had expected some sort of egregious demand, but *this* . . . ?

"What you are proposing," Thale said, barely reining in the fury in his voice, "amounts to nothing less than the absorption of the NAA into the military chain of command. And what is to ensure that the military is better able to determine the best interests of this nation?"

Upon the NAA rooftop, a rioter burst into flames, staggered backward, and fell fifty feet into the midst of a horrified, enraged crowd.

"When has the military failed in its duties to this country?" Pale asked. "When have we incinerated our fellow citizens?"

How was the NAA best to survive, Thale asked himself—as a beast hunted down or caged?

Upon the roof, he could see a rioter split open someone's head with a club and, an instant later, erupt in flames.

The wizard turned away from the square. Behind him, he found the ever-taciturn figure of Pale's Underminister, Agon Celwan, watching them both carefully through eyes that betrayed not a hint of judgment.

"Send in your men, General Pale," the wizard said.

"As soon as you take the oath yourself," the general whispered. "And to be sure, I require an Oath of Binding."

CHAPTER 12

The Druzem had disappeared long since, wading across the Woodblood and plunging into the thick forest of oaks that crowded the opposite shore. For nearly half an hour, they could hear the cracking of ancient tree limbs as the still more ancient Druzem shouldered its way into the woods, bellowing in pain and rage as it clutched the severed stump of its arm. Before leaving, it had searched for survivors among the ruined blocks of Happar's tower, seated like a stricken child among its toys. The remnants of the toppled tower stretched to the river itself, within which the monster thrice washed its wound. The Druzem never thought to search the oak tree that had remained standing at the northwest of the tower's base, and the three humans who hid within its branches hardly dared breathe for fear of attracting the creature's attention.

Finally, the sounds of the Druzem's passage faded beyond hearing and Miranda stirred within her arboreal haven. Somehow, while the others had landed in the oak in desperate postures, bruised and cut by their fall, the witch had fared better, able to sit primly while waiting for the Druzem to depart. *Magic, no doubt*, Marwick thought, wondering whether he had gone into the wrong line of work.

The Belfarian thief, however, had little cause for complaint. He had crashed through twenty feet of high, slender branches, suffering no worse than he would in a typical bar brawl in Blake's Warren. But then, more agile than most men, he had caught a broad limb with the surety of a trapeze artist, swung himself atop it, and sat straddling the oak, using a handkerchief to staunch the bleeding from a broad cut

across his forehead. From his vantage, he could see Roland
twenty feet below him. The aged warrior's great bulk had
shattered the high limbs that could hold a lighter man like
Marwick. Roland had plummeted through the foliage until
he struck the crotch of two stout branches. He lay there quietly as if in a hammock, and for a time, Marwick had been
unsure of the old man's condition. But when Roland caught
the thief's eye, he winked, signaling that he was well.

"Mouse says the Druzem is gone."

It was Miranda's voice, calmer than Marwick could imagine himself sounding under the circumstances. He wondered
what this mouse was that Miranda so often talked about.
Perhaps he would ask her, he thought, just as soon as he
helped Roland down from the tree.

Deep and swift from spring flooding, the Woodblood surged along its channel, carrying Brandt Karrelian
among the assorted debris of the Druzem's making. It was
cool beneath the waters, and strangely peaceful. Brandt liked
the feeling of being swept along, of abandoning himself to
the current rather than fighting. There had been altogether
too much fighting, he thought, wrapped in the Woodblood's
embrace. This was better.

But when his mouth opened and he swallowed water, his
lungs rebelled against the river's dangerous lull. Without
conscious direction, Brandt's limbs struck out against the
current, pushing him upward until he broke the surface, sputtering as he gulped the air. Blinking the Woodblood from
his eyes, he twisted about and saw only the dark mass of the
Ulthorn clustered close by each bank. The clearing and the
ruins of Happar's Folly had disappeared upriver. Best that he
try to make for the southern bank and hurry back to the tower
to check for survivors. The current was too strong to swim
against directly, he knew, but if he slowly angled toward the
southern bank, he might be able to make it out of the river
before being carried another mile away.

It was only as he took his first stroke that he noticed a tiny ball bobbing in the river far ahead—someone's head, although from this distance he could not say whose. He hesitated for a moment, then struck out strongly toward the other swimmer. Whoever it was might be hurt and in need of help, considering how far he or she had been carried toward the northern riverbank. With a little effort, Brandt thought, he would get there before long.

A few long strokes brought him farther toward the northern bank and into a rougher, swifter current. This seemed suddenly like a different river—a hungry one. The water buffeted and sucked at him, every now and then pulling him under for a few seconds before he could kick back to the surface. His waterlogged boots began to feel like boulders strapped to his feet, and his sword tugged at his hip like an anchor. Any thought of reaching the other swimmer vanished as Brandt struggled merely to stay afloat. For the first time he wondered whether he would make it out of the Woodblood alive. The current dragged him under again, deep enough that his foot grazed the river's rocky bed, and when he finally broke free he was sputtering, his lungs burning. Ahead of him, the other head bobbed up once more, and the moonlight glinted deep red in reflection.

Imbress, Brandt thought, swearing at himself. He had gotten his fool self killed for Imbress.

But from the corner of his eye, Brandt could see a stout oaken limb, twisted at one end where it had been rent violently from the trunk—an unintentional gift from the Druzem. If only he could reach it before the current swept it past him, perhaps the thing would buoy him to safety. Swimming with all his strength, Brandt fought against the relentless rush of the Woodblood. Every yard he gained toward the northern bank seemed as difficult as pushing a mountain before him. The tree branch, carried lightly by the waters, had quickly drawn even with him and had started to edge ahead. Brandt struggled against the current, but the oak was moving too quickly, and as he lunged desperately forward, the last broad leaves slipped past his fingers.

Brandt's hand splashed beneath the surface and, to his surprise, closed around a slim twig that had been trailing the rest of the branch underwater. Quickly, Brandt used that wooden shoot to reel in the rest of the branch, throwing his arms above the wood. The stout limb half-submerged beneath his weight, but was buoyant enough to keep his head clear of the Woodblood. Gasping, Brandt clung to his buoy and rested his leaden legs, wishing there was some way he could kick off his heavy boots. But one way or another, he swore, he would get out of this damned river, and when he did, he would need those boots.

Hain, you bastard, you haven't killed me yet.

Calador, it turned out, made his way easily down from the oak as soon as Miranda gave them permission to move. In a few moments, the Caladors and Marwick stood at the base of the tree.

"What about the others?" Marwick asked as he watched Miranda strip Roland of his shirt.

"I have sent Mouse to look for them," she informed the thief curtly as her delicate fingers probed her husband's bruised left side.

"I'll be fine," Roland muttered, as if embarrassed by his wife's attention. He lowered his shirt and took a step away.

"Mouse?" Marwick repeated, remembering the question he had meant to ask.

"Her familiar," Roland explained. "An owl. One with execrable manners and a poor sense of humor."

Marwick arched his left eyebrow and grinned, but before he could reply, Miranda's dark look shut him up.

"If you're both feeling so well," she proclaimed, "you might as well head downriver along the bank. Mouse says she has found someone. The bear-man, she says."

"Bear-man?" Calador asked.

"Callom Pell," Marwick explained, thinking of the woodsman's voluminous beard. "You know, Duke Calador, you may not be giving the creature enough credit for its humor."

The old warrior shrugged and strode off toward the riverbank, Marwick only a step behind him. The thief peered nervously down the path the Druzem had cleared to the north, but there was nothing to be seen in the Ulthorn's darkness besides shattered trees. It seemed the monster would not return soon.

While his keen eyes searched the underbrush for signs of Callom Pell, Marwick thought about the Druzem. An hour ago, he had come closer to dying than any other moment during the last decade or more—in fact, since a certain Brandt Karrelian had left Belfar. Marwick had seen danger enough in his life—indeed, even the best-planned heists could go awry—but the Druzem bothered him. As a thief, he could plan his jobs, analyze the risks, prepare for obstacles. Now, death came suddenly in the form of myths made flesh, of monsters that an army could not slay. Yes, it bothered him deeply, he realized . . . this lack of control, this vulnerability to dangers beyond anticipation. And yet Marwick did not once consider turning back toward the safety of Belfar, for that would truly be the greater danger. Neither well-known streets nor his painstakingly acquired cache of gems would help him when the horrors of the Ulthorn arose from their slumbers and ventured south once more. Madh had awoken one monstrosity already. Marwick did not want to consider what else might arise if the Binding was undone.

As they followed the river to the west, the clearing ended in thick woods that grew to the very edge of the steep bank. There was no room to walk along the water's edge, so the pair had to fight through the thick underbrush instead. Calador led the way, shouldering past shrubs and vines that Marwick would have needed his knife to part. The giant old soldier did a passable imitation of the Druzem, in his way.

Eventually, the Woodblood began to bend slightly toward the south. They had walked half a mile, yet there was still no sign of Callom Pell and Mouse.

"You don't suppose we missed them?" Marwick asked.

And then, from their right, came Pell's low, gruff voice. "Hsst! Is that you, city boy?"

There was an edge to Pell's tone, a hint of danger, and

Marwick instinctively drew his knives as he edged toward the riverbank.

"The Druzem?" Pell whispered urgently from wherever he lay in the darkened woods. "Is it about?"

"No," Calador replied. "It has withdrawn from the scene of its defeat."

"The Druzem is never defeated, merely discouraged," Pell corrected, his voice half-obscured by the gurgling of the river. "We must hurry before it returns."

"Well, then," Marwick said, "show yourself and we'll go."

"A wonder I hadn't thought of that," replied the woodsman's voice, its stoicism replaced by a surprising sarcasm. In a moment, as Marwick and Calador finally reached the riverbank, they could see why.

Callom Pell was immersed in the Woodblood up to his nose. Indeed, every few seconds a swell would sweep along, covering the woodsman to his brow, where every vein seemed ready to burst from strain.

"My foot is caught," Pell explained, struggling to lift his mouth above the waterline.

It was a wonder that the man hadn't drowned, pushed under by the river's current. But somehow, he had managed to lift his axe free and, with one desperate stroke, sink it into the trunk of a tree close by the riverbank. His grip on the axe was all that prevented the river from sucking him underwater, and the quivering of the man's corded muscles bespoke the last half hour's silent struggle.

Without a moment's pause, Roland knelt at the water's edge and wrapped his hands around Pell's wrist, pulling him upright against the current. Slowly, the woodsman came out of the water up to his chest. Truly, he had only been an inch from drowning.

"Can you pull your foot free now?" the old warrior asked.

Pell struggled against whatever had trapped him, writhing left and right, but to no avail.

"Let me try," Marwick suggested, quickly stripping down to his blue silken drawers. The water would most likely ruin the drawers, he thought ruefully—and they were a favorite pair. But a strange sort of modesty before these two veteran warriors kept his mouth sealed against complaints.

"Beware the current," Pell warned.

Marwick grinned cheerfully and lowered his foot into the water. The Woodblood was cold, so he jumped from the bank and plunged in—

—and immediately was swept away by the rushing waters. The current drove him hard against the bank, his breath exploding from his lungs in a cloud of bubbles as the water poured in. His hand struck against something—a tree root projecting out of the bank underwater—and he grabbed for it desperately, anchoring himself against the current. He pulled himself above the surface, coughing the Woodblood out of his lungs, feeling it run out of his nose.

"Fool city boy!" Pell called out. "I warned you!"

Marwick slicked back his hair as he crawled onto the bank.

"Faster than I thought," he muttered between fits of coughing.

Calador stared at him from his place on the riverbank fifty yards upstream.

"I can't hold him here forever, if that's what you think," the old man said, shaking his great mane of white hair for emphasis.

Dripping wet and still coughing, Marwick pushed his way through the underbrush back to Calador's side.

"The current is too strong," the thief said. "I don't think I can hold myself in place."

"*I'll* hold you in place," Pell said, extending his rough hand, "as long as the nobleman holds me."

There was an edge to the way Pell said "nobleman," unable to forget the Pells' age-old grudge against Chaldean nobility even as one of that nobility served as Callom Pell's last link to life. Marwick frowned but held out his hand to receive Pell's crushing grip. Then he slipped slowly beneath the water, this time using his spare hand to brace himself against a small projection beneath the riverbank. The water sucked greedily at him, but Pell's grip never wavered as Marwick descended to the river's bottom. After a few moments,

Pell felt Marwick squeeze his hand, prompting him to pull the thief back to the surface.

"Your foot is caught in a tree root," Marwick explained, gasping for breath. He had discovered this more by feel than by sight, for the moonlight barely penetrated the murky river. "Only a small loop of the root is exposed before it grows back beneath the riverbed. Your weight pulled the root taut, which is why you can't wriggle out. Easiest solution would be for me to cut the root itself."

Careful to keep his balance, Calador removed a knife from a small sheath at his belt and handed it to Marwick, hilt first. Nasty, serrated teeth ran along one side of the broad blade.

"It is a hunting knife," Roland explained. "It should cut through the root easily enough."

Perhaps with Calador wielding it, Marwick thought, after he had lowered himself back to the bottom to start sawing at the gnarled wood. His breath gave out long before the root did, and Marwick had to keep coming up for air between attempts. On his fifth try, the knife finally severed the wood, but it was only the root that had kept Callom Pell's foot so firmly in place. Now the current swept Pell's feet out from under him, swinging him downriver, and like a whip cracking round, Marwick felt himself spin past Pell. The sudden shift in weight caught Roland off balance, and the old warrior was almost jerked headlong into the Woodblood. He abandoned his two-handed grasp of Pell's wrist, flinging his left arm around the bole of the nearest tree just before he would have toppled over. Then he dug in his heels and slowly began to pull, the muscles in his thick, bare arms bunching from the strain. The Woodblood was loath to abandon its prey, and for a moment they fought to a stalemate, Calador bending his seven-foot frame against the thousands of gallons that fought to wash them all downstream.

Roland dug his heels farther into the yielding earth and squatted down, groaning as he levered himself away from the river. Slowly, as Roland's back straightened, Pell was pulled inch by inch from the water, until finally he could swing one knee onto the ground. Immediately, Roland abandoned his grip of the woodsman and rushed to get hold of Marwick. With Pell helping now, the two men pulled the thief quickly from the water.

"Mother always said, the honest man never bathes daily," the thief muttered, falling exhausted to the forest floor. "Now I know why."

Roland chuckled, leaning against a nearby willow as he regained his breath, but Callom Pell wasted no time on humor. Instead, he wrenched his axe from the tree and replaced the weapon on its belt hook. Then he gathered Marwick's clothes in a ball and deposited them on the thief's supine belly.

"Best we get moving," the woodsman growled, "before the Druzem decides one hand is all he needs for the likes of us."

One hand, Brandt found, was all he needed to hold on to his branch. With his other arm and his legs, he could slowly kick and stroke his way downstream. For a while, he had tried to maneuver himself back toward the southern bank, but the currents were too strong. The Woodblood kept bending slowly, almost imperceptibly south, and for some reason that curve kept buffeting him toward the northern bank. Ultimately, he abandoned his hopes of returning to the southern bank and concentrated instead on catching Imbress. He had closed enough on her to see that she, too, was clinging to a large branch. Apparently, she could not or would not turn around, for she never saw him.

His progress toward her seemed impossibly slow. While the banks rushed by on both sides, the bobbing head in front of him seemed determined to resist pursuit. Perhaps he gained a yard or two every minute—time was difficult to measure. It seemed that he had been in the water hours before he could make out her features beneath the wet red hair that was plastered to her head.

Finally, Brandt drew within ten yards of the agent. Imbress looked exhausted, her head pressed against the rough bark of the branch, eyes closed and teeth chattering. The water, Brandt thought, was indeed cold. A few weeks earlier and the newly melted snows would have frozen them to death after only half an hour. Now, cold though he was, the exercise had helped to keep the deadly chill at bay, and Brandt felt that if only he could get out of the river soon, he would be fine. Whether the same held true for Imbress, he had no idea.

"Imbress!" he called out, coughing as the Woodblood splashed into his open mouth.

The agent's eyelids flew open and she wrenched her head around, astonished to find Brandt only a few yards behind her. He could see her lips form his name, but no sound carried to him.

"I'm going to try to come alongside you," he cried. "This branch is bigger than yours. I think it can support us both. Grab on when I come within reach."

She nodded, her eyes coming a bit more alive as Brandt kicked against the water, driving himself a few inches closer with each surge. Imbress slowly removed one of her arms from her own buoy and grabbed the end of Brandt's. When she let go entirely of her own, she disappeared for a moment beneath the water, but her grip remained firm on Brandt's branch, and a moment later she pulled herself up, violently coughing water from her lungs.

"We need to get to the northern bank," Brandt gasped, staring at the haven that lay only thirty yards away, its oaks and willows rushing by in quick succession. "I can't do it alone."

Elena nodded, too tired to answer, and began to scissor her legs against the current. Brandt started to swim again, and ever so slowly, they inched their way closer to the riverside. Despite the burning fatigue that consumed his limbs, Brandt began to think they would make it. Then the rushing sound of the river began to mount ahead of them toward a crescendo.

He hadn't imagined that the Woodblood could offer rapids worse than the ones they had already traversed.

For a moment, gravity seemed to fail. Brandt's stomach leaped toward his throat, and he realized dimly that he was falling. Their landing was a crash of spray and foam, a plunge into turbid waters, and then a sharp jerk upward as the branch sought the surface. Brandt had only managed to blink the water from his eyes and ascertain that Imbress, now white as ice, had somehow kept her grip, when movement caught the corner of his eye. Turning, he saw a huge boulder rushing toward them. He kicked out with all his strength, but their course hardly changed. There was nothing that could prevent the collision.

In an instant, Brandt's end of the branch crashed into the rock, mere inches from his hands. The branch swung around, slamming Brandt's legs into the boulder's base before the current caught the wood again, sweeping them back out into the center of the river. Their backs were now downstream and if there were any other boulders about, mercifully, they would have no warning before being crushed to death.

But the roar of the Woodblood seemed to have been left behind them. To each side, Brandt could see the banks widening quickly. The hungry suck of the current slowly gave way to a gentle pull, and to Brandt's surprise, he found the surface of the river growing calm. A few moments later, his heels began to drag along the pebble-strewn riverbed and he finally released his grip on the branch. Imbress did the same, losing her balance and splashing wildly beneath the calmer waters before she struggled to her feet. Brandt wearily waded toward her and slung her arm over his shoulder, helping her toward the northern bank of the river. Her teeth were chattering wildly and he could feel her muscles shivering as she coaxed each step from her legs.

Together they stumbled onto dry land, dragging themselves past the pebbly shore to a stand of tall grass before they collapsed to the ground. Brandt struggled with his waterlogged boots, too tired even to curse before he managed to wrest them off his swollen feet. Then he stripped off his shirt and pants and tossed them away.

Imbress had curled into a ball on the ground, her head lost

in the deep grass, her arms pulled tight around her curled
knees. It was actually a warm spring night; Imbress's clothes,
soaked with the chilling water of the Woodblood would serve
only to keep her cold. Sighing, he reached for her feet, tug-
ging at her laces and removing her boots. Then he pried her
hands away from her knees and began to unbutton her shirt.

"Stop," Imbress stuttered, teeth still chattering.

"You'll be warmer," he replied curtly. "Trust me."

She was too tired to resist and let him undress her, until
they were both bare save for their cotton briefs. Immediately,
she rolled back into a tight ball and fell asleep. Brandt realized that, even had she been paying attention, he did not
have enough mischievous energy to summon up a leer. If
tomorrow, Imbress insisted on resuming her superior airs, he
could always remind her that he'd seen her in a far more
compromising position. For now, all he wanted was warmth
and sleep. He lay down behind the woman, curling his body
tightly against the contours of her own, feeling their shared
heat begin to rise.

And just before he fell asleep, he realized how very long
it had been since the last time he had just wanted to *hold* a
woman.

A few hours before dawn, Elena Imbress awoke
and, with a shudder she could not suppress, disentangled herself from Karrelian's arms. Quietly, she sought her still-damp
clothes in the dark and pulled them on. Then she staggered
a dozen paces away and lay down in the tall grass to finish
her sleep.

CHAPTER 13

The sun's swollen belly had just risen above the tree-tops when Elena Imbress awoke again. The Woodblood called musically from its banks, between which shifting facets of water gleamed like jewels in the morning light. But farther to the east Elena could see the twenty-foot waterfall that had almost killed her last night, and she reminded herself never to listen to this particular river. The Woodblood cooed like a lover, but one that you could be sure would betray you.

She turned toward Brandt, who seemed like little more than a hump within the tall grass. He had not awakened yet and, in fact, was snoring softly. Elena's nose wrinkled in disgust as she walked over to his side, preparing to kick him awake.

She paused, though, as she caught sight of his face. In the weeks she had known him, Karrelian harbored a perpetual look of distrust—a certain crease of his brow, a slant of the lips that lay only a twitch from a sneer. Indeed, Elena had noted once before that Karrelian's sour look did not even desert him in sleep. But now, wholly exhausted by the last days' exertions, he looked peaceful, his lips slightly parted, his black hair scattered across his brow like a child's. She supposed that even he deserved better than being kicked awake.

Elena bent over and shook him by the shoulder.

Slowly, Brandt came awake, realizing first that he lay in the grass, then remembering how exactly he had come to be there. Looking up, he saw Imbress. Her back was to him, arms crossed, as she contemplated the river.

"Get dressed," was all she said when she heard him stir.

Frowning, Brandt searched for his clothes and began pulling them on, angry at himself for not waking before her. He remembered how, even in last night's exhaustion, he had looked forward to ribbing Imbress about undressing her—how little she had resisted. But now, who knew how long she had been awake, staring at him? He flushed at the thought.

And then Brandt cursed himself further as he realized how far his mind had drifted from what was important: whether Marwick or any of the others had survived, whether any chance remained to catch Hain, whether their escape from the Woodblood was only a temporary reprieve from the deadly Ulthorn.

Imbress's thoughts, it turned out, were running along the same lines.

"Did the others escape, do you think?" she asked, her eyes following the Woodblood back to the east. She pulled her nails through her auburn hair, absently working at the tangles.

Brandt shrugged as he pulled on a boot. The leather was still waterlogged, and Brandt had to fight to haul it past his ankle.

"Who can say?" he muttered, his frustration building at not knowing. His nemesis, not knowing. "The fall alone might have killed them, and if not, the beast . . ."

His voice trailed off as the Druzem's image sprang to his mind—wounded, enraged, toppling a tower by sheer strength.

"Perhaps we were the lucky ones," Imbress replied softly, "despite almost drowning. At least the river carried us away from that thing."

A crisp morning breeze was blowing along the riverbank, but Brandt supposed that the wind was not responsible for Imbress's shudder.

The agent suddenly turned around, her green eyes fixing on Brandt with an intensity that made him feel more naked than he had before he had dressed. She was reappraising him and she didn't care whether he knew it or liked it.

"I've never liked you," she said bluntly, but without rancor. A simple statement of fact. "And I've never trusted you."

Brandt finished pulling on his other boot and stood up, but he felt no less uncomfortable.

"That leaves us even on both counts," he said, eyes narrowed.

Elena pondered this for a moment, then nodded. "Fair enough," she said. "But I'm beginning to fear this foolishness will get us killed.

"I want to catch Madh and Hain. You want to catch them. But they've been playing us for fools thus far. They know where they're going; we don't. They set the traps; we blunder into them. If we have any chance of catching them, Karrelian, we have to work together."

"Isn't that what we've been doing?" Brandt replied, eyeing Imbress warily.

"Hardly," the agent said, her mouth twisting into a sour frown. "We haven't said ten sentences to each other since leaving Belfar, and those ten were insults." She paused for a moment, again letting her eyes dissect Brandt, as if she were ticking off items on a private list. Strangely, she began to smile. "Let's get it over with, Karrelian. You're a despicable man. You use your money—your dirty money—to disguise a sordid past. You manipulate good people, you corrupt government, you do nothing unless motivated by greed . . . or perhaps by some warped sense of personal loyalty that you consider a thief's honor."

Brandt laughed sarcastically. Perhaps drowning would have been the better option—at least for her.

"This is how you go about encouraging cooperation?"

"Shut up and let me finish," Imbress snapped, her eyes flashing. "You may be corrupt, but Madh is *evil*. You may make Chaldus a fraction less the decent place it ought to be, but Madh—and whoever he works for—threatens Chaldus's very existence. I've been stupid to let my distaste for you endanger the only goal that matters, which is apprehending Madh. For all your lousy qualities, you're damned determined, as shrewd as a professional thief should be, and not half bad with that sword. Although I never would have chosen you as my partner, Tarem Selod may be right: without your help, I may fail."

Brandt stood there, quietly seething. It was just that sort of lily-white self-righteousness that always brought the gorge to his throat. "I'll spare you my character analysis of Elena Imbress," was all he said. He glanced up at the sky, wondering what time it was, but the sun was nowhere to be seen in the narrow swatch of sky that the Woodblood reclaimed from the Ulthorn's surrounding trees. "We're wasting time."

The agent pursed her lips and nodded. "True enough. What I'm suggesting is simple. From now on, we work together—and I mean *really* work together. I guard your back, you guard mine. We share ideas and agree on *one* strategy, rather than setting our own courses at each other's expense. I'm willing to bust my ass—and risk losing it—as long as we get another shot at Madh. If we can agree on that, we just may be able to help each other."

For a time, they both stood there, watching each other warily. "Whatever Hain's debt to me," Brandt said finally, "last night it may have doubled. You have a deal."

Elena Imbress held out her hand and squeezed Brandt's firmly as it met her own.

"We'll never be friends," she said, "but from now on, we're partners."

"You're better off that way," Brandt replied darkly. "My friends don't seem to fare too well these days."

But I promise you, Hain, he vowed, *my enemies fare much worse.*

Roland Duke Calador had been a leader of men since the first whisker had decorated his chin. Rule men, his father had said, and you will only be obeyed. Guide men and you will be respected. Know men and you will be loved.

The Lion of Calador had known men like no other general in Chaldean history. And though this man Marwick was a recent acquaintance—and clearly no soldier—Roland knew him well enough to see that he was troubled. Though it was little better than tatters now, that was a blue velvet suit that Marwick wore . . . and it was not the wont of a fop to brood. Indeed, Roland had seen enough of Marwick's true mettle at nightfall, during the battle with the Druzem, to get a clear sense of the man's character. Marwick had seemed more at ease fighting for his life than he looked now, simply riding a horse down a trail. And Calador suspected the problem.

Last night, after rescuing Callom Pell, the small party had quickly gathered their horses. Although Roland and Miranda's mounts had disappeared, the Ulthorn-trained horses of New Pell had responded to Callom Pell's summons, and Karrelian's and Imbress's steeds supplied the difference. With Harnor and Laz's horses, they had two mounts to spare. Without much discussion, Callom Pell had led them south to Beauty's Tress and a mile or so west along the trail before directing them to set up camp. Then the real talk had begun. Though Mouse had been searching the area in ever-widening circles, the owl had found no trace of Elena or Brandt.

"We've given up on them, haven't we?" Marwick had asked. "Otherwise, we wouldn't have left the river."

Callom Pell did not answer the question directly. "Madh and Hain are ahead of us on this trail," he said instead. "I suspected as much yesterday, but them willow doubles mislead me. Blasted fool I was. Anyway, I don't plan on losing their trail again. Yesterday's blunder gave them miles on us, but it could have been worse. And it will be if we start searching the Ulthorn at random."

"I thought you were the best tracker in New Pell," Marwick had said quietly, but with a slight edge to his voice.

"I am," Pell had replied, "but no man tracks through water. Finding where they climbed out of the Woodblood—*if* they climbed out—could mean searching both banks for miles. A week's work. And, let's not forget, there's an angry monster roaming them northern woods. You want to run into the Druzem again?" Pell scowled beneath his beard. "That beast scares my blood cold. The whole idea of the ancient days revived scares me sleepless . . . and that's the only reason I agreed to help you. To keep the Druzem and his like safely buried until the end of days. So I say we keep after the wizard. If your friends are alive, they'll be smart enough to head to Beauty's Tress and we'll find them soon enough."

And at that moment, Roland had come to understand that these men Tarem Selod had sent him to help knew exactly what they were doing, exactly what the stakes were. Callom Pell realized how close his world teetered along the edge of apocalypse, and judging by the way Marwick nodded grimly at Pell's words, the younger man understood as well. But this was Marwick's introduction to a misery that Calador had known since his first days as a soldier: the conflict between loyalty to a friend and loyalty to a cause. Marwick had chosen the latter, but he was not glad in the choosing.

Now, in the early-morning sun of a day that seemed to mock last night's danger, Calador nudged Ramus toward the left. Imbress's mount had proven a hand taller than Karellian's mare, although too small for Calador to feel anything but awkward. He had lowered the stirrups to their last notch, yet still his knees rode preposterously high. At least the chestnut gelding was well trained, and Roland's single nudge sufficed to send Ramus cantering toward Marwick's roan.

Marwick looked up as the giant old warrior approached, but his eyes retained their look of faraway thoughts.

"Quiet morning," Roland observed.

Marwick merely nodded.

"This is more the pleasant ride through the woods we anticipated when Tarem Selod bade us go to Happar's Folly. As ever, the mage omits most details."

At this, Marwick's interest seemed to heighten. "It was Tarem Selod that sent you?" he asked, remembering the mage's garish disguise as Old Hoot. Roland and Miranda's arrival last night had seemed too timely to be entirely fortuitous, but enough had happened in the hours since that Marwick had not cared to question good luck too closely.

"The old man told us the path Madh and Hain would take. Too bad," Marwick added more bitterly, "he didn't warn us what waited here."

But Roland shook his head, remembering his last meeting with the mage—how oddly insubstantial the man had seemed, more ghost than flesh.

"What little Tarem Selod saw of Madh's plans, he purchased at a price higher than we would care to pay. We each sacrifice what we can and cling to the rest." The old warrior sighed. "Miranda and I have fled our home and our peace. The same army I once commanded seeks my life. And even now, I fear my son believes us dead. That, for me, is the worst of it—to ponder Cail's pain."

Marwick shrugged. "Better he believe you dead and be mistaken than the other way 'round."

At that, Roland laughed, his mane of white hair shaking in the breeze as he threw back his head.

"You possess a peculiar wisdom, Marwick. By your accent, I'd say you are Belfarian, eh? What did you do there before you were embroiled in this mess?"

For once in his life, Marwick found words catching in his throat.

"I deal in gems," he said after a moment's pause, surprised by his own answer.

"Gems, eh?" Roland said approvingly. "A lucrative business. How were you mired in this mess? It seems you know Karrelian . . ."

And by the way Calador said that name, it was clear the Duke knew Karrelian as well.

They rode along in silence for a moment, Marwick's eyes focusing on a white spot on his horse's neck.

"I deal in *other people's* gems," Marwick explained softly, cursing himself for the blood that was rising to his cheeks.

Roland chewed on that admission for a moment before responding, although the confession had not surprised him. No merchant moved with the sinuous, inconspicuous grace of a man like Marwick.

"Before the Republic," Calador finally said, "a man in your profession would have been brought to my ancestors for judgment. But the Republic changed all that. We Caladors are not in the business of judging anymore."

Marwick said nothing, eyes focused on the ground as Roland continued to speak.

"When my father used to speak of those olden days, when the opinion of the House of Calador was also the law of the land, he told me what a tricky business it is to judge a man. As well to condemn a man for one mistake as to tear down a house for one broken window."

Marwick chuckled bitterly. "I fear, Duke Calador, that I'll prove a better-ventilated house than you'd care for."

But the warrior merely shook his head and smiled. "A man's faults are best measured in proportion to his valor," he said with peaceful certainty. "If your actions last night are any indication, Marwick of Belfar, dealer in others' gems and enemy of ancient evils, your valor may cast a long shadow on your faults. And if you fear I doubt it, you may make it your project to offer me proof."

Looking up, Marwick found no hint of mockery in Calador's steady blue eyes, and he slowly began to smile. "I may do just that, Lord Calador."

"I trust you shall," the old general replied, "and for pity's sake, don't call me Lord Calador. My dukedom ceased to mean anything centuries ago. Call me Roland, or simply Calador if you must." Suddenly, Roland's face cracked into a broad smile. "Or call me 'old man.' That seems to work well enough for my wife."

Whatever small enthusiasm had come from Brandt and Elena's new pact, it vanished as they peered east along the Woodblood, taking stock of their situation.

"Do we return to Happar's Folly?" Brandt asked quietly. He knew that this was the question on Imbress's mind as well, but it was a question more easily asked than answered.

"We agreed they might all be dead," she said slowly.

"True enough," Brandt said. "But we still need our horses and supplies."

Imbress laughed. "Do you suppose there's any chance of finding the horses?"

"No," Brandt sighed, "unless we go searching for them in the Druzem's gullet."

They stood there, brooding over the problem for a time. Imbress, Brandt noted, tended to grind her right foot back and forth in the dirt while thinking.

"Either way, we lose," the agent finally declared. "If we proceed westward on foot, we'll lose miles on Madh every hour. The only way to move through this forest is on horseback, along an established trail."

"Suppose we take a gamble, then," Brandt said, "and return for the horses. The Druzem did scare them away . . . and it was busy with us long enough to let them flee pretty far. If we're very lucky, the thing didn't get hungry enough to chase them down. If we're even luckier, we'll be able to find them ourselves."

Imbress shook her head.

"Still," she said, "in the thirty or forty minutes we were in the river, we must have been carried five miles downstream. Maybe more, for all I know. Without a trail, cutting back to the ruins could take half a day, while Madh continues west. Going back means giving Madh at least a full day's lead." She kicked the ground in frustration as she sorted through the mathematics of defeat. "There's no chance of our catching them either way."

Suddenly, Elena did the last thing Brandt expected. Her legs seemed to give out from under her and she fell into a sitting position, her head resting on her hands, her face obscured by a veil of lustrous red hair.

"Damn it, we're fooling ourselves. We've simply failed. The best we can do is backtrack out of here, contact the Ministry, and prepare them for the worst. At least we have agents in Yndor. We'll have to count on their finding Madh when he emerges from the forest."

After all her tough talk, the agent's sudden pessimism surprised Brandt. For him, there was no option of turning back. *He* had no agents in Yndor. As long as it took, he would chase Hain to the west. Especially when Imbress had unwittingly given him an idea.

"The river did carry us far from Happar's Folly," Brandt mused quietly. "Didn't Pell say the Woodblood flows all the way west to the Cirran?"

Elena looked up, a gleam of interest in her green eyes. "You're not thinking . . . ?"

But Brandt had already walked to the river's edge, dipping his hand into the clear, cold water.

"The Woodblood almost killed us last night," he said, "but it also saved our lives from the Druzem. I'm willing to gamble on it again." He turned around and surveyed the woods behind them. "If anything comes cheap in this forest, it's wood and vines. It shouldn't take too long to build some sort of raft. And as fast as this river is flowing, we should outpace any horse alive. All we need do is ride the Woodblood as far west as we can, then hike to the south and pray we find a trail. And pray that trail is Beauty's Tress."

Imbress stood up and moved alongside Brandt, surveying the river with both hope and suspicion.

"And pray that we don't get killed by another waterfall," she added, not yet sounding fully convinced. "And pray that Madh is still on Beauty's Tress, if we find it."

Brandt, however, had begun to smile. "But if he is, he's in for the biggest surprise of his life . . . and the last."

CHAPTER 14

Andus Ravenwood had ordered the shutters closed to accommodate his headache. He could swear there was tectonic activity taking place within his skull—continents of bone grinding together, throwing up interior mountain ranges that pierced his brain. And, Ravenwood knew, once Amet Pale arrived, not even the soothing dimness of the Council chamber would save his poor head from further eruptions to come. Not today, the day they were scheduled to vote on Pale's motion to declare war.

Pale had broached the issue a week ago, on the very day he had been disfigured by the assassin—the day they had learned that someone, most likely Emperor Mallioch of Yndor, had succeeded in capturing the last of the Chaldean Phrases of the Binding. Ravenwood had delayed the vote by one week, the maximum period allowed by the law when a minister chose to research an issue before putting it to vote. And what a week it had been ... Every time Ravenwood glanced up at the faces of his fellow ministers, he was painfully reminded of the turmoil the Council had suffered over the past few days.

Most disturbing, there were all the new faces—Seve Paxenay representing Finance, Lianna Holmaine for the Interior, and Jin Annard for Intelligence. In their first full meeting of the Council, Ravenood reflected glumly, fully half of the Ministers were new. Two weeks ago, Jame Kordor was the Minister of Finance; now he lay in his tomb, a victim of his own hand ... and Hazard's revelation that Kordor had for decades been a Gathon agent. Seven mornings ago, Landa Wells had been the Minister of the Interior; now she was missing—a fugitive from justice, Ravenwood supposed, since her long-time graft had been revealed by Hazard. Her Underminister, Tolbeck, had also been implicated in the corruption charges and had been found murdered, perhaps by a former benefactor who had feared Tolbeck would provide evidence for a criminal prosecution. The Council had been forced to confirm Lianna Holmaine as a hurried replacement.

The only familiar faces were Pale's grotesque version and Amet Thale's shrouded one . . . and they were late. Nothing Pale did surprised Ravenwood these days, but Thale never deviated from his obligations by a heartbeat or a hair. No matter. What was important was that Ravenwood could count on the wizard to oppose a vote for war. He had thought he had known that absolutely, after the talks they had conducted four days ago. But yesterday the army had intervened during the riot at the NAA. Such policing activities were no less than the army's obligation during periods of civil discord—the city guard was not equipped to deal with thousands of rioters at once. But Ravenwood wondered whether something else had occurred, whether Pale had somehow used the situation to his favor, opportunist that he was. And here were both the wizard and the general late—a further cause for worry.

If Thale remained safe, Ravenwood could count on Jin Annard and his own vote against war—three opposed. Even if the remainder of the Council were in favor, that left things at a deadlock . . . with Ravenwood's vote as prime minister breaking all ties. But if the general had somehow gotten to Thale . . . Ravenwood ground his teeth as he surveyed the room again. Lianna Holmaine, he thought—he could almost be sure of her. Always cautious as a tortoise during her career, he could not believe Holmaine's first vote as a minister would be in favor of war. If he was right, Ravenwood thought, Thale could go to hell if he'd sold himself to the general. There would still be at least three votes against.

When the door opened, Thale and the general walked in together. There was something about the wizard's posture that seemed off to Ravenwood—a hunch to the shoulders

that he had not seen before. The general walked just behind
Thale, as if ushering the man to his seat. And Ravenwood
knew he had his answer.

"Well, close the door and sit down," Ravenwood said to
Pale, working hard to keep the irritation out of his voice, "so
we can get on with this business of a vote."

The general glanced at his empty chair and shook his head
imperceptibly.

"I'm afraid there will be no vote today."

Ravenwood was not the only mouth to gape open.
"What—" He had been about to say "craziness," but he
stopped himself. Ravenwood realized that the stress was finally beginning to wear on even his decorum. "What are you
saying, Pale? You called for the vote yourself. Procedures
dictate we conduct it—or at least vote on tabling the motion
for some period of time."

The general licked his finger and idly rubbed a smudge
from his black lacquered breastplate.

"There will be no vote," he replied coolly, "because we
have no quorum."

"What *are* you going on about?" Lianna Holmaine interrupted. "We have more than a quorum, General. Each ministry is present and accounted for. Now explain yourself or
have a seat."

The general smiled. "I will explain myself gladly," he began. "There is no quorum because I have found evidence that
Mr. Ravenwood, like his predecessor, obtained his seat
through the help of rogue elements within the NAA, whom
Minister Thale has begun diligently purging."

The world spun on Ravenwood. Desperately, he reached
for the edge of the table, which seemed to be receding more
quickly than his hands could jump forth.

"Not only Ravenwood," Pale continued, "but all the top
officials in his ministry are implicated. And given Ravenwood's treasonous action, I'm afraid that this body cannot
recognize the authority of three new ministers, over whose
confirmations Ravenwood presided." Pale paused to make
eye contact with Holmaine, then Jin Annard, then Seve Pax-

enay. "This is not to say that you will not be confirmed *eventually*, but I'm afraid that in the present circumstances, further investigations will need to be conducted."

Somehow, Ravenwood found himself rising from his seat, trying to speak but doing nothing more than sputtering. How thoroughly Orbis Thale had sold himself had not been apparent until that moment. Ravenwood leaned over, wanted to reach across the table and throttle the wizard, but the table was too broad for that. Instead, his sweaty palms slipped outward against the polished wood, bringing his face inches from the table. He peered upward at Thale and something— the angle, some trick of the light—allowed him his first glimpse of the eyes beneath that cowl. Dark. Mournful. Hunted.

"It's not true," Ravenwood finally managed to say, and it was not. He knew that, Thale knew that, and the general himself knew it. But the truth did not matter. Amet Pale wanted his war and he had bought it, at the price of a single wizard.

"From this moment onward," Pale concluded, "this country will be governed by martial law, pending further investigations and trials. You, Mr. Ravenwood, are under arrest."

The footsteps sounded in unison as the soldiers marched in and led an ashen Ravenwood out of the chamber. The remaining ministers sat stock-still, all watching in horror, only too aware of Pale's implicit threat—that, subject to their good behavior, this could be their fate as well.

Amet Pale drew himself upright within his black lacquered armor as his disjointed features settled into a smile. At long last, it was the dawn of a new Chaldus, his Chaldus.

CHAPTER 15

Brandt Karrelian, child of the city, discovered quickly that building a raft was not as easy as he had supposed. Vines there were aplenty, and with a little patience the travelers' knives were able to cut through the tough stems. Vines were not nearly as pliant as rope, however, and Brandt soon began to fear that tying a simple knot would prove as difficult as building a horse out of leaves.

But before any knots could be tied, they needed something to tie them around. Although the Ulthorn was abundantly littered with fallen tree limbs, most of that wood was rotted. A branch as thick as Brandt's leg often weighed no more than a baby—and would break easily under a baby's weight. Had they Callom Pell's axe, procuring stout logs would have proved no problem, but Brandt had only his sword and he doubted that the light blade would prove equal to the task of felling one young tree, much less a dozen.

They would have had to abandon their plan if not for the recent tempest. The storm that had wrought so much havoc in western Chaldus had done its share of damage in the Ulthorn as well, capriciously blasting one stand of trees while leaving the adjacent forest untouched for a mile around. Brandt and Elena learned to look for the storm's work—trees shattered midtrunk, with the once-living wood twisted round as if by a giant's hand. There, they sometimes found a sturdy branch rent from its trunk, stout enough to withstand the pummeling of the rocks amid the Woodblood, yet light enough for them to carry to the river's edge. The work was tedious, slow, and exhausting, but one at a time they found the logs they needed and dragged them to the riverbank.

When they had collected fourteen of them, each a half-foot in diameter and five or six feet long, they decided it was time to begin assembling the raft. Using lengths of vine, they lashed each log to the next, laboring to tie knots that they hoped would withstand the savage currents. Construction took the better part of a day, and when they were done, the result looked less like a raft than a collection of wooden prisoners bound from head to foot.

"Perhaps," Brandt suggested, "we've erred on the side of caution."

"Would you rather take your chances on another dip in the river?" Imbress asked, laboring on yet another knot.

Brandt shook his head and bent over to help her.

Bound as it was, their bundle of logs had a disturbing tendency to flex and dip when they lifted up a corner. They were not certain whether that flexibility was bad, but ultimately they scavenged two longer tree limbs and cross-tied them to the bottom of the assemblage, adding lateral support. After only a short time more, they found two long, strong branches to use as steering poles, and then added a third for good measure.

Finally, they were ready to embark.

And they were also ready to sleep. Only a red sliver of the sun peeked above the treetops, and they were exhausted from their day's exertion. As they had searched the forest for what they needed, they had found some thorny, berry-bearing vines and some nuts, all of which they chanced eating, and a patch of green onions so strong that only that evening's hunger could convince them to try such pungent fare. Both Brandt and Elena had begun to realize that simply feeding themselves would prove more than challenge enough. Though the Ulthorn boasted birds and hares aplenty, neither Brandt nor Imbress had a bow, and without one, they were at an utter loss as to how to hunt anything.

Still hungry after an hour's scavenging, Brandt lay down in the tall grass for the night, damned if he would complain about hunger no matter how his stomach grumbled. A little thing like starvation was not going to cheat him of revenge, he vowed, and he tried to put the idea out of his mind.

Imbress's mood had turned equally grim as night began to fall. She had not said a word to Brandt in the last hour, and when she stretched out on the grass, she selected a spot several yards from his side.

But not half so far, though Imbress herself did not realize it, as the site she had chosen the night before.

After a full day's journey, Marwick had not stopped peering into the darkened canopy of the Ulthorn as if the Druzem might spring out at them at any moment. He had been apprehensive days ago upon first entering the Ulthorn, knowing its eerie reputation. Albeit older and darker than the sparse woods of southern Chaldus, the forest had at first lulled away his suspicions. Though gnarled and twisted, the ancient oaks and willows along Sorrowful Heart had possessed a sort of grandeur that he liked, and the excitement of chasing Madh and Hain—or their doppelgängers—had soon driven any real fear of the forest itself from his mind. Now, no matter how uneventful the day's ride had been, Marwick was not about to be fooled again. Let the Ulthorn smile as it may; he would remember the fangs such smiles concealed.

Even Callom Pell seemed more cautious than usual, leading them at a methodical pace. At the end of the day, he pronounced them to be eight or nine hours behind Madh.

"It's too far," he had explained when Marwick complained of the slower pace, "to drive the horses hard in hopes of overtaking them quickly. We'll succeed only in exhausting our own mounts and letting Madh slip away. Steady progress is our hope. If we can gain half an hour on them each day, we'll still overtake them a few days before they emerge from the forest."

But Marwick suspected another reason for Pell's deliberate progress, a reason tied to the gruff woodsman's single-minded concentration on the path ahead. Pell feared more false trails, more traps. And more than anyone else alive,

Callom Pell understood how lucky they were to have escaped the Ulthorn's clutches once. Such luck could not hold. His deep-set brown eyes never ceased scanning the forest, as if they could bore through the very trees. It was not long before such vigilance spread to the rest of the party. Though they traveled far before night fell and experienced no dangers at all, they did so without joy in the accomplishment. Each wondered when the Ulthorn would strike again.

After setting camp, Callom Pell instructed them to gather firewood for the night.

"Is a fire wise?" Roland asked. "It might give away our position."

"You think like a soldier," the woodsman replied, seeming to smile ever so slightly behind his voluminous beard. "Aside from Madh and Hain, who are miles ahead of us, there are no men to fear in this forest. But there are other things . . . and those things can probably smell our horses with ease. The fire may scare some of them off, letting them know that the horses are defended. There will be no easy meals here."

And then Pell set that night's watch, reserving the difficult, next-to-last watch for himself. Quietly, they ate their biscuits and cheese and dried meat, clustered around the fire, sweating from the heat but glad for the light.

"What can we expect on the trail ahead?" Roland asked, finally breaking the long silence. "You should know the Ulthorn as well as anyone alive."

"I suppose I do," Pell said simply. "I've read every traveler's diary and journal I've been able to find in order to learn more about this forest. I've tramped far and wide to talk to old men who've braved it and I've writ down their stories so they won't be lost. I've all but memorized my family's accounts of the forest—and my family is very old . . . and was once very large."

The woodsman paused to sip water from a skin.

"What you have to remember," he continued, pausing to stir the fire to a new height, ignoring the hot ashes that settled on his forearm, "is that all the stories and journals come from the men who *survived*. And that means their journeys were often the easy ones. Now, when you find the occasional lone survivor of a large expedition . . . those are the interesting stories . . ."

Callom Pell's deep brown eyes had taken a faraway look, as if he were somehow watching the scenes he had once read.

"And?" Calador prompted.

Pell's eyes flicked toward the soldier, registering an odd combination of humor and caution.

"Won't be happy," the forester asked, "without a list? So many bears, brown; so many bears, black; so many cougars and so many dragons."

At that last word, the blood drained from Marwick's face.

"There hasn't been a dragon sighting in the Ulthorn for ages," Miranda said quietly as she sipped her tea. She thought she liked this odd woodsman—after all, she liked anyone who respected the old things . . . among which she had lately begun to categorize herself; she was accumulating too many years, she thought, to spend her time pitching Fool's Fire at monsters. But she thought it slightly mean of Pell to be frightening Marwick with talk of dragons.

"Aliucius Pell claimed he saw one in the twenty-eighth year of the Republic," the woodsman countered. "Not so long ago at all, as dragons reckon time. But that sighting was much farther to the north. No, I do not think we will find any dragons."

Pell drained his cup and sighed. "What awaits us on Beauty's Tress? With a little luck, nothing more than Madh and Hain—and they may already be too much. This trail was originally cut because it skirts to the south of the worst areas, of Ulthorn Deep, which begins properly across the banks of the Woodblood."

"But we're only a few miles from the Woodblood," Marwick observed. "And being south of the river certainly didn't deter the Druzem from napping there for a few centuries."

"True enough," Pell allowed. He plucked a smoldering stick from the edge of the fire and began to scrape lines in the ground. "But here's Beauty's Tress, bowing gently to the south, and here the Woodblood arcs to the north. For a time, the river will run almost a hundred miles from the trail before it begins to bend southwest, back toward Beauty's Tress and back toward its mingling with the Cirran. Where the two rivers meet, they form a broad delta. Excepting flood seasons, that's easily forded. At least, so the old journals say. That's where Beauty's Tress once crossed the Cirran before making its final, brief run to the edge of the Jackalsmaw Plateau. But the delta . . . the delta has always proved dangerous."

"Dangerous? How so?" Marwick asked. But even as the question slid from his tongue, he was not entirely sure he would relish the answer.

"Few men have gone there and returned," Callom Pell explained. "Of the few who passed, there are only vague accounts . . . tales of being stalked, of their companions disappearing without a scream, without a trace. Consider the journal of Syndath Neem, a rug merchant who lived ninety years after the Binding. It was a time when Chaldus and Yndor had been skirmishing—one of the many times—and as usual, the borders had been closed to trade. So Syndath Neem loaded twenty carts with his finest rugs and hired thirty mercenaries as an escort. They fought off bears and cougars and even a griffin as they followed Beauty's Tress toward the delta. Once there, the men began to disappear one by one. Now, these were men walking in plain sight of one another—and just vanished. Even Syndath Neem himself disappeared. One of the mercenaries finished the journal—and somehow finished the journey by himself." Pell laughed—a quick, ironic bark. "Became a rich man. But the confluence of the rivers has acquired the reputation of the most evil spot in the forest."

"And we are headed for it?" Roland asked.

Callom Pell shrugged his broad shoulders. "We are headed wherever Madh is headed. After men began disappearing near the delta, another trail was cut. That spur skirts far to the south of the delta, taking a long detour toward the southernmost tip of the plateau. It made a more sensible route, anyway . . . that is, for anyone not headed directly toward the heart of Yndor."

Roland nodded, pondering this information. "Madh could reach Yndor most quickly by crossing the delta?"

Pell nodded. "It would save him four, perhaps five days."

The old warrior sighed and drew forth his own sword, reaching for the whetstone in his bags.

"I fear, Callom Pell, that you will soon pierce one of the great mysteries of your library. I only hope we all live to read what you write about it."

The raft floated slowly toward the middle of the river, where a faster current embraced it, bearing it swiftly to the west. From the side of the raft on which he carefully perched, Brandt lowered his pole into the water until only his hands remained visible. The current dragged the pole backward, making it difficult to probe for the river's bottom, but Brandt had the impression that, even had the water been still, he would have been unable to find the riverbed beneath.

Elena Imbress watched his efforts, frowning when Brandt finally lifted the long staff from the water and shook his head.

"Let's just hope we don't fall in," Brandt said.

Imbress turned her gaze toward the prospect before them. The banks were growing narrower and the current steadily deeper. Every now and again, usually close to a bank, the crown of a boulder would peep above the water like a whale breaching the surface for air.

"Let's just hope we don't have to steer this thing," she replied as they passed one of the submerged rocks.

Brandt nodded, laying his pole across the middle of the raft, where it was least likely to fall overboard. After a moment's thought, he realized that the pole was not all that was at risk, and he shifted himself toward the center of the raft until his shoulder all but brushed Imbress's. On the whole, though, their improvised craft felt sturdier than he had expected. Those two cross-beams had helped, he supposed, by tying everything together. Otherwise, the individual logs would probably be rising and falling in series beneath them as they passed over each eddy and swell of the Woodblood.

More, he suspected that those crossbeams were acting as rudders, keeping the raft from spinning around in the current.

"I guess all we need do now is relax," he said.

Elena snorted, unconvinced that she would ever relax while they remained in the forest.

"And what do we do," she asked, "when we want to get out of this river, if our poles are too short to touch the bottom?"

Brandt shrugged. "I guess we just wait until the water gets wider and shallower. And meanwhile count every mile as a blessing. We'll have overtaken Hain in no time."

Imbress turned to study Brandt, her green eyes narrowing as she pondered what he'd said.

Hain.

Brandt seemed unaware that he had said anything unusual. He was shifting about on the rough bark of the logs, searching for a remotely comfortable posture.

"We agreed to cooperate," Imbress said softly, working hard to keep the edge out of her voice. "I want to propose a deal."

A deal? Brandt sat up, turning for a better look at the agent. He thought they had already negotiated a deal yesterday, before building the bloody raft.

She would be pretty enough company, he decided, if she could only manage to shut up. But every time that mouth of hers opened, a new problem flew out. "Cooperation," to anyone who worked in Intelligence, seemed to mean, I tell you what to do and you do it.

Between Elena Imbress and the river, Brandt was not sure which was most overbearing.

"What sort of deal?" he sighed.

"You understand the danger to Chaldus should Madh succeed, no matter how you pretend that it's not your concern. It will be *everyone's* concern," she insisted. "You don't suppose Mallioch will leave Chaldean tycoons to their wealth when he overruns us, do you? Whatever comes, you will suffer with everyone else. And your friend will suffer as well."

Brandt closed his eyes. It was painfully clear where this was headed and it was a waste of Imbress's time. Patriotic appeals were not likely to sway the one person who knew more dirty secrets about Chaldean government than any other man alive.

"If you're about to start humming the national anthem—" Brandt began.

"All I ask," Imbress said, cutting him off, "is that you help me stop Madh. No matter what happens, our first priority is to capture or kill him."

Brandt tossed his head back and laughed. In her awkward way, Imbress could be genuinely funny.

"You call that a deal?" he asked with disbelief. "It's a good thing the Council Tower has a monopoly on Chaldean government, Agent Imbress . . . because, let me tell you, you wouldn't last a week in any real business."

Imbress's lips pressed together in a frown and she had to wait a moment before summoning the self-control to continue.

"The *deal*," she said, "is that after you help me with Madh, I will help you kill Hain. No matter what it takes, no matter how long. You have my word, Karrelian. If I have to take a leave of absence from the Ministry and spend five years with you tracking down the bastard, I will. Chances are, we'll find them together and this whole discussion will be moot. But in case they separate, Madh must be stopped *first*. Hain can wait. Your vengeance can wait. And I swear, if it does, I will then do everything in my power to help you."

The color had risen to her cheeks. As far as she was concerned, Brandt realized, this was no easy deal to make. She thought she was making a considerable self-sacrifice here . . . and that humorous consideration almost curled Brandt's lips.

"No deal," he said.

Imbress's green eyes flew open in shock and anger. "What?"

"No deal," Brandt repeated.

"Don't be coy, Karrelian," Elena warned. "I've given you my best offer."

"That's exactly the problem," he responded, suddenly grave. "I don't want your help. I don't want anybody's help. *Hain is wholly mine.*"

Imbress leaned back, covering her face with her hands. After a moment, she ran her fingers through her hair and shook her head, as if awakening.

"Don't you have any loyalty?" she asked. "Even a speck of patriotism?"

Brandt laughed. "I'm loyal to Carn," he replied. "As for patriotism, not a speck. What has the government of Chaldus ever done for me—aside from an orphanage in Belfar where a child could be beaten on any excuse, and harshly enough that the streets seemed a safer place?"

Elena turned away from him, a bitter taste in her mouth. So Karrelian was one of those boys who'd had a sour childhood, and so remained a boy for life. As if the fool was the only boy ever to be whipped, as if that pain outweighed the pain of the world.

She said nothing more, and suddenly, the Woodblood seemed to Brandt very peaceful indeed.

CHAPTER 16

At first. Carn had tried to work out of Masya's little house on the outskirts of the city. Carn was used to doing business away from the nerve center of Karrelian Industries. Indeed, both he and Brandt had always worked out of the mansion, rather than using the offices reserved for them at the factory where the generators were assembled. Initially, Carn had assumed that it would be just as easy to have papers delivered to Masya's house as the mansion, so he'd seen no reason why there would be a problem.

Masya had seen the problem right away. Indeed, it would have taken a blind man to miss it—the towering piles of contracts and forecasts and reports that had threatened to displace the furniture in her small, two-room house. It had taken only hours for her to put her foot down and evict Carn for the duration of every working day. Besides, she had pointed out, the change of scenery would be good for him—it was unhealthy to spend his life cooped up in a two-room house. So every morning the carriage arrived to bring him back to the mansion.

Today, however, no change of scenery would be good enough. Carn had been sitting at his office desk, staring at the same letter—an account of how labor shortages in the Ellenden Mountains were going to drive up the cost of copper wiring—without the least idea of what he should do about it or why he should care. His mind could not get past the news that Katham kept bringing in from much closer regions—news of suicides and murders and riots, each one of them the direct result of one of the damned black files whose distribution he'd orchestrated days ago. Somehow, he'd thought that publishing those files might bring some sort of justice, but if this was justice, Carn could not tell the difference from mere revenge. He had hoped for a fresh start and found, instead, only the start of fresh miseries.

Just this morning, Katham had brought the news from the final day of Andus Ravenwood's trial. It had been a quick affair—two days of evidence presented before a military tribunal, then a few hours of deliberation this morning. The result was that Andus Ravenwood's head would be decorating the end of a pike planted in front of Council Tower by dawn tomorrow. And somehow, Carn was certain that the responsibility for that could be traced by some tortuous trail back to his very own hands. A decent man's life he was somehow accountable for . . .

Baley cleared his throat in the doorway to catch Carn's attention. There was something almost offensive about the crisp lines of the man's uniform on a day like this, when the rest of the world seemed to be disintegrating all around them.

"Sorry to disturb, sir, but there's a visitor for you. An old man who says his name is Barr Vin . . . but I can swear I remember him, sir. I think I saw him here a week or two ago using a different name."

Barr Vin . . . Carn knew well enough who it must be, but he wondered what on earth the old Minister of Intelligence might want with him. He glanced down at where his lap blanket had slipped to the floor, leaving his useless legs visible as they leaned awkwardly on the wheelchair's footrests. Already, Carn thought, he could detect the first signs of atrophy. Before too long, his legs would look like a skeleton's.

Baley traced Carn's stare to the blanket puddled on the floor and lurched into motion. "Sorry, sir. I didn't realize . . ."

Grimacing, Carn leaned over and hooked the blanket with one finger. Baley stopped in midstride, then resumed the upright posture of a servant awaiting a command. Carn sighed. He wanted to see no one, but it would be unwise to turn this particular visitor away.

"Send him to the library," Carn muttered wearily as he began to wheel himself in that direction.

*   *   *

Barr Aston was wearing simple clothing and a broad-rimmed hat that all but concealed his face in shadows. He could have walked the streets of Prandis all day and not been known for anything other than a poor old pensioner. But when he removed the hat and bowed in Carn's direction, there were those eyes—like gems against the plain setting of his sere, weathered face.

"I've come to see how you fare, Master Eliando," Aston began, his tone cordial but guarded. "Well, I presume?"

"Well enough," Carn replied somewhat sourly. "You needn't have come on my account. I'll manage as I always have."

Outwardly, the former spymaster smiled, but in his mind— the only place he could ever express himself fully—Barr Aston sighed. Carn was defensive about his crippling. A pity. The man was really too bright to wallow in self-pity, and Aston especially hated to see it in someone who had been hurt on his own behalf. More to the point, no one had time for self-pity these days: neither Carn Eliando nor Barr Aston, both of whom had seen their hopes for a peaceful retirement shattered in one stroke.

But Carn would remain useless as long as he insisted on dwelling on his crippled legs. The very fact that the man had tracked him down in the Atahr Vin bespoke Carn's resourcefulness and persistence. Aston suspected he might have use of those traits in the future, but now, when Carn spoke, he did not bother to meet Aston's eyes.

"I'm sure you will manage," Aston replied pleasantly. "But it is a lot of responsibility, running Karrelian's empire while he's off to play."

Aston was rewarded by the momentary confusion that registered on Carn's face as he realized that Aston's first comment was not directed toward the crippling, but the daily rounds of business. *Good*, Aston thought. Let him see how he has become obsessed with his own grief. A necessary first step.

"How did you know I was running things," Carn finally said, "or that Brandt is away?"

Aston chuckled. "Let's just say there are some jobs you can never retire from *fully*. Which is my other reason for coming. I'm curious about . . . shall we say, the change in management policy since Karrelian left."

Carn's eyes angled upward, looking for some hint of what the old spymaster was getting at, but Aston's pursed lips revealed no trace of his thoughts.

"What do you mean?" Carn asked, the question sounding more curt than he'd intended.

Aston shrugged, as if the answer were obvious. "Karrelian hoarded his secrets, milking them like cows for years. You, on the other hand, have managed to bring down a government in little more than a week."

"*I* haven't brought—" Carn paused, regaining his composure, and regarded Aston anew. Clearly, the old minister knew everything there was to know about Carn's part in releasing the files. There was no profit in trying to fool him.

"The files I released never said a word about Ravenwood," Carn continued quietly. "He was innocent. At least, he was innocent as far as I know. But what was I to do? Wheel myself up to a military tribunal and introduce myself as a spy? My head would be keeping Ravenwood's company on a pike's point tomorrow, with nothing gained."

Aston absently adjusted the brim of his hat. "You're right, of course. Right about Ravenwood's innocence and right about not getting involved. Pale has been conducting a show trial, not a search for truth. And anyone getting in the general's way would have found himself dragged before a similar tribunal as an accomplice—if not killed outright in some quiet manner. But I haven't come here to argue about Ravenwood's sentence or even about why you did what you did. We can't change that now. For whatever reasons, you published your files—some of them, at any rate. And a lot of people got what they had coming. Others got *more* than what they had coming. And plenty of innocents have suffered things they never deserved."

Carn wanted to protest, but Aston was speaking the simple truth. His fingers fretted at the edge of his lap blanket, but he said nothing.

"The reason I'm here," the old man went on, "is to ask you a simple question. Now that you've brought down the government, what do you intend to do next?"

Carn ran a hand through his curly gray hair, wondering whether everyone would have been better off if Aston's aim had been sharper—if that statue in the Atahr Vin had broken his skull instead of his back.

"I don't intend anything," Carn sighed. "I never intended anything. I certainly didn't mean to cause this mess. And there are no more files to release, if that's what you mean. All the others have been destroyed."

Aston's left eyebrow arched upward with interest. "Is that so? Well, you may not have meant to cause any of this mess, but like it or not, you did. So my advice is, you'd better *start* meaning to do something, before you cause something even worse. Powerful people, Master Eliando, require a good deal more foresight in their actions."

Carn laughed bitterly. "You've come to the wrong place if you're looking for powerful people."

Aston took a step forward and, before Carn could react, snatched away the blanket that had covered his legs.

"Pity yourself if you want," the old minister snapped, "but don't fool yourself. Pale has been able to get away with this much only because no one has raised a serious protest. He's been feeding the common folk enough demagogic nonsense— like this Ravenwood thing—that they see the military as the only institution they can trust. For the time being, at least, he's safe on that front. But just as important, he's been quietly telling every major industrial leader in Prandis that the moneyed elite have nothing to fear from him. The last thing he wants is a worried merchant class organizing dissent."

Carn's brow furrowed, but he said nothing.

"But he hasn't come round to talk to you yet, has he?" Aston asked. "Karrelian's holdings are as large as any in

Prandis—and at least as strategic. Why do you think you haven't heard a word?"

Now Carn smiled slightly, waving his hand as if brushing away an idle problem.

"You're thinking of our steel mines in Desh? I have few worries there."

The statement took Aston by surprise—and it was a very pleasant surprise. It seemed that Master Eliando was not entirely absorbed in his own tragedy. He had somehow heard or guessed at Pale's program to equip three crack divisions with the best weaponry available.

"Pale means to have that steel," Aston said quietly. "I have no doubts of it."

"Perhaps so," Carn allowed. "But is he prepared to meet our price?"

"Are you familiar with our laws regarding eminent domain?" Aston replied.

"Naturally," Carn replied. "As familiar as you are with the simple fact that Desh lies beyond the boundaries of the Republic, in the northern territories. Whether or not Brandt and I are Chaldean citizens, those mines cannot legally be seized by the government."

Aston nodded with some gratification. Carn, it seemed, was warming to the game.

"The rule of law," the old man said regretfully, "is the first casualty of war. For proof of that, simply think of poor Ravenwood."

The last thing Carn wanted, he reflected, was to think of Ravenwood. In his mind's eye, it was all too easy to imagine the headsman's axe whistling down . . .

"We've taken precautions," Carn answered, forcing himself to concentrate on Aston's meandering train of thought. "The mines have been prepared for . . . let's say, for an abrupt closure should any sign of Chaldean troops appear."

The old spymaster nodded. "A wise precaution. Speaking of precautions, you may be curious to know that General Pale has announced that he will form a tribunal of three citizens—business leaders, of course—to serve as a type of ombudsmen, adjudicating complaints about the way his martial law is being administered. He knows, you see, that he can wage his war only by the sufferance of the people, so he's going to extremes to reassure them that he is their man."

Talking with Aston, Carn decided, was the verbal equivalent of whiplash. He could never quite put together the connection between one sentence and the last.

"Why do you mention it?" he asked, genuinely puzzled.

Aston shrugged as he pulled his hat low over his eyes with a slight twisting motion.

"No reason," he said as he turned to leave. "In the meantime, you might want to spend some time considering, when General Pale comes calling for his steel, what price you intend to ask."

When Aston had disappeared from view, Carn slumped down in his wheelchair, closing his eyes. The old spymaster had been kind to come, kind to warn him. But he could see little more to do than what he had done already to protect the interests of his business. What nagged at him most, however, was the way Aston always seemed to be implying more, that Carn should somehow be working harder to protect the interests of his country. Wheeling himself back to his office seemed challenge enough.

How could Barr Aston ask him to carry the burdens of the nation when his legs could not even carry the burden of his own weight?

CHAPTER 17

Their second day on the Woodblood, Brandt and Imbress dragged their raft upon the northern bank two full hours before sunset. They cut the day's journey short not so much because of the broad shallows that made coming ashore easy, but because of hunger—the sharp, wracking hunger that Brandt had not felt since his Belfarian youth. All they had been able to find the night before was a blackberry patch half-strangled by a flowering fern that infested this part of the Ulthorn—pretty, with its four-petaled white flowers, but of absolutely no use in filling the gnawing hollows within them.

Searching until sunset, they found only a few nuts to share between them. The great overhanging canopy of the trees was so thick here that few things prospered in the shade of the forest floor save moss and ferns, bright red mushrooms, and coarse weeds. Half-starved, they returned to the bank of the river, discussing the possibility of roasting some roots they had found. The tubers were large enough to look nutritious, but neither Brandt nor Elena had seen their like before, and they determined to postpone gambles until they were truly desperate. Instead, Brandt found a long, narrow branch and began whittling its end to a point, suggesting that they try to spear a fish.

"No one catches fish with a pointed stick," Imbress scoffed.

Brandt glared at the agent, muttering something about cooperation, before he returned to his work, but the sun fell before the experiment could be made. They spent a few dark hours in their still darker thoughts, saying nothing to each other, before sleep finally claimed them.

The next morning, as Brandt awoke, he felt something soft and warm against his left hand.

"Imbress?" he muttered, wondering how cold she must have been during the night to move to his side.

But opening his eyes, he found only a fat, bloody hare.

Elena, hearing her name, arose from the grass a half-dozen yards away.

"What on earth . . . ?"

Brandt seized the hare by its long gray ears and held it up in the morning sun. It was still so warm, it must have been killed only moments earlier.

"This can't be your doing," he muttered.

Shaking her head, Imbress knelt by his side, examining the long, jagged tears in the rabbit's coat.

"A predator did this," she said slowly, still rubbing the sleep from her eyes, "but why on earth would it leave its kill here?"

Brandt lifted the hare a little higher, as if testing its weight.

"I have no idea," he concluded, "but I'm willing to entertain any guesses . . . just as soon as we get it cooking."

"I'm not sure I trust this," Elena muttered, looking at the hare suspiciously, but her reservations disappeared as soon as the aroma of the hare's roasting curled into the cool morning air.

An hour later, they set the raft into the current again, noting how the river kept veering somewhat north of west. They might be left with more of a southward trek than they had hoped, Brandt thought, but at the rate they were moving, they should still be able to beat Hain to the forest's edge. With a bellyful of rabbit, he felt more optimistic than he had for days past.

Stretching out along the edge of the raft—the river was peaceful here—Brandt closed his eyes and remembered the dream he'd had just before waking. Scarily enough, he had been dreaming about Imbress. The dream hadn't been sexual, and that almost disturbed Brandt more. Simple frustration he could understand; after all, the last few months had been dry enough that he wouldn't have been surprised to fantasize about anything with legs, whether two or four. Hell, another few months like the last and Callom Pell would start looking attractive . . .

But Brandt's dream had been weirder than that: he and Imbress sitting in a little park he knew near Council Tower, eating a picnic meal and laughing—laughing outrageously, beyond control, so that the food was spilling out of their mouths.

Brought on by the hunger, Brandt thought.

Every now and then, back in Prandis, Brandt would dream about Carn—perhaps a dream of their thieving days in Belfar, or their espionage in Prandis. Or sometimes he would dream of something that had never happened. He used to tell Carn his dreams and they would make joking attempts at interpretation.

Not that he considered telling Imbress his dream. Let her know his subconscious mind registered her existence at all? Far too humiliating to consider.

He opened his eyes and turned toward her. She was sitting cross-legged near the front of the raft, her face concealed by the lustrous red veil of her hair. She had washed her hair quickly that morning while the rabbit cooked. He suspected that she desperately wanted to bathe, but she was not about to do so in his presence. Nor he in hers. They got wet enough dragging the raft into and out of the Woodblood, and though their clothes were becoming overripe, neither of them would be the first to suggest a remedy.

If yesterday had been any indication, Brandt knew that Imbress would remain in that posture most of the day, face pointed determinedly downriver—not so much in search of hazards as focused upon whom she sought at the river's end. Really, Brandt mused, Imbress was more like him than he cared to admit. Committed. Driven.

But there was one difference he could not comprehend.

He had embarked upon this mad quest because Hain had crippled one of the very few people Brandt had cared about in his entire life. Thinking about that even fleetingly consumed him with rage, made his fingers twitch toward his sword. Back in Prandis, Brandt had considered himself invulnerable. Had Hain stolen a fortune from Brandt, there were ten other fortunes hidden away. Had Hain burned down a factory, Brandt owned plenty more. But his whole life long, Brandt had known only two men he could call true friends, even if one was infuriating company. Now Carn was crippled and the other one, for all Brandt knew, lay dead beneath the ruins of Happar's Folly.

Again, a surge of regret swept through him, that he had not been kinder to Marwick while he had been given the chance. But that had always been the way with him, hadn't it?

Brandt could not begin to comprehend Imbress's motives in all this. For all he could see, she had no personal stake in the matter. She was *hired help*, for god's sake. And yet here she was, risking her life simply because Taylor Ash told her so. As if Brandt's factory workers would put their lives on the line to boost production—absurd. Was it something about Ash? Did the man somehow command blind obedience? Brandt didn't think so. Elena Imbress acted as if something greater was at stake than her own career, than pleasing her boss. She was somehow *compelled* to do what she did. All her blather about war—even about the unlikely possibility that Yndor truly wanted to unmake the Binding—how could she become so worked up about it that her life, in the balance, was cheap? Yndor and Chaldus had fought a hundred wars before the Binding and a hundred more since. Wars were fought and soldiers died all the time. All the more reason to stay out of government and make enough money, if need be, to pay off the draft board.

The longer Brandt stared at Elena Imbress's back, the more an enigma it seemed.

*   *   *

He tried to nap, he counted boulders in the current, he stabbed his spear futilely at the few fish that swam nearby, but whatever he tried, the calm of the day and the incessant babble of the river were oppressive. Finally, Brandt leaned forward and abandoned his battle with curiosity.

"So what made you join the Ministry of Intelligence?" he asked.

Imbress's head jerked around, so surprised was she by Karrelian's sudden question. Given his utter contempt for her job, she could not imagine why he was interested. If the man was simply bored and sought idle chatter, Elena had no intention of providing him entertainment. And if he meant to make greater sport of her . . .

She fixed her eyes on him, expecting to find that juvenile trace of ridicule upon his lips, but Brandt was avoiding her gaze, staring studiously at the passing water. Whether he was making fun of her or not, Elena could think of nothing safer than the honest answer.

"If you must know, Karrelian," she said, her tone cold, "I joined the Ministry because the army takes no women, and because even if it did, I can be more productive at Intelligence than I would sitting along the banks of the Cirran, waiting for the Yndrians to decide they want another war. I joined the Ministry because, unlike you, I think most Chaldeans are decent, hardworking people. And I'm convinced that the Republic, screwed up as it is, still treats us better than an Yndrian monarchy would. Or a Gathon theocracy, for that matter."

Brandt cocked his head as if contemplating the matter.

"That explains why we might want *a* Ministry of Intelligence," he conceded. "That's what I pay such vast taxes for. But why would you want to work *for* it?"

"Do you really care, Karrelian?" Imbress asked, laughing.

Brandt said nothing. He simply sat where he was, staring at the changing facets of the water. There was no need to go on, Imbress thought.

But she did.

"I was raised in Athor, Karrelian, so I don't suppose that you're acquainted with the Imbresses. My father made a pretty fair amount of money trading cloth. There's more money in cloth than you'd think. Not *your* sort of money, but enough for my father to accumulate many things."

For a moment, the waters of the Woodblood mingled in Elena's mind with the River Pammon that ran behind her father's estate, gurgling in spring past the formal garden with its manicured shrubs and deserted gazebos, with its weather-stained statuary huddled like hermits amid thickets of myrtles and azaleas, a small girl's only friends.

"That's what my father did, Karrelian. He accumulated things. Houses, horses, carriages, a wife, two daughters, a half-dozen mistresses. Some bastards, I suppose. The wife died, so he accumulated another one. They both died, in fact, and by-and-by, so did he. I let my sister keep the things—hers is more the curator's temperament than mine—and I came to Prandis."

Brandt looked up from the river and was a little put off by the intensity of Imbress's expression. Was it bitterness?

"I don't understand," he said.

Imbress smiled sourly. "I didn't expect that you would."

Brandt dropped his eyes back to the water. Satisfied that the conversation was over, Imbress bent her attention once more to the west and was surprised to hear Brandt speak again.

"That deal you proposed?" he said quietly. "You'll get what you want. Madh first."

She turned back in surprise. She hadn't really thought Karrelian capable of surprising her. Not, at least, like this.

Perhaps, she thought, there was a speck of honor buried in the man after all. Or perhaps he just wanted to get into her pants and this was the only route he could imagine. Either way, Elena reflected, his help was indispensable. She would take it . . . and deal with the consequences as they arose.

"Then you have my word," she finally replied. "After Madh, Hain."

Brandt looked up and shook his head, and she thought that his eyes looked sad. For the second time that day, he surprised her.

"Madh first, but Hain is still mine. Alone."

Madh first. Hain behind him. had become the accepted riding order as the two men made their way through the Ulthorn forest. Beauty's Tress was sometimes wide enough that two men could ride abreast, but Madh and Hain never made the effort, having nothing to say to one another. Ultimately, Madh was the only one who knew this trail, so it made sense that he ride first, but that was not his reason. Ultimately, Madh had no wish to *see* Hain even a moment more than necessary. When Madh tried hard enough to ignore the assassin, he could almost believe he was riding along Beauty's Tress alone, as he had come to Chaldus months ago.

The only drawback, he reflected, was that he disliked leaving Hain behind him. Madh's intuition told him with great certainty that the assassin had never stared at anyone's back quite so long without itching to stab it. But he would resist the urge, Madh knew, for Hain was not only greedy; he was now scared. Of course, Hain hid away that fear, carefully rolling it into a crevice of his soul that was shrouded by sadism and an evil sense of humor. Only an eye as practiced as Madh's could discern Hain's well-disguised vulnerability. But there it was, hide it as Hain might try: the assassin feared this forest. He had seemed happy enough at first, but since two evenings ago, when they could hear the Druzem uprooting trees and demolishing the remains of Happar's Folly, Hain had understood that the Ulthorn contained creatures far beyond the power of his paltry blades.

And Hain did not know the half of it.

As he rode along, Madh's mind flew nimbly among the trees, brushing through the grass, sniffing hints of things long forgotten. Buried like the Druzem, tucked away in caves, covered by moss, sunken to the bottom of ponds, long slumbering but alive, the creatures of the ancient days clung to their faded existence. Without the greater magic of the time before the Binding, most would persist as they were now, pitiful shades, growing fainter with each century as they rotted into myth. But others, like the Druzem, retained a measure of their old power, needing only something to wake them—blood, or a spell cast too close, where they could snare it and feast.

Occasionally Madh reflected that the power to unleash all this horror lay within the gem that rested by his hip. At the thought, the little hairs on the backs of his hand would stand up, wary but excited. With the Phrases of Unbinding in Yndor's possession, Chaldus would have to yield before almost any demands. Even the merest chance that Yndor would unmake the Binding was a trump card that the House of Jurin—and Sardos—could play until the end of their days.

A small smile flickered at the edges of Madh's lips. It was all that he would allow himself to betray of his triumph, even though the assassin behind him could not see his face.

"Can't we move any faster?"

Madh sighed. He had explained this to the assassin every day, but Hain was not the sort of man to be happy when he was neither killing nor complaining.

"If we push the horses too hard now," Madh said wearily, "we will only lose time in the end. The quickest way through the Ulthorn is the steady way. And that is also the safest. If we maintain this pace, I can avoid the dangers ahead and outdistance those behind."

Frowning, Hain slapped the side of his mount with the long leather reins and quickly drew even with Madh.

"What do you mean, dangers behind?"

"Karrelian, perhaps, and the rest."

The assassin ground his teeth together before replying.

"I thought your pet back there was supposed to take care of them."

Madh shrugged. "Quite likely the Druzem did. At least, I presume the beast killed some of them. After these long centuries, his hunger was palpable miles away—for those with the wits to be looking. But Hazard and his friends are not witless, and more disturbing still, I felt the use of magic back at Happar's Folly. Hazard is no mage, nor is that tiresome spy who accompanies him. Therefore, someone new has entered the mix. After your last meeting with a mage, Hain, I should think that you wouldn't care to meet another."

Hain's scowl deepened as he recalled his encounter with Tarem Selod. "Why don't you send one of your disgusting little friends back there to see?"

The smile again flickered at the corner of Madh's mouth. If Hain so dislikes the homunculi, Madh thought, perhaps I should let them linger longer by my side when they return from their expeditions.

"The homunculi serve me best by scouting ahead," Madh said dryly, "or would you rather we stumble into one of the Druzem's distant cousins? As long as we keep riding, we are safe from the Chaldeans, even if they all survived the Druzem. My main purpose in luring them to Happar's Folly was to slow them down, and that was certainly accomplished."

Unable to find any answer for Madh save a curse, Hain let his horse slow down and drop behind the Yndrian. This slow pace was like torture to Hain, who wanted nothing more than to drive his mount into a lathered gallop.

He glanced to the side, through the broad leaves of the oaks, his sharp eyes detecting movement . . . but there was nothing there. Just this damned forest that went on and on forever, always watching him, always waiting.

Hain ground together his teeth and concentrated on the trail ahead of him. It would not be half so bad, he thought for the hundredth time—if they hadn't been forced to flee Belfar before he had been able to score more veridine.

*   *   *

Callom Pell squatted by the tracks for a moment, brushing his finger across the U-shaped curves that continued toward the west.

"Are we gaining?" Marwick asked hopefully.

Since Brandt's disappearance, the thief had lost much of the exuberant spirit that Callom Pell had come to expect. Marwick's humor came only sporadically now, and half-hearted even then. The Caladors had adopted him, in some small measure, trying to fill the hours with small talk. But they had not, it seemed, succeeded in distracting him. With Brandt gone, Marwick had grown quiet and more focused on the chase.

Pell brushed his fingers again along the marks of Madh's passage, wishing at least that he could answer Marwick's question. It would be a small comfort, but the only one that Pell could offer.

"I cannot say," the tracker finally sighed.

Marwick's shoulders slumped, as if the news amounted to defeat.

"A trail," Pell explained, "is not a clock, not a note left behind by the quarry, announcing, 'We passed here half an hour past dawn, if you please.' I look at a track to see how distinct the edges remain, how much the wind has smoothed and erased it. These tracks were left between seven and nine hours ago. Perhaps we have gained an hour on Madh, perhaps we have lost an hour. Perhaps we match him stride for stride. Be satisfied, Marwick, for that is all anyone can tell you."

Marwick turned back toward his horse, his eyes dark, but Miranda stopped him, saying his name softly. Much of that morning she had spent staring off into the sky, as if day-dreaming, or absorbing the woods. But now her attention had snapped back.

"I have information you may want," Miranda announced, although Marwick could not imagine what she might have to say. She had not even dismounted to examine the tracks like the rest of them. She had simply been sitting astride Karrelian's old horse, watching the clouds.

"I've found Karrelian and Imbress," she announced simply.

And that swung everyone's heads about.

"Or rather, I suppose I should say Mouse has found them. It's my fault that she didn't find them sooner. I told the owl to search the forest when it should have been searching the river. They've built a raft, it seems. They're already forty leagues downriver of us."

For a moment, Marwick just stood there, astonished. Then he blinked and ran his hands through his wiry, carrot-colored hair, as if just waking up.

"They're safe?" he asked.

"So far," the woman replied, watching a sigh that had built up over two days escape from Marwick's lips.

"Well," Marwick said to himself, "Mother always said, the uglier the weed, the harder it is to pull. And I guess she was right."

The thief swung back up into his saddle, his lopsided grin back on his lips for the first time in two days.

"Let's get back on the trail," he said.

But Callom Pell hesitated a moment before climbing aboard One-Eye's back.

"Perhaps," the woodsman suggested, "you can send this owl of yours in search of Madh. We might find out more accurately where he is."

But Miranda shook her head.

"I'm afraid not," she replied, not bothering to explain how dangerous such a task would be. A mage could recognize a witch's familiar in an instant . . . and do things quite terrible if the familiar were caught. But even that did not matter. Mouse had other, more important work to do.

"I can communicate with Mouse over a limited distance," Miranda explained. "When last I spoke with her, she was at the edge of that distance, and she asked me whether I wanted her to return or to follow those upon the river. I chose the latter. I may not hear from Mouse again for days."

Callom Pell nodded and they pushed the horses onward, in better temper than they had enjoyed since Happar's Folly, passing the endless oaks and willows, and Madh's ambiguous tracks.

The next morning, when Brandt and Imbress awoke, another freshly slaughtered hare awaited them.

CHAPTER 18

The sky above was blue and large, large in a way that Elena Imbress had forgotten. Ten days upon the Woodblood, ten days borne upon those dark waters beneath trees darker still, trees that conspired to choke the river beneath the great overhanging arcs of their limbs. Ten days of fighting the current with their feeble poles and arms, catching upon submerged rocks and crashing against boulders that reared above the surface. Ten days with only rare glimpses of the open sky, and those glimpses usually alerted them to a waterfall ahead. They would have to steer their way out of the Woodblood when they could hear the telltale cataracts before them. Pausing atop the edge of each cliff, the water roaring down alongside them, there was a moment each time when Elena could stare out at the vast, verdant expanse of the Ulthorn's canopy, the forest conquered by the still vaster sky above. And then there came an hour or two of back-breaking labor, dragging their makeshift raft down to the lower banks where they were swallowed by the trees again.

But now, after ten days, the sky had returned.

Day by day, the Woodblood would receive tributaries—creeks and streams that surrendered to the small river, merging in the common dash toward the Cirran. With each tributary, the Woodblood had grown wider and the forest had receded a little farther from its banks. And with every yard the forest retreated, Brandt and Elena had breathed more easily. They mistrusted the Ulthorn, from which twice they had been surprised by *things* springing out at them. Once a bear, or so it had seemed, but for its greater size and its dark, malign eyes. The second time, five days ago, it had been something worse yet: something large and gray that charged from between the trees on four legs, sending great gouts of water spraying into the air as it breached the current, two ravenous mouths gnashing at them as the river swept them by.

Since that day, they had slept on the water, waiting for a gentle stretch of river where they could lash their raft to a rock or fallen tree that lay midstream. Whether that strategy had saved their lives, they would never be able to say. The only thing it changed for certain was the state of their necks and backs, as they woke each morning more sore and creaky than the day before. But each day they found another mysterious, providential meal lying between them. They would go to the shore only long enough to prepare their breakfast, saving what they could for a cold lunch or dinner upon the raft. Safety, they understood, came from speed, from moving quickly past the forest's dark banks before its residents were made aware of their presence. And speed meant not only safety. With each day, they derived the grim satisfaction that they had moved farther than Madh and Hain, that they had long ago overtaken them and would have plenty of time to find Beauty's Tress. Plenty of time to arrange their ambush.

The idea of lying in wait in the Ulthorn was troubling. Elena could not help but think that there would be other things, predators far worse than she, lying in wait for her.

But such fears skipped quickly past her that morning. The Woodblood had widened into a small delta, a quarter-mile in breadth, with dozens of channels splitting off and returning to its sides. The black oaks and willows had yielded their sovereignty to swamp grass and short, twisted shrubs. Here, the rivers and the sky ruled, and the Ulthorn could do nothing but shrink back, impotent. This morning, the river was almost pleasant.

In fact, Elena realized with a start as she sat cross-legged at the front of the raft, she had been humming. She glanced back quickly at Karrelian, surprised to find no waiting sneer, no jibe. Rather, the man lay on his back, his boots by his side as his feet hung over the edge of the raft, trailing in the river. He was looking up, as rapt by the broad blue sky and wispy cirrus overhead as she. Such a sky was a sight that neither had entirely expected to see again.

Relieved, Elena turned back toward the west. Really, she reflected, Karrelian had been perfectly civil for quite some time. Not friendly, exactly, and certainly not talkative. He remained as obsessed by his quest as she was by her own, but he felt keenly how he had gained a step on Hain, and that seemed to have taken some of the sharp edge from his tongue.

"I suppose we'll have to land soon," Elena said, half to herself.

Brandt rolled over and looked ahead. A foot-thick layer of cool mist hugged the Woodblood's surface, defying the sun to burn it off, although a haze of heat already shimmered in the distance. It was an odd sensation, the mist kissing his limbs, leaving wet traces of its presence, and the sun beating down like some jealous wife to wipe away the offending evidence. Weird that a sun so strong had not already burned off the thin cloak of fog, but everything about the Ulthorn was weird.

Because of the mist, Brandt could not see the Cirran in the distance, but he fancied that he could hear it, a hissing rush half-hidden beneath the Woodblood's amiable gurgle. The Cirran, he suspected, would make the Woodblood seem a tame stream by comparison—far too fast and treacherous for them to navigate on their battered raft. Besides, although he enjoyed the speed of traveling on the river, what they needed now was care. What would it profit them to move quickly on the Cirran if it sped them, unknowing, past Beauty's Tress? As soon as they could see the great river, it would be time to strike south on foot into the forest.

And best, Brandt thought, that he let nothing foolish happen until then. He had been so content to lie on his back and stare at the sky that he had not noticed the mist thickening. It was dense enough now that they could only see the water for a few yards around the raft. Beyond that, everything was lost beneath the foot-thick blanket. He pulled on his boots and reached for his pole, fearing that a rock would slide out of the mist at the last moment, requiring a spot of last-second steering.

But his hand never found what it sought, for just then, a rock did rise out of the mist.

A black rock, almost a quarter-mile wide, that split the Woodblood in two, upon which stood a fortress equally dark, as if hewn from the dead stone.

Beside him, Elena Imbress gasped.

Impossible, Brandt was thinking, that they had not seen it until now, when the thing was all but looming over them, a dark stone face disfigured by crooked arrow slits and jagged machicolations.

The mist was still only a foot deep . . .

But Brandt had no time for this puzzle. Something dark rose quietly from the river by his side, reaching out for the tattered remnants of his shirt, and suddenly he was dragged beneath the water.

Marwick had taken to looking at the tracks him-self, sliding down the flank of his horse to brush the imprinted dirt or mud with his blind fingertips. He scowled as he did this, never knowing what to make of the tracks. But this one evening, fourteen days into the Ulthorn forest, Callom Pell was glad for the thief's meddling.

As long as Marwick and the others were trying to decipher the traces of Madh's passage, they would not notice the dark turd that lay amid the trampled ferns a few yards to the north. As long and as thick as Pell's forearm, the mottled thing stared as balefully at Pell as a tombstone. Beside it, a small depression in the ground had collected a pool of that morning's rain. The size of a horse's head, none of the others would recognize the depression as an animal track.

Manticore, Pell thought.

He had never seen one and never wanted to. His ancestors had described them well enough, sketching the beasts and their tracks in the journals that neatly lined Pell's shelves. Yes, he thought, an encounter in a journal was close enough, as manticores went.

He checked that the others were still puzzling over Madh's trail before he allowed himself to glance again at the spoor. Partially decomposed by the rain, it was difficult to tell how old it was. Two days, he thought. Perhaps three. Pell swore softly to himself, cursing that none of his ancestors had demonstrated the courtesy to study a manticore's territorial range. Perhaps the creature was a dozen miles away by now. Perhaps it awaited them in the next thicket. All Callom Pell knew was that less than half an hour of twilight remained— he had planned to camp here before he'd seen the spoor— and that was not time enough to go far. It was nearing full darkness already, the moon low in the sky, a mere crescent that was too feeble to fight through the thick weave of the Ulthorn's foliage. But even with a full moon above, Callom Pell would not have dared press on. Two days ago, Madh had laid a false trail down a long-abandoned northern route, toward a part of the forest thick with bannacks—creatures that looked like grizzly bears, but that possessed cunning, evil minds. Pell had uncovered that ruse easily enough; there was no trail to the north that he would trust without checking it ten times. But under no circumstances dared they move at night and risk missing another of Madh's subterfuges. They had been drawing steadily closer to the Yndrian—five hours behind now, if his guess was right. Steady work and they would catch him yet.

If the manticore did not catch them all first.

Pell led them a mile farther into the forest, until all trace of the sun had disappeared beneath the horizon and they would have to set up camp by the bloody glow of the western sky. Then he set the watch for the night, sternly reminding everyone that their luck thus far was no substitute for proper vigilance.

And before he crawled beneath his blankets, silently he prayed.

*   *   *

The shriek woke them during Miranda's watch, sending the men tumbling from the blankets in their underclothes, scrambling for their weapons. Marwick, a knife in each hand, was spinning around, scanning the darkened forest for some monstrosity. Roland, his great mane of hair whipping about chaotically, moved instantly to Miranda's side, his great sword already bared. And it was there that he saw what Callom Pell already knew to expect.

Though his heart had leaped at the sudden awakening, even coming from a dead sleep, Callom Pell could recognize the shriek of an owl. It was a fairly small owl, Pell noted. But it had healthy lungs and it seemed more than a little agitated. The witch's familiar—and despite that, he'd barbecue the bird himself if it panicked them in the night again. It sat upon Miranda's right shoulder, its brown and gray wings still fully spread, as if to shield the pair from the prying eyes of Miranda's companions.

"What's going on?" Roland asked, though Miranda ignored her husband. The old warrior peered suspiciously at the strange colloquy between woman and bird, as if he were being cuckolded.

For a few moments more, Miranda and Mouse remained where they were, the two heads bent together in ineffable conversation. Finally, the owl tucked its wings to its side and nestled against the woman's neck, its round eyes blinking rapidly in the dim moonlight.

"Imbress and Karrelian are gone," Miranda announced quietly, looking at Marwick as she said it.

"What do you mean, gone?" the thief asked, clearly disturbed by the news. Since learning of Brandt's survival, he had assumed, with the certainty of prophecy, that they would meet again at the far side of the forest. Now . . .

"They disappeared," the woman replied. "There is no sign of them or their raft."

Marwick took a stumbling step backward, then sat heavily on the ground, his head in his hands. Roland slipped his

sword back into its sheath and knelt by the younger man.
Pell could see Marwick shaking his head, resisting whatever
words of false comfort Calador offered.

Certainly false comfort, Pell thought, for he suspected he
knew what had happened . . . or at least where it had happened.

"Does the owl say where they vanished?" the woodsman
asked, his brows knit in consternation.

Miranda shrugged. "Mouse is nocturnal," she said, though
she suspected the woodsman knew an owl's habits as well
or better than she. "Every day their raft would float ahead
and Mouse would catch them at night. All Mouse could say
was that the last time they had stopped, they were within half
a night's flight of the swift water, by which it means the
Cirran."

Callom Pell frowned, unhappy to have been right. The
confluence of the Woodblood and Cirran rivers. He thought
again of the journals—the mysterious disappearances, the
dark hunters that a few claimed they had glimpsed, the unexpected fogs that were sometimes said to billow through the
trees. Whatever lurked there, it had claimed Karrelian and
Imbress. And Pell had no doubt they were dead.

The woodsman glanced at Marwick. The thief looked
stricken, but there was nothing to be done about it. *Better
that the Druzem had killed Marwick's friend*, Pell thought.
Then Marwick would have grieved but once. That was the
Ulthorn, though, toying with you like a cat before it struck.

Beauty's Tress dipped ten miles below the rivers' junction.
Far enough, Pell hoped, that they would not discover what
fate had claimed Karrelian and Imbress. A few more days
would tell the tale. Pell thought of the journal he kept in the
oilskin pouch in his pack. He had been adding dozens of
pages in the past few days—meticulous details of the land,
the vegetation, the fauna—all scribed by firelight during his
late watches. Better, perhaps, to leave the journal here on
Beauty's Tress. If he survived this journey, he could reclaim
it on the return trip. If he did not, perhaps someone would
find it in the decades to come and bring it back to New Pell,

adding yet another mite to the Pell's long-stewarded hoard of knowledge.

A few more days, he decided. At least he could hope for a few more days.

"Two hours until first light," Pell announced gruffly as he turned and headed back toward his bedroll.

The rest of them followed him stiffly, as if already sleeping while they walked. But Pell was the only one of them to sleep again before dawn.

They rose quietly from their sweat•dampened bedrolls with the first glimmer of light—like vampires in reverse, beings who waited eagerly for the sun in order that they might move again. Little was said as they broke camp and slung their saddlebags over the haunches of their mounts. They ate cold breakfasts as they rode—hard biscuits and dried strips of salt beef so tough that it gave them another excuse for silence. Marwick looked in vain for the owl that had brought last night's bad news, but the creature had disappeared. Sleeping with the daybreak, he supposed. Marwick envied the bird; he doubted that he himself would ever be able to sleep again.

Callom Pell set a brisk rate, leading them at a trot along the dew-dampened twists of Beauty's Tress. As if, Marwick thought, a faster ride would shake their minds from the deaths of Brandt and Imbress.

But Callom Pell had already shaken his mind free of those deaths; there were other and more imminent deaths to consider if they didn't swiftly leave the manticore's territory—namely, their own. It was important that they not let the Ulthorn distract them, that they press on hard after Madh and Hain. And so Pell frowned beneath his prophetic beard when he saw Miranda draw her horse even with Marwick's roan.

"Don't despair," Pell overheard the witch whisper to Marwick. "Mouse knows only that your friend is *gone*—not dead—and I've sent her back to search. For all we know, they simply fled one of the Ulthorn's nasty inhabitants and, in the process, evaded Mouse as well."

Pell shook his head in disgust. What was the point in raising the thief's hopes? That the Ulthorn had spared Karrelian and Imbress at all after the Druzem's attack was a singular stroke of providence. That their luck could continue forever, Pell refused to believe. And, in the meantime, such talk only distracted the others from the real task at hand. If Marwick proceeded along Beauty's Tress looking for Brandt Karrelian, then he would *not* be looking for Madh . . . or any of the Ulthorn's other surprises. The farther they proceeded, the less Callom Pell knew the forest. Even here, he had only ventured once in his lifetime and, in such unfamiliar territory, the vigilance of the others was essential. But he said nothing, knowing that time alone would numb Marwick to his loss— and harsh words now might be worse than none at all.

"How did you come to know Brandt Karrelian anyway?" Miranda was asking. "I thought you had lived your whole life in Belfar."

Marwick opened his mouth to answer and then closed it as quickly again, his eyes narrowing suspiciously as he returned Miranda's gaze. But there was a kindness in her bright eyes that refuted any hint of snooping. Here was only a dignified lady trying to ease the pain of a fellow-traveler, and Marwick sighed uneasily, ashamed of his initial reaction.

"I suppose it doesn't matter anymore," he muttered. When Miranda said nothing in response, he quietly went on. "Brandt and I were brothers, you might say. Children of the streets of Belfar—he from a younger age than I. After my mother died, it was Brandt who showed me how to survive out there, saved me from the youth prisons they like to call orphanages. Never lose your first friend, my mother used to say, for he shall be your purest." Marwick sighed. "Only thing she ever said that really made sense, I suppose. For twelve years, I thought I had lost him—to Prandis and his empire of lights and motors. This, I thought, was my second chance . . ."

Miranda leaned toward the thief and smiled. "The Ulthorn

forest might swallow a thousand businessmen like Brandt Karrelian," she mused. "But I suspect Galatine Hazard will stick longer in its craw."

For a moment Marwick's eyes opened in surprise. It seemed everyone knew his friend's most closely guarded secret. But then he remembered that he was talking to a council minister's wife and few people were more likely to know such things than she.

After a moment more, he began to think about the meaning of her words, and then he, too, began to smile.

Shortly after noon. Callom Pell called a halt for lunch. He would have preferred another hour's travel or more, but the spring-fed pond by the side of the trail was too convenient to ignore. He vetoed a fire for fear the manticore was still nearby, though he only said that they had no time to cook. Roland grumbled about another meal of biscuits, cheese, and jerky, but Callom Pell supposed the warrior would rather chew on tough beef than have a manticore chew on him.

Pell was leaning by the noisily gurgling spring, refilling the water skins, when One-Eye whinnied nervously. Pell spun around toward the stallion—it was stamping its front hooves impatiently as it gazed toward a thin spot in the nearby foliage.

A very thin spot, Pell realized—too thin. The sort of patch that grows bare because too many branches for too many years have been broken off by large visitors to the pond. And judging by One-Eye's unease, Pell knew that another such visit was imminent. He cursed himself for his carelessness. They should have pressed on even if a catered feast had been left for them by the side of the spring; after all, if the pond was a convenient lunch spot for them, it would be equally convenient for the Ulthorn's darker residents.

"To the horses!" Pell called, trying to keep his voice low enough that it would not penetrate into the forest.

Marwick, however, mistook the urgency of the command

because of its low volume and began to wrap the large wedge of cheese that sat by his side. Pell snatched the thief's collar and dragged him to his feet, sending him stumbling toward Andus.

"Now!" Pell hissed through his beard as he pulled free One-Eye's tether and swung up upon the saddle.

The other horses were shuffling anxiously now and Pell's companions began to understand there was something wrong. Leaving food scattered about upon crumpled wax paper and overturned tins, they scrambled toward the horses. Only Roland, who saw Pell unhook the broad axe from his belt, bothered to keep an eye on the forest behind him. The old man retreated steadily toward his horse, drawing his enormous sword as he walked.

Pell could now hear the snapping twigs that heralded the approach of something from the south. They would have a scant head start on the beast. He wondered whether a horse could outrun a manticore in flight. It was not an issue that any of his ancestors had written about and thus, Pell concluded grimly, the answer was almost certainly no.

He glanced about. The clearing was no great place to make a stand, nor was the trail. They would be best off keeping to the thick of the forest where a manticore could not get at them from the air, where the close-growing trees might hamper its movement and allow them more safety from flanking attacks.

Pell had just begun to look for a likely route when the sparse foliage beyond the pond darkened with the silhouette of something huge. Young branches swept back, bearing their fan-shaped leaves like swinging doors and leaving the party face-to-face with the manticore.

As One-Eye shifted nervously beneath him, Pell's first impression was simply the immensity of the creature. Nine feet tall at the shoulder and almost equally broad, the manticore was a dwarf in comparison to the Druzem . . . but at such close quarters the beast seemed huge. A great shag of mane hung around its lionish head, the maw of which was large enough to bite a man in half. Although most of the creature was still obscured by the bushes, Pell could make out the wings that were drawn up against its flanks and, farther still, the deadly foot-long spikes that adorned its tail.

The manticore lifted its tremendous paw and took another step into the clearing, its yellow eyes fixed on the pond. It did not seem to have noticed the humans yet. Somehow sensing this, everyone had frozen in place, holding their breath in their lungs as they watched the manticore advance.

The great nares of its monstrous black snout dilated as it lifted its shaggy head toward the remains of the meal that the party had left by the pond. For the first time, it seemed to understand that it was not alone. Taking another step into the clearing, the manticore turned its almond-shaped pupils toward the men and horses, and suddenly it roared.

The noise was monstrous and polyphonic, as if the voices of a thousand lions had been lifted at once in anger, many of them deep and rumbling, but others the high-pitched shriek of a banshee. Callom Pell swore he could feel his hair fluttering in the wind of that roar, but perhaps it was simply One-Eye who took a few skittish steps backward. Another horse would have reared and fled, its spirit broken, but the New Pell horses gave only a few feet before the manticore's fury.

When Pell had quieted One-Eye and brought his attention once more to bear on the monster, he found that the beast had fully entered the clearing near the pond. He had expected as much . . . and more. Such an unnerving roar was a natural weapon for taking enemies off guard: shake their concentration and then pounce for the kill. But the manticore kept its distance, its dull yellow eyes moving from man to man as if counting its opposition.

Callom Pell, too, used the time to study the enemy. Now that the entire manticore was inside the small clearing, it seemed even larger than before. But the beast's body was no longer obscured by the forest's leaves and shade, and Pell noticed things he had not expected to find. The tawny fur that covered the monster was not so thick as he had at first supposed. In many places, the golden fur had turned a sickly gray, and in a few spots, mange had bared the manticore's skin entirely. The thing's wings were sparsely feathered, more gray than white, and Pell suspected that it had been years—perhaps decades—since the manticore had possessed the strength to fly.

With sudden certainty, Callom Pell understood that this manticore was dying.

The creature took another tentative step into the clearing, to the very edge of the pond, keeping its eyes on Pell's axe, the blade of which was flashing in a stray beam of forest-filtered light. For a long moment, the humans and the manticore watched each other, no one moving, the only sounds the gurgling of the spring and the ragged breathing of the manticore as its great chest expanded and contracted.

Slowly, the creature lowered its massive head to the pond and its pink-brown tongue curled out, lapping at the water. It drank for several minutes, never turning its haunted eyes from the humans.

Not every creature of the Ulthorn, Callom Pell thought, *had withstood the centuries as well as the Druzem.* And suddenly, he understood why they had been able to travel so far, so quickly, with so little trouble. Pell had attributed their relative success to his own skills as a woodsman and, equally, to luck. Neither was negligible. But there was a third factor as well, one of equal importance.

The manticore had finished drinking and backed a step away from the pond. It looked at the mounted party, then back over its shoulder toward the forest path by which it had come. It turned back toward the party again and did not move.

"It's afraid to turn its back on us," Pell whispered incredulously. Now that it had watered itself, the manticore wanted to leave, but it did not trust the men behind it. That left them in an odd sort of standoff.

Slowly, Callom Pell backed One-Eye toward Beauty's Tress, signaling his companions to do likewise. When they had all but reached the trail, Pell wheeled One-Eye about and set the horse off to the west at a gallop. In only a few minutes, the manticore had been left long behind.

But not forgotten. As they continued their relentless pursuit of Madh that day, Callom Pell continued to think of the dying beast. How long it had been in such condition, he could not say. How much longer it could continue to survive was equally a mystery. Now that he thought about it, he realized that it had been three centuries since a Pell had recorded seeing a manticore in the forest. From what he remembered of that account, the manticore had been healthy. The absence of the beasts from the journals since then had spoken misleadingly to Pell. He had thought no one wrote of them because no one survived an encounter. But perhaps some manticores had died off and the few survivors shunned the dangerous company of men.

The manticores were remnants of a world of magic, a world before the Binding when a beast that weighed five tons could fly through the air and hunt men as easily as deer. Since the Binding, some of those creatures had hibernated like the Druzem, conserving their strength toward a distant day. Others, like the manticore, were apparently dwindling away. Perhaps, Callom thought, the day was not far off when Happar's dream would be realized, and the citizens of New Pell would settle by the banks of the Woodblood, the new masters of the Ulthorn.

But it would be an Ulthorn without manticores, without the dozens of strange beasts that his ancestors had so painstakingly studied. And so it would not be the Ulthorn at all.

Strangely, Callom Pell realized he felt sad.

Then he remembered the disappearance of Karrelian and Imbress. This forest was not yet a tame and defeated place. And Callom Pell remembered that a certain man named Madh was headed toward Yndor, bearing the Phrases that could unmake the Binding. Then the manticores and the Druzem and everything else could feast again. Pell thought for a moment of how the afternoon's encounter might have turned out had that been a healthy manticore in search of prey.

Beneath his beard, the woodsman's mouth set into a hard line as he rode on.

Carn stared listlessly at the mountain of folders that had been stacked neatly upon his desk. Since Aston's visit, those Deshi holdings had been weighing upon his mind—though why he would want to read all these reports, Carn could not say. As a limited partner in all of Brandt's enterprises, Carn had a vague idea of what those reports contained: a copy of the contract by which Brandt had purchased a vast tract of land from a prominent Deshi tribe; records of the ore extraction over the past decade; estimates of the mines' future productivity; reports on labor relations with the imported Chaldean miners (even if the wild Deshi would have labored for any man other than a Deshi chieftain, they never would have consented to work beneath the ground); and blueprints of the foundry that they had built thirty miles northeast of Prandis, where the valuable Deshi steel was purified and cast into parts for Brandt's expensive generators. Now, that plant lay within Chaldus proper and was subject to laws of eminent domain. Best, Carn determined, to begin shipping ore to the foundry only as demand dictated . . .

His head hurt even thinking about it.

Carn rolled backward from the desk, spun his chair around, and began wheeling himself toward the door. "Paxon!" he called.

Immediately, a neatly dressed young man appeared in the doorway. It had been Paxon who had brought the reports for Carn, Paxon who worked (like so many others) at the ceaseless task of preserving and augmenting the Karrelian fortune. And the Eliando fortune, for that matter. Carn forgot rather easily that he owned some thirty-odd percent of all Brandt's

businesses—actually, one hundred percent, if the contract
Brandt had left with the lawyers was to be believed, but Carn
intended to rescind that as soon as Brandt returned. Whether
thirty or a hundred percent, the money had not mattered to
him for years—ever since there had been too much to keep
in his own pockets. Accumulation had been Brandt's fetish,
not his own.

"Master Eliando?" Paxon asked.

"You may replace the files. I've seen them."

And, Carn thought, *I've no wish to read them.*

He ignored the look of astonishment on Paxon's face.

Was the throbbing in his head the pulse of a tumor? He
considered packing it in, heading back to Masya's, but it was
far too early in the afternoon. She was doing washing today
and he'd only get in her way. Or worse, she'd insist on knowing what was wrong, why he had come back so early. Staying
in the office until the end of the day—or at least, staying in
the mansion—maintained the illusion that all was well. Carn
smiled wryly. Ultimately, he knew that Masya knew that he
lived under some strange cloud of depression these days,
even if she did not understand why. That he was haunted by
that damned old Minister of Intelligence.

"I'll be going to my room for a spell. I have a headache.
See that I'm not disturbed."

Paxon did not so much nod as bow, bending ever so
slightly from the waist. Why was it that the staff seemed so
much more deferential, now that Brandt was gone?

"Certainly, Master Eliando."

Carn had had the rugs removed from the corridors
throughout the mansion. They impeded his wheelchair. Now,
he glided easily along the second floor by the balustrade that
overlooked the great atrium below. If he wished to descend
to the marble floor, he would have to call two of the servants
to carry him down the sweeping, curved stairs. A third would
follow them with the wheelchair. Three servants so that one
man might ascend or descend a simple flight of stairs. It was
ridiculous. If such a calamity had befallen him earlier, during
the days when he made his living on the streets of Belfar

and Prandis, he would have been dead already. Money, Carn thought, thwarted the ways of nature. And he was not sure that was such a good thing.

He had to push a little harder to force his chair onto the thick rug of his room. Carn had ordered the servants not to open the drapes—he had found that he liked retreating to the darkness, and he breathed more easily after he closed the door, plunging himself into shadow.

He considered for a moment the idea of his bed, perhaps a nap. But he was reluctant to sleep, to dream. In truth, he was not haunted so much by Barr Aston as by Andus Ravenwood. The day after Aston's visit, Carn had traveled into the city to witness the execution. What a crowd there'd been, the milling citizens of Prandis crowding in toward the elevated platform and the executioner's block. It had been one of the warmer days of spring and the tightly packed masses smelled something other than human, like some starving animal horde whipped into a frenzy.

He could no longer remember what Amet Pale had said, though he remembered the punctuating cheers of the crowd. From their vantage—atop the front stairs of a brownstone that the servants had commandeered so Carn, in his wheelchair, could see over the heads of the people—he had not been sure how to read Ravenwood's expression. Impassive, he liked to think, though he feared he would have seen otherwise if he had been closer, close enough to hear the axe bite into the wood beneath the prime minister's neck, rather than the strange, silent puppet show it had appeared in the distance. Better that he had left then, but Carn had insisted on seeing Ravenwood's face—a kind of perverse punishment, making himself confront up close what he had wrought. Long after the crowd dispersed, they had returned to Council Tower to see what remained. Amet Pale had not, after all, mounted Ravenwood's head from a pike. Pale, it turned out, somehow knew that the trickle of blood to the ground inevitably invited ants to the flesh. And for whatever cruel reason, Pale wanted to preserve Ravenwood's head as long as possible, to keep it recognizable, as a more powerful reminder—*here, this man who was clearly the prime minister, is dead for resisting me.* He had hung the head high above the entrance to Council Tower, where neither ants nor men could reach it, in a fine mesh sphere that protected the gruesome relic from the birds. The minister's eyes had been open . . .

It would be nice to lie down, at least, if not to sleep. Nice to get out of the chair, but he didn't want to call a servant to help him. From experience, he had found that he could wheel the chair to the side of the bed and, using only his arms, pull himself onto the mattress. The process resembled a desperate crawling, and it always pulled the blankets and sheets askew. Worse still, it was virtually impossible to make it from the bed back to the chair alone, and so he would have to call for a servant eventually.

Instead, he slumped down, letting his head loll over the polished wooden chair back, his eyes staring toward a ceiling lost in darkness. A soft sigh issued into the room's still air.

But the sigh had not been Carn's.

His head snapped to attention, his eyes searching the shadows. There was nothing—no, there was a faint silhouette in the far corner of the room, nestled against the heavy serge drapes. It seemed to be a tall man, and slender, but Carn could see nothing more.

With a quick thrust of his wheels, he backed his chair up, banging it into the wall. His hand groped along the plaster until it found the small switch that triggered the electric light.

Carn expected the usual flood of harsh, merciless light, but the bulbs in the wall sconces responded only with a fitful, yellowish glow. The bulbs buzzed angrily, as if they housed bees rather than slender wires.

"My apologies," a soft voice said. "I'm afraid my presence upsets your lamps."

As the yellow light sputtered through the room, Carn stared at the intruder. It was a man, it seemed, more than six feet tall but possessed of a delicate, almost feminine grace. His bald head was long and narrow, his features soft. He wore a white robe that fell to his ankles, beneath which Carn could see long, sandaled feet.

"Who are you?" Carn asked, his voice sounding more hoarse than he might have wished. As he waited for an answer, he let his hand slide down from the light switch toward the handle of the nearby door.

The man smiled gently, though his dark eyes seemed sad. "I am Atahr Vin."

The voice was rich and musical, and somehow oddly accented, as if speaking a foreign language.

Carn's hand hesitated by the doorknob.

"The Atahr Vin is a place, not a man."

The intruder's long, spidery fingers spread slowly, expressive, it seemed to Carn, of a shrug. There was something unnerving about the man's grace, he thought. To look at him was to be reminded all the more keenly of one's clumsiness, crippled or not.

"When the scholars first came to my home," the intruder said, his voice almost a song, "and translated the runes by my door, they assumed the words named the place. But the way of the Khrine is different. The words name the man."

Carn said nothing for a moment, stunned. This man implied that he was no man at all, but Khrine! And not any Khrine, but the owner of the strange, underground dwelling in which Carn had been crippled. The idea itself was absurd, but here stood this impossible man, his cheeks as smooth as porcelain, his dark eyes as deep as the well Carn had descended to find Barr Aston. A deep chill crept through his body, stopping only at his legs, where he could feel nothing at all.

"I thought—" The words hardly left his mouth. Carn coughed and tried again, but he was hardly less hoarse. "I thought the Khrine were dead."

"For the most part, we are," Atahr Vin replied, sounding sad yet not regretful. "Dead utterly or dead to the world. For centuries, there has been little difference. Those of us who survived the Devastation and the Binding retreated to our homes, to sleep the centuries away in our grief, to flee from the face of a world we had harmed so grievously. Occasionally, I have risen and walked unseen among men, observing what you have done with the world that we bequeathed to you. I suppose some of my fellows have done the same, although I have seen none in my brief, infrequent journeys. It is not surprising that the race of men thinks us dead. And I would be sleeping still in my cold, empty palace, if not for a group of trespassers."

Carn's fingers twitched against the doorknob. *He's come to kill me,* he thought, *for violating the sanctity of his bloody home.*

But Atahr Vin did not move from the corner as the sputtering yellow light played softly over his features.

"I watched from my chamber," the ancient Khrine said, "as I have watched everyone who visits my house. Not long ago came the man whom I had liked so much when he was a boy, and I could feel that he was running for his life. I was saddened by his danger, but I decided not to interfere. His life was almost used already, I thought, and it would be unwise to reveal myself, to uncover such a long-kept secret on his behalf. You came next, followed closely by the evil one."

Atahr Vin sighed again and momentarily closed his eyes, as if remembering something that Carn could not comprehend. "I could feel that there was no harm in you, and a gesture of mine might have turned aside the statue that broke your back. But Khrine meddling in human affairs brought on the Devastation and it was to avoid more such tragedies that we retired to our lonely homes. I did nothing but watch as the evil one tore his secret from the one I had known as a boy, and then I watched further when your friend arrived and saved your lives. He is confused, that one, like a lake beset by a storm, its surface so troubled that he cannot behold his own depths. But he loves you, and he fought away the evil one, and so I was glad of his coming."

Atahr Vin paused, soaking up Carn with his deep, unreadable eyes.

If this being can see so much about Brandt in a few moments, what does he know about me?

The thought made his hands tremble, tightly though they gripped the handles of his wheelchair.

"Why have you come?" Carn asked, his voice barely audible.

Atahr Vin smiled sadly and traced his finger along the soft surface of the drapes.

"For all our power, we are prone to err. That was the lesson of the Devastation. Now, after the Binding, our power is far less, but we are still prone to err. My belief that separation from the world would make it better was one such mistake. I have hidden myself away and that was mere cowardice. Many times over the centuries, I might have come forward and offered great aid to mankind, and yet I did not. One afternoon, not so very long ago, without even revealing myself, I might have disposed of a supremely evil man who had been foolish enough to place himself within the very palm of my power. And yet I let him work his evil and walk away. I see my error. I see the pain I have caused you. And," Atahr Vin concluded, "I have come to make amends."

To make amends. With those words, all other thoughts fled Carn's mind. The Khrine had come to make him whole.

"My legs," he said, pushing the wheelchair with one urgent thrust toward the middle of the room.

But Atahr Vin shook his head.

"I am sorry, my friend. I cannot heal you, if that is what you think. Parts of your body are dead now, and even before the Binding, the Khrine could not make the dead live. Your legs will remain as they are."

The Khrine's words struck Carn as heavily as the statue had, and Carn's arms fell limp to his side.

"There is nothing else," he whispered.

Smiling sadly, the Khrine shook his head again. "There are two things that I can give you. The first, I am almost ashamed to offer. It is no replacement for what I have taken away, but it is an ancient token of esteem, of a sort we Khrine sometimes gave to a close human friend. It is a ring. Most of them were destroyed, along with their owners, in the Devastation."

And then, suddenly, Carn felt something cold in his hand. He looked down and found a simple stone band in his palm—seemingly made of the same yellow rock from which Atahr Vin had created his home. Like most things Khrine, it seemed to be entirely unadorned.

"It is but a small thing," Atahr Vin explained, sounding embarrassed. "A small thing that loves the truth."

The Khrine sighed again. When he began once more to speak, his voice was soft and worn, like a stone worn down by millennia's storms.

"I can offer you nothing else save a few words, Master Eliando. In my grief, I shut myself away for centuries while I might have done good. You are a man, Master Eliando. You do not have centuries to waste in mourning. I pray you, do not follow my poor example."

And without warning, Atahr Vin disappeared, leaving nothing in his wake but a faint breeze and the ring that still lay in Carn's palm.

The lights immediately burst forth into their customary brilliance.

"Don't go," Carn said, his voice choking at the base of his throat, but he was alone again. He sat limp in the chair, awash in light as his mind wandered vaguely for longer than he could tell. And then, finally, he noticed a leather-bound book that lay upon his bed. He remembered leaving nothing there. His eyes narrowed as he scanned the title.

It was the same volume that he had committed to the fire only last week.

Slowly, he placed his hands upon the plush, upholstered armrests of the chair and pushed himself upright.

"Paxon!" he bellowed. "Katham! Where are you, you slackers, when there's work to be done?"

CHAPTER 20

Being returned reluctantly, by a dark and circuitous path. The distant knowledge of a fingertip. A breath of air whispering across the brow, cold as stone. A tingle spreading over the inside of a thigh. And by and by, Elena Imbress came to know once again that she *was*, that once more the Woodblood had failed to claim her.

But something had claimed her, for she lay on her side in the midst of a great darkness—a blackness so complete that she could not say whether walls lay inches from her hands or miles away. Feeling disembodied, she lifted a hand to her face, seeing nothing, and when her fingers brushed across her cheek, they felt like a stranger's.

She pushed herself to a sitting position, feeling the cold, even texture of finished stone beneath her palm. She was indoors—that much was certain. And judging by the way the sound of her breathing returned to her, as a delayed, hollowed sibilance, she decided she must be in a fairly large chamber.

As if starved for sight, her mind replayed the last, chaotic images it had seen: skeletal figures rising amid gouts of water, striped black and white in crazy, intercrossed patterns; the raft capsizing; Karrelian drawing his sword; a hand scratching across her face before it found purchase in her hair and dragged her under.

Strangely, her clothes did not feel damp at all. She wondered how long she had been out.

"Karrelian?" she whispered, aware that, for once, she would be glad for his company.

Her question was greeted by a laugh that held all the warmth of an open coffin.

"You are concerned for your male?"

The voice was a knowing, leering rasp that filled Imbress with dismay. That voice, she understood instantly, contained reservoirs of ageless cruelty that she had no wish to plumb.

And yet she would not seem so easily cowed.

"He's not *my* male," she answered, trying to invest the answer with the full measure of scorn that this particular question would ordinarily have yielded.

Again, the dry, mirthless cackle. Elena wished she could determine where it came from, but it seemed to fill the chamber, echoing within the unseen walls.

Her entire body felt sore, as if every limb weighed twice what it should, but she pushed herself to her feet, thinking that it was somehow important that she stand on her own.

Immediately, the bony back of a hand smashed across her cheek, knocking her back to the cold floor. She could taste the warm, salty trickle of blood within her mouth.

"I did not ask you to stand," the voice explained, sounding not the least bit angry, but cruelly amused.

He must have been standing right next to her, Elena thought, though she had heard nothing—not a breath, not the slightest hint of motion. She could not even smell him. It was as if the creature existed only when and where it willed.

Suddenly, there was light—a soft lambency that came from no particular source, but simply suffused the room. As Elena had guessed, the chamber was large, almost thirty feet square, carved it seemed out of black rock, with neither windows nor doors. But the room did not hold her interest; the creature above her did.

He was standing astride her, one foot on either side of her hips, staring down dispassionately with eyes eerily robbed of color. Although he was six feet tall, she could not imagine him weighing more than a hundred pounds, he seemed so skeletally thin. His only clothing consisted of black leather bands, an inch in width, that crossed his body haphazardly, covering most of him, but leaving hundreds of tiny patches of pale white skin exposed. Where the leather did cover him, it was wrapped so tightly that every rib, every cable of muscle was defined beneath. It was almost as if the black hide had become a part of his own, as if he were entirely naked, some bizarre black-and-white ghoul of a man leering down at her. The leather straps crossed once beneath the emaciated purple-black lips of his mouth, then rose diagonally across his cheek and brow, and covered parts of a hairless head.

Directly above her, Elena could see the tightly bound bulge of his genitals, and it was there that she aimed her kick—a blow hard enough to be paralyzing, had it found anything but air. With an unnatural grace, Elena's captor pirouetted over her leg, spinning nimbly in a full circle, the completion of which brought his foot sharply across her chin. Her head snapped to the left beneath an arc of bloody spittle. The entire room seemed to lurch on its axis, and it took her a moment to realize that the man had grabbed her by the shoulders and lifted her from the ground. It was ridiculous, she thought as she fought her head from lolling helplessly backward. She must outweigh this macabre scarecrow of a man by twenty pounds, and yet here she was, her feet dangling inches above the floor, as if she were the one who weighed nothing.

Where his nails bit into the flesh of her arms, her tattered sleeves darkened with blood. His pale eyes darted toward the stain, his nostrils dilating with excitement. Suddenly, he thrust his face into the auburn mass of her hair, his icy, purple lips coming to rest at the lobe of her ear.

"Yes," he whispered in a tone of sickening intimacy, "we shall enjoy you greatly before you are spent. Your fear is delicious and your death shall be a great rapture. Alas, we must await the new moon."

Elena shuddered and struggled in his grasp, desperate to escape, desperate somehow to find the Ulthorn again. But with nauseating certainty, she understood that no one escaped from this dungeon within the Woodblood River. She would die here, and worse yet, Madh would go free.

Her captor pressed his face closer to her own, so she could

feel against her cheek the lines that separated the black leather from his cold flesh.

"What's this?" he hissed with interest. "An Yndrian in the forest?"

Elena gasped. Somehow, he had plucked from her mind the very image of Madh.

"And others as well," he went on, pleased. "Ulthorn teems with guests these days. Better, then, the feast. Aemon Goeth will be pleased."

And suddenly Elena was released, crumpling to the ground as if every bone in her body had been rendered liquid. At the same moment, the light disappeared . . . and with it, perhaps, Elena's captor, gone to tell his news to this Aemon Goeth.

But it was many minutes before Elena Imbress dared again move.

Imbress had fallen asleep, but the flash of light woke her as surely as a trumpet blast. It came from behind her: the narrowing beam of a closing door that silhouetted a jumbled mass of forms. Then utter darkness again. But there was someone with her now—she could hear breathing. Quietly, she began to creep away from the direction of the door until she realized that, since she *could* hear breathing, the newcomer was not the same sort of eerily silent creature as her captor.

In fact, not silent at all.

"Damn!"

The softly spoken curse accompanied the sound of someone picking himself off the floor.

"Karrelian?" Elena asked, uncertain. "I thought they might have killed you."

"Sorry to disappoint you," Brandt laughed.

"That's not what I meant," she replied, scowling. "It's simply that the last I saw of you, you were drawing your sword . . ."

She heard him stand up and brush himself off.

"Funny thing about swords. They're remarkably difficult to use when you're underwater. I wasn't able to put up much of a struggle. I got a good knock on the head, though—good enough, I thought at first, to knock me blind."

"They aren't much for windows, are they?" Elena sighed. "Do you have any idea who—or *what*—they are?"

Brandt paused before answering. "I may. Did you get a look at the architecture here?"

Elena shook her head, then realized that Karrelian could not see her. "Not really, but what does the architecture have to do with anything?"

Brandt laughed. "It's somewhat distinctive. No windows, all stone—and no seams showing anywhere, as if the whole place was carved out of one large rock. High ceilings, simple square rooms. Reminds me a lot of the Atahr Vin."

A chill swept through Elena's body.

"You think we've been captured by *Khrine*?"

"I didn't say that. Khrine were supposed to be loners, I thought, but this place is crawling with them, whatever they are. Perhaps they're descendants. Or perhaps they're squatters in an old Khrine home. Or maybe they're just admirers of the style and built something like it. In any case, they don't seem entirely human. And they're definitely not friendly."

Elena sighed. She had hoped that Karrelian could offer more encouraging information than what she herself possessed.

"I think they plan to kill us during the next new moon," Elena said quietly.

"Nice of them to wait," Brandt observed. "That gives us nine or ten days. What for, I wonder. Skinny as they are, maybe they plan on eating us. It might take a week or so to fatten us up properly—"

"That's enough!" Elena said, interrupting Brandt sharply. "Sarcasm won't get us out of here."

Brandt laughed. "What will?"

For a long while, Elena was silent.

"Well, we might as well try to search this place, see if we can find anything."

For what seemed an interminable time, they crawled across the floor and traced the path of the walls, exploring every surface with their fingers. Three times, they bumped into each other, recoiling quickly and proceeding on their way. But they found nothing useful—not a seam or a crack in the stone, not even a hint of the door, although they knew more or less where they should find it. Save for themselves, the only thing in the chamber was a small wooden bucket, the use of which was obvious. They left it in a corner so it could be found more easily, then wandered about for a few minutes more before settling down onto the cold stone, across the room from each other.

They sat.

And after the first hour, when they realized fully that they were trapped in utter darkness, with nothing to see and nothing to hear and nothing to do, they began to wonder whether nine days' reprieve before the new moon was such a very good thing after all.

Almost. Madh thought. he had won. Another day or two and they would be out of the Ulthorn, into Yndor where Madh need fear nothing. The Chaldeans were still three or four hours behind, far enough, Madh knew, that they had no chance of catching up in the short distance remaining.

Almost, Madh thought, he had won . . . but not yet. Two things bothered him. First, as always, there was Hain. As the assassin's supply of veridine had run short and finally, two days ago, run out, Hain had grown withdrawn. In fact, this spared Madh the assassin's usual sarcastic banter, save an occasional irritable question. But the man's behavior was growing more erratic, and every night, Hain seemed to take greater pleasure in stalking and torturing whatever small things of the forest came near. And some things not so small. Two nights ago, Hain had slain a bannack—one of the malevolent bear-things that ruled much of Ulthorn—and eaten its heart. As if he meant to remind Madh of how dangerous he remained. Time and again, Madh debated whether it would be best simply to dispose of the assassin now. He had almost decided that the answer was yes.

The deciding factor was the second thing that gave pause to Madh's thoughts of victory: he had always hated this part of the forest, so close to the Cirran. Something, he knew, lived not far to the north—something active, powerful, and malevolent, for he had often felt its mind searching the forest for prey. On the trip west, Madh had closed his mind to such prying, hiding himself from any intelligence that sought to scour the woods for easy game; it was a trick of his, taught to him as a child. But he could hide himself, not Hain, and thus, in this area of the forest, Hain was doubly an encumbrance.

He would obscure himself, he decided, and at the first hint of the other's probings, he would slay Hain, projecting the image of a bannack. That should do.

Behind him, Hain shifted uneasily in his saddle.

"I don't like this," the assassin murmured, moving a hand to the hilt of his knife.

"This?" Madh replied, but as he shifted his attention from his reverie to the trail ahead, he understood immediately what Hain meant. Though nothing looked or sounded out of place, although nothing even presented itself to his keener arcane senses, there was, nevertheless, a distinct feeling of *wrongness*. He should send a homunculus to investigate, he thought, but there was only Sycorax, still in his saddlebag, recovering from Karrelian's cruelty. The others were already gone scouting . . . gone for a long while, he realized.

And then, abruptly, a dozen figures appeared amidst the foliage—skeletal blurs of black and white racing toward them, bearing long black staves that terminated in a curved blade on one end, a wicked fork on the other. As they came upon him, Madh reached swiftly into his pocket, retrieving a pouch and tearing at its drawstrings. Most of the gray powder spilled to the forest floor—certainly a shame, but there was no time to worry about waste when such needs pressed.

Madh rubbed the gray powder between his palms, feeling it warm to his touch as he began to chant.

Out of the corner of his eye, he could see Hain dismount, nimbly sliding back along the haunches of the horse. As the assassin reached the ground, he ran the edge of his blade across the horse's flank, spurring the beast into a mad charge that made their ambushers scatter ahead of them. *Such a contemptible man,* Madh thought, *but clever.*

Five or six of the men approached Hain again, more warily this time, their bladed staves spinning ominously before them. "Surrender," one of them said, his voice a gravelly command. Used to being obeyed, this one.

And Madh suddenly realized why. The black-and-white patches that he had at first taken for some ragged, motley clothing were no clothes at all. Rather, it was the effect created by a black leather band wound at crazy angles across emaciated bodies. *Like mummies wrapped by a blind man,* Madh thought. But these were no mummies. He recognized them now, for he had read about them once, although he never expected to see one alive. If they truly could be considered alive.

Nistashi.

The word rang like a bell in his mind, though his lips continued his ancient chant, and he kept rubbing the powder between his palms.

"Surrender," the leader repeated, but Hain only laughed. Of course, the assassin had no idea these were Nistashi—no idea, most likely, what a Nistashin was—but Madh suspected that Hain would have little cared had he known. This was the fight he had been spoiling for during the past weeks, ever since his last duel with Karrelian had been cut short in Belfar. The prospect of taking life was too strong, too alluring for Hain to control himself. Hain would not surrender, and most likely, Madh thought, the Nistashi would save Madh the trouble of eliminating the assassin himself. Almost a neat conclusion.

Hain launched his knife with deadly accuracy at the nearest of the Nistashi, drawing his sword as he did so. The knife struck at the center of the abdomen—a fatal blow, except for the ribbon of leather that crossed the Nistashin's body there. The man smiled as the knife bounced off the leather and fell harmlessly to the ground.

Hain's eyes widened, but only for an instant. Then he was crouched, ready for an attack.

Madh's mind, meanwhile, searched for what he had once known of the Nistashi. He had read something about those leather bands once: how Nistash Mar had fashioned them as armor for the final battle, how only certain rites could remove them, and only then in the dark of the new moon. The bands were supposed to be impregnable—and so they seemed—but they had their costs as well . . .

The first of the Nistashi sprang forward, a contemptuous smile upon his lips as he brought his staff around in a round-house blow at Hain's head. With speed the equal of the Nistashin's, Hain ducked beneath the blow and behind the man, swinging his own sword in an arc that should have severed the Nistashin's head. But the blade struck one of the innumerable black bands and rebounded harmlessly, shivering in Hain's hands.

Laughing, the Nistashin whirled about, leveling another blow at Hain's skull. The assassin parried the staff mere inches from his shaven head and exchanged a series of lightning-quick cuts and ripostes. Then, without warning, Hain let himself drop flat on his back, thrusting upward with his sword as he fell. This time, unerringly, Hain's sword found a tiny patch of exposed skin near the bottom of the Nistashin's stomach. The blade slid inward without protest, great gouts of black blood spurting to the ground.

A clever move, Madh thought, but Hain had been forced to expose himself in the process. Before he could regain his feet, the other Nistashi were upon him, pinning the assassin's limbs to the ground between the razor-edged blades of their forks.

At the same instant, the first Nistashin reached Madh, reaching a gaunt hand toward the unarmed Yndrian. But as his fingers closed around Madh's sleeve, the Nistashin's body erupted in orange flames. He fell first to his knees, then toppled to the forest floor, writhing in silent pain. In a moment more, his struggles ceased. Slowly, the flames guttered out, leaving only a blackened corpse, surrounded by leather bands that seemed entirely unharmed.

Madh smiled slightly as he continued to chant and rub his hands together; he suspected he had made his point. He wondered when was the last time two Nistashi had died on one day. Not, he suspected, since the Devastation itself, and three hundred had perished that day, it was told.

The leader of the group—the one who had spoken first to Madh—plunged the foot-long blade of his weapon into the ground, leaving the staff quivering behind him. Without the slightest hint of apprehension, he walked directly to Madh, until his colorless eyes were mere inches from the Yndrian's own. From this distance, Madh could see the Nistashin's skin more closely, yellowed and cracked like ancient parchment. There was no sign of stubble on the few patches of skin that peeked out between the leather that crossed the Nistashin's skull and cheeks, nor could Madh find any sign of hair on the Nistashin's arms. As if the centuries had eroded away anything the black bands did not protect.

"You are a mage?" he said quietly, offhandedly, as if he already knew the answer to his question.

Madh's smile only widened as he continued to chant and rub his hands.

The Nistashin sighed. Then, suddenly, he whipped his arm upward, breaking Madh's hands apart. The Yndrian smiled apologetically as he glanced down at his empty palms.

"The spell consumes the powder the first time," the Nistashin said, his gravelly voice sounding vaguely disappointed. "We played these tricks a millenium ago. You think to fool us with them now?"

Madh shrugged and pointed toward the corpse near his feet. "He was fooled."

"He was an imbecile," the Nistashin sneered. "If he had no time to listen to your chant, he deserved the final sleep."

Madh nodded.

"If you have time to listen to other things I may say, it may profit the Nistashi greatly. Does Aemon Goeth still live?"

The Nistashin's eyes narrowed. "Aemon Goeth will never let the final sleep claim him. Whether he chooses to speak with you before he reaps your soul . . . that is another matter. It has been a long while, though, since we have had news of the outer world from a mage."

The sound of scuffling feet drew the Nistashin's attention back toward Hain. The assassin had been lifted upright, each arm pinioned by an impassive Nistashin. His feet kicked out at his captors but did no harm.

The leader turned back toward Madh.

"A tool of yours?" he asked.

Madh inclined his head silently.

"Unruly," the Nistashin leader observed with cool contempt.

"The most potent tools often are—a lesson you should have learned from the Devastation."

The leader's bleached pupils fixed angrily on Madh for a moment, then turned again to watch one of his men approach Hain.

"Zemon Hoth intends to have some sport with your tool," the leader said. "You are not, I trust, a jealous man."

Madh did not reply, watching as the tall, gaunt Nistashin named Zemon Hoth came to stand next to Hain, the Nistashin's nose a mere finger's breadth from Hain's own. The Nistashin's nostrils widened as he drew in air, as if sampling the aroma of a stew.

"So very vital," the Nistashin hissed. "Yes, you will be mine on the night of no moon."

And then, without warning, the Nistashin's tongue snaked out of his mouth, as purple-black as a bruise, and rasped upward across Hain's cheek.

Madh caught only the quick flash of a smile across Hain's lips before the assassin spun his head to the left, biting viciously at the Nistashin's exposed tongue. They were locked for a second in a violent kiss before the Nistashin wrenched himself away, black blood spurting between his withered lips. Hain, his face painted wildly with the other's blood, grinned maniacally for a moment before spitting something out—an inch-long mass of darkened flesh that oozed liquid when it hit the ground. Hain struggled again against his captors, hoping that the distraction had loosened their grips, but met with no success. The other Nistashi seemed unmoved, save for regarding Zemon Hoth with what seemed to Madh an air of subtle amusement.

The leader turned back to Madh, a slight scowl on his thin lips.

"Whether Aemon Goeth will speak with you is for him to say, but your tool, I promise, is ours. He will not leave the house of Nistash Mar alive."

Madh shrugged, following the Nistashin as the man took a firm grip of his arm and led him north. He had hoped to reach Yndor without such difficulties. But all in all, he supposed, things could be far worse.

CHAPTER 21

In his bare feet, Katham advanced cautiously across the
ebony-stained floorboards. His toes knew these boards
now, knew where he could or could not place his weight
if he wanted to move without a trace of sound. A few catlike
steps brought him to the edge of the second-floor landing,
allowing him to look down between the balusters to the mansion's empty atrium below. So far, so good. In the distance,
he could hear the faint murmur of Baley and Tomas talking—perhaps playing cards in the kitchen, judging by their
distance. Those sixty feet gave him all the time in the world,
so long as he kept quiet.

Katham nimbly hopped onto the beginning of the stairway's handrail, just beyond the massive newel post that announced one's arrival upon the second floor, and pushed off,
sliding down the polished banister. It was amazing, he'd
found, how much speed you could achieve while riding those
thirty curved feet of mahogany—which made it all the more
essential to leap away at just the right moment, before one
crashed into the newel post on the first floor. In Katham's
estimation, he had now perfected the maneuver, springing
outward from the banister with lithe grace, landing softly on
the marble tile of the atrium. And the soft landing was crit-
ical. Even the hint of a noise would bring Baley running out
of the kitchen to scold him for the dozenth time that rail
slides were dangerous.

So Katham's heart nearly stopped when he landed with an
awful clatter—a clatter it took him a moment to realize was
the banging of something very hard against the front doors.
At this time of night, visitors were quite unexpected. And

predictably, the commotion was bringing Baley and Tomas at full tilt from the kitchen. Katham cast a venomous stare at the door. Whoever it was, they almost certainly spelled the end of banister slides for the time being.

Katham straightened himself and walked toward the door, intending to look as if he were being useful as Baley and then Tomas careened into the atrium from a side entrance.

Again, there was a clattering knock at the door.

"Would you like me . . . ?" Katham began, gesturing toward the door.

Tomas rolled his eyes; Baley simply grimaced.

"What are you doing up at this time of night?" the tall doorman said. He was half out of his uniform now, wearing a simple white shirt, open at the collar, and his black pants.

"Get to bed, Katham," Tomas said, trying to sound stern, glancing up at the second floor as if to remind the boy where his bedroom was.

Whoever was outside was out of patience, for the door visibly rattled at the knocking this time.

"Where's Dannel?" Baley growled as he buttoned his collar. On evenings when no one was expected, only a single doorman was stationed outside—tonight, Dannel. It irked Baley that the man was incapable of doing his job.

Baley paused a moment more to ensure that he was looking respectable before he turned the cylinders of the door's two massive locks and swung the portal open. Katham retreated backward into the shadows behind a long hallway table, presuming that Baley and Tomas were now sufficiently distracted that they would not notice him if he stayed. Provided, of course, that he stayed inconspicuously.

Katham was not sure what he expected to see as the tall door swung open, but it was not a half-dozen armored soldiers standing over Dannel, who lay across the front steps, rubbing his left temple. The two foremost soldiers had their swords out. They had been using the pommels to pound upon the door. And, it seemed, upon poor Dannel's head.

Baley drew himself up to his full, considerable height and growled in his most forbidding voice, "What on earth is going on here?" The doorman spared only a moment to shoot Tomas a sidelong glance—upon which the coachman retreated rapidly into the interior of the mansion to make preparations of some last-resort kind.

Two of the soldiers picked Dannel up and pushed him through the doorway. Katham could now see an ugly, eggplant-colored bruise rising on his forehead.

"They want Master Eliando," the man explained, his voice strained. "I explained he wasn't home, but they insisted on coming in."

And come in they did. Six soldiers in black lacquered breast plates, followed by two officers—one that Katham did not recognize, but another whom he'd seen too much of lately, at least for his liking. There had been Jame Kordor's funeral, then Ravenwood's execution, and now this. But no one needed a prior acquaintance, these days, to recognize the features of a man whose face had been carved like a festival pumpkin. Their intemperate visitor was General Amet Pale.

"Master Eliando is not home," Baley confirmed, doing a good job of betraying no particular reaction as he came face-to-disfigured-face with the man. He sounded as if he expected that to settle the matter, as if the de facto ruler of the nation would simply take him at his word and retreat.

Pale smiled, contorting his longitudinal scars, and stepped inside the atrium. He was followed by another soldier, someone Katham did not recognize, who looked uncomfortable in his armor, like a turtle in a borrowed shell.

"Perhaps we shall await his return," Pale said. His small eyes darted about the marble-clad space, quietly appraising. "At this hour, he can't be far from home."

"We do not expect him home tonight," Baley said, his voice as stiffly formal as Katham had ever heard it. Baley glanced at Dannel, who was just now picking himself up unsteadily from the steps. From Katham's vantage, he could see the muscles in Baley's broad shoulders bunch. He was a man made of duty, Katham knew—a type the boy had run into rarely in his brief life. The kind of man who did what he must because he could not live with himself if he did

anything else. A silly kind of way to live, the boy thought.
And that silliness was about to cost Baley his life, Katham
suspected.

"And you would not be welcome to stay," Baley added,
"without Master Eliando or Master Karrelian in residence."

Pale's smile twitched upward, continents of flesh drifting
in unexpected directions. Katham recognized this as something like the look on the face of a child who was about to
pull the wings off a butterfly.

"And where is Master Eliando?" the general asked, a clear
threat suffusing his voice. His right hand came to rest lightly
on the pommel of his sword as he stepped closer to the doorman.

"I cannot say," Baley replied, unflinching.

"Cannot," Pale asked, "or will not?"

The man's fingers slid around the leather-wrapped hilt of
the blade.

Quickly, Katham stepped forward from the shadows of the
stair. "I know where he is."

There was a moment of surprised silence as the soldiers
seemed to notice the boy for the first time. General Pale
smiled with what seemed like genuine amusement.

"You have rats in the walls, it appears," he muttered to
Baley before turning his full attention upon Katham. The boy
felt something tingle in the small of his back beneath the
weight of Pale's scrutiny. "And where might that be?"

Katham shrugged, working a bit to sound at his ease. "I
can show you. I can't tell you. I can't read the street signs,"
he lied.

The general reached forward and placed his hand on Katham's head—not patting it but gripping the skull as if he
were taking possession of it.

"Well, my little homing pigeon, let's be off."

As the general spun him toward the front door, Katham
caught a glimpse of the flesh that lay hidden beneath Pale's
sleeve—a view that no one but a four-footer could have seen.
An angry rictus of red flesh circled the general's wrist—a
recent scar—and he thought he could glimpse another

scarred loop just an inch beyond it. Odd, he thought. He'd heard the stories of the general's maiming, but no one had ever mentioned anything beyond the man's face. Had the assassin also carved orbits around the general's arms as well? The general noticed Katham's attention and tugged his cuff back below his wrist. The pad of the man's forefinger and thumb were stained red, as if he'd been dying clothing. Or shelling bettem nuts. Some of the ghetto rats Katham knew chewed bettem for the slight buzz they gave. And old women used it sometimes to relieve their aching joints . . .

Baley was scowling at him, Katham realized. Best he lead the soldiers out of the house before the doorman's foolish principles awakened bloodshed.

"Let's," Katham agreed. And with a wink toward Baley, he added, "I have to be back home in time for my bath."

Masya was unaccustomed to anyone banging on her door, much less banging on her door in the middle of the night so vigorously that all the windowpanes rattled. Astonishingly rude, she thought, as she opened the door. But the procession of soldiers who filed inside, with Katham trailing behind—that she had no words for at all.

Carn, on the other hand, did. Whatever surprise he felt was hidden quickly behind his narrowed eyes. After his discussion with Aston, Carn had expected General Pale to come looking for him. Just not this soon . . . nor at this particular place. The look of fear on Masya's face made Carn furious at the general's intrusion. This was his business to bear—not Masya's. His love knew nothing—and wanted to know nothing—of affairs of soldiers and state. But the soldiers would not disappear by wishing them away.

Carn swung his arms downward so his fingers came to rest against the wooden spokes of his chair. He wheeled himself away from the table, glad now that he and Masya had stayed up a bit late playing cards, rather than retiring. It would have been awkward to meet the general had he already been abed. Crawling from beneath the sheets toward his wheelchair was not the way to meet anyone, least of all Amet Pale and his black-armored minions.

"Good evening, General." Carn hoped his voice sounded as unsurprised as if Pale had come by invitation for a spot of tea.

Pale stepped forward from his men and inclined his head slightly by way of greeting. In the dim light of Masya's house, the general's scars faded from view, almost giving Carn a view of the man as he'd looked before his encounter with Hain. Only weeks, but a world ago.

"So you know me," the general said.

"Your reputation," Carn allowed, "precedes you."

Andus Ravenwood's head swinging in a cage, Carn thought. *Soldiers marching down the streets.*

The general raised a finger to his cheek and traced the equator that Madh had left above the bridge of his nose.

"Odd how reputations grow," Pale observed. "Two months ago, no one would know me, running across me in the market."

Carn shrugged. "I would have known you then. I know you now."

But it was odd, he thought, to have this much in common with the general, whom he had good reason to despise. Not many weeks ago, they had both been living their lives within the bounds of expectation. And then the assassin—whether directly or indirectly—had thrown those lives out of orbit. So he expected he shared this much with Pale—that each understood the fragile fiction of a life, of a future suddenly made unclear. No, not *made* unclear, Carn thought. What Hain had taken from them was only an illusion of certainty, a fool idea that a life can wear a groove so deep that nothing can kick it from its track. Hain was the jarring truth—that there was no gravity holding those orbits in place, no laws to stop the single, daring act. Amet Pale had learned Hain's lesson well. He'd been a snake before, Carn reflected, but the kind of snake that hid in the underbrush and attacked men by their heels. Now, Pale was another species entirely.

And he was poised to devour all of Chaldus, if not the

continent. That had led him to this modest, two-room house in a part of the city where only day-laborers lived. Amet Pale had an appetite for conquest now, and that meant an appetite for steel.

"You've come to discuss Desh," Carn began, wanting the general to know that the subject of this visit was no surprise.

The general raised an eyebrow.

"I've been examining our inventory," Carn continued. "Almost seven tons refined, though the wrong gauge for using as stock for arms. Resmelting would mean two weeks' delay. But all told, enough to equip six divisions."

"More than I had expected," Pale mused. Then his manner became darker, his voice more formal. "That steel is a strategic asset that should be properly protected. What would happen should Yndor attempt to seize it?"

Carn was tempted to laugh by the sheer geographical absurdity of the question. For Yndrian troops to seize Deshi mines, they would have to ride across the full breadth of Chaldus—in which case, they would have already accomplished the end for which the steel was the supposed means. Or they would have to traverse a thousand miles of mountains . . . and drag seven tons of steel back over the same peaks to get it home. But the question was disingenuous, Carn knew—simply Pale's way of trying to pry loose information about the security of the mines, which, though far from Yndor, lay only a scant hundred miles from Chaldus's northern border.

"No need to fear, General. The steel is very well protected. The single pass that leads to the mine entrance is well fortified and the Deshi have rigged the tunnels to collapse at a moment's notice. Given five minutes' warning, all that ore can be buried as deeply as it had been for millennia before the Deshi found it."

Pale wiped the back of his hand across his lips, as if the answer had literally been distasteful. He paused for a moment, looking down at Carn with open annoyance. Of late, Carn knew, the general had become used to taking what he wanted, with little regard to what anyone else thought. The general knew Carn as little more than an obstacle to the steel he wanted, and Carn imagined that the general was simply trying to determine whether the steel would be more easily had with Carn alive or dead.

Finally, the general released a long-held breath. "Your country has need of that steel, Master Eliando."

"That steel, General, is my livelihood. And it resides in Desh, where you have no legal claims upon it. However, I'm happy to sell it to you for a fair price."

Carn paused for a moment and then quoted a price appropriate for the poor-quality iron that was commonly available on the market, rather than impeccable Deshi steel.

"Done," Pale said quickly. He had expected more of a battle over this and, in all likelihood, the need to coerce Eliando. Indeed, even at the fair market price for Deshi steel, Eliando would be losing a fortune through this deal. Without steel, Eliando's factories would be idled. "You are a credit to your country."

Carn smiled. "I live to serve. Indeed, I understand that you've convened a panel of ombudsmen to oversee civil matters while the city is under martial law. I will be honored to serve upon it."

Carn's choice of verb was not lost upon the general.

"The panel is fully staffed," Pale observed.

Carn lifted his hands from the wheels of his chair, spreading them palms-up for the general's inspection.

"Many hands lighten the load, General."

"Indeed, they do," Pale agreed warily. He did not intend to leave without his steel—but Eliando, it seemed, did not intend to let him leave without the promise of an ombudsmanship. Not that it mattered a damn how many industrialists he had on the panel, so long as he owned them all. "Well," Pale concluded, "it seems then that we'll be seeing much more of one another."

Carn inclined his head in a slight bow of gratitude as Pale turned to take his leave. But now, he would not be leaving for long or far . . . and that was just the way Carn wanted things.

The best place to keep a snake, he reflected, *is in plain sight.*

CHAPTER 22

Twelve paces wide.

Twelve paces long.

That had become the measure and rhythm of Brandt Karrelian's world, his eternity. At first, the distances seemed to vary. Sometimes it would be only eleven paces, sometimes thirteen before his outstretched fingers would meet the cool rock of the cell wall. But he had plenty of time to practice, and before long, his body had learned to make twelve even steps from one wall to the next. Soon enough he dropped his hands to his sides, walking with perfect confidence, stopping on the twelfth step because he could almost feel the wall inches from his face. A crisp turn and he could proceed with his endless circuit.

Forty-eight steps made a complete lap.

Each stride, he calculated, occupied a little more than a full second, provided he came to a brief, complete stop at the completion of each step. Thus, every complete lap of the cell occupied a minute.

Sixty laps to the hour.

During one stretch, he had counted two hundred laps—three hours and twenty minutes, he believed, and he would have been willing to bet much of his fortune on his accuracy—before the pacing became maddening even to him. After that, he continued his walking only as exercise, to stretch his limbs a few hours each day. Lately, he had begun walking the cell on his hands. It was more difficult to maintain even progress and he had the strength only to complete a few circuits at a time. But it had proved, at least for a short time, a reasonable distraction.

Twenty-one paces long, twenty-one paces wide, if you walked on your hands.

As he took another measured hand-step forward, his biceps just beginning to tremble, he realized that the room was very close to the dimensions of his study at home. He had paced through that room as well—paced long enough around its perimeter that he had worn through a good Deshi rug. But there was a difference. Back in his mansion, he paced from boredom; he had conquered Prandis and built a monument to his triumph, and the very dimensions of that monument had become the suffocating horizon of his life. Three months ago, if a pack of crazy zebra-men had broken in to kill him, he was not quite sure he would have minded dying. At least it would have saved him the pacing. But now there were things to be done; Brandt, rich as he was, could no longer afford to die. And each upside-down step he took was a measure of controlled fury.

"How long?" Imbress asked abruptly. Her voice sounded rusted from disuse.

Brandt paused in his pacing. He did not consciously think about it, but he knew that he had just finished the fourth hand-step along the northern wall, a mere two paces shy of the door they could never find. He knew his location as surely as any blind man knew his home. No matter how many circuits he made now, he retained a sure sense of which direction he faced, where he was relative to the door, to Imbress, to the bucket. There was nothing else to know, so those few things he knew very well indeed.

Only he could not be sure that the "northern" wall was truly northern. It was easier to visualize the room if he lent it direction, and so he had decided arbitrarily that the door was to the north. As if north or south would ever matter again.

"How long," Imbress repeated, her voice still hoarse.

Brandt laughed. It was more a cackle than a laugh, he realized, as the sound returned to him from the austere walls.

"*How long?* How long until what? Or *from* what? How

long have we been here? Or how long will we be here? How long is this accursed room?"

Elena let icy silence be her first reply, hoping it would jog Karrelian from his childishness.

"How long until the new moon?" she finally said.

It was the only question that mattered.

Brandt lowered himself to his feet, leaned back against the wall, and sighed, closing his eyes against the dead darkness of the cell.

"I don't know. I suppose that depends on how long we've been here and how many days there were to the new moon when we arrived."

"Ten," Imbress replied quietly. "I think there were ten days left. Or perhaps eleven. But the moon had been full only a few nights before we were captured. It had already started to wane."

Thinking back, Brandt fancied he could see a fat, gibbous moon hanging above the Woodblood—but he could not say whether it was memory or imagination.

"Well," he replied, "I think we've probably been in here eight days."

Imbress was quiet for a moment. "What makes you think so?" she asked, sounding skeptical. Whether she believed his estimate too short or too long, Brandt had no idea.

"The way they feed us . . ." Brandt began. "I think we're fed daily."

"But we've only been fed six times," Imbress responded sharply. "That would be six days."

Brandt shook his head, although he knew the effort was wasted in the darkness.

"We weren't fed the day we were captured. At first we were separated, then they threw me in here with you. It was still a long time after that before the first platter of food came. I know because I was starving. I think they feed us once, every morning, and since we weren't captured until mid-morning, we missed out that first day."

"All right," Imbress conceded. "I see your point. It's been a long while since our last meal. It will probably come any minute now. So you think this is the eighth morning of our captivity."

It was hard for her to imagine it as morning, but Elena knew that her body's rhythms had been destroyed by the darkness and isolation. She had slept at least two dozen times and not once did she have any idea how long her disjointed, nightmare-ridden naps had been.

"What makes you assume they feed us once a day?" she asked.

Brandt laughed. "Twelve by twelve," he replied.

Imbress's silence demanded that he explain.

"This cell is precisely square . . . and unless I miss my guess, it's exactly as tall as it is long or wide. Whether our jailers are Khrine or just creatures who liked the look of Khrine real estate, I'm willing to bet that order appeals to them."

"Not judging by those crazy straps they wear," Imbress muttered.

"Mm," Brandt agreed. "There's a point. But if we're not being fed daily, then I have no idea how long we've been here. Does that make you feel any better?"

"No," Elena replied with a certain odd sharpness to her voice. Granted, she spoke sharply often enough, but there was a wrong note to it here. None of her usual sarcasm and superiority. Without thinking, he took a few steps in her direction.

Elena heard him come nearer and, for her part, pushed herself backward. If he was done with his maddening pacing, at least she could lean against the wall again without his stepping over her legs every time he came near. As her back met the cold stone, she shivered.

"We have to get out of here," she muttered.

"There is no way out," Brandt replied with finality.

Of that he was sure. Yesterday, in what he took to be the morning, he had stood by the door, awaiting the meal: the brief, dazzling flash of light, the wooden tray scraping across the stone. He had planned no escape, yet . . . He merely wanted to be close enough to get a good look into the corridor, to see who brought the food and how many there were, whether they were armed, and what the corridor looked like beyond. And so he had stood there for what seemed an eternity, his fingers laced loosely over his eyes so that, when the light came, it would not blind him. But the light never came. And the longer he stood there, the more he became convinced that his jailer stood on the other side of the door, waiting with devilish patience for him to move away. Finally, as if he'd decided to take a casual stroll, he turned around and walked toward the center of the room. Immediately, the light had burst in, the tray was inserted, and the door closed again. The entire process had taken all of a second. From it, Brandt had learned that, despite the contemptuous ease with which they had overpowered him the first time, his captors were not about to underestimate a desperate man. He would never be given a chance to make for the door.

"No," he repeated, "no way out at all."

Elena almost said it, the question that had preyed on her mind for so long: *What will they do with us?* But she bit it back in her throat. Brandt Karrelian was a violent man and so she knew what he would answer: they will kill us. And of course, she agreed. Whatever her captors were, they *would* kill her . . . but that was not all they intended to do, and that was what Karrelian would not understand. But she knew. She knew from the way the creature had looked at her that he wanted more than just her life. There had been a strange, horrible lust in his voice. Not a sexual lust, she thought, for his strange, colorless eyes had not once wandered across her body; they had remained locked upon her own eyes the entire time. This was a lust that she could not understand, a lust that transcended physical pleasure, or compounded it with something she did not recognize. And Elena Imbress was scared.

Karrelian had come closer, she suddenly realized. She could hear his breathing above her, a few paces away. She could not think of anything to say that might drive him away.

"Doesn't this damned darkness bother you?" she asked, unable to think of anything else.

"You get used to it," he replied.

Imbress ground her teeth together. His casual tone was infuriating.

"Actually," Brandt went on, "I lived someplace like this a long time ago."

"You're not funny," Imbress snapped.

"That's appropriate," he said, "since I'm not joking. I don't mean I lived in some strange dungeon in the Ulthorn forest, but I *did* live in an old underground storeroom in Belfar. It was beneath a grocer's shop, but it had been bricked off from the shop itself. It flooded during heavy rains, so I guess that's why they sealed it. The grocer— Pelman, his name was, though he never knew me . . . Well, Pelman was tired of having his wares spoiled, or maybe just the smell from the basement had been driving off business. Before he bricked it off, though, he had dug through the basement's floor to a storm sewer that ran beneath it. He had been hoping the place would drain, I guess, but the floor was so badly laid that the puddles were a foot deep in the corners. Anyhow, that's how I learned to get in, through the storm sewers."

"Charming," Imbress muttered, her nose wrinkled in disgust.

To her surprise, Brandt laughed.

"It was, to a seven-year-old."

Funny, but he could almost smell the place, now that he was thinking about it—a rich, mossy odor, like a rock-strewn riverbank in perpetual shade. The soles of his feet remembered the uneven cobblestones beneath him, his fingers remembered the rotted wooden stairs that led upward to the brick rectangle that had once been a door.

"For me it was more than charming. It was my own. It was safe, a place that only I knew. At least, only I knew it until I met Marwick. That was a couple of years down the road, still. For a while it was all mine, and it was just about this size."

He turned and pointed upward, toward the middle of what

he'd decided was the eastern wall, imagining in the darkness the scene his memory painted.

"There was a grate up there, originally built to let in some light and some air, I guess. Just a couple feet long and maybe four inches wide. Every morning, the sun would rise and I could look up through the grate, see the grocer's storefront above me, the roofs of the houses across the street, and a little patch of sky. Just about half an hour each morning, on a good day. Then Pelman would open the shop and he'd put some crates of produce out on the street. Apples, usually, or pears. Sometimes plums or Gathon peaches in summer. Anyway, the boxes covered the grate and it would be this dark inside, all day. The old man never closed shop until the sun was down. Maybe, during summer, you'd catch just a glimpse of a purple sky above. But in winter, the days were shorter and Pelman would open before sunup, close after sundown. The winters, I could go a whole season without a shred of light. Like this."

Brandt sighed and took a few more steps forward, turning instinctively when he knew he was by the wall, and then sliding down its smooth drop until he was sitting on the floor, only a few feet from Imbress.

"Yeah, you get used to the darkness," he said. "But the days I really lived for . . . Well, every once in a while, maybe only twice a month, Pelman wouldn't snug those crates of his right up against the wall, or right up against each other. Just a few inches off, but a seven-year-old has skinny arms. The walls in that place were made of big, rough-hewn blocks—not this smooth, seamless stuff—and I could climb them easy as pie, grab on to the grate, pull myself up until my nose was pressed against the iron bars, and hold on just long enough with one arm to reach up and snatch a piece of fruit. Only in the mornings, when the crates were full; after that, I couldn't reach."

Suddenly, the room exploded with light. Both Brandt and Elena threw their arms over their eyes, but by the time they'd done so, the door had already been snapped back. A wooden

tray, Brandt knew, would be lying on the ground, filled with
hot food. But he let it be.

"What I wouldn't give for one of Pelman's apples now,"
he sighed.

Then, finally, he moved, just pushing himself across the
floor.

Toward me, Imbress realized with a start.

He was next to her before she could say a word, though
she knew that she would hit him if he so much as laid a
hand on her.

But all he did was slide back down into a sitting position,
the very tip of his shoulder slowly coming to rest against her
own. Her whole back and the bottom of her legs had gone
cold, pressed against the stone, but this one tiny part of her
was warm.

They both remained there, quiet, letting their food grow
cold.

"Here." Callom Pell growled. lowering his fingers
to the dark puddle in the uneven ground. "Here there was a
fight. And no one cared a whit to disguise the fact."

He lifted his forefinger to the light of the dying sun. Even
in the glare of sunset, the blood looked more black than red.

"Whatever was bleeding, it wasn't Madh or Hain," Pell
announced. "But it doesn't seem that the Yndrians won this
particular fight."

"What makes you think not?" Marwick asked, dismounting before he approached the woodsman.

Pell shrugged. "Suddenly, the tracks lead north, toward the
Woodblood, rather than west along Beauty's Tress."

Or, Pell corrected himself mentally, more proper to say
they head a bit northwest. Toward the confluence of the Cirran and Woodblood rivers. More disturbing still, the only
tracks Callom Pell could discern leading northward into the
thick woods were the prints of Madh and Hain's horses.
Whatever they had fought along the trail, whatever had
forced them or led them northward, left no tracks of its own,

except black blood. And strange, paired holes in the ground, perhaps a finger's breadth each and six inches apart. Not the work of an animal, Pell knew. It was the trace of some kind of tool.

"Perhaps," Roland speculated, "the Ulthorn has done our job for us and finally disposed of the Yndrians."

"Except the blood is not theirs," Pell sighed.

"Of course," Roland allowed, "I assume nothing. We shall press on, until our own eyes find Madh's corpse."

Callom Pell glanced at the darkening sky. The moon had already cleared the trees—an emaciated crescent of silver that shed no light worth mentioning. Tomorrow, Pell judged, there would be no moon at all.

"We don't dare travel tonight," he announced, heading toward One-Eye to unsaddle the horse.

"At first light then," Marwick said. "At first light."

For days, the only sounds in their cell had been those they made themselves: their hoarse breathing, their pacing steps. Otherwise, it was quiet as a tomb, whether because the walls were too thick or because their captors moved with such unnatural silence, they could not say. It came as a surprise, then, a few hours later when they heard noise approaching the door. They had not moved in all that time, but now they both got cautiously to their feet and walked across the room as quietly as possible, trying not to obscure the low sounds that whispered through the stone.

A man's voice, raised in anger, though otherwise indistinguishable.

"One of our jailers?" Brandt asked quietly, concentrating on the sounds as they drew even with him, just on the other side of the wall.

"I don't think yelling is their style," Elena whispered in reply, thinking of the coolly contemptuous demeanor of her strange interrogator.

The sounds passed them, continuing down the hallway. Brandt and Elena followed as far as they could, until the far wall of their cell brought them up short. The voice slowly faded into the distance, followed a moment later by the remote sound of a door being slammed closed.

"Sounds more like another captive," Elena said, more life in her voice now than there had been in days. "How many people do you suppose are traipsing through the Ulthorn this time of year, Karrelian?"

"Very few indeed," Brandt replied.

For a moment, she was silent as she considered the possibilities.

"What do you think?" she finally asked.

Brandt pondered the question for a moment.

"I think," he finally responded, "that if they've captured Hain and Madh, I'll die a happy man."

"And if not?" she asked quietly.

If not, he thought, *it meant that Pell had been captured. Or Marwick.* He thought of Carn and felt the blood drain from his face.

"*If not*, I hope there really are such things as ghosts," Brandt said quietly. Because, he reflected, his business on earth would not yet be done.

The tracks followed no trail, meandering through the landscape along the path of least resistance, pushing through spots of light vegetation, but skirting the dense thickets of foliage that often barred the way northward. It was impossible to hide the progress of two horses breaking through virgin woods, so Callom Pell hurried them along, following the path easily. He stopped only a few times in midmorning, examining broken twigs with the tip of his finger. He found no fresh sap, the breaks already sealed, at least ten or twelve hours old.

"They did not stop to sleep last night," he finally announced.

"Perhaps they were fleeing something desperately," Marwick suggested hopefully.

Pell shook his head, his great, grizzled beard swaying over

his chest. "The hoof marks tell a different story. These horses were proceeding at an easy walk."

"Then what do you suppose happened?" asked Miranda.

"They were being escorted," Pell rumbled, "by something that did not plan to travel too far—otherwise it would have stopped for the night. Anyone who travels by night in the Ulthorn forest feels very comfortable indeed. Someone—or something—lives close by . . . and Madh and Hain stumbled into its backyard."

Marwick glanced around at the silent trees before replying. "And so have we."

The instant the door opened. Brandt was on his feet, knowing that a full day hadn't passed since the last tray of meat and cheese had been slid through the door. Rather than the momentary flash of light and a return to utter darkness that they had come to expect, this time the light remained. Compared to day, it would have been dim, but to their eyes, the beam that pierced their chamber seemed brighter than any electrical torch Brandt's engineers could devise. And in the midst of the beam, framed as an utterly black silhouette, stood one of the Nistashin.

"It is your time," he said. "Come."

Brandt turned around. Imbress was still sitting against the wall, blinking in the harsh light. He stepped over to her and offered his hand, helping her to her feet. Releasing his hand, she strode toward the Nistashin in the doorway, her back straight. Brandt followed.

Their eyes adjusted quickly to the dimly lit hallway. It reminded Brandt strongly of the Atahr Vin, with its lofty ceilings and precise angles. Unlike the Atahr Vin, there were actual doors in this hallway. Though they appeared to have neither handles nor locks, Brandt knew from experience that they worked well enough without them. Like that other Khrine dwelling, this place was fashioned out of unseamed stone, as if the whole place had been carved from a single rock. But unlike the Atahr Vin, this rock was black, and it seemed to suck away the light from whatever mysterious source shed it.

The Nistashin who had spoken to them led the way, but two more followed after Brandt and Elena, each armed with odd pole-arms: a curved spear at one end, a nasty-looking fork at the other. Neither was an extremity that Brandt wanted any part of. And so, without objection, he followed the Nistashi along a route of intersecting corridors. At first, he thought he would be able to remember his way back, if need be; there had been no stairs to reckon with and each intersection seemed to form a perfect right angle. But after ten minutes of winding his way through the rock passages, he had to admit he was lost. He had no particular desire to return to the cell, but he harbored an uneasy suspicion that it was preferable to whatever awaited them.

What did await them was a broad, arched opening that led to a circular stairwell. The stairs stretched upward as far as Brandt could see, a hundred feet or more. Before he could get a proper look upward, one of the guards poked his back with the fork end of a staff. Brandt shot a dark look over his shoulder at the skeletal guardsman behind him, but he began climbing. The unbroken spiral of stairs made it difficult to say how far they had ascended, but the stairs finally terminated at another great arch, beyond which they could see the ebon night sky.

And a vast host of Nistashi.

"Out," one of their guards whispered.

Reluctantly they proceeded onto the keep's vast, square roof and into the midst of dozens of blank-eyed Nistashi, each wrapped in their crazy-angled leather straps, very few of them armed. But Brandt suspected they didn't much need arms when, all totaled, there must have been two hundred of them spread across the roof of the keep. They all turned with a certain cool interest as Brandt and Elena were led toward the middle of the roof, at which point stood a huge black chair—a throne, one might have thought, except that the mammoth seat was entirely unadorned.

But it was not unoccupied. Sitting upon it was a large

Nistashin, as obscenely thin as the rest, each whip-cord muscle defined beneath the tightly stretched straps of leather that crisscrossed his body. Unlike most of his brethren, this Nistashin's straps seemed to have been arranged with some sort of complicated pattern in mind, though it defied Brandt's ability to comprehend it. Only the Nistashin's head straps were simply symmetrical: an X that crossed at the bridge of his nose, leading up to a solid skullcap of wound leather. The face beneath was cadaverous, etched deeply with creases that intersected at more crazy angles than the Nistashin's black straps. His nose was a thin plane of bone, almost two-dimensional, with an upturned edge that suggested a skull's missing nostrils.

"What do you want with us?" Brandt demanded as he was led before the man, the guard's blade poking him in the back with each step.

"Quiet," the enthroned Nistashin commanded. His voice was the hollow echo of stone being scraped over stone, as if his vocal cords had been eroded by centuries of harsh storms.

After a few moments, it became apparent that they were waiting for something. And Elena Imbress was content to wait. She peered upward at the sky, a black pincushion for the stars, the moon absent. A new moon: the night in which the Nistashin's promises to her would be fulfilled. A shiver scratched along her spine as she thought of it, and Elena hoped Karrelian did not notice, although she had no idea what difference it would make. They were both dead now, or worse.

With Elena and Brandt's arrival, the scattered Nistashi had begun to gravitate toward the center of the roof, making it difficult for Elena to see beyond them. In each corner of the keep stood a low, square tower, through which led stairs like the ones she had just climbed. Between the four towers, a low stone wall guarded the perimeter of the keep, beyond which she could barely discern the dim, pulsing reflections of a broad river far below her, like a vast swarm of black snakes racing through darkness toward some distant goal. Too broad, she thought, for the Woodblood. She must be looking westward toward the Cirran. She turned around, trying to catch a glimpse of the Woodblood in the other direction, but a solid mass of Nistashi blocked her view. They were even closer now, beginning to cluster tightly about, and Elena felt suddenly claustrophobic, as if their presence stole the air from her lungs.

Suddenly, the host of Nistashi parted, and turning, Elena saw the tower by which she'd entered. A Nistashin was just emerging upon the roof, followed by four darkened figures. The last pair carried Nistashin pole arms, which identified them easily enough. But the two in between . . .

Madh and Hain.

With a howl, Brandt sprang forward through the first few ranks of Nistashi, but in an instant two curved blades brought him up short. He had not, in fact, been able to stop himself before the very tip of one blade bit through his shirt into his shoulder. The linen began darkening slowly with a trickle of blood, and this, it seemed strangely to him, drew the Nistashi's attention. Just in front of him, Brandt saw a dry, purple tongue flicker eagerly between dark lips. It took no further prodding for him to return to the small circle that remained clear around the leader's throne.

"Yes," said Aemon Goeth as he slid his hands along the smooth, cold armrests of his stone chair, "our party is now complete."

A strange bed of mist covered the confluence of the Woodblood and Cirran rivers, even creeping beyond the waters over the ground itself. The sun had long ago gone down, the last dim trace of its presence erased from the sky more than half an hour ago. Ordinarily, Callom Pell would have begun to set camp for the night. He knew, even now, that he was wasting his time, staring out at the fog-shrouded waters, but he expected something here, at the meeting of the rivers. What he expected, he could not say, but the fate of too many men throughout the centuries had led to this mysterious point, and that list now included Madh and

Hain—Karrelian and Imbress, too, if the witch's familiar was to be trusted.

And now he was here.

Yet there was nothing.

Frowning, he walked the remaining yards to the Woodblood's edge, his legs disappearing in the mist up to his knees with each step. When his toes splashed down into the river, he turned left and followed the course of the riverbank west toward the Cirran. Perhaps a quarter-mile remained before the southern bank of the Woodblood and the eastern bank of the Cirran would merge. There, with luck, he would find something.

As it turned out, Pell had no need to go that far. He stumbled as, unexpectedly, his right foot descended farther than he had expected before reaching the muddy bank. Reaching down to catch his balance, his fingers found the mud beneath him to be unexpectedly smooth. He ran his hand along the ground, finding a deep, even furrow of compacted mud, closing to an angle as it came inland. Glancing to his left, Pell found a telltale loop of damaged bark around the nearest tree.

A small boat had been moored here.

They had crossed the river. And since the boat had been moored on the banks of the Woodblood rather than the Cirran, logic dictated that they had crossed to the north. Pell peered across the waters, but between the fog and the moonless night, he could see nothing of the far bank. With a quickened step, he returned to the others.

They had retreated a hundred feet or so, to the point where the mist gave out. Although they had not begun to set camp without Pell's orders, the horses had been tethered. Roland and Marwick sat together against the trunk of a large, ancient oak, Roland sharpening his tremendous sword, Marwick honing a knife. Miranda seemed to be in deep conversation with the owl that sat on her shoulders, its wings half-spread as if to keep their discussion private.

"Yes," Callom Pell growled, "Mouse."

Miranda looked up, her eyebrows arched, and Mouse's head swiveled one hundred and eighty degrees around, cocked at exactly the same curious angle as the head of its mistress.

"Yes?" Miranda asked.

"They've crossed the Woodblood," Pell announced, keeping his voice low. "Can the owl scout the other side?"

Miranda merely looked at the bird before Mouse launched itself from her shoulder, catching a cushion of air between its spread wings. Slowly, it circled and rose, disappearing to the north.

"And in the meantime?" Marwick asked, looking up anxiously from his blade.

"In the meantime," the woodsman replied, "we wait."

They did not have to wait long. Within ten minutes, Mouse returned, landing softly on Miranda's left shoulder, its beak bent close to her ear. Although the owl's posture always made it look as if it were speaking to her, Callom Pell never heard a sound from the little bird. He wondered how they did communicate.

"Well?" Pell asked. "Did it find anything on the far bank?"

Miranda paused a minute, her head cocked, as if listening.

"The far bank is like this bank, Mouse says. Wooded, full of game. Squirrels, rabbits. No men."

Pell's brow furrowed in frustration.

"Useless creature," he muttered.

Miranda did not seem to catch the insult. Her eyes had acquired a faraway look.

"Mouse does want to know, however, if you have any interest in the island."

"What island?" Pell growled, louder than he'd intended.

"The island," Miranda replied slowly, as if she could not believe the words her tongue was forming, "with the fortress on it."

"Fortress?" Pell thundered, enraged. "There's no bloody fortress in the middle of the Woodblood River."

And he turned on his heels, stomping off into the mist, toward the riverbank. Immediately, the others were off in pursuit, catching the woodsman just as his feet splashed into the Woodblood.

"There!" he said, stretching his arm out toward the river when the others joined him at the bank. "Nothing but mist and water."

They peered into the darkness. The fog might have obscured a small sandbar or two, but it could not hide an island, much less an island with a fortress on it.

"Mouse says we must look harder," Miranda whispered.

Pell turned, glaring at the witch, but she did not notice. Her head was tilted back somewhat, as if to catch a breeze, and she was humming something. Her fingers were gently rubbing something . . . one of the owl's feathers, Pell thought.

Suddenly, her humming stopped.

"Hell and damnation," Miranda whispered.

The three men gathered around her, Roland towering over her back protectively, as if to protect her from whatever invisible menace she saw.

"What is it?" the old warrior asked.

"A fortress," Miranda replied, "just as Mouse says. As tall as Council Tower and black as Amet Pale's heart."

Marwick took a few steps forward, not caring that the Woodblood rose to his thighs. He stared out to the north as if he, too, could see the fortress.

"Then we must get inside," he said. "We'll find Madh there. And perhaps Brandt as well."

Roland's long arm shot out and dragged Marwick back from the river.

"Just because we can't see them," Roland cautioned, "doesn't mean they can't see us."

Callom Pell inclined his head in agreement.

"As it is, it's far too quiet here to suit me. Who builds a fortress without setting a guard?"

Marwick shrugged. "What's the point of an *invisible* fortress," he argued, "if not that it spares your having to guard it?"

"Perhaps," Pell allowed, "but I'm still uneasy. The river

dwellers ambushed Madh and Hain fifteen miles to the south, yet they don't know we're here? It makes no sense."

"Unless," Miranda suggested slowly, "they knew Madh was coming . . . and wanted particularly to catch him."

"Why?" Marwick asked, but even as the question passed his lips, he understood. They all understood. There was only one reason on earth that anyone would want to ambush Madh:

The Phrases.

"The last thing this game needs is another player," Miranda observed quietly. Particularly the sort of player that lives in an invisible fortress in the middle of the Ulthorn. "All the more important that we get over there."

Marwick frowned. "The only question is how."

The thief stared in frustration at the fog-shrouded water. Somewhere in its midst was a keep that only Miranda and her familiar could see, and yet they were supposed to get there, in blackest night, without a boat.

"Mouse says that there are caves at the base of the island," Miranda said quietly. "Docks and boats to be had. I'll have to swim over there and bring back a boat."

"Out of the question," Roland interrupted. "You haven't had to swim any real distance in years."

The small woman spun around, and even though Roland towered a foot and a half above her, there was something in Miranda's posture that made her seem every bit his equal.

"Don't be an old fool. I'm the only one who can *see* the blasted place!"

Roland grit his teeth in fury. "If anyone gets into that river, it will be me."

"You'll sink like a length of lead pipe," Marwick said.

The Caladors turned as one, as if the argument belonged to them alone, only to discover that the affair had already been settled. The thief had somehow stripped down to his silken boxers and was busy strapping his sheathed knife, which he'd removed from his trousers' belt, to his upper arm.

"I was born a river rat," he explained. "Still spend half the summers in Belfar swimming in the Lespar, just to stay cool.

If you ask the owl to fly above me, it can guide me to the island without problem."

Both Roland and Miranda looked as if they wanted to argue, but there seemed to be nothing to say.

"Will he be able to see the fortress when he's atop the thing?" Callom Pell asked.

Miranda pondered the problem for a moment.

"It's a powerful warding," she mused, "but I've never heard of a warding so powerful as *that*. At some point, once he's close enough, the island should become visible."

"Where exactly is the thing?" Marwick asked.

Miranda turned and pointed dead north. "About two hundred paces, or perhaps fifty more.

Marwick nodded and waded into the Woodblood, trailing his hand in the water to judge the current. Then he walked back to land and followed the bank five hundred paces upstream. The one thing he wanted to be sure of was that the current did not sweep him past the island, into the Cirran. That, he suspected, might be a fatal mistake.

Then, ignoring the shock of cold as he slid entirely into the water, he began to swim.

"I see nothing." Roland muttered, sounding worried. "I should have gone . . ."

"It hasn't been twenty minutes yet," Callom Pell cautioned. "There may be activity upon the docks. He may have to wait before he can steal a boat."

"There's surely enough activity upon the roof," Miranda said to no one in particular.

"What?" Roland asked.

For the past few minutes, his wife had been staring absently into space, or so it seemed. Roland's hand moved automatically to the hilt of his sword. He disliked this inability to see his enemy.

"At first I wasn't sure," Miranda explained. "It's just so dark. But now I'm certain. There are people upon the roof—a lot of them."

"Looking down?" Roland asked. "Marwick will be caught as plain as a beacon if anyone is watching the river."

Miranda sighed and squinted harder against the darkness. "I don't see anyone against the parapet itself. They all seem gathered toward the middle of the keep, or perhaps the far end. That's why I only catch occasional glimpses of movement."

"Let's pray they stay there," Callom Pell began, but his next thought was cut off by the sudden sound of an oar dipping into water, far closer than they had expected.

They turned their gazes toward the Woodblood and, after a moment, were able to make out a dark spot moving against the fog.

It was Marwick's head, bobbing back and forth as he rowed a craft that was almost entirely lost in the mist. Only the very tip of a prow could be seen floating ghostlike toward them. A shallow boat, Pell thought, to keep its owners well hidden within their unnatural mist. Perhaps that very subterfuge would now work against them, whatever they were.

In a few minutes more, Marwick was within reach of land. Pell and Roland waded waist-deep into the Woodblood, catching hold of the low gunwales and leading the rowboat to shore.

"Are the docks clear?" Pell whispered.

Marwick said nothing, clearly out of breath from his exertions, but nodded.

"Get dressed," Roland said gently. "I'll row, this time."

But as Calador made to climb into the boat, Pell laid a restraining hand on the warrior's shoulder.

"The fog is our friend tonight," the woodsman explained, "and you will tower over it. Marwick is tired, so I will row the boat. The rest of you will lie beneath the fog."

Roland nodded and helped Miranda into the curved angle of the prow, where she fit snugly. Mouse glided out of the darkness above to nestle down in the crook of her arm. It took only a minute for Marwick to pull on his clothes and climb back into the boat, lowering himself into the space behind Pell. Roland remained in the river and helped the craft push off, then climbed in and crouched down in the remaining space between the plank seats as Pell began to row. It was a simple boat, Roland noted, fashioned from black oak and completely unadorned. He had hoped that, somehow, it would offer a clue to the identity of its owners, but it revealed nothing.

There was nothing to do but lie there, cringing every time that Pell, himself hunched down into the fog, let an oar splash audibly into the Woodblood. Every now and again, Miranda would peek over the prow into the inscrutable darkness ahead and issue Pell a direction, a bit more right, a touch left. Cramped down against the wet planks of the boat, Roland and Marwick could do nothing but stare into the quiet sky.

And suddenly it was there—a tremendous black fortress perched upon the back of a craggy island, as if the keep had been sculpted of the island's stone and the sculptor simply grew tired at the base, leaving the rock there unworked. Two thousand men could lie in wait in such a keep, perhaps three thousand, but the thing had appeared as suddenly as if it had been dropped out of the sky. Apparently, the fortress's wards operated until fifty or sixty paces, for the island could not be much farther away than that.

"There are three arched openings at the waterline," Marwick whispered. "I took the boat from the one farthest upstream. Best that we return to that one, as well. For all I know, the others could be manned."

Pell peered at the black rock until he thought his eyes would fall out, and gradually he made out what Marwick was talking about: against the vast darkness of the island's sheer rock face, there were three semicircles of still greater darkness. As his slow, steady strokes brought them closer, Pell could see the evenness of the arches. These openings were made of smooth, worked stone—not quite the caves Mouse had called them.

As the boat drew near the mouth of the opening, the curved chamber inside caught the sound of the oars, magnifying and echoing each stroke. Finally, Roland allowed himself to rise fully above the mist, searching the darkness for enemies. What he saw instead was only the water stretching deep into the bowels of the island. Although the archway was a semicircle fifty feet wide and twenty-five feet high, the channel broadened as soon as they passed inside. Here, they saw, was a large docking area. The water broadened into a harbor a hundred yards wide and twice that in length. On each side ran stone piers forty feet wide, meeting in a broad U at the far end of the channel. Once, a harbor such as this might have held dozens of ships, and this, Roland reminded himself, was only one of three docks that they had seen. Now, however, the piers stood almost empty. Only a half-dozen boats were visible, four of them rowboats like the one they had stolen. The other two were larger vessels, broader in beam and deeper in draft—built to sail down the mighty Cirran and, unless Roland missed his guess, seaworthy as well. Their masts had been lowered so that they could fit beneath the arch, and there was something about how neatly they'd been stowed that made Pell think they had not been used for a very long time.

Pell began to work his right oar more vigorously, steering them toward the eastern pier. Marwick had the boat's line in hand, and as soon as the gunwale tapped against the stone, he sprang onto the pier and secured the craft. One by one, they climbed onto the pier, and though the place was perfectly deserted, by unspoken agreement the men each bared a weapon. Miranda paused only to whisper a brief command to Mouse, who winged quickly beneath the arch back toward the Ulthorn.

"If you think it's safer for the owl there than here," Marwick muttered, "then we're really in trouble."

Pell raised a finger to his lips and led the party along the length of the dock. At the far junction between the eastern and western piers, he could just make out another arched opening and what he thought was a stairway beyond. It was indeed a stairway, he decided, as he drew near, and there seemed to be some dim source of light in its upper reaches. They would not have to climb in utter darkness.

Then, suddenly, Miranda drew in her breath.

"Oh, my."

Pell turned back and saw the witch looking upward, at the top of the arch that led to the stairs. Pell had been concentrating so fiercely on the stairway that he had not noticed the spidery characters that had been engraved in the stone above, all but lost in the darkness. His lips formed the words soundlessly.

"What is it?" Marwick asked impatiently, his foot already on the first step.

Callom Pell shook his head, as if he refused to believe what his eyes insisted was real. He had seen those letters before in his books, but had never expected to see them anywhere else.

"What indeed?" Roland asked, taking hold of Miranda's arm.

"Nistash Mar," Pell said hoarsely.

"What's that?" Marwick asked.

"Who," Miranda corrected.

Finally, Callom Pell sighed and turned his attention from the inscription to the staircase beyond it. "Nistash Mar was a Khrine—a Khrine who could be happy only in proportion to the blood he shed. The Devastation was, in many ways, the handiwork of Nistash Mar, who goaded the continent into a broader war. Histories of the Devastation say only that he came from the north . . . relative, that is, to Kirilei. Not very specific, the word 'north.' Now we know precisely where they meant."

"There's a *Khrine* awaiting us up there?" Marwick asked, half-disbelieving.

"No wonder he would want Madh and the Phrases," Miranda mused. "To set things back as they were . . ."

"Nistash Mar is dead," Pell said, somewhat pleased that the noblewoman's knowledge of the olden days was not so extensive as his own. "The histories are clear. He was killed not by another Khrine, but by a man, oddly enough. Tarem Hamir."

But Pell was still looking at the staircase before them as if death awaited at the top.

"If Nistash Mar is dead," Marwick asked, "then who did Miranda see on the roof?"

"The Nistashi," Miranda whispered, and the word seemed to linger longer in the air than it should. "Surely they are dead."

"Surely," Pell replied, "they are not. I've always wondered why this particular bit of the Ulthorn acquired such a dangerous reputation, and now I know."

"Who—" Marwick began.

"The Nistashi," Miranda explained, "were men, the followers of Nistash Mar."

Marwick's brow creased in consternation. "But if they were men—during the Devastation—they would be long dead."

"Nistash Mar," Pell sighed, "led a thousand men into battle on the day of the Devastation. Not ordinary men, but followers whom he had endowed with special powers. Some of them were mages in their own right, others merely warriors of uncommon skill and ferocity. For every five that took the field, the histories say, four were overcome by the forces led by Atahr Vin and Tarem Hamir. The remainder fled the Devastation, like so many other creatures, and I suppose it natural that they fled to Mar's keep. The Binding followed soon after, and the Nistashi must have found their powers dreadfully reduced. They were never heard from again. Whether these are the original Nistashi or, what seems more likely, descendants of those men, I don't know. But if Lady Calador is right, we can find them on the roof."

And without another word, Callom Pell began to take the stairs by twos.

"**Aemon Goeth, it is you!**"

Madh seemed pleased by his discovery as he strode willingly toward the throne in the center of the roof. In truth, his heart rang like a church's bell within his chest, hard enough, it seemed, to bruise his ribs. He would have been far happier had his master been here, but his master was not. Only Aemon Goeth. And to make matters worse, Galatine Hazard. If there were two men more dangerous to him, Madh could not think of them. But Aemon Goeth did not know what Madh knew, and as long as that held true, he had the chance to turn danger into opportunity. His master would be most pleased to learn that the men of Nistash Mar walked the earth still. No doubt, there would be uses to which he would want them put. For two reasons, then, it behooved Madh to tread very carefully with Aemon Goeth.

The Nistashin upon the throne chuckled as Madh approached.

"Child," he said, his ancient voice coolly amused, "you cannot possibly know me."

"Certainly not," Madh allowed, "but I know *of* you. I have read about you in the histories, in the pages of Grendin and Tarem Hamir—"

"Tarem Hamir!" Aemon Goeth fairly spat the name from his tongue, but then he leaned forward, intrigued. "Tell me, child, does Tarem Hamir live still?"

"He died centuries ago."

The Nistashin's head swung backward as he cackled toward the sky. His dry laugh rattled through the air for a full minute before he finally turned back to Madh.

"Then I have won the longer battle," he said with sinister satisfaction. "For Nistash Mar loved us more dearly than Atahr Vin loved his pawn."

Madh shook his head. "I do not understand you."

Aemon Goeth laughed again. "No? A pity, for it concerns you. Let me explain, child." Then his colorless eyes flashed from Hain to Elena to Brandt. "Listen well, you all. How think you that I have survived the countless dry centuries since Kirilei was destroyed? We were men, once, as you are men now. But Nistash Mar loved us, and it saddened the Khrine, who live without natural end, to watch their mortal friends wither and die so quickly. And so Nistash Mar taught us a way to cheat death, and we have cheated it thus more than a millennium."

Madh's hand twitched at his side. Nervous, Brandt thought.

No, not nervous. The Yndrian's fingers were as quick as his own, Brandt realized. Madh had retrieved something that had been secreted within his clothes.

"Do you wish to learn the ritual?" Aemon Goeth asked. Suddenly, his eyes flashed toward Hain. The assassin had leaned forward eagerly at the Nistashin's words, as if he refused to lose a precious syllable.

"Yes," Aemon Goeth said, still looking at Hain, "you burn for the secret of eternal life. You are much like us, child. Nistash Mar may have found favor with you, so long ago." Aemon Goeth leaned farther forward in his chair, lowering his voice to speak with Hain. "Well, child, you shall learn the secrets of the ritual *intimately*."

Slowly, the leader of the Nistashi rose from his seat, standing on the broad stone platform upon which the throne rested, and lifted his skeletal arms toward the sky.

"On the night of the new moon," he explained, "the ritual may be enacted, by which we tease the souls of living men from their bodies and share them between us."

Aemon Goeth moved his hands to the top of his head, his fingers working curiously as he continued to speak. "The four of you are young, vital. Between you, there must remain two hundred years of life. After the two Nistashi you killed, we number two hundred and eight." Aemon Goeth smiled. "Almost a full year's feast for each of us."

Suddenly, the end of a black strap had appeared in Goeth's hand, and he slowly began to unwrap the leather ribbon that covered his head. Fascinated, Brandt watched as the leather came loose. Beneath, each inch-wide swath of skin was clearly delineated, as if the edges of the straps had bitten deeply into the Nistashin's flesh. The skin itself was gray beneath the leather—the pallid color of death.

Aemon Goeth turned toward Brandt, his teeth a ghastly white behind his purple lips.

"Yes, child, we pay a price for our bindings, which protect us so well from the winged years. You are privileged to see us thus. Few are the mortals who do."

Nervously, Brandt realized that all the other Nistashi were removing their bindings as well. He had no idea what the strange leather straps did, but he felt with certainty that their removal had something to do with his own approaching death.

"Your pardon, Aemon Goeth," Madh said, without a trace of uncertainty in his voice, "but I am worth more than fifty years to you."

The Nistashin inclined his head, the trace of a condescending smile beneath the X of dead flesh that marked his face. The bindings had been unwound from his neck and arms, and now the Nistashin was removing them from his chest.

"Really, child?"

"Your question about Tarem Hamir shows that you know little of the world since the Devastation. Let me be your teacher. My master is a mage of great power, like the magi of old, and he would honor the Nistashi as they were honored once before. His men are as numerous as the leaves of the Ulthorn—centuries for you to feast upon openly, rather than hiding in your forest like an old spider desperate for flies. By his side, you could conquer much of the land you once desired—"

Elena Imbress took a step forward, her voice sharp as she interrupted the Yndrian.

"Kill us all and be done with it."

Aemon Goeth's head snapped around, curious to see why the woman was so eager to die. His empty eyes bore in upon her own.

"You are afraid, child . . ."

Elena desperately sought to close her mind to him, but she had no idea how.

". . . afraid that this man . . ."

She turned her mind to the Woodblood, to the feeling that she had briefly experienced of surrendering to the waters, being swept away.

But it was no good.

". . . afraid that this man possesses the power to unmake the Binding."

Now Aemon Goeth turned back toward Madh with legitimate interest.

"Can you truly possess such awesome power, child?"

The assault was astonishing in its speed and ferocity, like an oak falling upon his head. But Madh gnashed his teeth and pushed Aemon Goeth out of his skull. He wanted nothing more than to reach over and tear out the heart of the Chaldean fool. Didn't she realize that, while no sane Yndrian would wish to unmake the Binding, this was exactly the hope that Aemon Goeth had harbored these long centuries? Madh might want the Phrases for political leverage, but for Aemon Goeth, the Phrases possessed power of a far different sort.

Time and again, Aemon Goeth tried to batter his way into Madh's brain, but the Yndrian mage stood there, trembling only slightly, and repulsed each attack with a strength he knew was born entirely of desperation.

"Very good," Aemon Goeth chuckled, and the assault vanished as suddenly as it had begun. "You protect yourself well."

The trace of a smile rose upon Madh's lips . . . until he realized that the ancient Nistashin had turned his attention toward Hain.

Hain, whom Madh had bade memorize all the Phrases, lest the assassin become suspicious that all Madh truly needed was the gem that remained in the pouch beneath his shirt.

But all Aemon Goeth needed was Hain.

Hain took an uncertain step backward, as if physically propelled by the force of the two wizards' gazes. He felt nothing, really, just the mere whisper of voices too low to be discerned. Certainly, he did not feel the struggle of two mages to possess his mind.

But Madh knew Hain's sick mind better than he cared to ponder, and he dove beneath the assassin's skin as easily as one of Hain's needles, coursing along the same path to the assassin's brain. It was an ugly place, Madh realized, more gruesome than he had even imagined, chambered with bloody corpses after which Hain still lusted. Aemon Goeth would have felt himself at home.

Except that Madh got there first. And he slammed down his will like a portcullis, just in time to meet the battering force of the Nistashin's raid.

"Better still, child," Aemon Goeth said, undisturbed. "But I fear you cannot protect both your tool and yourself for very long. And be assured, after I take what I want, I shall feast on you both, slowly, beneath this moonless sky."

Brandt had lost the thread of the ancient Nistashin's conversation. How Madh was protecting himself, and from what, Brandt had no idea. The Yndrian was simply standing there, the muscles of his jaw bunching against some unseen strain. Aemon Goeth, meanwhile, continued to unwrap his bindings. He was down to his thighs now, having uncovered his shriveled, blackened genitals. So contented he was with his unwrapping, that he still hadn't noticed what was in Madh's hand.

It looked something like an acorn, Brandt thought, except for the spines. They looked nasty, pin-sharp, but if Madh thought a fistful of pins was a weapon against the Nistashi, the Yndrian had lost his mind.

The last of Aemon Goeth's wrappings slipped from his feet and the Nistashin draped the long leather straps almost negligently over the throne behind him. Aemon Goeth's followers had finished their demummifying as well, it seemed. Brandt glanced about, looking desperately for an escape route, but he and Imbress were surrounded by a sea of hungry, naked corpses.

Suddenly, Madh thrust his hand into the air. Brandt expected him to hurl his spiny weapon at Aemon Goeth, but instead, he closed his hand into a convulsive fist. The spines bit deeply into Madh's flesh, one of them piercing the fan of skin between his thumb and forefinger. Blood ran freely down the man's arm.

For a moment, nothing happened. Madh remained there, his entire body trembling in a seizure, his teeth chattering.

Slowly, Aemon Goeth leaned forward, his narrowed eyes suspicious that his feast had been stolen.

And then the lightning struck.

The bolts were blue, jagged, and short, not descending from the clouds but rising from the black stone beneath them. In an eerily silent ballet, Nistashi scattered to all sides, most avoiding the sizzling strokes with graceful ease, but a few were not so lucky. Their flesh charred and turned black where the lightning touched them, and four or five, hit more directly than the others, fell to the ground, quivering.

Too much, it seemed, was happening at one time for Brandt to comprehend it all. Close by him, one of the Nistashi had been felled by the lightning and his comrades sank to their knees around him—not to help him, as Brandt had at first surmised. Rather, they bit down hard on their own tongues or lips until blood spurted freely. Then one of them reached a jagged fingernail toward the tongue of his dying brother and ripped a gash in it. With fingers long-practiced, they were brushing blood onto their naked bodies and that of the dying Nistashin, chanting something as they scribed ancient characters across their ribs and thighs. Suddenly, the Nistashin lay quiet, and in the darkness of the moonless night, Brandt thought he discerned something vaporous rising from the dead man to the eager mouths of those gathered around him.

But he had no time to satisfy his curiosity about Nistashi feeding, for only a few dozen of the creatures were engaged in the process. Some, disciplined enough to forestall their hunger, had begun to reapply their bindings and several others, though naked, had leaped forward with their weapons, willing, it seemed, to forgo the feast entirely for bloodsport of a different kind.

As the first of the armed Nistashi reached the throne, Hain bent down and retrieved something from the side of his boot—a steel needle, eight inches long, with a small cross at the end that gave his fingers purchase. The assassin spun around with savage grace, bringing his arm upward in a compact swing as the Nistashin sprung upon him. The needle pierced the Nistashin's skin beneath the jaw, biting upward toward his brain. Black blood trickled from the Nistashin's ears and mouth as he fell, and this sight was too tempting to several of his brethren, who stooped down to steal the weary centuries that the dying Nistashin had first stolen himself.

Brandt spun around and found what he wanted by the side of a feeding Nistashin: one of their curious pole-arms. Testing the curved blade at one end, he swept the staff around, neatly severing the head of its former owner. Brandt nodded with satisfaction. The Nistashi chose their weapons well.

And they knew how to use them. A naked Nistashin aimed to skewer Brandt on the fork of his staff, and Brandt sidestepped the thrust only narrowly. The Nistashin swung the weapon around, the curved blade now whistling toward Brandt's head, but then Imbress was there, kicking out at the Nistashin's exposed knee. With a sickening crack of ancient bones, the man fell to the stone and was set upon by a group of diners who had just completed their last feast.

Imbress snatched a weapon from the floor and took a position covering Brandt's back. Off to the right, Hain was still causing havoc, but the initial bloodlust of the feeding frenzy seemed to have abated, as had the lightning, which now only shot sporadically from the stones beneath them. Aemon Goeth was shouting orders as he restored his bindings and the Nistashi were moving forward again.

Then a cry came from the rear—not the odd sibilance of a Nistashin voice, but a full-throated war-cry that Brandt had heard once before, near the base of Happar's Folly.

"Calador!"

There, toward the southeast tower, Brandt saw a huge sword flash above the crowd, followed closely by the broad swipe of an axe.

"Pell!" Brandt called as he kicked a naked Nistashin out of his way and, grabbing Elena's arm, spun her toward the southeast.

One final, tremendous bolt of lightning split the air, followed by a deafening explosion that knocked everyone to the roof, men and Nistashi alike. The air was filled with smoke, thicker than a fog, and it was only by luck that Brandt retained his grasp of Imbress's arm. He dragged her back to her feet and stumbled through the press of Nistashi bodies toward what he prayed was the southeast.

As the smoke began to clear, Brandt caught sight of Aemon Goeth behind him—not chasing him, but busy tearing Nistashi from their fallen brethren.

"Only the mortally wounded—" he was shouting.

Madh and Hain were nowhere to be seen.

"Brandt!"

At the sound of Marwick's voice, Brandt's head whipped around. The Belfarian thief was only a few yards away now, flanked by Callom Pell and the giant warrior who had appeared at Happar's Folly. The Nistashi had become cautious now, aware how very vulnerable they were without their eldritch bindings. They gave way to the men's sharp, swinging steel, and in moments, Brandt and Imbress had slipped by them.

Across the roof, near the northwest tower, a huge sheet of flame shot into the sky.

"Madh!" Brandt growled.

"Not now, Karrelian!"

It was a woman's voice, and she seemed to know him, though he did not know her. No, he had seen this older woman at Happar's Folly as well.

"If we give the Nistashi a chance to recover, we're all dead. Back to the stairs!"

Indeed, more than a few of the ancient ghouls had wrapped their bindings back over their chests, and they were glaring dangerously at the intruders as they hurried to cover their shoulders and heads. Pell and Calador began to fall back now, and Marwick herded Brandt and Imbress toward the tower. The Chaldeans rushed down the stairs, taking two and three steps at a time. They could hear nothing behind them, but Callom Pell shouted, "They're after us!"

They sped past several landings, always following the curving steps downward until Brandt was convinced they must be far beneath the waters of the Woodblood. Then, abruptly, the last landing was before them and they tumbled out past an arched opening onto a tremendous dock. Brandt paused for a moment, surveying the Nistashi's craft, until Marwick caught his sleeve and pulled him toward a rowboat docked at the very end of the pier. It was a wonder they didn't capsize the boat, jumping into it as they did. As Marwick untied the mooring rope, Calador and Pell each took an oar, sitting shoulder to shoulder in the cramped rower's seat.

"They're here!" Miranda shouted, and Brandt turned to find a group of Nistashi pouring through the archway.

It was too far to see, but the one in the front revealed he was Aemon Goeth by his voice.

"Such an insult I have not suffered for a thousand years! You shall each die by my hand!"

Brandt stood in the boat and hurled his weapon at Aemon Goeth, but the thick staff was not meant to fly. It wobbled a few dozen yards through the air, then plunged harmlessly into the water.

The last sound Brandt heard as the craft pulled past the black stone arch into the current of the Woodblood was Aemon Goeth's humorless laughter.

"Do you think they'll come after us?" Roland asked between clenched teeth as he pulled mightily at the oar.

"Very likely," Miranda answered as she combed her fingers through her long hair, as if nothing very disturbing had happened. But her voice betrayed anxiety. "Us *and* Madh, unless I miss my guess."

"Aemon Goeth is nothing but grand talk," Brandt sneered. "He blustered half the night away before you arrived, but once the fight began, he did nothing. He won't follow."

"*You* may not have noticed," Miranda corrected, "but Aemon Goeth did quite a lot up there. I'm not sure how Madh conjured that lightning, but it was a powerful spell—a dozen times more potent than anything I could manage. And it would have been much worse, except Goeth was fighting the conjuring the entire time. I sensed an enormous power there, held in reserve. If Aemon Goeth had cared to, I suspect he could have done much more to hinder our escape."

"Then why didn't he?" Brandt asked, wishing he knew who this woman was, and how on earth she knew the answers to his questions.

Miranda shrugged. "I suspect that Aemon Goeth is much more interested in Madh—and those Phrases—than he is in us. The entire time we were on the roof, he and Madh were locked in a struggle that none of us could see. Madh, I think, barely escaped alive, and he probably would not have been so lucky if not for the distraction of the Nistashi turning on each other. Aemon Goeth has a limited number of troops at his disposal and we caught him at a particularly vulnerable moment. The Nistashi will pick the next fight at their own pleasure."

Thoughtfully, Miranda turned toward her husband. "If only Selod had been here, he might have made the difference. Somehow, we must let him know that the Nistashi still live . . ."

Suddenly, Brandt sat bolt upright in the boat, pointing to the northwest, across the waters.

"Hain!" he hissed.

Callom Pell stopped rowing, turning his head to follow the line of Brandt's arm. There, just barely visible against the dark waters, was another boat, pulling steadily toward the west.

"We follow," he announced grimly.

"The horses—" Roland began.

"The horses will have to be sacrificed," Pell said sternly. "We're only a day or two from the Yndrian border. Fortune has given us one last chance to catch Madh. We must make the best of it."

And so they steered the boat around, letting the waters of the Woodblood bear them eastward toward the still swifter waters of the Cirran, toward Hain and toward Madh.

CHAPTER 23

It had not taken long for Hain to remember his predator's leer. Not long at all, Madh thought, for a man whose mind had almost been raped—whose soul had almost been reaped—by Aemon Goeth.

But on more mature consideration, Madh was not entirely sure that Hain possessed a soul. He possessed a predator's leer—that was certain—and a predator's mind to go along with it. Madh had occupied that mind himself for a few distasteful seconds and he now knew only too well what the assassin was thinking as he rowed the boat.

Madh had seen Hain humbled, however temporarily. In fact, Madh had saved Hain's life from the Nistashi.

For a man like Hain, there was only one way to repay such a debt.

In blood.

And so Hain continued to leer at Madh as he rowed toward the west. The Cirran's swift current was taking them fifty yards south for every yard they traveled toward shore, but Hain was not concerned with geography. The assassin's eyes were on neither the river nor the shore, nor even the spot where the Nistashi fortress had so strangely disappeared a few minutes ago. No, Madh could feel Hain's eyes on *him*. Madh's limbs were trembling within his spray-soaked cloak and he knew that Hain was contemplating that weakness. Use of the kahanes root cost Madh a dear price—no man, no matter how inured, could take such a dose of lethal poison without some effects. Use of the root made Madh a hundred times stronger than he would be without it; it had saved his life already a dozen times. But it would also, someday, kill him.

Unless, Madh reflected, Hain killed him first.

But there was one thing holding Hain back—one thing that weighed against his desire to kill the man who had seen him mastered—and that was the untold fortune that Madh had promised him. The fortune that awaited Hain in Yndor. The fortune that he would never see without Madh to lead him to it. And so, Madh judged, Hain would struggle with himself—struggle to wait long enough to collect his pay before indulging his bloodlust.

But just in case Hain lost that struggle, Madh motioned toward the third occupant of the boat, the occupant that Hain could not see crouched invisibly upon the prow of the boat behind him. Inclining its head in acknowledgment, Sycorax, Madh's last homunculus, jumped fluidly into the air, landing on Hain's back, although the assassin felt nothing. Slowly, the homunculus sank into Hain's flesh, its translucent green form melting into Hain's solidity until only a clawed hand remained raised above Hain's shoulder, like the last glimpse of a man drowning at sea. Then the homunculus was gone, tucked inside the assassin entirely, seeking Hain's abdominal cavity. In case Hain misbehaved, Madh would simply instruct the creature to materialize at once. It would take Sycorax's life as well, that way.

That would be a shame, for Sycorax was Madh's very last homunculus.

But, he reflected as the boat ground against the muddy shore of the Cirran's western bank, he could always bear another.

With Callom Pell and Roland Calador pulling mightⲟ ily at the oars, they had gained momentarily on the boat ahead, but then the swift rivers of the Cirran had caught Madh's craft and carried it into the impenetrable darkness beyond.

"We need to get close to the western bank as soon as

possible and keep an eye out for where they land," Pell
grunted as he continued to row. But his own back was to the
west, and so his eyes faced the Nistashi fortress, now invisible again. For a moment, he thought he glimpsed movement
in the fog behind them. Calador raised a shaggy, white eyebrow and caught Pell's eye; the old warrior had seen something as well. But by silent consent, they said nothing. They
were already rowing with all the strength they could muster,
and when they reached land, they would move with all speed.
There was no sense making the others nervous about shadows in the fog.

The whole craft spun toward the south as the current of
the Cirran devoured the Woodblood. The Cirran was far
swifter than its cousin; a long ride in a small boat was out
of the question. Pell and Calador straightened the prow toward the west and renewed their efforts against a river that
was determined, it seemed, to sweep them to the Bismet
Bogs. They were carried four miles downstream before they
drew close to the far bank and Callom Pell realized that, for
the first time in his entire life, he had left the confines of the
Ulthorn forest. Four decades he had spent in New Pell, wandering about the outskirts of the forest, venturing into its
interior when it seemed to slumber. The Cirran, however,
was the Ulthorn's western boundary at this latitude. Glancing
over his shoulder, Pell could see how the landscape changed.
A few pines grew close by the river, but most of the vegetation was low and scrubby, unable to find purchase in the
rocky soil that marked the eastern spine of the Jackalsmaw
Mountains.

It was a misnomer to call them mountains, really. The
western range of the Jackalsmaw—jagged spires rising in the
midst of the Yndrian plains—surely deserved the title, but
this area was nothing more than a rocky plateau. For twenty
miles, Pell knew, the land should rise before terminating in
a cliff face that fell to the fertile plains below, eons ago an
inland sea. Twenty miles left to catch Madh.

"There they are," Marwick announced with excitement,
pointing toward a dim speck on the river to the south.

Pell's eyes narrowed as he studied Marwick's find. A boat, certainly, tossing about on the current. Tossing about, he decided, a bit too freely.

"It's a ruse," Pell announced. "There's no one in that boat. They've already gone aground and set the boat adrift."

Roland glowered at the distant craft, then at the bleak, dark landscape a few dozen yards to the west. Dozens of rocky gullies disappeared into the black night, and Madh could be in any one of them.

"We'll never be able to track them," the old warrior swore.

Pell frowned beneath his beard, unwilling to admit that Roland was right. But privately, the fact had to be acknowledged. Pell had been counting on their catching a glimpse of Madh, or at least finding a beached boat. If Pell knew where the Yndrian had disembarked, he would have at least a slim chance of tracking the man through the dark. But now . . .

"We'll have to make for the west as swiftly as possible," Pell grumbled, "just as Madh must be doing."

"Mouse can track them," Miranda said simply, drawing every eye toward the prow of the boat, where the owl had just landed.

Roland glanced at the bird, then at his wife. "The mage is dangerous," he said hesitantly.

"We all must take our chances in this venture," the witch replied, "Mouse no less than the rest of us. But unless he possesses inhuman strength, that display before Aemon Goeth should have exhausted our Yndrian friend. With any luck, one more owl in the night sky will draw no attention."

"Then send the bird off," Pell growled as he jumped over the side into the knee-high surf, "for we've arrived at the Jackalsmaw."

It was as frustrating a chase as Brandt had ever experienced. Hain was so close, he could almost smell the assassin, and yet here they were mincing through the darkness, moving like blindfolded children at a party game. Dark as the moonless sky had seemed upon the Cirran, it was darker still in the ravines that rose twenty feet above their heads. The gullies twisted and turned in a tortuous manner, never running straight toward the west, intersecting dozens of other crevices at crazy angles. If not for Miranda pointing the way at each crossing, they would have been hopelessly lost. They rushed on as best they could in the blackness, hunched over, their arms spread wide to find obstacles. Even still, a minute did not go by without someone tripping or ramming into a rock that jutted unexpectedly from a nearby wall. Brandt could feel the blood flowing from a dozen cuts in his shins, but he said nothing, grimly pressing on. The others, he knew, must be suffering the same.

They were lucky, Brandt suspected, if they were covering two miles each hour. Every step was a challenge, a wager against a broken ankle. They said little, breathing heavily as they drove themselves forward, slowly forgetting why they were there, their limbs working automatically as their minds drifted into the numbing haze of concentrating upon blackness. Time became meaningless, something that could not be counted in minutes or hours, but only by gullies crossed, tumbles taken. The gashes across Brandt's shins were the closest thing to tally marks for a night that stretched toward eternity.

Finally, a glimmer of pink filtered into the blackness, so gently that at first they didn't notice it. But in a few minutes, the ravine began to glow with the approach of dawn. They paused for a moment, blinking, looking at each other as if for the first time. They were haggard, their hair pasted to their skulls with sweat, their faces gray with rock dust, their clothes hanging in tattered, bloody ribbons about their legs.

Miranda sat down heavily on a nearby boulder. She looked older, Brandt thought, than his first impression of her. "I've sent Mouse away," the witch said. "An owl during daylight would catch Madh's attention. Mouse says, however, that they are no more than ten minutes ahead of us."

Imbress caught Brandt's arm and squeezed it. He turned toward the agent. Her red hair hung in a sweaty tangle that half-obscured her face, but beneath the veil, her green eyes burned. "Remember," she whispered too quietly for anyone else to hear. "Remember your promise. Madh first."

Miranda pushed herself to her feet, rubbing her hands against her eyes as if she had just awoken from a nap, and set off at a brisk pace toward the west. "On the other hand," she said, "Mouse says the Nistashi are no more than ten minutes behind us."

The day was a mad hike through a crazy, rocky maze. What force of nature had carved the earth into this warren of twisting ravines, each only a few yards wide and ten or fifteen yards high, Brandt could not say. He yearned to race forward and catch Hain, but Callom Pell had held him back.

"Ten minutes is a longer lead than you might think," the woodsman had said, "especially in this terrain. If we exhaust ourselves by running, we only deliver ourselves to the butchers behind us."

Brandt thought about the Nistashi, considered the prospect of spending twenty-seven days in a cell before the next new moon, and fell in by Callom Pell's side, matching the woodsman's brisk, steady stride. It was the Caladors who suffered the most. A sheen of sweat covered Roland's tremendous frame. He had lost his plate mail when he threw it at the Druzem, but he still wore a coat of finely wrought chain that must have weighed thirty pounds by itself. Brandt wondered why the old soldier did not simply discard the heavy, hot armor. He himself would be dead, Brandt thought, if he'd been forced to trek this far with thirty pounds of metal on his back. But Calador's long legs took two strides for every three of Brandt's, and the old man kept the pace without complaint, a veteran of longer marches than Brandt could have guessed.

Roland's attention turned frequently to his wife, though, for Miranda was clearly in pain, breathing heavily as she pressed on, using the Nistashi weapon that Imbress had taken as a walking stick to help support her weight. Pell gave no thought to Miranda as he set the pace, striding steadily through the ravines. His broad back did not turn, indifferent to whether the others were keeping up. But there was nothing he could do. If they stopped to rest, Madh might get away.

If they stopped to rest, the Nistashi would be upon them.

The sun rose until it was visible above the lip of the tall ravine walls, and then it began to disappear again. Brandt had no idea how far they had walked, but it seemed as if he could have hiked back to Chaldus by now. Twenty-five or thirty miles, he had heard Pell tell Marwick not long ago, but the distance meant nothing to him. For all he could tell, their many turns had brought them back to the same ravine they had started in. At any moment, Brandt expected to turn a corner and find the Cirran River rushing before him.

"—not far—"

The words sounded far-off, not simply because they interrupted Brandt's reverie, but because the voice whispered to him from a distance. Madh's voice. Brandt stopped in his tracks, concentrating, and detected another sound—the click of a boot's heel against rock. And it was coming to him from *above*.

"Damn!" he swore. "They've changed ravines on us."

He glanced at the craggy wall of the gully, no more than forty feet high. For Brandt and Marwick, who had climbed sheer facades of buildings, the jagged rock looked as navigable as a formal staircase. In an instant, Brandt was scrambling up the rock face, Marwick not far behind him. As he neared the top of the wall, he could see the others making more careful progress at the base of the ravine.

From the top, the Jackalsmaw seemed a very different place indeed. In the distance, the plateau seemed almost smooth, except for the spidery black lines that traced broken paths against the white rock. They looked like insignificant cracks in the distance, Brandt knew, but they were in fact the deep, irregular ravines that divided the plateau into a maddening labyrinth. And this, standing atop the plateau, was like traveling across the top of the walls of a roofless maze. Brandt stood on a long pier of rock, twenty yards wide, that rose between the ravine he'd just left and the next one to the south. The spine of rock curved another hundred yards or so to the northwest, where the two ravines met. Just beyond that juncture, yet another wall arose. But as Brandt looked to the west, he saw the white expanse of rock end in a premature horizon against a clear blue sky. They were near the edge of the plateau.

Near Yndor.

Madh and Hain, however, were nowhere to be seen. He wondered whether his ears had played tricks on him. The way sound might echo in the gullies . . .

Marwick had arrived at the top, along with Imbress. Pell, Roland, and Miranda were within a few yards of the summit. Marwick bent over to offer Miranda his hand—and froze.

Rounding a corner in the ravine they had just vacated, four Nistashi strode into view. An evil smile crossed the leader's face as he lifted his skeletal hand, pointing toward the humans that clung to the rocks only a hundred yards away.

Brandt sucked in his breath as he, too, noticed the advancing Nistashi. The only consolation, as he peered down, was that none of them was decorated with a symmetrical cross of leather on his face. Aemon Goeth had not come to see personally to their doom.

"I would hurry up," Brandt warned. Roland and Pell were still a few yards beneath the top.

"Madh!" Imbress cried, and Brandt spun around. There, two ravines away, Madh and Hain were climbing to the top of the next ridge. As Hain pulled himself up, he paused to survey the activity behind him. Grinning, he touched his hand to his brow and bowed, the sun reflecting off his stubbled head.

Madh, meanwhile, was in no mood for courtesy. He had turned to the west and started running along the long, rocky island. Brandt traced the path with his eye, wondering why Madh had bothered to climb across two ravines to that particular prominence. As his eye traced the ribbon of white to the waiting blue horizon, the answer came to him: that particular stripe of the plateau wound its way to the edge without any other ravines crossing its path. What Madh intended to do when he reached the Jackalsmaw's edge, Brandt had no idea, but the man was burning to get there.

Brandt turned back momentarily to find the Nistashi at the base of the rock wall, two of them already beginning to climb upward, their long weapons clenched between their teeth. Marwick was just pulling Miranda onto the top of the ridge. Pell and Calador had both got a hand to the top. Cursing, Brandt slipped a knife out of the sheath at Marwick's right hip and turned to follow Hain.

Imbress moved to the opposite edge of the ridge. looked down into the ravine on the other side, and started cursing. Like the wall they had just climbed, there were plenty of jagged ledges and scrubby plants available for handholds. But then they would have to climb up the next ridge, down its obverse, and back up another to reach the ribbon of rock upon which Madh was escaping. It would take far too long, even if the Nistashi did not overtake them.

A scream of utter self-abandonment pierced the air and she whirled around, expecting to see the Nistashi upon her, wicked blades raised above her.

Instead, it was Brandt Karrelian who was sprinting toward her as fast as his legs would carry him. Instinctively, Imbress spun around and ducked . . . but Karrelian had not been charging at her.

He had been charging at the very edge of their rocky peninsula, and as he reached it, he launched himself into the air, his arms wind-milling wildly as his body soared above hungry, jagged rock. And then he cleared the abyss, landing in an awkward roll on the rocks of the next ridge. There was blood on his face now, but he didn't seem to notice it. Without hesitation, he pushed himself to his feet, a mad glint in his eyes as he caught the fleeing figures of Madh and Hain, still another ridge beyond him.

Elena took a few steps backward, measuring the width of the ravine. Fifteen, maybe sixteen feet. She took another few paces backward, almost to where Callom Pell was finally pulling himself up upon the ridge. She had no idea how far she could jump, but this certainly seemed farther.

One way or another, it would be quicker than climbing.

Callom Pell watched Imbress clear the void, barely arriving safely on the far side. Pell knew his wide, dense body, built for plodding endless miles through forests, built for battling creatures even larger than he.

He was not built to fly.

The broad-bladed battle-axe felt good in his palm as he tested its familiar weight.

"I'll remain here," he announced gruffly, glowering at the advancing Nistashi.

Beside him, Roland drew his five-foot blade from the sheath across his back and took a fighting stance. A fleeting, ironic smile crossed Pell's lips as he realized that finally, after centuries, a Pell and a Chaldean nobleman would knowingly stand together against the monsters of the Ulthorn.

Beneath them, impassive as ever, the Nistashi continued to ascend.

Miranda turned toward Marwick.

"We'll be fine here," she said, her voice brooking no argument. "Go after Madh. He's all that's important."

Marwick hesitated no longer, turning on his heels and sprinting toward the empty air.

Elena Imbress watched Karrelian clear the second gulf, landing more heavily this time, but forcing himself quickly to his feet. Hain was only thirty yards ahead of him, Madh a few more than that. Imbress steeled herself and began to sprint toward the edge of the ridge. A part of her mind was telling her that this ravine was even wider than the first, which she had survived by mere inches. That internal voice was screaming at her to stop, that it was madness to propel herself into the void—

But then she was flying, white and gray rocks a blur to each side, the next ravine springing toward her, but not quickly enough.

The breath exploded from her lungs as she crashed into the top of the ravine wall and began to fall. Desperately, her hands scrambled for purchase, found a tiny ledge, lost it, found a small rocky protrusion, and held fast. Beneath her, her feet kicked out in search of the ravine wall, but she found nothing but air. Almost afraid to look down, she found a concavity beneath her. The wall curved inward just two or three feet, but that was far enough to leave her dangling from the precarious knob of rock that she clung to. She tried to pull herself up, but her trembling arms would not obey the command. She was exhausted.

And she would fall.

For a few moments, at least, she could hang here, fighting gravity to a draw before she fell forty feet to the ravine below.

As she let her head lean forward against the sharp rock, she prayed that Karrelian would honor his promise.

Madh first.

The Nistashi had reached the midway point of their climb before Miranda began to hum her little tune, hands casually in the pockets of her dress as if she were out for a stroll through the garden. But her eyes were focused fiercely on the ancient killers scaling the rocks below. Grinning, the closest of the Nistashi reached for the next convenient handhold and began to pull himself up.

Abruptly, the rock came loose in his hand and he plummeted more than three stories to the bottom of the ravine.

One by one, each of his companions followed him. The fall was far enough to kill most men.

"That should give them something to think about," the witch said softly.

"They're not thinking too long," Callom Pell observed.

The Nistashi had pulled themselves to their feet, dusting

themselves off casually as if they had nodded to sleep and fallen off a chair. There were a few scratches and a little dark blood in the spaces between their black bindings, but that hardly seemed an inconvenience.

This time, however, two of the Nistashi remained on the ravine floor, their hands pressed together by their chests as if they were praying, while the other two began to climb. Again, midway through their climb, Miranda began her little tune.

Abruptly, the air was expelled from her lungs as if she'd been punched in the stomach, and she fell into a sitting position. Roland turned toward her, a dangerous look in his eye.

"I'll be fine," she assured him, but her voice was weak and she made no attempt to rise.

Pell watched as Roland took a long step toward the very edge of the ravine, his long sword pointed down toward the advancing Nistashi. The old warrior's face was set in a grim frown that promised death for any who approached. For the first time, Callom Pell understood how Calador had led the armies of Chaldus for so many years.

The Nistashi, however, were indifferent to Roland's rage. Warriors far more ancient than he, they were pressed by other needs. Near the top, they took their staves from their mouths, continuing their climb one-handed. Their brethren had abandoned their praying posture, moved a few dozen yards farther down the ravine, and begun to climb as well.

Cursing, Roland dropped his sword and bent over a large stone that stood near the ravine's edge. The stone was as big as a wolf, Pell thought; three hundred pounds, at least. Roland's arms wrapped around the contours of the rock and his seven-foot frame began to straighten. He took a few small steps to the edge, then let the missile plunge down at the nearest of the Nistashi. The huge stone struck the creature full in the face and both tumbled down to the ravine floor. The Nistashin lay there unmoving for a moment, then shook its head and began to sit up.

"They'll keep this up all day," Pell spat, "until we die of fatigue."

The other Nistashin was near the top. Pell lashed out with his axe, but this Nistashin was clever, remaining just beyond Pell's reach. Every time Pell would swing, the Nistashin would stab upward with the forked end of his staff, trying to catch Pell's wrist.

Meanwhile, the other two had almost reached the summit, ten yards west of where Pell and Calador had made their stand. His sword back in his hand, Calador strode toward them.

"Don't cut," Miranda called behind him, still sounding weak. "Thrust! And aim only at the open flesh between their bindings."

There wasn't much of that, Roland thought, as he surveyed the crazy quilt of black leather straps that covered the climbing Nistashi. Just small patches of white skin; not much to aim at. As if they understood Roland's frustration, the Nistashi grinned as they came within feet of the ridge. Instantly, Roland thrust downward, aiming at the closest of those grins. His stout blade broke teeth as it slid between the Nistashin's purple lips, piercing the back of the throat and the brain stem, halting only as it smashed against the leather straps that covered the back of the Nistashin's skull. A gout of blood erupted around the blade as the Nistashin's eyes went wide with shock.

And now it was Roland's turn to grin as he watched the corpse fall forty feet to the rocks below, its twisted, mummified limbs embracing the death they had so long eluded. But Roland's grin quickly faded, for the next Nistashin was upon him.

Pell saw the Nistashin's fall from the corner of his eye. Rather than feeling satisfied, he wondered whether three to two made better odds. While one Nistashin kept Calador occupied, another now climbed unhindered to the top of the ridge—the one that Calador had knocked down with the boulder. In only another moment, he would be out-numbered . . . and dead. Desperately, Pell reached with his left hand for the mace that hung from his belt. He hurled the weapon awkwardly at the Nistashin who clung to the rock beneath him. The ancient creature had to jump backward to avoid the blow and it fell back to the bottom of the ravine.

Pell knew the Nistashin would start climbing again im-mediately, but he had no time to watch its progress. Only a few yards to his right, another Nistashin had reached the summit and turned toward Pell. Twirling its staff lightly in its hands, the creature advanced, and Pell turned to meet its charge. They traded a dozen quick blows, the Nistashin using its weapon sometimes as a cudgel, sometimes as a spear or a fork. It pressed relentlessly, uncaring of the little openings it allowed. Pell's broad-bladed axe glanced harmlessly off the web of black leather that protected it, at best cutting a patch of open flesh superficially. An axe was no good against these creatures, he realized; only a sword or a spear would do.

Pell fended off two thrusts by the Nistashin's spear blade, all the while searching for a part of the creature that might be vulnerable to his axe. Ribbons of leather encircled the Nistashin's wrist and the backs of its hands, but its fingers . . .

As the next blow came, Pell did not strike it away so much as catch it upon his axe, letting the momentum of the Nis-tashin's swing carry his axe blade down the length of the staff until the steel bit deeply into the Nistashin's fingers. The creature howled in fury, but Pell gave it no time to recover. Dropping his axe, he grabbed the Nistashin's weapon with both hands, kicking out savagely at his at-tacker's chest. Surprised, the Nistashin fell roughly on its back and, an instant later, was pinned there by its own curved blade, thrust roughly through an exposed patch of skin on its abdomen.

Pell spared only a moment to glance at Calador. The old warrior was trading heavy blows with another Nistashin, but he seemed to be growing tired. A sheen of sweat mingled with blood from a half-dozen superficial wounds as Calador brought his tremendous sword around time and again, each cut met surely by the Nistashin's staff. But Callom Pell had no time to help the old warrior, for the last Nistashin had just regained the plateau, come for a return encounter with Pell. There was a slight smile upon the Nistashin's face, as if it were assured of a victory. And perhaps it was, Pell thought, as he met the creature's savage attack. Slowly, Pell felt himself giving ground before the Nistashin's roundhouse blows. The Nistashi, it seemed, never weakened, but Callom Pell knew that he himself had very little strength remaining.

A shadow flew over Imbress's face, followed by a shower of rock dust, and she looked up to find Marwick sprawled on the rocks above her, his feet dangling over the cliff's edge, but most of him on safe ground. He scrambled onto the top of the ridge and disappeared.

Above her, Elena Imbress could see a few wisps of white clouds in a glorious, blue sky—the sort of sky she never thought she would see again during her trip through the Ulthorn. Now, she supposed, it would be her last sight.

But then Marwick's face thrust itself into view, his curly copper hair in wild disarray. His hand reached down.

Imbress shook her head.

"Madh," she muttered. She could not tell if he heard her. She had so little breath left.

Marwick glanced over his shoulder, a look of pure determination crossing his face.

"Damn you," he muttered, reaching lower. "Give me your hand."

Brandt slowed to a trot as he realized that he had them. Madh stood at the very edge of the Jackalsmaw, a sheer drop of two thousand feet to the fertile Yndrian farms that lay below. There was nowhere to go, no way down. Madh's back was pressed against the sky and Brandt could advance leisurely.

Hain stood a few yards from the very edge, his eyes flickering from one possibility to the next: the abyss behind him, Madh's impassive expression, the long jumps over the ravines on either side—too long for even him to make. And Galatine Hazard advancing. Hazard had a knife in his hand, probably taken from a companion. Hain reached down and drew his slim steel needle from its hiding place in his boot. It was still stained black with Nistashin blood.

"Come, Hazard," Hain growled, "I'll make short work of you."

Brandt glowered at the assassin, and images of Carn, lying crippled in the Atahr Vin, sprung again to his mind, as vivid as if the butchery had occurred that hour. The weeks had dissolved—the hallucinatory ride to Belfar, his encounter with Old Hoot, the conflagration at the inn, the long chase to the Ulthorn, and then the trickery at Happar's Folly.

It had all been forgotten, dismissed as easily as a dream . . . all except the nagging memory of a misbegotten oath he'd made on the Woodblood River.

His gaze traveled from one to the other—Hain feral, Madh impassive—and Brandt knew that Hain needed killing far more than Madh, like a rabid dog needed killing.

He lifted the knife in his hand.

Hain dove neatly to the side, surprised that Brandt would risk his only weapon on a throw, but the knife sailed far wide of where he'd been. A lousy throw, the assassin thought, rolling back to his feet, until he realized that the blade had been aimed at Madh.

A brief look of shock crossed the Yndrian's face as the knife came speeding his way. He had not expected that Hazard could master his bloodlust. And then Madh bowed ever so slightly backward, letting the knife pass through the space that his throat had a moment ago occupied, and he watched the blade fall through empty space to the plains a half-mile below.

Leering, Hain seized the opportunity and sprang forward. Brandt caught him around each wrist and allowed the assassin's momentum to bear them both to the ground. They tumbled one over another for a few seconds until Hain finally braced himself on top, straddling Brandt's torso, bringing all his weight to bear on the tip of the needle that was aimed at Brandt's throat. The assassin felt his prey struggling wildly beneath him, as wildly as prey always struggled . . . and as ineffectually. Hain was the larger man, and stronger, and more gloriously ferocious. The tip of the needle kissed the hollow beneath Hazard's voice box.

Yes, Hain thought, watching this needle pierce Hazard's skin would be almost as satisfying as the needles full of veridine that so often pierced his own.

Madh's dark eyes glittered as he watched the two men struggle. It would be interesting to see which of these two men hungered most for the other's blood. A tidy drama to conclude his stay in Chaldus. And then he remembered Sycorax, lodged in Hain's belly.

Come, Madh instructed, *it is almost time to leave.*

Behind him, Hain could feel Hazard's legs kicking out, wild to unseat him, but the assassin had spread his weight across Hazard's belly, leaving the man little leverage. The needle dipped a little lower and a red bloom spread across Hazard's throat.

Hain smiled.

And then he felt something—just a twinge, a tiny flicker of pain in his stomach where he expected to feel nothing. He looked down, expecting treachery, some little knife that Hazard had hidden, but there was nothing there.

Brandt didn't question the shadow of doubt that passed over Hain's eyes; he merely used it. With both hands, he twisted at Hain's wrist, forcing the needle's point away from his throat and up toward the sky. Then, with both feet braced solidly against the rock, Brandt thrust his body savagely upward. Hain was thrown over onto his back, and before he could regain his feet, Brandt had swung himself atop Hain, reversing the position of a moment before. Their hands and wrists locked in a tangle around the deadly needle, and its tip wavered like an uncertain compass, trembling between the two men.

Above him, Hain could see the muscles in Hazard's jaw bunching with effort, his eyes furious for blood. Hain had never seen before how he himself looked when the lust was upon him.

Slowly, the tip of the needle inched downward, tapping Hain's brow, tracing a ticklish path to his left eyelid. A surge of strength had come over Karrelian and Hain suddenly understood that this was a fight he would not win. The assassin could not move his head, but his eyes flickered toward the Yndrian mage who stood quietly at the edge of the precipice, watching the battle as if it were a play staged exclusively for his amusement.

"Madh!" Hain hissed through clenched teeth. "The Phrases will die with me."

For the first time that Hain could remember, a tiny smile curled the edges of Madh's mouth. The Yndrian was holding something in his hand, holding it up to the light of the sun, where it flashed blue and green in succession.

"I'm afraid you're mistaken," Madh replied quietly.

And then Brandt drove home the point of the needle through Hain's eye into the depths of his bare skull. As the assassin's blood jetted over his hands, Brandt released the needle and jerked convulsively away. Slowly, he pushed himself to his feet and turned toward Madh. The mage remained at the edge of the cliff, his heels a finger's breadth over the side, as if he dared the abyss to claim him. In one hand he held a large gem; in the other, the odd, spiky ball that he had used against Aemon Goeth the night before.

Brandt bent into a crouch, ready for lightning to spring up around him. His only chance, he thought, was to throw Madh over the precipice, and he sprang forward.

But the mage was too quick. He did not summon his lightning. He did not try to dodge. He merely stepped backward into the empty air, spreading wide his arms as if he were falling into bed.

Brandt stopped short at the edge of the Jackalsmaw, watching as Madh fell, not plummeting against the rocky cliff below, but wafting toward the ground, rocking gently back and forth as he fell, like a sheet of parchment dropping to the floor. Even now, he was only twenty feet below Brandt.

And there was that damned oath.

Brandt's muscles coiled as he crouched, ready to spring into the void, cursing himself even as he measured the distance of the jump.

And suddenly he was being choked, spun backward by his collar away from the precipice until Marwick's grim face swung into view.

"Are all you morons so eager to die today?" the thief muttered wearily, finally releasing Brandt's shirt.

For a moment they said nothing. Then they stepped back toward the edge and peered over the side. It took minutes, it seemed, until Madh's body dwindled into a distant dot, barely distinguishable against the white cliffs below. At the very base of the plateau, a broad, bowl-shaped plain bellied out toward the Yndrian horizon, covered in the near distance by a patchwork of green farms. Far below, toward those farms to the west, Madh began to make his slow, steady way.

Ωith leaden arms, Pell and Calador did their best to fend off the blows of the Nistashi. Each of the men bled from a half-dozen wounds where the ancient warriors had evaded their guard. It was only a matter of time before the men made more serious mistakes, and paid with their lives.

Callom Pell prayed that it would not be wasted, that Karrelian had been able to catch Madh . . . although what Karrelian could do with the mage, after what Pell had seen last night, he could not begin to guess.

The Nistashin swung its curved blade toward Pell's throat and the woodsman brought his axe wildly upward, barely knocking away the thrust. But the force of his own parry sent Pell listing off balance and the Nistashin swung his staff around in a sweeping windmill of a blow that knocked Pell to the ground.

It was a simple choice, now: the fork to skewer him or the curved blade to slice his throat.

But the Nistashin paused, cocking its head as if listening to a far-off voice. Then, inexplicably, the Nistashin turned on its heels and walked calmly toward the end of the rocky pier. Not far away, Roland's attacker disengaged as well, springing nimbly backward into the ravine. Roland staggered to the edge of the gully, propping himself up upon the hilt of his sword, and watched as the two Nistashi retreated into the distance, never once glancing back.

"They had us," Pell gasped in disbelief, climbing shakily to his feet.

"But they didn't want us," Calador replied.

Pell shook his head. It made no sense.

"Then why . . . ?"

Years of studying military strategy provided the answer. The old general sighed, glad he was still alive, but not sure he was glad what that implied.

"A feint," Calador said, "a delaying tactic. Something to draw our attention, occupy our time."

"Draw our attention from what?"

But even as he asked the question, Pell had turned to the west. A hundred yards away, Marwick and Karrelian stood staring over the edge of the Jackalsmaw into oblivion. A single corpse lay near their feet.

A bald corpse.

"Madh got away," Pell rumbled.

Elena rolled onto the top of the stone island, her chest heaving. Marwick sat down heavily beside her, also gasping for breath. A few minutes earlier, he had pulled Imbress up to a small ledge a few feet beneath the plateau. Then he had gone to help Brandt, assuming the agent would make it the last couple of feet by herself. It had turned out that, totally exhausted, Elena Imbress could not even accomplish that. And so, after stopping Brandt from hurling himself over the edge of the abyss, Marwick had returned to help Imbress.

"My mother used to say," Marwick panted, "that if children were meant to fly, mothers would be catapults . . ."

Imbress ignored the thief, pushing herself to her hands and knees. Slowly, she stood, swaying dangerously near the edge of the ravine. Twenty yards away, Brandt Karrelian was walking back from the precipice toward Hain's corpse. Elena's eyes surveyed the assassin's remains, then turned coldly toward Brandt.

"The Yndrian?" she asked.

Brandt shook his head. "I did what I could."

Imbress turned around and walked past Marwick.

"It that's all you could do," she said quietly as she traversed the broken stones, "then you've betrayed us all."

Epilogue

The setting sun shone through the jagged spires of the Jackalsmaw's western range, washing the peaks red like bloody teeth. Miles ago, the farms had given way to rocky badlands as the plains rose toward the mountains. Occasionally, a shepherd and his flock wandered over the rough terrain, seeking better grazing. But for the most part, Madh was once again alone, blissfully alone. He had ridden hard on a succession of horses across the broad fields of Yndor, but slowed his latest horse to a walk when he reached the badlands. He was not worried about the creature's breaking an ankle, which it could easily accomplish here whether walking or trotting. Rather, he was home for the first time in months and he wanted to enjoy the isolated, brutal beauty of the badlands. He had been given until sundown. Then his master would arrive.

Only a few miles remained between Madh and the foot of Mount Eihr and he savored them, thinking about all the work he had done since last winter. The research and the dangerous trek through the Ulthorn, the search for a tool in Chaldus and the subsequent difficulty of controlling the one he had found. He smiled as he thought of how that had turned out. Hazard had spurned his offer in the beginning, but had proved useful nonetheless, sparing Madh the distasteful task of killing Hain. If Madh had any taste for blood, after all, he would not have needed Hain in the first place . . .

Madh shook his head, trying to dismiss further thoughts of the boorish assassin. All such unpleasantness was over now. He rode easily toward home, he reminded himself, in new clothes, with the gem safe in the pouch beneath his tunic. His master would be most pleased, Madh reflected. Together, they had performed a great service for Yndor.

Mount Eihr towered above him now, its great twisted roots cutting the landscape into a dozen steep valleys. Madh chose the northernmost valley and plunged into the mountain's shadow, headed straight for the crotch of the two converging ridges, at the very heart of which was his home. After only ten minutes more, he could discern the dark opening in the rocks that was the mouth of the cave.

He dismounted, tethering his horse to the twisted bole of a nearby pine, and took a moment to look around. There was no other sign of life, not that that meant anything. His master would not have come by horse; it was impossible to tell whether or not he would be inside. Madh brushed the dust from his new cloak and straightened his tie. They were not the garments he would have preferred, but the farming towns of the plains had offered little variety. Aginath lay only a hundred miles to the south, and perhaps, if his master had no further tasks for him at this time, he would travel there. In Prandis, Madh had discovered that he had a taste for opera. There was an opera house in Aginath, and Madh yearned to try it. A small enough reward for all that he had accomplished.

He could feel the chill of the mountain seep through his cloak as he took the first step into the cave. After the first two turns, the darkness became impenetrable, but Madh knew every twist of the tunnel as well as he knew the lines of his master's face. When the echo of his boots suddenly became broader, more hollow, he knew that he had entered the main chamber. There were no lights; he was early.

He uttered a word, and the oil lamp that rested on the table sputtered into flames. Nothing had changed: the cot and the trunk in the nook on the left, the pine table and two chairs in the middle of the small, main chamber.

But Madh was surprised to find the enormous silhouette of his master between him and the light. The master had been sitting at the table, in the dark; for how long, Madh could not say. The chair pushed back and the man began to rise, foot after foot of black velvet straightening along his back.

Slowly, Sardos turned around.

"You have succeeded."

It was not a question. Sardos knew that Madh had been victorious. Madh would not have returned otherwise.

Madh smiled.

"Yes, my lord. Each of the Chaldean Phrases is ours."

Madh walked the few remaining steps between him and Sardos, then pulled the pouch from around his neck, emptying the gem into his hand. He proffered it.

For a moment, Sardos merely stood there, his black eyes boring into the gem's faceted surface. Then a flicker crossed his face, his brow knitting, and a smile rose to his lips. A wave of pleasure ran through Madh's body; he could not remember his master ever having smiled before.

"Have I pleased you?" Madh asked.

Sardos reached out and took the gem between his fingers, holding it up, although his back was to the light.

"I am very pleased indeed," Sardos rumbled. "Your discovery of the Nistashi was fortuitous as well."

The gem disappeared into Sardos's hand as the mage walked to the mouth of the tunnel.

"How long before you are ready to travel?" Sardos asked, his deep voice almost betraying a hint of eagerness.

Madh sighed. The opera at Aginath, it appeared, would have to wait. But the good of the country must come before his personal pleasure.

"I am ready at your command, my lord, as always."

Sardos inclined his head in acknowledgment.

"Good. I sail in five days from Thyrsus, but you will not have time to meet us there. We will stop for provisions in Khantoum. There you shall come aboard."

Madh nodded. "But where are we traveling?"

The word had a liquid sound, like blood, as it came from Sardos's lips:

"Gonwyr."

And for a moment, Madh's heart froze within his chest.

Gonwyr, the Devastation of the Magi—the dead land.

Gonwyr, which had once been the garden of Kirilei, the home of the Khrine, and which had also been the home of their final slaughter. Gonwyr, where nothing lived that had not been warped beyond nature's laws. No one went to that poisoned place, for there was nothing in Gonwyr that any sane man could desire.

There was nothing in Gonwyr at all, Madh thought . . .

Nothing save the doomed city of Tythoom. And the chamber, in the heart of the city, in which Atahr Vin and Tarem Hamir had crafted the Binding. The chamber in which the Binding could be unmade.

Madh's voice sounded strangely hollow as he spoke, his hand strangely distant as his fingers groped through his pocket.

"You said the Phrases were for protection, merely to compel Chaldus to our will . . ."

"I did say that once," Sardos rumbled, finality in his voice.

Madh almost inclined his head in obedience, as he had been taught, but his mouth could not contain the reply. It came slowly at first, then burst forth like a dam breaking.

"You said that Yndor would never seek to return the world to the chaos of the days before the Binding."

"Enough!" Sardos thundered, his dark brows gathering in rage. "Be in Khantoum in two weeks."

The blood was pounding through Madh's head; he felt drunk.

"I cannot let you do it," he breathed.

Sardos laughed and took a step into the tunnel.

"Khantoum," the mage repeated.

And then sharp pain exploded through Madh's palm as the kahanes needles pierced his flesh—an intimate agony, as familiar as the spasms that wracked his body, as the words that spilled through the rictus of his lips. He saw Sardos turn just as the first crackling bolt of power erupted from the floor, playing over the mage's seven-foot frame, illuminating in blue the deadly fury on his face. As the next bolt struck, Sardos's long black hair reached out to meet it, burning at the tips, but the mage paid the attack no mind. He raised both his hands above his head, his tongue forming a word with lethal precision, his eyes directed not at Madh but at the cavern's ceiling.

Too late, Madh looked up, just as he realized the source of the tremendous groaning he heard, barely in time to watch the roof of the cave in which he'd been born come tumbling down upon his head.

Sardos stepped back from the destruction, his black eyes piercing the lesser blackness of the cavern. Beneath the great cloud of dust, the heaping pile of rocks would make a fitting cairn for a worthy tool.

It was a pity to waste such a resource, the mage thought as his lips began to form the spell that would return him to Thyrsus. But after the world was his own, there would be time enough to sire another son.

PENGUIN PUTNAM INC.
Online

Your Internet gateway to a virtual environment with
hundreds of entertaining and enlightening books
from Penguin Putnam Inc.

While you're there, get the latest buzz on
the best authors and books around—

Tom Clancy, Patricia Cornwell, W.E.B. Griffin,
Nora Roberts, William Gibson, Robin Cook,
Brian Jacques, Catherine Coulter, Stephen King,
Ken Follett, Terry McMillan, and many more!

Penguin Putnam Online is located at
http://www.penguinputnam.com

PENGUIN PUTNAM NEWS

Every month you'll get an inside look at our upcom-
ing books and new features on our site. This is an
ongoing effort to provide you with the most
up-to-date information about
our books and authors.

Subscribe to Penguin Putnam News at
http://www.penguinputnam.com/newsletters